Praise for L. R. Braden's Magicsmith series...

Winner of:

Eric Hoffer Book Award—SciFi/Fantasy category

First Horizon Award for Debut Authors

Next Generation Indie Book Award—Paranormal category

Imadjinn Award—Best Urban Fantasy (for multiple books)

Colorado Authors League Award for Writing Excellence—
Fantasy and Paranormal categories

Finalist: *Colorado Book Award*—SciFi/Fantasy category

Finalist: Chanticleer International Book Award, Paranormal and
Fantasy categories

———

"Magic, Murder and Romance, oh my! This is an amazing fantasy in which every character is more than they appear."
—Winchester Public Library on *A Drop of Magic*

"A riveting world filled with amazing characters and a tightly woven plot."
—Richelle Rodarte, Netgalley reviewer on *Chaos Song*

"This is one of my favorite fictional worlds to visit. . . . I devoured this like a reader starved for every word, gulping yet somehow managing to savor the delightful taste of the story."
—Lucretia, Goodreads reviewer on *Of Mettle & Magic*

Other Titles
by L. R. Braden

The Magicsmith Series

A Drop of Magic, Book 1
Courting Darkness, Book 2
Faerie Forged, Book 3
Casting Shadows, Book 4
Of Mettle and Magic, Book 5
Chaos Song, Book 6
Lies and Illusion, Book 7

The Rifter Series
(set in the Magicsmith Universe)

Demon Riding Shotgun, Book 1
Personal Demons, Book 2
A Demon Faerie Tale, Book 3
Dancing with a Demon, Book 4

Lies and Illusion

The Magicsmith - Book 7

by

L. R. Braden

Magical Realms Press

This is a work of fiction. Names, characters, places and incidents are either the products of the author's imagination or are used fictitiously. Any resemblance to actual persons (living or dead), events or locations is entirely coincidental.

Magical Realms Press
PO BOX 24
Broomfield, CO 80038

Print ISBN: 978-1-968414-13-9

Published in the United States of America.
Previously published by BelleBooks

We love to hear from readers!
Contact us at:
MagicalRealmsPress.com
LRBraden.com

Cover design: Debra Dixon
Interior design: Hank Smith
Photo/Art credits:
Woman (manipulated) © Viorel Sima | Dreamstime.com
Columns (manipulated) © Aliaksandr Kudlakou | Dreamstime.com

:Lilo:01:

Dedication

For the outcasts.

Chapter 1

I GRIPPED THE half-inch shard of silver between my finger and thumb, closed my eyes, and opened myself to my magic. The rosy glow of liquid light at the center of my being sloshed and bubbled as I dove into it, and the familiar tide of my emotions washed over me, as they always did when I tapped into the fae side of my powers. I'd done this so many times today that I no longer felt overwhelmed when I called the magic. The worry—dread, even—at the impossibility of my task had become, well, not comfortable . . . never that . . . but tolerable.

The edges of the silver scrap dug into my skin as I squeezed tighter, focusing on my goal. One more impossible task on the road to peace, but I'd accomplished the impossible before. I could do it again. I pushed my awareness into the metal, diving deep. Its core was cold and hard— a tangle of steel cables rather than the ribbonlike threads found at the center of living things. The shard's core sang of the deep earth, of moonlight, and of a flexible strength that was happy to change its form to the need at hand. That's why I'd chosen silver; of all the metals, it was the most accommodating. I peeled off a thread of the hazy pink light of my magic and wove it into the shard's core, binding, coaxing, telling the metal what I needed it to be.

I twisted together strands of silver with ribbons of magic as I pictured the beat of light and heat against my skin. At the same time, I wrapped the image of a protective cage around the silver shard. Pouring magic into the metal, I twined the feelings, linking them, syncing the cage to the feeling of heat and expanding the protective shell to encompass my hand. The silver grew warm. My fingers shook, pinching harder so as not to drop the smooth shard. The cords of its core deformed and rearranged as I pushed my magic into it. Changed it.

Yes, I whispered to the metal, as it gave way under my will and the force of my magic. *That's it.* The cords solidified. I choked off the trickle of magic connecting me to the metal, let my awareness sink back into my own body, and opened my eyes.

The walls and tools of my studio surrounded me, a comforting embrace, but I kept my attention on the half-inch shard of eighteen-gauge silver I'd cut for the purpose of this experiment. It looked like a perfectly normal hunk of metal pinched in my hand, its polished surface a bit clouded by the heat and moisture of my skin.

Please work. I pushed that prayer into the metal, not with magic but with hope. Lifting a lighter from my workbench, I lit a flame and brought it slowly toward my hand. If my magic worked, the spell locked into the silver would save my fingers from being burned.

The flame wavered as I moved the lighter closer to my skin. So far so good. I brought my hands together. Heat seared my knuckles. I jerked my hands apart.

"Dammit." Flipping the lighter closed, I slammed it to the desk and threw the useless silver shard onto the pile of failed attempts heaped at the edge of my workbench. It clinked against its companions, mocking me with their growing numbers. A guttural snarl built in my throat, erupting as an inarticulate shout as I swept my arm across the table. Silver shards scattered like confetti across my studio, bouncing off cabinets and the bricks of the cold forge, sliding over the smooth concrete floor to hide in the shadows of my larger tools. The tinkle of metal connecting with other objects echoed through the studio like wind chimes in a tornado for one brief moment. Then all fell still and silent. Only the angry huff of my breath filled the space as I covered my face with my hands and let myself wallow in the frustration of failure.

The earthy smells of fresh wood and metal dust mixed with the old char scent baked into my forge and the various chemicals used to color, clean, and otherwise treat metals. The puffs of my breath came a little slower as my pulse eased off the throttle. I tipped my chin to my chest, burrowing my fingers into the tied-back strands of my auburn hair. My gaze found and followed the whorls of wood grain across my workbench. Every scratch, scorch, and divot lifted my spirits a little higher. Hundreds of projects had come to life in this space. Tools and sculptures. Practical pieces and flights of fancy. Even before I knew I had magic. Especially then. Before fate, friendship, and long-lost family ties had dragged me into this impossible situation. This was my sanctuary. My kingdom. Here, I could do anything . . . eventually.

"But maybe not today." I pushed to my feet with a long, deep exhale, grabbed a broom out of the corner, and went to work cleaning up my tantrum.

As I swept, my mind drifted, teasing out possibilities about why the imbuing hadn't worked. Was it a shortcoming of power on my part? I'd managed to forge sunlight into metal before, so trapping a single property within a piece of silver should have been well within my abilities. Of course, that time I'd had my fae friend Kai to bolster and help direct my magic. I'd also turned a crumpled knot of fabric into a blazing handful of pure sunshine and shoved it into the face of an angry vampire, and I'd done that entirely on my own. I knew I could trap the heat of a flame, but somehow, despite weeks of trying, I still hadn't managed to. I'd thought perhaps the issue was with getting the silver to absorb something that wasn't there to begin with, which was why I'd poured heat into the heart of the metal first—like called to like. Clearly that hadn't been the solution. Perhaps the problem came from expanding the field beyond the shard itself?

I crouched and brushed the collected shards onto a dustpan. "I just don't know enough about the way my fae magic works." The studio's silence pressed against me in quiet agreement. My practitioner magic, the magic I'd inherited from my father, was newer, but it was more instinctive. I'd think of something, focus a bit of power, then the *something* would happen. The magic I'd inherited from my fae heritage had a lot more rules, but mastering them was necessary if I wanted any amount of permanence to my spell. I sighed and dumped my failed attempts into the scrap bin.

After propping the broom back in the corner, I retrieved my sketchbook from the floor, where I'd knocked it, and opened it to the sketch of a stylized sun pendant layered with notes and angry red scribbles. I'd thought today, with the implementation of my latest insight, I might finally succeed, might actually be able to dig myself out of the debt hanging over me like an avalanche poised to fall. I scoffed at my own optimism and snapped the notebook closed. Weeks of work and I was no closer to trapping sunlight . . . no closer to replicating the daywalking amulet that had protected James for years . . . no closer to fulfilling my oath. Tucking my journal of impossible tasks under one arm, I turned off the studio lights and stepped into the crisp mountain breeze.

A ceiling of gray clouds, heavy with rain and slightly paler in the west where the hidden sun was on its way down, kissed the tops of pine trees. Dim light blurred the shadows of the forest. The yellow-green of new growth dotted evergreen branches, while the fuzzy white tufts and round leaves of waking aspens filled in the gaps. Most of winter had melted away, save a few patches of gray slush tucked into the deepest shadows.

Soft dirt slicked with moisture clung to the tread of my boots as I left the oversized shed that served as my studio and retraced my earlier tracks across my property. My stomach grumbled as the front door to my modest ranch home drew closer, as if my physical body had suddenly woken from the trance I seemed to fall under whenever I focused on my work. Breakfast had been a very long time ago, and lunch had been a hasty granola bar. The extra energy I'd burned tapping into my magic, successful or not, came roaring into my awareness, sapping the strength from my limbs. I stumbled, dizzy, and pressed a hand to my gut. The cool breeze blowing through the valley ruffled my ponytail and snuck through a hole in the knee of my torn jeans. I hurried my steps, patting the rust-flecked blue paint of my sleeping Jeep as I passed, and pushed through the front door.

The TV in my living room played *Aladdin* for the umpteenth time. The genie was singing about what an amazing friend he was. That sentiment also applied to Emma, whose slippered feet peeked above the nearest armrest of the couch. I kicked off my boots and stepped around the sofa. Emma's head was propped on a pillow against the other armrest. The dark fluff of her buzzed hair topped her pale face. A dozen silver rings and studs pierced her ears, her eyebrow, her nose. Her eyes were closed. Her hands were folded over a tie-dyed T-shirt, rising and falling with her breath. She looked as if she were sleeping, but as soon as I rounded the end of the couch her eyes opened. Her milky-white stare found me.

It was disconcerting to have that blind gaze focus on me, not that Emma's eyes really had anything to do with her sight these days. Her practitioner magic had been damaged, then twisted—an unintended side effect from an encounter with an immensely powerful fae—resulting in a new form of magic that we were still trying to understand.

"Any luck?" Emma asked, grabbing a remote off the coffee table to pause her movie.

I shook my head, trusting her sonar-like awareness to convey the motion.

"Victoria's not going to be thrilled about that."

I rolled my eyes at mention of the vampire who ruled over the Denver metro area. "Thanks for the reminder." As if I could forget the threat looming over me if I didn't keep my promise to deliver amulets that neutralized sunlight—a delivery that was already overdue.

I dropped my sketchbook on the coffee table and continued past Emma, through the dining area dominated by my thrift-store oak table, and around the bar-height counter that acted as a boundary line for the kitchen. "I think I've got the *how* of imbuing down okay. It's *what* I'm trying to imbue that's the problem. It's too complicated."

"Bael did it," Emma pointed out.

Another reminder I could do without. Thoughts of my fae grandfather and his skill with our family magic irritated me on the best of days. Today was not the best of days. I opened the refrigerator door with enough force to make the condiments rattle and pulled out a leftover burrito from dinner two nights ago.

"Maybe you should pop over to Enchantment and ask for another lesson?"

I sighed. "If only it were that simple." The single lesson I'd had with Bael constituted nearly everything I knew about using my fae abilities. Of course I would love to learn more, and I was sure he'd be happy to teach me . . . for a price. Nothing came free with the fae. Least of all with Bael. He was the lord of the fae realm of Enchantment after all. "I'd rather steer clear of fae realms for a while."

"You may not have a choice if you want to keep your promise to Victoria," Emma said. "No one gets *everything* they want out of life. At some point you'll have to decide what's most important to you, and compromise on the rest. Besides," she continued, "you'll have to go back eventually, if for no other reason than to tell Kai it's safe for him to come home."

I made a noncommittal grunt and shoved my burrito in the microwave. My second roommate, Kai, had retreated into the faerie realms—along with any fae with a sense of self-preservation—while the dust settled after a conflict with a powerful rogue siren and her enchanted army brought humans and fae to the brink of open war. There'd been casualties on both sides, and it had seemed smart for my non-human friends to make themselves scarce until we knew what the fallout would be. It had taken weeks, but official pardons were offered to those of us who'd helped end that conflict. The human world wasn't exactly *safe* for fae at the moment, but Kai would no longer be arrested on sight if he came home.

"In fact," Emma continued, "maybe Kai could help you with the amulets." She sat up and pivoted to face the kitchen. "He helped you make zombie-killing bullets and that anti-vampire knife."

The microwave dinged. I retrieved my steaming burrito and carried the hot plate to the table, inhaling the spicy aroma. "Maybe," I said, but I didn't hold out much hope that Kai could help. He was fae, but young and inexperienced, and he couldn't imbue. That skill was unique to only one bloodline. Bael's. "I'll ask him before I ask Bael, anyway, but I'm not sure *any* fae will help me make artifacts that eliminate the vampires' biggest weakness, seeing how they're not thrilled that vampires exist in the first place."

Emma shifted suddenly, twisting to look at the front door.

I froze with my fork halfway to my mouth. A string of melty cheese stretched from the promised bite. "What is it?" I whispered.

Then I heard it—the rumble of an engine.

"We're about to have company," Emma said.

I glanced mournfully at the temptation on my fork, then set the bite down on the plate and stood up. "Anyone you recognize?"

Emma squinted as though she could see through the building's wall, which I suppose she kind of could. She shook her head. "Just one. Human. No magic."

A car door closed outside.

I crossed the living room and waited. Three solid knocks sounded on the front door. I took a breath and pulled it open.

A short woman with a messy blond bun stared at me through thin, rectangular glasses. Her green eyes were the color of spring grass, but they seemed unfocused, as though she were staring at something slightly behind me. She wore high heels and a pinstripe dress suit in shades of gray. She held a clipboard against her breast.

I raised an eyebrow. "We don't get a lot of solicitors out here."

"Alyssandra Katherine Blackwood?" The woman's voice had a singsong quality, but the use of my full legal name grated like nails on a chalkboard.

"Who wants to know?"

She glanced at her clipboard. "Are you Alyssandra Katherine Blackwood?"

I narrowed my eyes. "Yes."

"Then I am here to collect you."

I took a step back. "Excuse me?"

Emma stood in my peripheral vision, circling the couch in case I needed backup.

"Your presence is required at an emergency conclave of the council."

"Which council?" I asked. "The council of the Unified Church? The PTF directors? Have they finally set a date to begin treaty negotiations with the fae?"

She shook her head. A rumble of thunder pealed through the overhead clouds. When the sound died, the woman spoke into the silence of the hushed forest. "The Council of Seven."

I staggered as though gut-punched and grabbed the door for support. My chest refused to expand. The Council of Seven, also known as the Council of Sin. The vampire council. Part of me had hoped I'd never have to meet the bogeymen that kept the rest of the vampires in line, but that had been a thin hope after James's cameo on the evening news when he'd been recorded defending the local PTF headquarters from rogue forces. A well-known vampire—at least well known in the paranatural community—standing bare-chested under the midday sun. How could the council not take notice? And it wouldn't have taken much poking around for that trail to lead them to me.

I forced myself to inhale. At least they'd sent an envoy rather than the assassin James had predicted. Perhaps there was still a chance for me to talk my way out of serious trouble. I cleared my dry throat and asked, "When is the conclave?"

"It will begin as soon as you arrive. We need to leave now."

"They're already in town?" I pressed a hand over my racing heart to suppress its rib-jarring pounding while I considered the implications of having a large group of incredibly powerful vampires visit my already volatile city. "Where exactly is this happening? How long will it take?"

"For the security of the council, I cannot answer those questions."

"You can't be serious." Emma pulled the door open wider so she could stand beside me. "You expect her to just drop everything and come running at a moment's notice without having any of her questions answered?"

"Yes." The woman frowned. "This invitation will not be offered again. If you refuse to come with me now, you will forfeit your chance to present your case before the council."

I set my hand on Emma's shoulder. "It's okay, Em. I got this."

The truth was I didn't have it. I was a fisherman in a rowboat who'd accidentally caught a shark and been dragged out to sea. I was adrift without oars or a compass, but letting Emma see that wouldn't change the situation. It would only make her worry more.

"I expected something like this might happen," I lied. After James's description of the council, what I'd expected was for them to slide into my bedroom like smoke and slit my throat while I slept. I slapped a smile on my face and tried to project optimism. "This is a good thing, really. I'll be able to clear up any misunderstandings they may have about me. Maybe I can even convince them to join the paranatural alliance."

She scowled at me. "Then I'm coming with you. You'll need backup."

"I'm only going to talk."

"The last time you said that, you were snatched off a public dock and sucked into an underwater fae realm for three days."

"Vampires can't cross realms."

"That's not the point."

The woman cleared her throat. "Only Ms. Blackwood may come, but her safety will be guaranteed for the duration of the conclave."

"There." I indicated the woman and fought to keep a straight face. "You have the word of this creepy total stranger that I'll be safe."

The corners of Emma's mouth twitched. I watched her trying to fight her smile as I struggled with my own. We both burst out laughing. Sometimes the world was just too ridiculous to do anything but laugh or scream. I'd spent plenty of time screaming. Laughter felt better.

I wiped tears from my eyes. "Seriously though, if the vampire council wanted me dead, I'd be dead. The fact that this invitation isn't coming on the tip of a knife means they want something from me. So long as that's true, I'm safe enough. The same can't be said for you."

Emma crossed her arms with a *harrumph*.

The woman looked from one of us to the other, her expression neutral. "Are you coming, or not?"

I nodded. Dubious as this woman's guarantee of safety might be, I doubted she was lying when she said this invitation wouldn't be offered again. If I turned the council away now, their next envoy wouldn't be so polite. "Can you give me an *estimate* of how long this meeting will take? Hours? Days?"

"The conclave will last as long as necessary. It will adjourn once the council is satisfied."

I twisted my lips, trying to dislodge the sour flavor her useless answer put in my mouth. My experience with politicians—and vampires or not, that's what the council members were—was that they were *never* satisfied. "Can I at least pack a bag in case I want to freshen up between sessions?"

"Everything you need will be provided for you."

"No offense, but I prefer to wear my own underwear."

She looked at her watch. "Five minutes. No weapons."

That last comment smothered any lingering mirth like a plunge through an iced-over lake. The thought of being completely at the mercy of unknown vampires brought back memories of my time as a captive of the previous master of Denver—trapped in my own head, looking through the windows of my eyes as a stranger moved my body like a puppeteer. I shoved those memories back and slammed a steel door in my mind. Not all vampires were evil, and not all thralls were victims.

I didn't invite the woman in. I simply turned and walked toward my bedroom. Emma closed the door in the woman's face and followed me. As soon as I crossed the threshold to my bedroom, I pulled out my cell phone and speed-dialed James. Setting the phone to speaker, I set it on the end of my bed to free my hands for packing.

"I don't like this," Emma said from the hall as I shoved clothes into a teal-and-black backpack.

"Neither do I, but this honestly isn't the worst way this could have gone." I crossed to my attached bathroom to grab a few essentials. "We knew there'd be a response to James's public daywalking. If explaining the situation to the vampire council is the worst to come out of this, I'll be happy."

"And if it's not?" she asked, voicing my concern that a group of power-hungry immortals probably wanted more from me than a simple explanation.

"Then I'll deal with it." I shoved my toiletries in the bag. My phone call rolled over to James's voicemail. Scooping up the phone, I waited for the *beep* then said tersely, "Call me asap." I pressed the "hang up" button with more force than was strictly necessary, stuffed the phone in my pocket, and zipped my bag closed. Finding the magical thread that connected me to James where our souls had been twined together, I strummed it like a guitar string. A deep vibration thrummed through me, carrying the chant of *I am here*. That echo tugged me like a compass needle in the direction of Boulder, the direction of James.

"You should delay until you hear from him," Emma said. "Maybe he'll have an alternative to this near-kidnapping."

"If the vampire council wants to talk to me, chances are they want to talk to him as well, and I don't think even James would dare turn them down. These folks scare some of the most dangerous people in the world."

"That's comforting."

"The most likely reason James isn't answering is that he's already at, or on his way to, this conclave. In which case I'll see him there." I would have liked the chance to talk to him without an audience, but at least the side effects of our interlinked souls gave us options, assuming we could get close enough to each other.

Emma crossed her arms. "And if it turns out he's not there?"

"Even better." I slung my bag over one shoulder. "If by some miracle this isn't about James and his newfound ability to get a tan, then the council must want to talk to me about joining the paranatural alliance. If that's the case, I'd like to make a good first impression. Having James go all white-knight protector on my behalf isn't likely to accomplish that, so it'll be easier all around if he's left out of this."

"I'd still be happier if you had backup."

"Me, too. But you heard the talking statue out there. The vampires' dubious promise of safety doesn't extend to my friends." I set my hand on her shoulder. "I don't really have a choice here. I have to go, or face worse consequences down the road, but I won't put you in danger."

Emma pursed her lips but thought better of whatever else she wanted to say.

"Call David and let him know what's going on. He can work with Garrett and Sarah to cover any emergencies that might come up while I'm . . . otherwise occupied." I cast a wistful look at the light-imbued knife on my dresser—my only battle-tested protection against vampires—sighed, and pulled Emma into a hug. "Will you be okay on your own?"

"Will you?" She shot back.

"Touché." I stepped away. "Don't throw any wild parties while I'm gone."

"Only if you promise not to do anything reckless."

I wrinkled my nose. "That's a tall ask, considering my track record."

"Just come back safe."

When I opened the front door again, the woman who'd been sent to collect me was standing in the exact same place she had been, as though time had simply frozen on that side of the door.

"Ready?" she asked.

"As I'll ever be."

She backtracked to her car and climbed into the driver's seat. She didn't offer to pop the trunk, so I tucked my bag on the floor between my feet on the passenger side. She backed up and swung the car around before I'd gotten my seat belt clicked.

I twisted to see my home, tucked between towering pines with my rusted Jeep out front and my studio hunkered nearby. When the driveway curved and stole my view, it felt as if a hollow had been scooped out of my chest. I faced front and stared into the growing darkness. "What do I call you?"

"You needn't call me anything. I'm an extension of the conclave steward, Zuri Yahaya."

My limbs turned to ice as all the warmth in my body seemed to retreat from that statement. I studied the woman's profile. She was a thrall—a person whose sense of self had been completely overridden by a vampire. That's why her gaze seemed so distant. Her personality wasn't really in there.

More memories threatened to surface. I shuddered and rubbed my arms to dislodge the phantom sensation of teeth against my skin. Those thoughts were reserved for my nightmares; I refused to let them plague my waking world.

"Do you remember who you were before?"

She cast me a condescending smile. "I do."

"What was your name?"

"Helen Oswald."

"And you're okay with . . . this?" I gestured to her body, unsure how to indicate the wrongness I felt when I looked at her.

"I am."

I slouched against my seat and turned my attention back to the window, unable to frame a response that didn't sound like an insult. Gravel gave way to pavement as we left my driveway, and I wondered just where this ride would take me. A fat raindrop exploded against the windshield. Then another. Then all at once, the rain let loose as the long-threatening storm broke over the mountain.

Chapter 2

MY HEART SKIPPED a beat as Helen left the highway and steered the car toward a small airport just east of Boulder.

I sat up a little straighter and peered through the intermittent swipe of the windshield wipers. "I thought we were going to Denver." I glanced at my chauffeur. "Aren't the council members staying with Victoria?"

"You assumed incorrectly." She slowed the car as a burly man in a plastic poncho pushed open a wide, iron gate for her to pass. A sleek white jet waited on the airport tarmac.

"Where are we going?" I couldn't help but repeat my earlier question, hoping against hope that this time, without Emma as an audience, I might actually get an answer.

Helen stepped out of the car and closed the door behind her. She left the keys in the ignition.

Swearing at the sky, I grabbed my pack and followed her into the rain. It wasn't a downpour, but the fat drops were steady and stung when they hit. Coupled with the onset of night, the storm dropped my visibility to almost nothing, save where small globes of light marked the edges of the runway. I squinted at Helen, already halfway up a set of stairs built into the plane's door. "Are we going to be able to take off in this?"

She passed into the cabin without comment.

I muttered an insult that was lost to a peal of thunder and set my foot on the first step. A cone of light flashed over me. I turned to find its source. Headlights. A silver Porsche pulled to a stop beside the car that had brought me. I raised my hand to shield my eyes from the glare.

The man who stepped out of the driver's seat was easily seven feet tall, with broad shoulders, bronze skin, and straight black hair that hung to his waist. He tugged the lapels of his indigo suit and fixed his gaze on me. He started forward.

My attention shifted to the still-running Porsche. I knew who was in the passenger seat before I saw him. The constant thrum in my heart that sang the promise of souls reunited tethered me to James like the pull of a magnet, stronger the closer we came. The passenger-side door opened, and my vampire boyfriend stepped into the rain. All hope that this summons might be about anything other than James's televised midday display vanished. He stared at me over the silver roof of the sports car. The anxiety I sensed through our bond told me he was as torn to see me as I was to see him.

The massive man stepped around me without a word and climbed the stairs to the jet's dry cabin. I didn't spare him a glance. I was rounding the hood of the Porsche by the time James closed his door. He wasn't nearly as tall as the walking mountain I'd just passed, barely topping six feet. His lithe frame, hidden in the strategic cut of his long coat, belied his strength. Even standing in the rain with his short, black hair plastered flat to his forehead, he was beautiful, and seeing him brought a thrill to my heart despite the dire circumstances of our meeting.

James caught me up in his arms, pulling me into a tight embrace.

I see you received a summons as well. I spoke the words inside my head, trusting the magical bond between our shared souls would convey them to James. Touching as we were, I didn't have to try very hard to project. *I thought you probably would.*

But you hoped I wouldn't, came his silent reply.

Swells of emotion shifted between us. Mine, his, it was hard to tell when we were this close.

I stepped back and met his gaze. Staring into his impossibly blue eyes was like falling into the sky on a clear summer day. "Your being here doesn't leave much room for interpretation. This has to be about your daywalking."

"We knew they'd come. It was inevitable."

"But not quite the worst-case scenario you predicted," I pointed out in a falsely cheerful tone. "We're both still alive."

"Indeed. Which means we have something the council wants enough to bargain for. Do you remember what I told you about the council members?"

"That they're selfish and manipulative, but they'll always do what's best for the survival of the species."

"And what's best for their survival right now," he said, "is you."

"Until they find out daywalking isn't something I can turn on in them like flipping a switch."

He wrapped one arm around my shoulders and steered me toward the plane. "Let's keep that little detail to ourselves for now."

"Do you know where they're taking us?" I asked. "My kidnapper wouldn't answer any of my questions."

"Canada, I'd imagine. That's the closest."

"The closest what?"

"When the council convenes, they do so in a neutral location set aside specifically for that purpose and maintained by impartial stewards. There are three that I know of. Though they certainly could have changed them since my time on the council."

I couldn't swallow past the sudden lump in my throat. It was so easy to forget that James had once held a seat on the vampire council, that he'd had centuries of life, dozens of identities, before I was even born.

"Do you think we'll be able to talk our way out of this?" I whispered as we approached the stairs.

"I honestly don't know. The council has never been known for its mercy." He squeezed me closer. "But whatever comes, I promise, I won't let any harm befall you."

There's that white-knight syndrome rearing its head. I poked him in the chest. "And what if it's *you* they intend to harm."

We stopped at the base of the stairs. He smiled at me. "I won't go down without a fight."

"Just remember, we're in this together."

"Always." He kissed me on the lips. Just when my knees turned to jelly, he nudged me to ascend the stairs.

I glanced left as I boarded the plane, toward the cockpit. Mr. Mountain sat in the pilot's seat with a pair of large black headphones over his ears. He was flipping switches on the console. I wasn't sure how I felt about having the equivalent of a puppet fly the plane. Then again, Helen had managed the car okay. I made a mental note to identify the emergency exits, just in case.

I hadn't spent a lot of time on private planes, but this was definitely the nicest I'd seen. It had wide leather seats that reclined, permanently affixed tables, and enough space to stand up and stretch on a long flight. All the windows were closed, making the space feel a bit claustrophobic despite its luxury.

I walked past Helen, tossed my soggy pack and wet jacket onto an empty seat, and sat down near the back of the plane. James sat beside me and twined his fingers with mine.

I glanced at the still-open hatch, then at Helen, who didn't show any indication of closing it. I cleared my throat. When she looked at me, I nodded to the open door. "Why aren't we taking off?"

"We're expecting two more passengers."

I looked at James, whose expression reflected my surprise and concern. Who else was coming?

The rain beat a jig against the exterior of the plane while we waited. I shifted in my seat, trying to find a position that wouldn't press the wet sections of my clothing against my skin. I glanced again at Helen. She stared into space, seemingly oblivious. Her pilot counterpart was out of sight in the cockpit. I squeezed James's hand. *Can we review the council members and what to expect from them?*

He also glanced at Helen, frowned, then answered aloud. "It should be fine to discuss what you can expect from the council. Their anonymity is as good as gone now that you've been summoned."

I watched Helen for some reaction. She gave none.

James tipped his face toward the ceiling and exhaled. His gaze grew distant. Lines of tension creased the corners of his mouth and eyes as he dredged through memories from his time on the council. I'd seen a few of those memories myself. I hated to make him relive them, but the cursory explanation he'd given when he warned me of the council's inevitable attention suddenly didn't seem like nearly enough information.

"Hanzo holds the seat of Pride. He's probably going to be the biggest problem for us. He's very traditional and believes in honor above all else. He's never forgiven me for, as he sees it, abandoning my duty. The Greed seat is held by Fatima. Her title tells you pretty much everything you need to know about her. She'll vote whichever way brings her the most personal benefit. Chae-Won is Gluttony. Unless something has changed in their relationship, she'll follow Fatima's lead. Esteban represents Sloth, and he embodies it well. He rarely takes much interest in events and often seems to vote on a whim. The final seat is held by Cecil Greenwick. I don't know him except by his reputation as a ruthless businessman. His seat of Envy was empty while I served on the council. He's not only the newest council member but also the youngest."

I nodded. Two seats on the council would be empty. Wrath belonged to James—or had before he abdicated. The seat of Lust had been held by James's creator until he killed her nearly five hundred years ago. I'd experienced enough of James's past to know better than to mention either.

I opened my mouth to ask for more details on what the conclave proceedings would entail, but a flash of headlights swept across the cabin opening. All my focus snapped to the entryway. Car doors closed outside—four, no, five thumps. Voices drifted through the rain. Three more thumps, then one, two, three sets of headlights flared and faded, leaving the cabin entrance dark compared to the interior. A flash of lightning framed a woman's silhouette under the cover of an umbrella. She stepped into the cabin on a roll of thunder. I gripped James's wrist.

Victoria's emerald gaze met mine. A smile curved her crimson lips. "Good evening, Alex, James. So lovely to see you both." She swept down the aisle like a dancer, all fluid grace and promises. Only a few scattered drops of water dotted the fibers of her brown fur coat, but she slipped it off her shoulders and draped it over one of the empty chairs near the front of the plane. Glossy black hair that looked almost purple in the cabin lights cascaded around her shoulders and over a tightly laced bodice that pushed the creamy swells of her breasts into prominent view. A tight skirt with a flared hem hugged the curves of her hips and legs. Glittery scarlet sandals with ankle straps and four-inch heels peeked under the blood-red fabric.

I suddenly felt dingy in my torn jeans and damp T-shirt, wet hair plastered to my neck and dripping down my back.

Victoria smoothed her skirt and perched on one of the seats facing James and me. She looked ready to accept an award at a red-carpet event. And James, in his sharp suit and silk tie, would look perfectly paired on her arm. Even the rain, which had turned my auburn strands to spindly straggles, only cast a pleasant sheen on his dark locks once he'd run a hand through it. I squinted to make sure he hadn't cast an illusion to make himself look better when Victoria came in, but no, he was only rocking his natural sexiness.

Stupid beautiful creatures. Between the vampires and the fae I'd so often found myself dealing with lately, I was in danger of developing a full-blown inferiority complex.

James's free hand covered our joined ones, sandwiching my fingers between his palms. Feelings of comfort flowed into me.

You are the most beautiful creature in this room.

I laughed out loud, unable to wallow in my pity party with the warmth of how James viewed me wrapped around me like a hug.

Victoria narrowed her eyes. The smallest frown creased her mask of amiability.

She probably thinks you're laughing at her. James's voice coiled through my soul, projecting thoughts without words.

Serves her right. She's certainly laughed at me enough times.

Her presence here does not bode well for us.

Do you think she reported us?

Maybe. I sensed a hesitation. *Probably. There is, however, a small chance that she was holding out for the amulets you promised, and she's being reprimanded because she* didn't *turn us over to the council. Her silence would be considered a betrayal.*

I pursed my lips. *She doesn't seem worried.*

She wouldn't, even if she were.

I shifted my gaze to the person who'd followed Victoria onto the plane. The petite brunette was struggling to stow a soggy umbrella, a large suitcase, a small duffel, and a garment bag. No wonder Victoria had been the last to arrive. She seemed to have packed her whole wardrobe. I glanced at my backpack and smiled. There were perks to being practical, even if looking like a movie star wasn't one of them.

The brunette finished stowing Victoria's luggage and took a seat. Meanwhile, Helen closed the hatch and said something to the pilot. She paused before sitting back down and glanced at the three of us clustered near the rear of the plane. "*Now* we can leave."

The whine of the engines grew louder. The plane started moving.

"Oh shit," I blurted. "I don't have my passport." I'd been so caught up in the rush and worry of being summoned by the vampires that the rules of human travel had completely slipped my mind. "I can't get through customs."

"We control the customs office in Calgary," Helen said. "You won't have any trouble entering the country."

"I was thinking more about the trip back," I muttered.

Victoria tittered, the high-pitched sound filtering through her nose. "As if a piece of paper could get you home safely should the council deem otherwise."

I tried to keep that thought at bay as the plane picked up speed, pinning me to my seat, and its wheels left the ground.

"ALEX." SOMETHING soft and warm caressed my cheek, bringing with it a familiar smell of cloves and blackberries. "Wake up. We're here."

James's words sank into my sleep-addled brain, and my eyelids fluttered open. The plane cabin was dark except for a few dim LEDs marking the aisle and emergency exits. A sudden *thud* rocked me as the plane's wheels touched down.

I rubbed my grit-crusted eyes and stretched. I'd dozed off somewhere over Montana. All the windows were still closed, so there was no way to tell if the sun was coming up yet. I glanced at Victoria. Probably not sunrise, since I was traveling with vampires.

"Are we in Calgary?" I asked through a yawn.

James shook his head. "This is a private airstrip."

"You slept through Calgary," Victoria said. Her eyes twinkled with laughter. "Snoring, I might add." She pointed to my chin. "You may want to wipe the drool."

My hand came up before I could stop myself, but my chin was dry.

Victoria's smile widened, showing perfect, pearly teeth.

"Ignore her," James said.

The plane came to a complete stop. The whir of the engines died down. Silence fell over the cabin.

Helen stood and pressed a button on the wall to open the hatch and lower the stairs. A gust of freezing air surged from the inky black beyond the door and swirled through the cabin. She turned to us and said, "Welcome to Canada. Please watch your step."

I hugged myself and shivered. I was used to Colorado winters, but this was worse. The air hurt to breath, crystallizing the moisture in my throat and lungs with every inhale.

James handed me my coat, which, unfortunately, was still damp from my time in the rain. Victoria lifted her fur coat and sauntered to the exit as if the cold didn't bother her in the slightest despite her inappropriate dress. Which, to be fair, was probably true. Along with being unfairly beautiful, my vampire companions didn't have the same sensitivity to temperatures that I did, nor my pressing need to breathe.

James reached for my pack, but I snatched it from the seat before he could claim it. He glanced at me, then closed his hand and withdrew his reach without argument. I didn't need our connection to feel his frustration. Mostly James was good about letting me be my own person, fight my own battles, carry my own luggage, but it was a struggle for him. He'd come from, and lived through, different times. He'd done his best to keep up with societal changes through the centuries, but sometimes he needed reminding. Especially about things that were relatively recent developments.

Slinging the bag over one shoulder, I followed Victoria off the plane. She, of course, had left her luggage for someone else to deal with. When I reached the doorway, I froze on the top step. My mouth dropped open. The night was alive with color. Ribbons of green laced with pink rippled across the starry sky like oil swirled through water. Orange streaks silhouetted treetops against the horizon.

I made my way slowly to the ground, feeling for my footing while my focus remained on the light show. Ice-crusted snow crunched under my boots. The aurora's lights reflected off the frozen ground, making the land glow. I took a few more steps away from the plane and stopped, staring skyward. The cold stung my skin, burned my lungs, and dried out my eyes, but this silent spectacle was worth the discomfort. I could have stood there for hours.

"You're lucky to witness them," said an unfamiliar voice.

I spun toward the source of the words. A woman slightly taller than myself stood beside me. She wore a pale coat patterned with darker patches and lined with fur at the collar, cuffs, and thigh-length hem. Her features were hard to make out in the shade of her hood, even with the aurora lighting the night.

She gestured, drawing my attention back to the glowing ribbons in the sky. "The nights here are shrinking. In a few weeks, these displays will be chased away by the midnight sun until the end of summer."

"They're beautiful," I whispered.

James came to stand beside me. I quietly took his hand, and together we watched the sky dance. Even Victoria seemed entranced.

I'm not sure how long we all stood there, lost in the beauty of the sky, but eventually the stranger cleared her throat. "It is time to head inside. The council waits."

Reference to the council dropped me back into my body like a rock sinking to the bottom of a pond. I took one last wistful look at the playful freedom of the aurora, embedding its beauty in my memory, and forced my focus back to earth.

The three people who'd accompanied us from Colorado were nowhere in sight. The hatch to the plane was closed. I turned a slow circle, finally taking in the land below that hypnotic sky. We seemed to have landed in a snowy field in a wide valley. A high ridge swelled nearby, speckled black and white by snow, trees, and exposed rock. A sea of darkness coated the far side of the valley, where dense forest blocked the glittery reflection of the snow. Another mountain rose to cup the bowl we were in. I hugged myself and felt some of the tension in my chest ease. The place felt comfortable, familiar even though I'd never been there. Other than the lights in the sky, I could have been standing on my own mountain property on a winter night.

"This way." The stranger started walking.

"Who are you?" I asked as I scrambled to follow.

"Zuri Yahaya." She glanced at me. White teeth flashed in her dark hood. "I am the steward of this conclave."

I missed a step. This was the woman who'd enthralled Helen, who'd programmed her like a robot to come and get me. That meant she was a vampire, and a powerful one at that. I walked a little slower, letting some distance grow between me and my guide.

"What's the matter?" James whispered when he noticed my pace slow.

I shook my head. I'd known before stepping off the plane that most of the people I was about to interact with would be vampires. It wasn't a surprise. So why was my heart hammering so hard? Why had the realization that I was walking next to a vampire triggered my fight-or-flight response?

Because vampires are predators, I thought, *and humans are their prey. Somewhere deep down, on an instinctual level, I can't shake that truth.* I glanced at James, glad that he wasn't touching me, that I didn't have to shield my feelings for fear of hurting his. I loved James, but he was definitely the exception to the rule when it came to vampires. Of the others I'd met, I wouldn't want to spend time alone with any of them.

But the paranatural alliance is about creating a safe way for all the species to interact, I reminded myself. I rubbed my frozen fingers together and exhaled, leaving a trail of crystallized breath on the air. *I have to be bigger than my fear. The vampires are a powerful group. I can't afford to alienate them.*

"How much farther?" Victoria's question tore me from my thoughts. She was bringing up the rear, struggling for balance as her impractical heels sank into the snow with every step.

I turned away to hide my smile.

"Not far." Our guide didn't look back or even slow. It seemed Victoria was on her own.

"Allow me." James backtracked to Victoria, who wrapped her arms around his neck. He swept her off her feet in one smooth motion and continued forward with Victoria nestled comfortably in his arms.

Jealousy rippled through me. I tamped it down. *He's just being kind.* I clenched my teeth and stared resolutely at the ground in front of my feet as I tromped on. James was chivalrous by nature. He would have rescued any woman in Victoria's position. *But Victoria isn't just any woman,* whispered my insecurity. *She's James's ex-lover. They've known each other longer than you've been alive.*

I shot a covert glance to the side. With James in his suit and Victoria in her dress, coupled with the ageless youth of their unfairly beautiful features, they looked like a pair of movie stars out on a date.

The jealousy twisted with something darker. Victoria had likely betrayed James to the council for her own benefit. How could she snuggle against him as if she hadn't just offered him up on a silver platter? And how could he forgive her so easily?

James cast me a disapproving look, as though responding to the pettiness of my thoughts. We weren't touching, so he shouldn't have heard them, but I'd always been an open book to James. Even before he shared his soul with me.

"Here we are." Zuri's words split the silence and drew everyone's attention to a log cabin nestled at the center of a ring of evergreens. It was smaller and simpler than I expected, considering who was supposed to be waiting inside. Again I was reminded of home and my own secluded house. This building looked to be about the same size. I couldn't imagine how I would handle sharing such a tight space with Victoria, let alone the vampires on the council. I wrapped my arms around my torso and squeezed. I definitely wasn't going to get any sleep on this trip.

Chapter 3

ZURI PAUSED ON the front stoop of the cabin until I caught up and James had set Victoria back on her own two feet, then she pushed open the door and gestured for us to precede her inside. The interior space matched the simple architecture of the exterior. Woven rugs with colorful, geometric patterns covered hardwood floors. The stripped and sealed timbers of the cabin walls were left visible, the rafters exposed in the ceiling. A pair of overhead lights lit the interior, suspended from crossbeams by their power cords. A simple kitchen with a large iron stove that probably doubled as a heater filled most of the main area. One couch and two wooden chairs occupied the rest. The back half of the cabin seemed to be split between a bathroom—which I glimpsed through an open door—and what I assumed would be a bedroom through a closed door on the same wall. The decorations were rustic—antlers, animal pelts, and more geometric weavings hung like tapestries. A bookshelf made from split logs held a smattering of well-worn paperbacks. There didn't seem to be any personal items.

"Welcome to the Canada conclave." Zuri closed the door behind us and pushed back the hood of her parka. A mass of black curls parted slightly off center fluffed around her face, as if excited to be free from the confines of her hood. Gray threaded the black in pale streaks. Zuri smiled, and her teeth shone in contrast to her dark skin, as they had in the shadow of her hood. Her long nose hooked down at the tip over full lips. Her brown eyes carried a metallic sheen, as though swirled with molten bronze. She stomped her calf-high boots on a thick mat just inside the door to knock off the snow stuck in her treads and strode through the room toward the closed door on the far side. "Come along."

We all filed into what was indeed a bedroom. Two sets of bunk beds lined one wall, separated by a narrow dresser under a curtained window. Another rested against the back wall, its lower futon folded into a couch.

My jaw dropped as I imagined sharing not only this cabin but this very small bedroom with multiple unfamiliar vampires. "You have got to be kidding me."

Zuri looked at me and arched an eyebrow. Victoria covered her mouth with her fingertips as if to stifle a laugh, or possibly to imply, "What an embarrassment you are."

James took my hand and offered a sympathetic smile. "This isn't the whole building."

I glanced behind, into the cabin's main area, then at the back wall of the bedroom. Together they seemed to account for the length I'd seen from the outside, but I held my tongue. Clearly I was missing something, and I didn't want to look any dumber than I already did.

Zuri pulled open a louvered door and stepped into what looked like a cedar closet. Victoria followed her inside, and James tugged me along like a reluctant puppy. I wasn't naturally claustrophobic, but sharing such a small space with three vampires was an exercise in self-control. With a deep breath, I pressed shoulder to shoulder with Victoria and waited for whatever was going to happen.

James pulled the closet door closed. The darkness became oppressive as we bumped against each other, and the air grew slightly warmer from our body heat. There was a soft *click* followed by the hum of machinery. The room lurched, flinging my stomach into my chest and sending my heart to live in my throat. I gasped and grabbed James for support as we plummeted into the mountain.

The closet-slash-elevator jerked to a sudden stop that buckled my knees. Only James's arm around my waist prevented me from ending up on the floor. Light once more filtered through the louvered slats of the closet door.

"Jeez," I muttered, steadying myself and looking at the wood-panel ceiling of the little room. "How far did we just drop?"

"Around forty feet," Zuri said. "Mr. Abernathy, if you would?"

James shoved the door open.

Bright light made me wince and shield my eyes. James stepped out, towing me with him. I blinked a few times to let my eyes adjust, then lowered my hand. My breath lodged in my chest as my lungs momentarily forgot how to function.

This room was easily three times the size of the cabin above. It had a cathedral ceiling at least two stories high, carved from white marble with sweeping arches, sleek buttresses, and spiral columns. The elevator had deposited us on the topmost step of a half-circle staircase that descended into the center of the chamber. Intricately carved arches on the remaining three walls led to brightly lit corridors lined with what looked like LED sconces tailored to resemble medieval lanterns.

I stepped away from James, descended the stairs, and turned a slow circle, taking it all in. "This is incredible. How long did it take to carve all this out? Was the marble native, or did you ship it in?" Following the sound of trickling water, I slid my fingers along the smooth curves of a stone banister that overlooked a fountain set in one corner of the vast chamber. Clear water tumbled from the mouth of a stylized serpent that was carved to look as if it were swimming in and out of the wall, causing frozen ripples in the stone. The water tumbled along a series of basins before plunging into a blue-tiled pool.

Another corner held a monumental figure sculpted with its arms raised as though shielding itself from an attack. The way the light fell in the room cast that corner in shadow, making it appear as though the figure were retreating from the encroaching light. I gazed up and up, awed by both the size and craftsmanship. The drape of the marble fabric made it difficult to determine sex, and a peek behind the arms revealed an equally androgynous face, though the exquisitely carved expression was easily recognizable as pain. I reached out and set my palm against the giant toe of the cringing figure.

Emotions slammed into me. Terror. Confusion. The sensation of burning. A memory of blistered flesh. Then another, and another. I gasped, preparing to scream.

"Alex!" James's face hovered inches from my own. His fingers dug into my shoulders hard enough to hurt. "Snap out of it."

I took a shuddering breath. My eyes rolled, cataloging the space around me—the vaulted ceiling, the statue, the burble of water. Zuri and Victoria watched me from behind James, staring over his shoulder. Victoria's gaze narrowed. A small frown creased her mouth.

Zuri looked curious but not concerned. "What was that about?" she asked.

"Nothing." I patted James's wrist. "I'm fine."

He hesitated before letting go. More emotions, mostly worry, surged through me, this time from my bond to James.

"Hmm." Zuri didn't seem convinced, but what could she do? She turned down the left-hand corridor. "This way."

I slipped my hand into James's to hold him back while Victoria passed.

Did you feel anything when I touched that sculpture? I projected as we brought up the rear.

Just your panic. Another wave of worry washed over me.

That statue is imbued.

James cast a sidelong look at me, his expression troubled. *No fae has ever walked these halls, least of all Bael.*

I frowned. *Are you sure?*

He leaned closer, tipping his head so his cheek brushed mine. "It would be blasphemy," he whispered, perhaps not trusting the imprecise nature of our silent communication to clearly convey the depth of his sentiment. "This place is, above all, a sanctuary from the bloodthirsty bigotry of the fae. That statue is a depiction of our progenitor. It's as close to a holy figure as we have. Letting a fae near it would be like a priest inviting Satan to piss on a crucifix."

"That's . . . graphic."

"The point is there's no way a fae has ever been anywhere near that statue."

I resisted the urge to point out that *I* was part fae, but he heard it anyway.

"You know what I mean."

I thought back to when I'd first learned I was fae, to the reason Kai sought me out, told me who and what I was. He'd needed my help reading memories from murder sites, reliving the final moments of people's lives that had been seared into the nearest object at hand by the strength of their emotions as they died. *Fae magic isn't the only way an object can be imbued.*

If the statue was sacred, maybe some of the vampires who'd passed through touched it on their way to face the council as a sort of fervent prayer. Seeing as the statue clearly depicted a vampire hiding from daylight, they'd naturally recall their own experiences with sunshine— especially if they were facing vampiric punishment from the council. Those emotions could be strong enough to leave a lasting impression when piled one on top of another.

Zuri stopped ahead. We caught up in half a dozen steps. "Prepare yourselves. The council awaits."

Shock ran through me like a bolt of lightning. I looked at the double-wide doors as Zuri reached for the handles—doors behind which the governing body of vampire society waited—and realized I was not at all ready to face them. I'd been running on momentum and bravado, sure I could muddle my way through when the time came. Now that that time was almost upon me, my confidence wavered. I glanced at James. "We don't get to eat, or change, or anything?"

"Did you think I wore this dress for you?" Victoria said as she plumped up her breasts and pinched a bit of color into her pale cheeks.

"I figured you were slutted up for an orgy when the council goons arrived," I shot back.

The fact that she didn't rise to my bait or laugh at my ignorance, just stared fixedly at the door Zuri was opening, scared me more than anything in our trip so far.

James set his free hand against my cheek, turning my face until my gaze met his.

"Don't be intimidated." A swell of pride rushed through our connection. "You are the most amazing person I've ever known, and I met Joan of Arc. You do the impossible every day. You're going to be fine."

"Aw," Victoria crooned. "That's so sweet I think I might puke."

Come on, Alex. I gave myself a mental slap. *You've faced down fae lords and PTF directors. You've come back from the brink of death and survived falling through the Rift. Placating a few immortal politicians should be a walk in the park. Right?*

I took a deep breath and let it out slowly, bringing down my heart rate.

James squeezed my fingers. *Together.*

I squeezed back. *Always.*

Victoria, James, and I followed Zuri over the threshold, pausing for her to close us in. The marble bricks of the hallway ended in a crisp line, giving way to darker, rougher stones. The circular room beyond the double doors was much dimmer than the hallway, lit only by a few hooded sconces spaced around the outer wall. A ring of narrow arches created a passage around the edge of the room. While the high ceiling's specific architecture was lost to darkness, flickering streaks of weak light slashed the shadows across the wide stone floor of the inner circle.

My mind twisted what light there was to a pale, watery blue as memories of Merak's throne room, and the first time I'd been brought before an unfriendly vampire, flooded back to me. He'd used illusions to create a house of horrors, tormenting me while his followers watched and cheered from shadowed archways just like this. Then he'd trapped my consciousness in a living nightmare. My knees wobbled. My lungs grew tight.

James squeezed my hand so hard it hurt. *You are not alone this time. I'm right here.*

I took a shuddering breath and forced the memories back. They wouldn't go entirely, not while I was in this place. They circled like sharks waiting for my vigilance to weaken.

Zuri stopped under the central arch, which was wider than the others. "You will wait here until called upon."

She marched to the center of the chamber. The darkness between the arches seemed to breathe like a living thing. "Three petitioners come today to face the judgment of the council," she said in a booming voice that echoed and amplified around the room. "Will you hear them?"

They damned well better after dragging us all the way out here, I thought. Quickly followed by . . . *although I rather wish they wouldn't.*

"We will." The words came from the darkness, seeming to seep out of the very walls.

One by one, torches along the inner arches lit of their own accord, blazing like tiny suns that made me wince and cringe with each addition as their brightness seared my straining eyes.

A tall, narrow throne carved of black marble veined with gold flared into existence under one of the arches to my left. Another appeared from the darkness on my right. Both thrones were empty. The next one was not.

A slim woman with brown skin and black eyes rimmed in heavy makeup sat upon the third throne. She wore a red-and-gold sari that left her right arm bare below a short sleeve while entirely covering the other. Her lustrous hair fell in long waves around her shoulders. Large golden earrings like inverted peacock feathers hung from her ears. A thin gold chain connected one ear to a piercing in her nose, and a collar of gold and pearls that must have cost a fortune ringed her neck. A matching headpiece held a pearl-inlaid starburst pendant against her forehead. *Judging by the dragon's hoard of jewelry draping her, this has to be Greed.*

The fourth seat held a man with olive skin and shoulder-length dark-brown hair that framed his face in haphazard waves, as though he couldn't be bothered to brush it. A short goatee hugged his lower lip and accentuated his chiseled jaw line. His eyes twinkled a pale greenish-gold when he looked at me. Despite sitting upright, he seemed to lounge in his chair. His relaxed attitude was matched by loose, homespun trousers, a collared, pink shirt with the buttons undone to the base of his sternum, and brown loafers without socks. *Probably Sloth.*

Next came a fellow in a silk suit and tie. He was a bit on the thin side but intimidating in his intensity. The lines around his stern lips and flinty eyes spoke more of frowns than smiles. Close-cropped, black hair clung to his brown scalp and continued past his temples, merging with a well-trimmed beard. *Envy, maybe?*

A petite waif of a girl dressed like a K-pop idol perched in the next chair, one foot tucked under her while the other swung freely. The bottom half of her hair was dyed bluish purple; the top was pink. Most of it was twisted into a pair of fluffy buns, save two tendrils left out to frame her childlike face. She wore mismatched hoop and dangle earrings. An eclectic collection of silver chains iced her neck and wrists. Her clothes were as mixed as the rest of her, consisting of a pair of loose red pants, a billowy white shirt cut well above her navel, and a cerulean-blue vest. *If the Indian woman is Greed, this must be Gluttony. Though how someone that small can represent gluttony is beyond me.*

The final seat, dead center in front of us, held a brick of a man. He had a square face the same width as his neck. The narrowness of his eyes made him appear as though he were half-asleep, but the dark focus in them exposed that for a lie. Gray shot through the temples of his short, black hair. The corners of his mouth turned down. He wore a shirt that crossed diagonally over his chest and a jacket with wide sleeves. His pants were similar to those of the girl beside him, loose enough to be mistaken for a skirt if you didn't notice the split. He wore socks and sandals on his feet, which were planted solidly on the ground. *No doubt . . . this is Pride.* Condescension radiated from every inch of the stiffly postured man.

My attention ping-ponged back and forth as each new throne, each new threat, was illuminated.

"They do so love a show," James muttered under his breath.

I cast him a sidelong glance, then looked back to the empty seats. Once upon a time, James would have been sitting in one of those. I squeezed his hand and prodded our link, wondering how all this must be affecting him. But James had closed the door on his side of our bond. He was better than I was at shielding his emotions, and he was locked down like Fort Knox right now.

Zuri, standing at the center of the now-lit chamber, bowed deeply, then straightened and said in that resounding voice, "Victoria, Master of Denver, wishes to petition for a boon."

She stepped backward, never turning, until she was even with the rest of us. Glancing at Victoria, she gestured to the space she'd vacated.

Victoria handed Zuri her coat without a word, straightened her shoulders, took a deep breath that threatened to burst the seams of her bodice, and sashayed forward, swinging her hips like a runway model. When she reached the center of the chamber, she made a deep curtsy. Much as I disliked her, I couldn't help but be impressed by her grace and balance in that ridiculously tight getup and stilt of a shoe choice. "Praise to the council."

"What is it that you want?" asked the woman in the sari with an Indian accent.

"And why do you think you deserve it?" added the young businessman, who I was now fairly certain was Envy by process of elimination.

Victoria straightened. "It was I who brought the council's attention to the miracle of James's daywalking, and I who informed the council of the abomination's talent."

James squeezed my hand a little tighter. A thread of anger filtered through his blockade.

It took a second for me to register that he wasn't angry at Victoria's betrayal of him. He was angry that she'd dragged me into this as well. Then it clicked. When Victoria said abomination . . . she was talking about me.

A sour twist cramped my insides. The temperature seemed to drop a few degrees. I'd been called "abomination" before. By fae. By humans. Repetition didn't make it any easier to bear.

"You did your duty," said the serious-looking Asian man I'd pegged as Pride.

"And in so doing, alerted the council to a significant threat and opportunity," Victoria replied in her sweet, lilting tone.

Loathing burned like acid in my veins. I couldn't believe I'd actually let myself hope that Victoria's feelings for James might keep us safe. She'd helped us before, but only for a price, and the council had deeper pockets than I ever would. Merak had been terrible, but at least he'd been simple. I'd always been off-balance with Victoria, never quite sure if she was an ally or an enemy. Now there could be no question . . . but the damage was done.

Greed waved Victoria's comment away with one resplendently bedecked hand and said, "We know what you did. What is it you *want?*"

Victoria lifted her chin. "I wish to claim the seat of Lust."

Greed raised one eyebrow. Envy looked apoplectic. The laid-back man who hadn't yet spoken laughed, a resounding sound that filled the chamber and faded into the now-visible vault above.

Pride sneered. "Council positions are reserved for those who distinguish themselves in some monumental way, such as single-handedly turning the tide of a war or overthrowing a nation. You think racing ahead of a piece of information to reach us first is a worthy enough act to earn you a seat?"

"All due respect," Victoria said, "but time grows short. The seat of Lust has remained empty for nearly five centuries. Elise was my maker. What better heir to her seat than one of her children?"

"What does she mean 'time grows short'?" I whispered, then chided myself for not keeping a better hold on my tongue. Standing before people he'd once served with, hearing them discuss the woman he'd killed to get there, had to be hard enough on James without fielding my questions.

"Council positions must be filled within five hundred years of the seat becoming vacant." James's words were a brittle whisper in my ear. It seemed he didn't want to open himself up enough for silent communication at the moment. "In all the time since my mentor's passing"—his voice hitched, snagging on the memory I knew haunted him of golden-blond hair stained with blood and staring sapphire eyes—"no one has distinguished themselves enough to earn the chair. With the deadline fast approaching, the council is running out of time to name a successor. Victoria knows that. She's counting on it."

"What happens if they don't find someone within five hundred years?" I whispered back.

"They must."

"Why?"

"Because it is tradition," boomed the deep, Asian-accented voice of Hanzo, a.k.a. Pride. His dark, disapproving eyes focused on me. I took an involuntary step back. "Petitioners in the gallery will remain *silent* until called forth."

"Yet the girl has a point," said the businessman I'd pegged as Envy.

I might have bristled at the term "girl," except that I was so unsettled by Hanzo's intense stare and rebuke that I did, in fact, feel like a child at that moment.

"Maybe it's time to rethink our selection process," Envy continued. What had James said his name was? Cecil something?

"Of course *you* would think that." Hanzo finally shifted his focus away from me.

Cecil met the older man's gaze, glare for glare. "Massacring armies isn't the only measure of a person's strength. The council deemed *me* worthy."

"The council deemed you rich," Hanzo shot back. "I'm still not convinced that makes you worthy." Hanzo gestured to Victoria without looking at her. "I suppose you think being an opportunist is enough to warrant council status as well?"

"Children," drolled the bored-looking man who had to be Sloth, "perhaps we can put your bickering aside for the moment and get back to the task at hand?"

"The petition has been made," said the eclectically dressed woman who hadn't yet spoken. Her voice was high-pitched and carried a thick Korean accent. I had trouble reconciling the anorexically thin girl with the title of Gluttony. "Clearly we're going to need some time to deliberate your request." She waved a dismissive hand. The many bracelets on her wrist jangled like chimes.

Victoria opened her mouth as though she had more to say, but Zuri strode forward and handed back her coat, effectively diverting her attention. "A guide is waiting outside this chamber to take you to your room. Your belongings have already been delivered." She ushered Victoria back toward us like a border collie herding a stray sheep.

The double doors opened from the outside as if on cue. The brunette who'd struggled with Victoria's luggage earlier stood on the threshold. Light from the hallway slashed across the shadowed area beyond the arches, creating a bridge of light that connected the inner chamber to the exit. I fought the impulse to run across that bridge.

Victoria glanced in our direction as she passed. No, not ours. James's. She met his gaze for a moment, then looked away. I couldn't interpret her expression. She and James had been friends, lovers—they'd known each other for centuries. Surely she must have some regret over stabbing him in the back?

I studied James's profile, again prodding the walls he'd erected around his emotions. He wore a sad smile as he watched her go. He didn't seem the least bit angry. I would have been angry. Hell, I *was* angry. I guess I'd just have to be angry for the both of us.

Victoria passed through the open doors. Zuri pushed them closed behind her, cutting off the external light. The aisle beyond the arches grew dark again, making it seem as though the council sat on a glowing island in a sea of shadows. James and I waited in the shallows.

Zuri passed us, once again taking up her position in the center of the lit area. "James Abernathy stands accused of endangering the secrecy of our race and colluding with fae. He will now face the judgment of the council."

Gravity seemed to go haywire as my organs flip-flopped in response to Zuri's words.

James took a step forward, releasing my hand, but I grabbed his sleeve and pulled him back, clinging to his arm as if it were a life raft in the ocean. The calm I'd been struggling to maintain had cracked under the weight of the word "judgment." Panic flickered like red lightning at the edges of my vision as my racing heart made me lightheaded, and my legs turned to jelly.

James patted my hand. His blue gaze was steady, unafraid. "Let go, Alex."

I shook my head.

It's okay. James's voice was a caress inside my head, soothing my panic like balm on a burn. *They aren't going to decide a case as convoluted as ours on a whim. They'll accuse, and grandstand, and try to scare us, but in the end, none of them will throw away this opportunity.*

You really believe that? I knocked against his mental barrier to highlight the fact that he was hiding his emotions from me.

He exhaled. His feelings flowed into me, first as a trickle, then as a flood. He really wasn't angry with Victoria for contacting the council. He'd expected the betrayal. In some weird way he was even proud of her for doing it. He was also worried about her. Worried that she'd bitten off too much by asking for a council seat. A simpler request would have seen her back on the plane with a pat on the head. Instead she'd gone in search of honey and put her foot in a wasp nest.

Thoughts of the council turned his emotions to frustration, regret, grief. Fragments of memories flitted like fireflies through my mind. Bickering. Deceit. Secret deals and outright lies. The council was divided. Yes, they ruled over vampire society as a unified force, but they were all snakes looking for advantage, desperate to stay on top and constantly suspicious. *They can't trust each other. That's their greatest weakness. They'll each want to keep us safe from the others until they've had a chance to twist the situation to their benefit.*

How can you be sure?

Because that's what I would have done when I sat in one of those seats. Memories of manipulations, threats, and unfair deals played out in my head, many of which starred James as the villain.

I dug my fingers into his arm, feeling sick.

The walls went up, shutting off the flow of memories and feelings. *Just remember, we hold the winning cards. As long as there's a chance they can use you, your life is safe.* He cupped my cheek in his hand. *This is a game I've played before. Trust me.*

"James." Zuri placed one hand on James's shoulder, drawing our attention. She gestured to the center of the chamber, half invitation, half command.

He nodded, shot me a brilliant, confident smile, and took the stage, spreading his arms and bowing with a flourish like a performer stepping into the spotlight. "I, James Abernathy, answer the summons of the council." He turned, meeting each council member's gaze for a moment before moving to the next.

The tightness in my chest eased as "James-the-showman" made his appearance. I hadn't seen that side of him in a while, but I'd witnessed it often enough at gallery openings and charity events in the years before we'd grown close. With all the drama in our lives lately, I'd forgotten how charismatic James could be when he had a part to play. How he was able to draw people in with a look or a gesture and get them to dance to his tune.

Maybe convincing the council to exonerate James and join the paranatural alliance won't be so difficult after all . . . assuming they're as susceptible to his charms as the check writers who come to his gallery.

"Cocky as ever, I see," grumbled Hanzo with the warmth of a shifting glacier.

"It's good to see you again, James." This came from Sloth.

James nodded. "I only wish it were under better circumstances." He lowered his arms to his sides and turned to the man in the suit. "Cecil Greenwick. Congratulations on your appointment. It's an honor to finally meet you." He made a more reserved bow.

"The honor is mine." Cecil placed a hand against his chest and bobbed his head. "Stories of your accomplishments are legendary."

Murmurs and smiles spread among the council members as they, too, were reminded of James's reputation.

Hanzo swung his hand as though swiping the contents off a table to clear it. "Yes, yes, we all know who he *used to* be." His emphasis on the phrase "used to" created a knot in the pit of my stomach. "The problem is who he is now. Flouting our laws, doing as he pleases with no regard for the cost. Not only has he disrespected this council, he's endangered our very existence."

The knot in my stomach grew tighter, pulling in other organs and sinking lower with the added weight.

"Indeed," said Greed. She focused on James, who gave her his full attention. "For someone who left us to seek a quiet life, you've been making an awful lot of noise lately."

"Not on purpose, I assure you."

She frowned at him as a parent would at a child who was clearly lying. "When you left this council, you swore you would never again rule an area."

"And I haven't."

"Yet you overthrew Merak, the master of Denver."

"In self-defense. *He* declared war on *me*."

"Now," she continued, "you collude with the master who took his place. A woman well known to be your protégée. It does not seem unreasonable to see this as a puppet government that allows you to control the city without, strictly speaking, breaking your vow."

"That same protégée now requests a seat on this council." Hanzo picked up the narrative. "An honor *you* abandoned." He twisted to address his fellow council members. "Perhaps he's come to miss the taste of power."

Gluttony shook her head. "If that were the case, he could simply have come back. It's not as if he ever technically *stopped* being a council member."

Hanzo thumped a fist on the arm of his throne. "That's exactly what he did."

"Chae-Won is correct," Sloth interjected. "James stopped performing his duties, but technically he was never stripped of his title."

My heart fluttered as I absorbed the import of the exchange. James was still on the council? Could that help us? Maybe. But if he used that influence, he would surely be dragged back into this world that he'd sought to distance himself from. And that was assuming the council would allow such a return. Hanzo at least didn't seem happy to see him again.

"Even a council member should not be allowed to run amok as he has." This came from Cecil. "I am sorry, James, but holding hostage the PTF board of directors? Jumping out a fourth-floor window on national television? Dating the spokesperson for paranatural rights?" He gestured in my direction. "These are hardly the acts of a man seeking a quiet life."

"Top that off with your display in front of the Denver PTF building when that siren attacked . . ." Greed's words rippled through the room like a stone dropped into a still pond. "You've put yourself at the heart of matters in the Mortal Realm. You have no one to blame for your current situation but yourself."

That's not true, I thought. *Everything James has done—threatening the directors, fighting the sorcerers, colluding with fae—it was all for me.* I bit my lip and took half a step forward, inching toward the light.

James's gaze snapped to me, freezing me in place under the shadow of the arch. For just a moment, his blue eyes looked silver. We weren't touching, but I didn't need our link to know he wanted me to stay out of this.

Zuri's hand settled on my shoulder.

I jumped. Focused as I'd been on the exchange happening in the light, I'd nearly forgotten she was standing in the shadows beside me.

"You'll have your chance to speak," she whispered. "But not yet. Listen and learn."

"And how exactly were you able to hold off those rabid werewolves and mind-controlled soldiers under the blazing afternoon sun?" Sloth asked. He spread his hands wide, indicating his fellow council members. "Most, if not all, of us were aware of the trinket given to you by the Lord of Enchantment all those years ago, but we all saw the footage Victoria sent. You were nearly naked in that fight. No magic amulet. Sun shining gloriously against your bare skin. Yet you weren't burning." He leaned forward, his relaxed air falling away. His narrowed gaze took on a sharp intensity. "Even the first of us could not boast such a feat."

And there's the heart of the matter. I tightened my hands to fists, arms pressed to my sides. These people, powerful and proud, had no idea how James had survived the sunlight. That was the trump card keeping us alive. As long as we held that secret, we had a strong bargaining position. The moment they discovered I could never do for them what I'd done for James, the polite hospitality of this conclave would vanish.

Cecil stroked his beard in an offhand manner and asked, "What can you tell us about your immunity to sunlight?"

Blunt as a bulldozer, that one.

"Is it a recent development, or was the amulet Esteban referenced merely a cover story for your ability?"

"I assure you, the daywalking amulet was real," James said. "Victoria used it, as well."

"So she claimed," Chae-Won said. "She also said it was destroyed."

James nodded. "In the battle with the necromancer at Arlington."

Fire and ice raged inside me, flaring in my cheeks and freezing my limbs, as happened anytime someone mentioned my father and the twisted magic he'd wielded.

"So your condition was already permanent at that point." Cecil concluded.

"It was."

"How?" Hanzo's gruff demand made goosebumps pop out along my skin.

James looked from face to face. "Since when is it the policy of this council to police individual assets?"

Hanzo's already stern face grew stony. He sat back. I could almost picture a cartoon thundercloud crackling above his head.

"We're not talking about a simple talent, James." Fatima folded her ringed hands in her lap, smoothing the drape of her sari. "What you can do . . . it could redefine our species. It could shift the balance of power in our favor. We might finally be able to come out of the shadows. You could put an end to millennia of vampires hiding for fear of being eradicated by the fae."

"Or don't you care about that anymore?" asked Sloth. His gaze found me in the darkness under the arch. "Perhaps your loyalties have changed?"

"I wish for nothing more than to see my fellow vampires take their place alongside the other species of this world," James said. "And I shall be pleased to discuss what possibilities my new talent might provide . . . once the charges against me have been cleared. I'm sure you can all see how the uncertainty of my current situation might prove distracting."

"He's playing us for fools," Hanzo said. "We should execute him now, as we should have when he walked away from this council."

"And lose this opportunity?" Cecil asked. "That's terribly short-sighted of you."

Fatima nodded. "We should not let past grudges influence our decision in this matter."

"Shall we put it to a vote?" asked Esteban. "All those in favor of summary execution?"

My breath caught in my throat. I stepped to the edge of the light before I realized I was moving. Zuri's hand wrapped my upper arm like a vise, stopping me from going any farther.

Hanzo's hand shot into the air. No surprise there.

My lungs burned, desperate for air but struggling to fill against the pressure in my chest.

Esteban's hand was slower to rise, but it too went up.

My heart hammered against my ribs, and the pounding of my pulse drowned out any possibility of sound. I swung my gaze desperately around the room, alert to any movement.

"It is decided," said Fatima. "James will be put on trial and allowed to defend himself."

Esteban and Hanzo lowered their hands.

"The trial will begin tomorrow," continued Fatima. "You will be shown to a room until then."

Once more the double doors to the chamber opened, creating that brilliant bridge of light to the outside world. The mountain of a man who'd flown our plane stepped up to the threshold.

James bowed to the council, then turned his back on them.

Zuri stepped away from me as James approached. I no longer had any desire to leave my place under the arch.

He cupped my chin in both his hands and pressed soft lips to mine. I wrapped my arms around his waist, pulling him closer.

That was too close. Even my mental projection sounded shaky.

I warned you about their grandstanding, he thought back. *They wanted to remind me what's at stake.*

One more vote and they would have killed you.

Exactly.

Hanzo wasn't bluffing. He's disappointed you're still alive.

Yes. We're going to have to do something about him.

"Let's go, James." Zuri's words broke into our private conversation.

I opened my eyes, which I hadn't realized I'd closed, and found myself staring into a sea of blue. *Remember, they will try to trick or scare you into giving them what they want. Don't let them.* He rested his forehead against mine. *You hold both our lives in your hands.*

Zuri cleared her throat. The guide-slash-guard who'd come to collect James stepped into the room, growing impatient.

James planted one last kiss on my forehead as he pulled back, trailed his hands over my shoulders, and walked away.

The doors sealed. The light of escape disappeared. I continued to stare into the darkness of his retreat.

"Alyssandra Blackwood," called Esteban from the glowing island behind me. "Step forward."

Chapter 4

MOISTURE SLICKED my palms. I dry-swallowed and wiped my hands on my jeans. My legs shook.

Move, I scolded myself, but I continued to stare at the spotlit center of the room where I was intended to stand.

Zuri nudged me forward when it became apparent my feet had grown roots.

I took one stumbling step, feeling the council members' eyes upon me as I approached the edge of the shadows. Filling my lungs as much as possible, I lowered my pack to the floor, straightened my shoulders, and stepped into the light.

Everything looked different from the center of the chamber. The lights that had illuminated the council members when I peered at them through the arches now blinded me, turning the daunting figures on their thrones to shadowy silhouettes. The vault of the ceiling created an echo chamber, causing every sound to boom in my ears.

This room is designed to intimidate. Somehow, that thought made the whole scenario a little less scary. I'd met monsters who didn't have to rely on tricks.

I cleared my throat and squinted at the backlit figures. "I am *Alex* Blackwood." I emphasized my chosen name. "And I have come to address this council on behalf of the paranatural coalition."

Hanzo snorted. "You have been *summoned* by this council to answer for your culpability in potentially exposing us to the human population and to clarify the part you played in James's current condition."

I took a deep breath and forced myself to relax so that my voice wouldn't shake or crack. "Then it seems we have *three* topics to discuss."

A soft chuckle drifted through the room, but I couldn't tell from which person it had emanated.

"Where to begin?" said Chae-Won. "Shall we start with your blatant disregard for our wish as a species to remain hidden?"

I lifted my chin. "I haven't told anyone about the existence of vampires who wasn't in a position to discover the truth for themselves."

Cecil scoffed. "You as much as outed us on national television when you told the PTF board of directors that they shared the world with more than practitioners and werewolves, that there were other species who hadn't yet revealed themselves."

I opened my mouth, but Fatima beat me to the punch.

"Then you handed James over to the PTF testing facility like some kind of specimen to be dissected." She shook her head. "Honestly, I can't understand why he still seems to care for you."

Her words punctured my heart.

"I assume it has something to do with Victoria's claim that she's responsible for his ability to walk unscathed in daylight." Hanzo said. "Perhaps his obedience is the cost for her protection, like the Church with their magic-dampening collars."

Hanzo's comparison lit a fire in my soul. I bunched my fingers into fists as the heat of his accusation flared through me. I was nothing like the bastards who'd taken my father away, made us believe he was dead, just so they could use his magic as a weapon against the fae in their pointless war. James wasn't a prisoner or a pet. He didn't owe me anything. I took a deep breath, ready to set these pompous jerks straight . . . then snapped my teeth closed on the first word as James's parting warning filled my head. *They will try to trick or scare you into giving them what they want. Don't let them.*

I couldn't afford to lose my temper. Not here. Not with both our lives on the line.

I exhaled slowly and shook out my tingling hands. Then I cleared my throat, faced Hanzo, and smiled. "My personal relationship with James is no one's business but our own." I shifted my gaze to the silhouette of Cecil. "As to my allusions to other paranatural species during my televised discussion with the PTF board, I never once used the word 'vampire'."

"James's show of force was on full display, fangs and all."

"As was his immunity to the afternoon sun," I countered. "Plenty of species have fangs. Do you really think anyone would look at him and think *Dracula*? If anything, having James tested by the PTF helped to *hide* the existence of vampires."

"At the very least, it confuses the matter," chimed Esteban. "One must consider that having a vampire who doesn't follow the usual conventions could be a useful tool. Especially in dealings with the fae."

"Perhaps," Fatima conceded, "but we are getting ahead of ourselves.

James's usefulness is a matter for *his* trial. Ms. Blackwood's crimes are her own."

"Agreed," said Hanzo. "I propose that Ms. Blackwood used her knowledge of our existence as a bargaining chip in her negotiations with the PTF, thereby endangering our secret, the sentence for which is execution. All those in favor of summary judgment?" He raised his hand. Cecil's hand shot up almost in sync.

Hanzo waited a moment. When no others joined their judgment, he and Cecil lowered their hands. "Those in favor of a full trial?"

Esteban, Fatima, and Chae-Won lifted their hands.

I exhaled noisily, having held my breath through the voting.

"We shall proceed with a trial to determine whether Ms. Blackwood's actions or comments constitute a violation of our laws," Fatima announced.

"All due respect," I piped up, my confidence momentarily bolstered by their pronouncement, "but how can you judge me by your laws? I'm not a vampire. I only found out you existed a few months ago. Why would you assume I knew your rules at all?"

"Ignorance of a law does not grant immunity from it," Esteban said. "You would not be the first ignorant human to die for a foolish mistake."

Fatima's voice cut through the room, tinged with . . . irritation? Impatience? "Regardless, the need for a trial has been established. Shall we move to the next topic?"

"Indeed," said Cecil. He leaned forward, bracing his elbows on his knees. The deep shadows cast by the angled lights created the illusion that he was draped in a living cloak of darkness.

I shivered, scratching a faint itch on my right arm. Startled, I glanced down. The spiral of tattoo hidden by my sleeve was reacting to the use of magic. Specifically, magic directed at me. I narrowed my eyes. Perhaps there was more to the trickery of light and sound in this place than architectural engineering. Vampires were masters of illusion, after all.

"Exactly what part did you play in James's sudden ability to walk in daylight?" Cecil continued, unaware that his attempt to appear dangerous had backfired. Not that he wasn't plenty dangerous without the creepy shroud—only an idiot would think a vampire was anything less than deadly—but the fact that he was trying so hard to intimidate me meant he doubted himself. Judging by the way he'd interacted with Hanzo, coupled with his current overcompensation, Cecil probably had an inferiority complex. *Not too surprising for the seat of Envy, I guess.* I frowned. *I wonder if they take on the traits of their titles after getting on the council, or if their personalities already matched their seat descriptions.*

"Well?" Cecil's irritation snapped me back to the present.

Taking a deep breath, I straightened my shoulders, lifted my chin, and reminded myself that I held a winning hand. "Frankly, I don't see how that's any of your business."

Chae-Won's sudden burst of laughter drew everyone's attention. She wiped her cheek, as if brought to tears. "You find a way around a millennia-old curse, and you can't see how that concerns us? Are you dense?"

I glowered. "Oh, I understand perfectly why you'd be interested in the knowledge, but you have no right to it."

That shut her up.

"You seek to bargain with the knowledge?" Greed's voice was low and dangerous, but also hungry. I had something she wanted. Something they all wanted. And now they knew I wasn't dumb enough to just hand it over out of fear.

Silence stretched.

Esteban shifted on his seat. The soft rustle of fabric carried like the crash of a cymbal. He cleared his throat. All eyes turned to him as he asked, "You desire that the vampires as a whole join your paranatural alliance, correct?"

I inhaled but didn't immediately confirm his claim. My time among the fae had taught me to measure my words. Knowledge was power, especially when making a bargain. Careless words could snare the unwary as surely as ropes or chains. "I've come to outline the potential benefits of such an alliance, both to the world in general and to the vampire community. I'm only acting as an intermediary."

Hanzo crossed his arms. "We have no interest in such an alliance."

"On the contrary," said Fatima. "I'd be willing to entertain such a notion if it meant walking in daylight." She turned to Esteban. "I assume that's the compromise you were implying?"

"Just so," he said, turning his focus back to me. "Our secrecy has always been paramount to our survival. With our current vulnerability to sunlight, we'd be at a disadvantage among the other alliance participants, not to mention the PTF, should our existence be confirmed. But if we could meet the other species on equal footing, we'd be much more likely to join them on the world stage."

"The whole point of the paranatural alliance is that we present a united front," I countered. "You don't have to stand strong alone. The

PTF couldn't move against you without going to war with the were-wolves and human practitioners as well. And they know that's a fight they can't win. Joining the alliance would grant you the protection of the other Earth paranaturals."

Cecil scoffed. "She would make us servants, ever dependent on the graciousness of others. Secrecy not only keeps us safe but keeps us strong. In the shadows we can shape the world. She would drag us into the light to dull our fangs and render us helpless. It is a trap."

"For once we find ourselves in agreement," said Hanzo, his voice booming off the walls. "There are other ways to get the information we desire than to entertain such absurd notions."

"Are you so sure?" asked Chae-Won.

"Torture can be quite effective," said Hanzo.

My breath caught. I stiffened my limbs to keep from shaking like a leaf as the council members discussed my fate as though they'd forgotten I was still in the room.

No. They're doing it on purpose. They want to scare me into folding. I clung to that thought as my imagination ran wild with all the things a group of sadistic vampires could do to a human.

"I say one of us enthralls her and be done with it," said Fatima.

"Assuming James hasn't already," said Esteban.

"She doesn't seem enthralled," said Fatima.

"And who would you suggest takes her?" Cecil asked. "Yourself?"

"Don't you trust me?" Fatima offered him a wicked grin.

I cleared my throat.

Five pairs of eyes swung in my direction.

"While I don't deny that you could torture me beyond my breaking point," I said with only a slight quaver in my voice, "my particular brand of magic won't work if I'm being coerced." I forced as much sincerity into the half-bluff as I could. I was fairly confident that being enthralled would screw up the level of self-awareness required for me to imbue, but I couldn't be certain. There was still an awful lot about my magic that I didn't understand.

Cecil shook his head. "Of course she would say that."

"That doesn't mean she's lying," retorted Chae-Won.

"I motion a vote," said Esteban. "All those in favor of at least *considering* alliance participation in exchange for the ability to walk in daylight?" Esteban, Fatima, and Chae-Won raised their hands. "Those opposed?" Hanzo's and Cecil's hands went up. "Then we're agreed that the subject is open for discussion," he concluded.

"Assuming she can actually deliver," Chae-Won added, shifting her childlike gaze to me.

I scrambled for something to say that would keep them interested without promising something I couldn't follow through on. Getting caught in a lie at this point would definitely come back to bite me, but I was only safe so long as they believed I could provide what they wanted.

"You all saw James," I said at last. "He's no longer affected by sunlight." I stood a little straighter. "I did that."

"Can you do it again?" Fatima gestured around the council chamber. "To us?"

My heart hammered against my ribs as I thanked the stars that half-fae weren't bound against lying like our full-blooded relatives. "I'm at least willing to *consider* the possibility."

"Touché," said Esteban. "Then I suggest we retire for the day. Negotiations can begin in earnest when we reconvene."

"I'd like to make something clear," I said, ignoring the dismissal.

Their irritation was palpable as the council members stared at the audacious human in their midst.

I cleared my throat. "If James dies, I swear that none of you will ever walk in daylight. That point is non-negotiable." Despite the fact that it went against every instinct in my body, I turned my back on the council and forced myself to walk slowly back to the arch where Zuri waited. The hairs on the back of my neck tingled. My shoulder blades itched. But I kept my head high and my steps even.

The door behind Zuri opened. The bridge of light unfurled before me.

"Helen will see you to your room," Zuri whispered as I passed, seemingly afraid of drawing attention to herself.

I lifted my backpack without pausing, slung it on my shoulder, and proceeded out the door. Not a sound escaped the chamber behind me. I could almost believe the room was empty except for the pressure against my back.

Helen stood across the hall, watching my approach. I kept my gaze fixed on her unfocused expression until I was over the threshold.

The doors swung on silent hinges. When they came together, the pressure around me eased. My knees buckled as though a tether had been cut. I stumbled to the far wall and braced against it.

Helen looked on in silence. After a moment or two of watching me gasp for breath, when my hands had finally stopped shaking, she gestured down the hall. "This way."

The underground compound was a labyrinth of polished marble hallways, twisting back on themselves in ways that seemed impossible to my anxiety-addled brain as I tried to map my path. I gave up after the sixth turn. I'd never find my way back to the council chamber without a guide, let alone the exit to the surface. Identical doorways with molded wooden frames disrupted the uniformity at random intervals. Testing the tether that connected me to James, I guessed he wasn't behind any of these doors. Every step I took following Helen stretched our connection thinner as I moved farther away.

At least he seems okay, I thought. We were too far apart to communicate directly, but I didn't sense any pain or fear. Just the reasonable amount of worry I would expect from anyone facing an uncertain future.

I suppose Victoria is behind one of these doors, too. I bunched my fists, picturing the haughty way she'd faced the council, as if she hadn't stabbed a friend in the back to be there.

"This is your room." Helen indicated a door, identical to those we'd passed, and handed me a rectangle of thick, white plastic with a metal clip attached to one end. "And this is your key. Don't lose it."

I took the keycard and gestured to the door. "This building is full of vampires. Do you really think a piece of wood is going to stop them if they want to come in?"

"This building was designed for vampires. Do you really think we didn't account for that?" She smiled a lopsided smile that made me think maybe her personality wasn't buried as deeply as I'd first assumed. "The walls, floor, ceiling, and doors are all reinforced. A vampire would be able to get through them eventually, but not before their efforts were noticed on the security cameras."

I tapped my keycard to the gray lock. There was a *whir*, a *click*, and a flash of green light. Turning the handle, I stepped inside.

The room looked how I imagined a posh hotel must be, and I turned a slow circle, mouth agape. The ceiling was a good twelve feet high. A crystal chandelier sporting hundreds of sparkling jewels reflected the light of two elegant floor lamps. Four velvet-cushioned chairs surrounded an oval table with cast-bronze dragon feet and a glass top. A pitcher of water and a tea service shared the surface with a tray of fruits, cheeses, and a loaf of bread that had to be oven fresh judging by the wisps of steam rising off it and the yeasty smell in the air. The entire back wall was dominated by a gas fireplace. Flames licked ceramic logs that looked just like the real thing. There was even an illusion of ash and glowing embers. The fire's lively light saved the stark stone walls and hardwood floor from feeling cold. A plush sofa and matching armchair sat on a thick Turkish rug in front of the fire. Bookcases with a collection of reading material in a wide range of genres framed the fireplace.

Two arched doorways, one on either side, exited the main room. One led to a white-marble-and-black-granite bathroom with gold fixtures that was larger than the combined living room, kitchen, and dining room of my home in Nederland. Bottles of oils and various dried plants lined a shelf above a clawed tub that promised to soak my troubles away. The second arch led to a bedroom.

A polished vanity with five mirrors and gold trim rested against one wall. Another held a six-foot, intricately carved wardrobe. A bed—so tall I'd probably have to jump to get into it—rested against the far wall. Beside the bed, an old-fashioned rotary phone with an elaborate black-and-gold receiver in a metal cradle sat on a mahogany nightstand.

"If you should need anything," Helen said, "use the phone by the bed. It can't be used to place outside calls. Rather, it will connect you directly with whomever is manning the help line in the security office. As an accused, you are prohibited from leaving your room without an escort. However, it's likely that some, if not all, of the council members will wish to speak with you at some point." She indicated a small black monitor anchored to the wall next to the door. A tiny replica of the hallway we'd just left was displayed on its screen. "You can identify visitors here before opening the door. Be aware that the security cameras do not cover room interiors for the sake of privacy. If you let someone in, you'll be on your own unless you call for help or exit the room."

I swallowed the sudden lump in my throat, picturing myself alone with any of the council members.

"Is there anything else you require?" Helen asked.

I shook my head.

"Then I'll bid you good day." She stepped out and pulled the door closed, sealing my gilded prison.

I let my bag slide to the floor with a *thud* followed by my still-damp coat. Turning another slow circle, I crossed to the table. The bread was as fresh as I'd hoped when I tore into it—a crisp shell housing warm insides as soft as air. The slightly nutty flavor was heaven itself. A small, silver cloche revealed butter and a variety of preserves. Making myself a small plate, I munched as I examined my surroundings in greater detail. Helen hadn't been kidding about not needing to pack. There were clothes—my size—in the closet for every occasion. A sealed toothbrush, toothpaste, and all the usual bathroom amenities, plus a few I'd never seen before, waited on the polished counter beside the sink. A navy-blue silk bathrobe draped the plush comforter in the bedroom.

I was barely halfway through my snack when the first knock came.

Setting down my plate, I examined the monitor on the wall. Greed—Fatima—stood outside my door. As I watched, she turned her face to the side, jewelry shimmering under the hallway lights, to look at something not captured on my screen. She knocked again.

My heart filled my throat as I wrestled with the decision of whether or not to answer the door. The last thing I wanted was to let her in . . . let any of them in, but neither could I afford to insult or offend her. Not when James's and my fate, not to mention the future of the paranatural alliance, rested on these negotiations. From what I'd gleaned from James's memories, most council deals were made outside of the official meetings.

I have to get as many of them on my side before the trial as I can . . . and this might be my only chance. Taking a deep breath, I opened the door.

Before I could speak, a bored, male voice said, "Isn't it past your bedtime, Fatima? Surely a woman of your advanced years requires her beauty rest."

I looked to the left, the direction Fatima had looked earlier, and found Sloth strolling toward us with his hands in his pockets.

"I see we all had the same idea," said an even deeper voice.

My attention swiveled in the opposite direction to find Envy approaching from the right.

Fatima snapped her fingers under my nose. "Let's get inside."

"Not so fast, Fatima," Cecil called. "Why should you get first crack at her?"

"Because I was the first to arrive," she shot back.

"But perhaps not the one Ms. Blackwood most needs to speak with," said Esteban with a twinkle in his green eyes.

"I'm surprised you bothered to visit at all," she said. "You've been up for what, two whole hours now? You must be exhausted." She turned to Cecil. "And you made your position clear in the voting. Why would Ms. Blackwood wish to meet with someone who clearly wants her dead?"

"Perhaps to change my mind?" he replied.

"Please"—I held up a hand—"call me Alex. And I'd like to speak with each of you . . . one at a time."

"Then I request the honor of going first." Esteban reached past Fatima to lift my hand, which he brought to his lips with a bow.

"Get in line," Fatima said, bumping him with her hip.

"I seem to be late to the party." Gluttony's high-pitched voice came from somewhere behind Sloth. The hallway was getting very crowded.

"I insist on speaking with you first, if you wish to speak with me at all," said Cecil. "I do not have time to simply wait around."

"As if your time is any more valuable than ours," said Esteban.

Chae-Won giggled. "When's the last time you were in a rush to do anything? It's amazing one of the lieutenants running your territory hasn't retired you yet."

"If I thought any of them could survive this viper nest, I might let them," he said with a smile.

"Enough of this." Fatima tried to push past me, but Cecil grabbed her arm, pulling her back.

Esteban took advantage of the distraction to step into the doorway, but Chae-Won seemed to have the same idea and wedged her tiny body in front of him.

I took a step back, still holding the doorknob, as the group in the hall pressed inside.

Fatima raised her hand as if to strike Cecil, but in drawing back she accidentally slapped Chae-Won, who'd stepped into the space beside her. Chae-Won reeled, knocking her head into Esteban's chin. All at once the hallway erupted into shouts and flailing limbs as the vampires jockeyed for space in the too-tight doorway.

An errant elbow caught me on the nose with a *crack*. I stumbled back and landed on my butt. Warm blood rushed over my lip.

The vampires froze. Four sets of metallic eyes focused on me. My heart beat like a rabbit's . . . a rabbit who'd just wandered into a fox den.

"Enough!" Zuri's command echoed off the walls. The steward pushed through the crowd until she stood between me and my visitors. She glanced down at me, her gaze lingering for just a moment on the blood making its way down my chin, then turned to address the gathered vampires. "As Ms. Blackwood's safety has been brought into question, I must insist that you all leave. This room is hereby off limits until further notice. Anyone who ignores this edict will be held in contempt of the conclave charter and punished accordingly."

The council members glared at Zuri, and at one another, as they each backed away.

Once the entrance was clear, Zuri slammed the door. She spun on me. "Do you need medical attention?" She kept her gaze somewhere in the region of my forehead, but I could see the hunger swimming in her eyes, the way she swallowed a little too often. With the coppery tang of blood scenting the air, I wasn't safe with *any* vampire.

"I'm fine." I pushed to my feet and grabbed a tissue from a box on the sideboard. The blood was already slowing, but I wadded the tissue under my nose just to be on the safe side. "Out of curiosity, what's the punishment for a vampire found in contempt?"

"A fine of one-third their total assets distributed among the other attending guests."

"And if one of them had killed me just now? What would be the punishment for that?"

"Same. They would have violated the rules of this conclave."

I stared at her. "If they kill me . . . they pay a fine?"

"If they kill you without permission," she amended. "For your own safety, I suggest you keep your door locked for the remainder of your stay. Should you wish to arrange a meeting with one of the council members, alert the security office and we'll relay your invitation."

I almost laughed. *Invite them back?* If the worst a councilor could be slapped with for my death was a hefty fine, there was no way I was letting any of them into my room. I'd just have to make my case during the trial and trust that the possibility of daywalking was enough to keep me safe.

"I doubt I'll be sending any invitations," I said. "Unless James is allowed to visit."

She shook her head.

"Didn't think so."

"If there's nothing else . . ." Zuri pivoted and opened the door. The hallway was clear. She stepped through and pulled the door closed once more.

My limbs started to shake. The aftereffects of adrenaline. A sensation I'd become disturbingly familiar with in the past year. Wiping the last trickle of blood from my nose, I tossed the crimson tissue in a waste-basket and glanced at the food on my plate. It still looked and smelled delicious, but the memory of having the councilors stare at me as if I were their midnight snack stole my appetite.

James's presence was a constant, comforting hum at the back of my mind, but my thoughts continued to tumble, turning over and over as I paced the room, cataloging all the worst-case scenarios of what had nearly happened . . . and what was yet to come. Moving to the bath-room, I filled the tub with scalding water, added a few drops of lavender essence, and stripped. There was nothing better than heat to relax mus-cles and melt stress, and despite the generous amenities, there wasn't a whole lot to do while locked in my room other than stress about what was coming.

I hissed as I sank into the just-tolerable water one inch at a time. There were no windows and no clocks, but it had to be well after sunrise on the surface. I wasn't thrilled at the prospect of sleeping during the day, but I was going to need all my wits about me for the negotiations I'd be facing that night, so a nap was definitely on the agenda. At least Zuri's edict meant I shouldn't have any more surprise visits. I relaxed in the soothing embrace of the bath until my fingers resembled prunes, then I dried off and set about distracting myself until my thoughts settled enough for sleep.

I GASPED, THRASHING against the constricting blankets of an unfamiliar bed. My chest ached. I scrambled off the bed, disoriented, looking for the threat that had woken me. The cold floor against the soles of my feet provided a welcome shock. My thoughts snapped into focus. I was alone in the extravagant bedroom provided by the vampire council. Sleep clung like gauzy cobwebs in my mind. I'd tossed and turned for hours, trying to convince my brain to let me rest, but clearly I *had* been asleep. *What woke me?*

The ache in my chest intensified. Panic, anxiety, fear . . . but not mine.

I reached along the tether that connected me to James. He wasn't where I expected—closer and in the opposite direction from where I'd last felt him.

Pulling the silk robe over the extra-large T-shirt I'd worn to bed, I trotted to the front room, opened the door, and peeked into the hall. Raised voices, too distant to make out clearly, echoed along the corridor. Something acrid stung my nose. I sniffed. *Smoke.*

Fighting down my panic, I called out with my mind, *What's happening? Are you okay?* The logical part of my brain knew we were too far apart for articulate conversation, but my heart still stuttered at the silence that answered me. Stepping into the hall, I turned toward the weight of James's presence and started to run.

My bare feet slapped against marble as I raced around turn after turn, trying to zero in on the distant shouts and the smell of smoke that seemed to grow thicker no matter which way I went. I skidded to a halt in a corridor I could swear I'd been down before. The rapid patter of racing footsteps sounded behind me. Spinning, I caught the barest glimpse of fabric streaking through an intersection. Reversing course, I raced after the retreating figure. The smoke I'd struggled to identify when I first woke now burned my lungs and made my eyes stream. Two more corners brought me to the heart of bedlam.

A wall of heat slammed into me, drying my skin and cracking my lips. I took a step back, raising one hand to shield myself. Shifting orange light filled the hall. Black smoke boiled along the ceiling. I hunched, trying to stay below the toxic cloud as I choked on my next breath.

Halfway down the corridor, a soot-streaked Cecil bellowed at an equally dirty, equally agitated James, while Fatima held them forcibly apart with a hand against each man's chest. The men's business suits were singed, but Fatima's red sari showed no sign of fire damage. On the far side of the doorway from which smoke billowed like a steam engine, a pale man in a black suit and tie crouched on the floor with his fingers gripped into his reddish-brown hair. He rocked back and forth, emitting a long, low moan. A young woman in a pale-pink business suit whose dark-brown hair was pulled into a French twist updo held him with one arm around his hunched shoulders. Her glossy pink lips moved, but I couldn't hear her words over Cecil's shouts of, "Don't deny it," and the crackle and pop of burning wood that came from the smoke-filled room.

"*Heol!* What is going on?" Chae-Won's high-pitched exclamation made me jump.

I spun and found the childlike council member standing beside me, eyes wide and mouth agape. She wore a black satin robe similar to mine, but the delicate precision of her hair and makeup made me think she definitely hadn't been sleeping.

The vampires in the hall ignored the question as they continued to bellow at one another.

"This isn't the time for accusations. Not while the room's still ablaze." Fatima's attempt to defuse the situation failed as Cecil rounded on her.

"Says the woman who came late to the party. All Tash got from your maid when she went for help was that you'd 'be along shortly,' but that was ages ago. Obviously you weren't in your room, so what were you doing?"

Fatima pulled herself to her full height, but the men still loomed over her. She glanced in my direction. Her gaze slid to Chae-Won. She turned quickly away. "That's got no bearing on this situation."

"Then why not tell us?" Cecil countered.

A loud hiss emanated from the room, followed by a massive plume of gray-white smoke. Four figures stumbled out with the cloud, coughing and fanning themselves. One, the petite, brunette thrall who'd hauled Victoria's bags aboard the plane, collapsed to her knees, coughing hard enough to make my ribs ache in sympathy. The hem of her nightgown—I thought it might once have been blue—was charred to halfway up her thigh, and one sleeve was missing. The mountain of a man who'd flown me here, still in the indigo suit he'd worn earlier, braced his forearms against the hallway wall and took deep, labored breaths.

The third figure was an elderly woman who held herself to a rigid posture despite her disheveled gray bun and the rumpled and singed purple sari wrapped around her plump frame. The final person to emerge was Zuri, wearing a hairnet and soot-streaked pink pajamas patterned with variously decorated donuts. She swiveled her gaze around the hall, taking us all in, and announced, "The fire is out. Hanzo is dead."

Chapter 5

ONLY THE ROCKING man's keening persisted in the silence of the marble furnace in which we all stood. Cecil ran a hand over his short hair and stepped away from Fatima and James. I coughed, covering my mouth and nose with the sleeve of my robe to try to block the smoke that was irritating my throat and making my eyes sting. James glanced in my direction, seeming to notice my presence for the first time. The panic and fear that had woken me, that had drawn me to this place, pinched off. He didn't want me to know how worried he was, and that freaked me out even more.

James had been losing his cool more often lately. No longer the calm, collected gallery curator I'd first met, he'd regained some of the volatility of his earlier incarnations when I'd used my magic to muck about in his fundamental makeup. He'd gained the ability to walk unharmed in sunlight, which had been my goal, but diving so deep into his core had unintentionally awoken long-dormant memories and personality traits that he'd previously suppressed—some stretching all the way back to his mortal life, before he became a vampire. I was still getting to know the new—old—James, but one thing that became obvious straight away was that he had a shorter temper, as evidenced by the shouting match he'd just had with Cecil.

Chae-Won took three steps forward. "Will someone please tell me what in the name of the Creator is going on here?"

"I think it's pretty clear," Fatima said dryly, gesturing to the burnt-out room. "Someone's murdered Pride."

The words rang like a bell in my head. I couldn't say I was sad exactly. Hanzo had been the steepest obstacle to my goals here. He'd wanted James dead. He didn't want vampires to join the paranatural alliance even if I could provide them with the ability to walk in daylight. With him gone, James and I might actually stand a chance of coming out of this conclave unscathed. And yet . . . the fact that someone had just murdered a member of the vampire council right under our noses. . . . Far from simplifying my position, I had a feeling things were about to get *much* more complicated.

"I think it's pretty clear who the culprit is, too," said Cecil, rounding once more on James.

"I could say the same," James shot back. "What were you doing outside Hanzo's door at this hour?"

Cecil lifted his chin. "*I* was invited."

"So was I." James pointed one slim finger at the keening man. "I was summoned for a meeting with Hanzo not five minutes ago. The room was already ablaze when I arrived."

The man, who must have been Hanzo's servant, looked up. Tear trails striped the soot on his cheeks. Gray ash speckled his hair. His wide eyes jumped from James, to Cecil, to Zuri. "What? I . . . no. Oh, how could this happen?" He rocked harder, gripping his hair tight enough that I wouldn't be surprised if he had bald spots later.

James frowned. A pang of worry trickled through our connection. He took a step toward the man, who flinched. "You told me to come to Hanzo's room, then proceeded to the feeding pens to collect donors for our breakfast."

Cecil turned on the confused-looking servant. "That's exactly what you said to me."

Zuri clapped her hands. The sound echoed oddly, louder than it should have, making us all flinch. "We don't have time to sort this out right now. I've lost contact with the security room, which means we have no idea what may be happening elsewhere in this facility. I need to get to the control room, and until I know what's going on, we're all sticking together. Let's go."

She turned and stalked up the hall toward me, passing without a word or glance. Her narrowed gaze seemed focused on something in the far distance.

Fatima grumbled about being forced to march, but otherwise the council members fell into step behind the steward. Cecil cast a scathing glance at James, who returned the glare. The elderly Indian woman who'd emerged from the fire walked at Fatima's shoulder. Zuri's petite thrall joined the woman consoling Hanzo's distraught servant. Between the two of them, they got him to his feet and, sharing his weight, guided his stumbling steps in the right direction. He stared blankly ahead, unblinking. Zuri's remaining thrall brought up the rear, head on a swivel as though guarding our flank from attack.

I turned when James reached me, matching his stride, and slipped my hand in his. *What happened?*

He shook his head. A muscle twitched under his clenched jaw.

I gave his fingers a squeeze. *Talk to me.*

He shot me an irritated glance. When his gaze met mine, his expression softened. He exhaled. *Hanzo is dead, and I believe someone intends to frame me for the deed.* Anger bordering on rage tinged the words that made their way through our bond.

I gathered that much from the exchange back there. What really happened to Hanzo?

He shook his head again. *I have no idea. He was already dead when I arrived. The room was in flames. I . . . I ran.* Shame, guilt, and more anger boiled just beneath the surface, leaking through the filters James was trying to hold in place. *I knew what it would look like if I was found there, but Cecil was standing just outside the door.*

You think he killed Hanzo?

I know I didn't. A deep scowl settled over his features.

I patted his knuckles with my free hand. *We'll get to the bottom of this.*

Zuri led the group through the winding hallways. She stopped in front of a section of wall that looked exactly like all the rest. Pressing her palm to the white marble, she popped out a section of wall. Zuri slid the section sideways to reveal a door that looked nothing like the clones in the rest of the facility. This door was made of thick steel reinforced with riveted cross bars. I stared at the section of false wall. I could have walked past that entrance a million times and never known it was there.

Blocking our view with her back, Zuri activated a security panel in the door. A distinct *click* sounded inside the door's mechanism. She pushed inside, swinging the massive door as if it weighed nothing.

Blank monitors lined two walls of the room beyond, their dark screens acting as mirrors. Storage lockers stood in front of the third visible wall. A plain wooden table and four chairs sat to one side. An overturned office chair rested on its side next to a simple black desk.

Zuri hurried into the room and crouched down. There on the floor, initially hidden from view by the table and Zuri's legs, was Helen. Blood coated one side of her face.

Gasping, I dropped James's hand and hurried forward. "Is she alive?"

Zuri nodded.

I sagged in relief. Helen wasn't a friend. I barely even knew her. Still, I was glad she was all right.

Zuri pointed to the cabinets behind the table. "There should be a first aid kit in there."

Skirting the furniture, I rummaged through the locker until I came up with a small box made of molded red plastic with a large white plus symbol on the front. My hands shook slightly as I pulled it out, the adrenaline of my wake-up call finally crashing.

Zuri had moved away from Helen. She stood beside the overturned chair, typing at the keyboard on the desk.

Frowning at the steward's apparent lack of concern for her human servant, I glanced at the doorway. Zuri's pilot thrall had stepped inside the room just far enough to hold the door open and block the passage. Everyone else remained outside. The vampires all wore strategically blank expressions. Zuri's third thrall continued to support Hanzo's servant. Tightening my grip on the first aid kit, I knelt at Helen's side and snapped the box open.

The blood on her face came from a nasty gash on her temple. Crimson life gushed from the open wound, cascading over swollen, purple skin. I glanced nervously at the vampires standing in the hall, just as they'd stood on the threshold to my room earlier. *Probably best they remain outside. Maybe that's why Mr. Mountain is staying by the door.*

Pushing that thought aside, I pressed a wad of gauze to Helen's wet skin, staunching the flow. "She needs a doctor," I said to Zuri's back.

"She'll be fine." It was the thrall holding the door who replied. Zuri continued to type at her keyboard, seemingly oblivious to the rest of the room.

"She probably has a concussion," I shot back. "And she's lost a lot of blood."

Chae-Won shuffled her feet. Cecil shook his head, as if lamenting the waste.

"She'll be fine," the pilot repeated. "Just get her cleaned up."

"Someone has erased all the surveillance footage from the past two hours," Zuri said to no one in particular. She frowned. "They scrubbed everything. Even the backups."

"So whoever killed Hanzo knew a thing or two about computers." Fatima cast a sidelong glance at Cecil.

Zuri continued to type. "I'm rebooting the system now, but it will take time. I need to physically check on the status of the other guests. There could still be an enemy in these halls." She pressed a small, black button set on the underside of the desk. A red light flashed on the wall. I felt like the bright strobes should be accompanied by some kind of alarm. The silent warning was somehow more concerning.

"Is that supposed to tell people to evacuate?" I asked, feeling that

I'd missed some kind of "in case of emergency" orientation.

"Quite the opposite," she said. "I've placed the facility on lockdown. The lifts will block the exit until I release them."

"Then you've locked the killer in with us?" Chae-Won asked.

Cecil gave her a condescending look. "More likely the killer *is* one of us." He shot a glare at James, then turned a speculative look back on Chae-Won. "Your room is next to mine, on the east side of the complex. What were you doing near Hanzo's room?"

Chae-Won's gaze darted toward Fatima then away. "I'm not required to answer your questions, Envy."

"But you will answer mine," announced Zuri as she stepped away from the keyboard. "As steward, it is my responsibility to get to the bottom of this."

"It was your responsibility to keep us all safe," Fatima said. "Fat lot of good that did Hanzo."

"And when my duties here are done, I will accept the consequences of that failure. But in the meantime, I am still the steward of this conclave, and no one is leaving until we discover the source of the breach. We need to collect everyone in one place to ensure there is no one unaccounted for. The east ballroom should be large enough."

"Then we'll meet you there once you've rounded up the stragglers," said Cecil.

"You will all stay together," Zuri said. "If anyone separates from the group before I return, it will be assumed that they are the killer. Do I make myself clear?"

The council members and James made sounds of agreement, though Fatima and Cecil both wore looks of resentment. I wanted to ask James why the council, the strongest, most influential, most feared vampires in the world, were deferring to Zuri's orders, but he was still in the hall and Helen's blood had soaked through a second stack of gauze.

"I don't think she should be moved," I said to Zuri.

The steward looked down at her unconscious thrall, worry wrinkling her forehead. "Neither can we leave her here." Her expression turned calculating. "I will take her to the food locker."

I blinked in confusion, then realization sank in. *Food locker. Vampires. That must be where they keep the people they're planning to drink . . . and maybe where they dispose of corpses when they're done.* I choked down my gag reflex and said, "I really don't think—"

"Enough," Zuri cut me off. "We've wasted enough time here. Everyone will head to the east ballroom."

I hastily tied off Helen's bandage as Zuri crouched to lift her. "Moving her could kill her," I growled through clenched teeth.

"She's stronger than she looks."

"I hope you're right." I set the first aid kit on Helen's stomach. Whoever took over her care would likely need it.

"Everyone out," Zuri said.

I joined the others in the hallway. Zuri waited until the man holding the door had sealed it behind her and replaced the secret panel, then she took off at a run, blurring with speed, Helen cradled in her arms.

"Let's go, everyone." This came from the petite thrall shouldering the weight of Hanzo's still-in-shock servant. She turned and led the parade forward. Zuri's pilot thrall took up his position in the rear. I fell in step beside James once more, but I didn't touch him. My fingers were sticky with Helen's blood.

THE EAST BALLROOM was certainly big enough to hold us all. It was big enough to hold, well, a ball. Carved pillars of the same white marble as the walls and ceiling marked aisles along the edges of the long room. Six crystal chandeliers hung overhead, tinkling slightly in the breeze of the ventilation system. The air here, while still carrying the slightly stale flavor of being recirculated, was cool and eased the tightness in my lungs and throat caused by the smoke. The floor in this room was black marble veined with gold and polished to a mirror finish. Multicolored specks embedded in the darkness created the illusion that I was walking across a starry sky.

The petite woman who'd led us to the ballroom settled Hanzo's servant against a pillar. The man allowed himself to be moved like a posable doll, staring at nothing. He seemed hollow. Chae-Won and Fatima moved farther into the room, whispering. The older Indian woman trailed behind. Cecil crossed his arms and began to pace, his expression clouding more with each step. The large thrall with the beaklike nose who'd brought up the rear sealed the ballroom doors behind us.

Cecil made a full lap of the room then approached James and me, his expression having transformed from irritation to full-on fury. "How did you get into the security room?" He spoke the words with such force that spittle flew from his lips. "How did you get the drop on the steward's thrall without alerting her? It shouldn't have been possible."

James, stately even when smeared with soot and ash, straightened to his full height and looked down at the slightly shorter man. "As I said before, I had nothing to do with Hanzo's death."

His voice carried through the room, drawing the attention of the others. Fatima and Chae-Won drifted closer.

"Do you really expect anyone to believe that?" Cecil demanded. "That with your life on the line, and Hanzo firmly set on ending it, you would not strike first? We've all heard the stories of Wrath, killer of his own creator."

James stiffened. "That's not who I am anymore."

"After centuries of life," said Fatima, "I think it's fair for me to say that people don't change very much."

James turned on her. "When I killed Elise, it was for the benefit of all our kind."

"Which is why you were rewarded rather than punished," said Fatima. "But if you've killed Hanzo simply to save your own skin—"

"I did not."

"Then why were you in Hanzo's room?" Cecil demanded.

James let out a long exhale. "I've already told you. I was summoned." He pointed to Hanzo's nearly catatonic servant. "By him."

The group turned their attention as one on the hapless man. He didn't react at all.

Fatima shook her head. "He's not going to make it."

"He's just in shock," I said.

James set his hand on my shoulder. "No, Alex. He's not. At least, not in the way you think. Thralls rarely survive the death of their master."

"The loss breaks them," Fatima said. "We should drag what information we can from him before he becomes entirely useless."

"Agreed." Cecil moved toward the man, but I stepped into his path. Raising both hands in a placating manner, I said, "Allow me."

"We need to know what he knows, and we haven't much time," said Cecil. To James, he said, "Get your woman under control."

James snorted. "And here I thought Hanzo was the chauvinist."

"Just let me talk to him first," I said, forcing as much civility into my tone as I could despite wanting to sock this asshole in the jaw. "The poor man has been through enough without you lot going at him."

"If she can get him to answer, let her try," Fatima said. "We can change tactics if she fails."

Cecil crossed his arms but settled back on his heels. He watched me through narrowed eyes.

Licking my lips, I hurried to the servant's side and crouched beside him. If this man held the key to proving James was innocent, I had to get him talking. I just hoped I could get what we needed before the immortals in the room grew impatient. I'd seen quite enough of vampire torture. Setting my hand against his shoulder, I pitched my voice to what I hoped was a soothing tone. "Hello. I'm Alex. What's your name?"

The man's gaze rolled slowly in my direction. "He's dead. My master is dead."

I nodded. "And we're going to find out who's responsible. I know it's hard, but I need you to talk to me about what happened tonight. Where did you go? Who did you talk to?"

His chin quivered. He lifted one hand to his chest, digging fingers into flesh. He whimpered as if in pain.

This guy must have really loved his master. I couldn't imagine liking, much less loving, the hard man on the throne of Pride. Then again, I wasn't his thrall. A memory bubbled up of fawning over Merak, the Master of Denver, when I was under his power. I'd let him hurt me, begged for it even, and loved every minute, even as I screamed my horror in the cage of my mind. The adoration evoked by a vampire's spell was intoxicating and toxic.

I perked up. If this man's grief wasn't natural but rather the lingering effects of the magic binding him to his vampire master, maybe I could ease it.

I set my free hand against his chest, beside his own, and called up my magic. Warmth filled me. My awareness disengaged from my physical form as I looked on the world through the purplish tint of my magic. The man in front of me was just a shell. Sinking beneath the surface, I dove toward the intricate web of entangled threads that made up the core of his being. Touching those threads was like touching a person's soul. I would see their memories. Their life. The moments that made them who they were. It was incredibly personal, and most people would fight to protect those threads with everything they had, sometimes without even realizing it. That was why I couldn't offer the vampire council the same solution I'd given James. He'd had to trust me enough to let me into the very center of his core, to lay himself bare before me and let me muck about in the most intimate parts of himself. I still wasn't sure that had been a good idea.

I didn't need to go anywhere near as deep as I had in James to find the source of this man's distress. While most of the threads of his soul were thin strands in varying shades of red, a thick black cord snaked through the rest, tangling, strangling. That dark ribbon trailed away to a ragged end that drifted like seaweed in a current. I guessed that was the link that had connected him to Hanzo, but why hadn't it vanished entirely with the vampire's death?

"What is she doing?" Chae-Won's voice prickled at the edge of my awareness.

"Shh." That had been Fatima.

The sounds of the physical world were like echoes from the far end of a canyon, faint and distorted.

Doing my best to ignore my audience and the pressure of passing time, I wrapped my spectral fingers around the toxic cord.

Memories rushed into my mind, drowning me in a life I'd never lived. Faces and places flashed past, a high-speed slideshow, too confusing to decipher without context. Hanzo featured prominently in every scene, his grim expression looking on as my blood-soaked hands carried out his orders. Men and women screamed from cages and died in darkness. I cleaned the stains and disposed of the meat. I participated in hundreds of back-alley deals and penthouse negotiations. Sometimes I exchanged money. Sometimes blows. My body was broken and put back together more times than I could count. Through it all was Hanzo, and the sure truth that I would do anything for my master.

I struggled to the surface, fighting the pull of the man's memories.

Calling on my ability to imbue—the power to change the fundamental nature of an object—I maneuvered the thick, dark cord between the thinner threads, separating the black from the red as if picking an errant stitch from a woven cloth. Occasionally, I brushed other strands, and untainted memories from his time before Hanzo drifted into my mind. His name was Ronald. He had a wife and two sons. He'd grown up in the countryside an hour from the sea. He loved the smell of heather. As a boy, he'd spent hours playing with his terrier in the field of heather that grew behind his house.

I tugged and pushed, feeding the thicker strand through loops and around twists. The cord fought back, whipping at me. Smaller threads tightened around the dark ribbon, fighting to hold it close even as it poisoned them. Pressure built in Ronald's core, trying to force me out. The whole mass surged, pulsing and contracting, rejecting my presence. But the attack lacked cohesion. Ronald's core was dying, strangled by the toxic cord of Hanzo's leash. He didn't have the strength to chase me away.

When I'd picked free the last knot—a tangle that locked the darker ribbon to Ronald's soul—the black tether snapped free. It writhed for a moment like a snake, coiling and curling as if looking for a target to strike. Then it fell to ash. Where specks touched the healthy red strands of Ronald's core, spots of darkness bloomed. Ronald would never be free of the memories of his time with Hanzo; they were a part of who he was, but Hanzo's stranglehold on Ronald's soul was broken. His onetime master held no more power than the memories he inhabited.

I withdrew my awareness from the raw core of Ronald's being, settling once more into my own body.

Ronald relaxed under my hand. He took a deep breath and exhaled, stirring the hair around my face with mint-scented breath. His chocolate-brown gaze focused on me, carrying none of the vague detachment I'd come to expect in a thrall.

"Please," I said, "can you tell us what happened?"

Ronald licked his cracked lips. He wiped his cheeks, smearing the soot and tears into gray streaks. "I . . . I was summoned by my master early this evening. He asked that I invite Councilor Envy to his room for breakfast, then go to collect the meal." His eyes darted over my shoulder.

I glanced behind me to find Cecil's satisfied smirk. James's brow was pinched. His mouth turned down at the corners.

"I delivered my message and had just reached the food storage when I felt . . ." His hand returned to his chest, as if remembering the pain.

"Thralls can feel when their link is broken," Chae-Won said. "Just as we can tell when a thrall dies."

Except your end of the tether doesn't come with a self-destruct trigger. I fought to keep my thoughts contained behind my gritted teeth.

"I ran back to the room as soon as I felt my master's distress." His gaze grew distant, remembering. "Mr. Abernathy and Councilor Envy were in the room when I arrived. My master was on the floor, unmoving. There was fire everywhere." He shook his head and began rocking again. "I tried to reach him." He lifted his hands to stare at his palms, which I noticed for the first time were covered not just with soot, but with burns and painful-looking blisters.

I glanced at James and bit my lower lip. Setting one hand against Ronald's shoulder I asked, "Did you invite James to Hanzo's room?"

He froze, frowned, and said, "I never saw Mr. Abernathy until he was standing over my master's corpse."

My blood turned to ice.

Cecil made a satisfied sound, sort of a cross between a chuckle and a purr.

"He's lying," James shouted, taking a threatening step forward.

Ronald shrank back against his pillar, and I couldn't blame him. As much as I loved James, I had trouble not flinching myself when I saw the look in his eyes—a look that promised death.

Cecil's hand flashed out, too fast for even my half-fae eyes to follow. He gripped James's arm, halting his progress. "Now, now," Cecil chided. "No killing the messenger just because you don't like what you heard."

Confusion and anger poured through my link to James. He'd really thought this man's testimony would save him.

I once again shifted my focus to the strands of Ronald's core, hoping to catch a glimpse of a useful memory, and asked, "Are you sure you never saw or spoke to James before you walked into Hanzo's burning room?"

Flashes of light sparked, making certain threads glow momentarily as memories were accessed. I raced through the web, chasing those sparks. Hanzo had spoken to Ronald of James, mostly complaints about his lack of honor and general disregard for the mantle of the council, but there were no memories of Ronald actually coming face-to-face with James.

"I never saw him before in my life." Ronald's words rang with truth, supported by the warm glow in his core.

Doubt stabbed like a knife in my heart. Dumbfounded, I released Ronald, stood, and turned once more to James. Pain and anger twisted his expression.

Cecil smiled. "Murderer."

Chapter 6

CECIL WAS ON THE ground before I could blink.

One second he was goading James, the next he was gone. By the time my brain tracked the motion, Cecil was back on his feet. Fatima blurred. Her sari left a fiery streak across my vision. She materialized beside Cecil, one hand wrapped around his wrist, halting the punch he'd been halfway through throwing. James shook himself, dislodging Chae-Won, whom I hadn't even seen wrap herself bodily around his torso. This wasn't like the playful-by-comparison jockeying for space I'd witnessed in the hall outside my room. Cecil and James were looking to hurt one another, and anyone who got in their way.

I reached down, but the light-imbued knife that might have given me a snowball's chance in hell of surviving a vampire brawl was sitting on my dresser back at home. The cotton T-shirt and silk robe I'd thrown on before leaving my room would be less than useless as armor. Keeping my eyes wide to track the streaks of movement that might give me some warning of an attack, I edged around the pillar Ronald had been leaning against.

Hanzo's servant was crawling away on all fours, head down. As if he could hide simply by not looking.

I licked my lips and wiped my sweaty, blood-smeared palms on the blue silk. The ballroom had become a battlefield. James, Fatima, Cecil, and Chae-Won appeared at random intervals, just long enough to land or block a blow, change direction, or hit the ground. It was like watching a movie with half the frames clipped out, jerking from moment to moment with no transition. The hiss of air, slap of flesh connecting with flesh, and occasional grunt punctuated the fight like an out-of-sync audio track, lagging behind the actual events and muffled by the pounding in my ears.

Fatima's human servant, along with the woman who'd been consoling Ronald earlier, had retreated to the far side of the room. Rather than trying to track the action as I did, they simply stared into space, seeming half-asleep.

Zuri's thralls, however, waded into the fray. It was no surprise when the petite woman went flying. She landed with a *thud* and skidded the remaining length of the ballroom on her side. The bodybuilder pilot fared little better. He managed to keep his feet, but he was always a step behind, dodging shadows and swinging at air while the vampires continued their fight as if he weren't even there.

White light suddenly filled my vision—a tiny supernova that swallowed the room. The sounds of battle and my own pumping blood were drowned by a sonic blast that melted my senses. I dropped to my knees, eyes shut, hands clamped uselessly over my ears. My stomach heaved. I curled tighter.

The light vanished. Silence rang like a bell. I was sweat-soaked and shivering on the cold, hard floor. But I wasn't the only one. Shapes wavered in my teary vision. All the combatants had dropped where they stood, strength and speed rendered moot in the face of the sensory onslaught.

My breath came in shaky gasps. My arms wobbled as I lifted myself to a sitting position. *What the hell was that?*

"Not even five minutes." Zuri's voice boomed in my ears, making me cringe. From their reactions, I'd say it was even worse for the vampires. Zuri strode into the center of the staggering vampires, pinning each with a glare. "There will be no more violence done this night. Do I make myself clear?"

Muttered acknowledgments trickled from the council members. James gave a curt nod.

I guess that's how she keeps the vampires in line . . . But how the hell did she do that? What even happened? I touched my fingers to my head, still dizzy from the experience. *And why isn't someone that strong on the council?*

"It seems we're quite late to the party." Esteban's voice drew my attention to the end of the ballroom, where he, Victoria, and a handful of humans I hadn't met—more thralls most likely—were filing through the ballroom doors. Esteban padded barefoot across the marble floor. Loose cotton pants covered his legs, but the hard lines of his well-defined abs, chest, and arms were bare. Long, dark waves of hair hung in unbrushed tangles to his shoulders. He rubbed his eyes as though checking that he wasn't still asleep. "Who wants to bring us up to speed?"

Victoria's high heels *click-clack*ed in Esteban's wake. Unlike the councilor, she clearly hadn't been asleep when Zuri collected her. Her red dress had been replaced by a green one that perfectly matched the emerald of her eyes, was just as tight as yesterday's, and had a plunging neckline that made it impossible to see anything but cleavage when you looked at her.

"As I told you," Zuri said, "Councilor Pride has been murdered. The conclave will remain on lockdown until I can determine who killed him."

"Or until we all kill each other." Esteban chuckled, but the deadly glares James and Cecil shot at one another were no joke.

"We know who the killer is," said Cecil.

I stiffened.

James bristled. "No, we don't. Even if the servant's story matches your claim and not mine, you know full well that a thrall's testimony cannot be taken at face value."

"Enough." Zuri's command brought everyone to attention. I shivered at the memory of . . . whatever she'd done. "With the security system down, it's impossible to say with certainty who did what. Or have you all conveniently forgotten the abilities of the people standing next to you?"

Everyone, vampire and human alike, looked at their neighbors as though seeing them for the first time. The humans were easy enough to dismiss, but even the weakest vampire had the power of illusion. And these were not weak vampires. With the security cameras out of play, and therefore no way to verify if someone had been wearing an illusion, any one of them could have used their magic to walk the halls unobserved or disguised as someone else. On the plus side, that meant James might have been telling the truth about someone who looked like Hanzo's servant summoning him to the room. Unfortunately, it also meant that every member of the council was now a murder suspect . . . and I was trapped in an underground bunker with them.

I swallowed.

"Have we ruled out an invader?" asked Esteban.

"I haven't ruled anything out yet," said Zuri, "but I've verified that there's been no suspicious activity on the surface. The lift had not been accessed since the most recent patrol went out, and no alarms were tripped before the system was disabled. That all implies the perpetrator was already inside."

"How could this even happen?" Chae-Won shot the accusation at Zuri with a glare. "Unless you were part of the plot against Hanzo."

"Perhaps she's also throwing in a bid for the seat of Lust," Esteban said. "It wouldn't be the first time a council member was chosen based on a daring murder." Several pairs of eyes shifted to James.

Zuri snorted. "And undermine my own authority as steward of this conclave? Hardly a solid plan."

"Then you are simply incompetent," said Cecil. "In either case, I call for a vote of no confidence in the steward to resolve this matter."

"Seconded," said Chae-Won.

"And who would you propose in her stead?" James demanded. "Yourself?"

"On the contrary." Cecil's smile dripped with malice. "I nominate Victoria as Truth Seeker. She shall find justice for the death of Pride."

Fatima crossed her arms. "Knowing Hanzo's stance on her ascension, she had as much reason to want him dead as anyone. Who's to say she didn't kill him herself?"

"No one," Cecil said, casting Victoria an appraising look. "But solving this case would give her a chance to prove her usefulness to the council, thereby earning the seat she wishes to claim. Either she admits to being the murderer, or she finds sufficient evidence to convict someone else. Either way, justice is served, and we on the council can make a more informed decision as to her value."

"Agreed," said Fatima. "All those in favor of letting Victoria handle the investigation?"

All four remaining councilors raised their hands. Zuri's gaze fell to the floor. Her shoulders sagged. The tendons in James's neck stood out, a sure sign he was clenching his jaw.

Cecil turned to Victoria, who stood a little straighter and inhaled enough to strain the fabric of her dress. "By unanimous vote, Victoria is tasked with bringing us irrefutable evidence of Hanzo's killer, preferably with a confession." He narrowed his eyes. "You have tonight and tomorrow, after which we shall make our final ruling and conclude this conclave."

"What of me?" Zuri's voice was small, especially compared to the boom of her earlier authority. Her gaze remained fixed on the stone universe under our feet.

"The conclave cannot be without a steward," said Fatima. "Until such time as Victoria finds you in some way culpable, you shall continue in your current role to facilitate the proceedings, but you shall not be allowed to investigate."

Zuri bobbed a stiff curtsy.

"Don't disappoint us again," said Esteban.

She nodded. "I suggest thralls room with their masters for the remainder of this conclave, as a precaution."

"Agreed," said Chae-Won, hooking elbows with a tall man with creamy brown skin and straight black hair. He wore silver slacks, polished shoes, and a black, button-down shirt with rolled cuffs. From the sheen in his ebony eyes, I assumed he was the servant who'd be sharing her room.

Curious, I shifted my focus, calling just enough magic to see the flows of energy in those around me. Gray-blue fog rolled in at the edges of my vision. I shrank my awareness to Chae-Won and her thrall. Like Ronald, the man whose arm Chae-Won gripped had a thick black thread tangled in his core. The tether snaked through his being and extended toward his master, whose core was such a tangled mess of darkness that I lost track of the pertinent thread.

I shifted my attention to the other human newcomers—a twenty-something Asian man sporting a dragon tattoo on one side of his shaved head and a person with a narrow jaw, shoulder-length hair with asymmetrical bangs, and dark, thickly-lashed eyes. The Asian man had a tether trailing from his core that drifted toward Zuri. It wasn't torn or broken as Ronald's had been, but the cord faded to invisibility across the intervening space. The other person's core seemed more muddled than the others. I squinted, trying to get a better look.

"James should be kept under guard." Cecil's words snapped my focus back to the physical world.

I met James's glacial gaze.

"If it will let you all sleep better," he said, "I'll welcome the protection."

Zuri nodded and turned to the newcomer I'd identified as her thrall. "Yichén, take him to his room, and remain there until further notice."

The man bowed and moved toward James.

James was at my side in a flash. My loose hair fluffed in the char-scented breeze of his arrival. He gripped my hand and placed his free palm against my cheek, smearing me with ash. "Believe me," he whispered. Hope and fear pounded through our bond. "Help Victoria prove I didn't do this."

I scrunched my nose, ill at the prospect of working with Victoria. "Of course I believe you, but . . . I'll work better alone."

"Not this time." He pressed his lips long and hard against mine. When he pulled away, the taste of blackberries lingered. "Don't let your guard down."

Yichén gripped the elbow of James's scorched suit, tugging him toward the exit.

My heart took up residence in my throat. My limbs tingled and itched with anxiety as the only friendly face in this room walked away. It took everything I had not to race after him.

Fatima clapped her hands once. The smack resounded through the ballroom like a gunshot. "In the meantime, we should all retire for breakfast before the trials recommence."

"Seriously?" I blurted, before I could think better of drawing attention to myself. "You're just going to move on like nothing happened?"

Fatima frowned. "Pride is dead. Someone has been assigned to identify his killer. What more would you have us do?"

I glanced from one inscrutable face to the next. Not a flicker of emotion met my inspection. I licked my lips. "Shouldn't we postpone the trials until we know who the killer is?"

"To what end?"

I stared at the Indian councilor, confounded. "To make sure no one else dies in the meantime." I spoke slowly, as though trying to convey an obvious fact to a stubbornly obtuse child.

"Hanzo had clearly grown lax to succumb to an assassination," said Chae-Won. "The rest of us will be on better guard."

I gaped at her callousness. "But—"

"Those who cannot hold their own have no place on this council," Cecil said with finality.

Remember who you're dealing with, I chided myself. *The lives of others mean nothing to them.* I tried to swallow, but my throat was swollen shut. *Even the death of one of their own means nothing beyond the political ripples it causes.*

"Come." Zuri motioned to me. "I will see you back to your room." She cast a warning glance over her shoulder. "I trust there will be no more brawls to referee."

Once we were in the hallway and past the first corner, I asked, "What did you do back there?"

She raised an eyebrow.

"The light? The noise?"

"Ah." She faced forward again. "Stewards are bound to their conclave, and vice versa. We control the building in, as I understand it, much the same way that a fae realm responds to the will of its lord. Therefore, in this place, I have more power than those who might otherwise be stronger."

"Like the councilors."

"Precisely. Otherwise, the stewards would not be able to maintain order during these gatherings."

"But how does that even work? I mean . . ." I stuttered to a halt. Asking a fae about the source and limits of their powers was incredibly rude. There was no reason to think vampires were any less sensitive to the topic.

Much to my relief, Zuri simply shrugged and said, "Through magic built into the structures long ago. When a new steward is selected, we are bonded to our conclave by a ritual that requires at least three council members to perform, ensuring no single vampire can claim the power." Her shoulders sagged. "I am the law in this place, but it is only by the will of the council that I remain so. Likely, I will be stripped of my position when this is over."

I cleared my throat in the awkward silence that followed her mournful pronouncement, eager to steer the conversation in a more productive direction. "How do you suppose the killer got into the security room?"

Zuri shook her head. "The door was not damaged, and only my thralls and I have access."

"Might Helen have let someone in?"

"That would be against protocol."

Tightening my jaw, I asked, "How is Helen?"

"She should make a full recovery." She cast me a sidelong look. "She does not know who attacked her, if that's what you're wondering."

"I just wanted to make sure she was okay," I said, though the optimist in me had hoped she could ID the killer. Luckily, I had other ways of finding things out. "Would it be all right if I looked in Hanzo's room before going back to my own?"

Zuri met my gaze, eyes wide with surprise. "To what purpose?"

"To figure out what really happened."

"It is Victoria who has been charged with that task. Not you." A hint of frustration edged into her voice. I could almost hear that last statement as "Not *me*."

"Maybe I can help."

Surprise turned to suspicion, then calculation. "In what way?"

I chewed my lower lip. Prudence told me to keep the details of my fae abilities secret from anyone who might seek to use me, and the vampires definitely fell into that camp. But I couldn't clear James's name if I wasn't able to investigate. "I have some experience investigating crime scenes. Maybe I'll see something that Victoria wouldn't."

Zuri pursed her lips and looked away, wavering.

Feeling only slightly guilty for playing on Zuri's wounded pride, I said, "I don't know about you, but I don't think Victoria has what it takes to solve this." Then I twisted the knife. "Wouldn't you like to find out how someone got around your security?"

Her steady gaze swung back to me, unmoved by my heavy-handed attempt at manipulation. "I no longer have the right to investigate this matter."

I deflated slightly.

"But I see no reason to deny you access to the crime scene." The corner of her mouth pulled into an almost-smile, and I found myself liking this woman despite her predatory nature. Maybe Helen hadn't been lying when she said she was okay with her arrangement as a thrall. Then James's warning bubbled up in my memory. *Don't let your guard down.*

I trotted to keep up with Zuri's swift pace as she veered toward Hanzo's room. Lingering smoke drifted through the halls, growing thicker as we walked.

"You don't have long if you wish to be presentable for your trial." She gestured through the charred doorway. "Whatever you intend to do, do so now."

Covering my mouth and nose with the sleeve of my robe to block the worst of the fading smoke that hung in the room, I stepped inside. My eyes immediately began to water. I let the tears fall, blinking to clear my vision. My sinuses, throat, and lungs grew tight despite my attempt at a silk filter. Trapped heat radiated from the marble walls. Ash drifts scattered around my bare feet where carpet had burned away to the cracked wood beneath. Steeling my nerves, I looked at the corpse on the floor.

Hanzo—what was left of him—lay on his stomach in the middle of the room, arms stretched as though he were trying to crawl out of the flames that consumed him. His flesh had turned to charcoal—black, cracked, looking as if it would powder at a touch. Thin bones jutted from the ends of missing fingers. His hair and eyes were gone.

I gagged as my stomach responded to the barbecue smell. Turning away from Hanzo's cooked flesh, I made a brief catalog of the rest of the room. A cracked vase lay on its side on the charred table, its former bouquet burned to blackened stalks and shriveled clumps of ash. Three sets of shoes, untouched by the fire, waited in a row by the door. Half the sofa was a ruined mess while the other side remained virtually untouched. The fire seemed to have jumped erratically, decimating some sections of the room while skipping others entirely.

Lowering my hand, I gave a delicate sniff. The smoke and cooked-meat smells were overwhelming, but I didn't smell anything chemical like gasoline or lighter fluid.

I glanced back at Zuri, who waited in the doorway. "How long would it take to kill a vampire with fire if there was nothing else wrong with him?"

"If there were nothing else wrong with him, no vampire would hold still long enough to burn to death . . . except in the case of sunlight, which is nearly instantaneous."

I frowned at Hanzo's corpse. "James said Hanzo was already burning when he got here, so the fire was probably used to destroy evidence and mask the actual cause of death. Ronald said he was getting Hanzo's breakfast when he felt his master die. He ran back as fast as he could but found James and Cecil already here."

"Then Hanzo's death couldn't have taken place much before the fire," Zuri said.

I knelt beside the corpse, thankful my sense of smell had been numbed by the smoke. I blinked. The tears that had blurred my vision had all dried up. Now my eyelids grated like sandpaper as the moisture evaporated from my eyes. "He wasn't dismembered, and his head is on straight." I'd once seen James buy time by snapping a vampire's neck . . . repeatedly. It really did take a lot to kill them, and anything short of sunlight was slow. So why hadn't Hanzo made it out of the fire?

Clearing my mind, I opened myself to the flow of my fae power. My emotions bubbled to the surface on a well of ruby magic. The dread of my coming trial and fear of what might happen if I was unable to find Hanzo's true killer coiled through me, weighing me down like iron chains as I struggled to find the calm surface of my magic—the state that would allow me to receive rather than project.

I took three deep breaths, in and out to a count of four. The tumultuous thoughts boiling on the surface of my mind stilled. The worry was still there, but as a whisper rather than a shout. The itching dryness of my skin grew more intense, as did the ache in my parched lungs. I felt as if all my nerve endings lay exposed to the caustic environment.

Gently, I swept my fingertips over the floor near Hanzo's outstretched hands. I touched the charred side of the couch, dragging my hand across the cushions until I crossed over to the slightly damp upholstery of the intact side. Walking as if in a dream, I trailed my fingers along a soot-blackened wall and down to the scorched tabletop with its overturned vase. My vision swam. The light in the room grew brighter, reflecting like ocean waves dyed the colors of a tropical sunset.

Heat cracks my lips and steals my breath as I cry out in shock. My master is on the floor, unmoving. Two figures stand above him, the seat of Envy and the traitor James. They argue and shove one another. Neither moves to help my master. I stumble forward, knocking into the table. The vase of flowers I'd arranged that morning topples. The porcelain cracks. The petals are black and curled. The desiccated buds burst apart when they hit the surface. I can't stop coughing. I drop to my knees beside my master's blackened body and reach for his hand. What was once flesh falls away under my touch, as dry and brittle as charred paper. The hollowness growing inside me swallows me whole.

Gasping, I yanked my palm from the smooth surface of the table. The cracked vase rolled. I caught it just shy of the edge. Luckily, the vase didn't hold any memory, only the table Hanzo's servant had grabbed for support upon seeing his master dead.

I swallowed, giving myself a little shake. I needed an older memory. Something Hanzo touched as he was burning. Not that I had any great desire to experience what it felt like to be burned alive. I shuddered, licked my parched lips, and continued around the room.

"What exactly are you doing?" Zuri asked from the doorway.

"Shh. I need to focus."

I made a complete circuit of the room. Ronald's imbued memory was the only one I found. Huffing, I glared at Hanzo's corpse. *Come on, you old bastard, even someone as stiff as you must have felt something when you realized you were dying.*

The angle of Hanzo's body made it seem as though he'd crawled from the bedroom, so I backtracked through the door on the left and sent a prayer into the universe that Hanzo had enough emotions to leave an imprint behind.

The fire damage was less severe in the bedroom. The black sheets on the king-sized bed were completely intact, the cool silk soothing against my dry skin. The smoke, however, was thicker, having no direct ventilation. *I'm definitely going to have a sore throat after this.*

I quickly pawed through the handful of books and decorations on the shelves in Hanzo's bedroom. No imbued memories. I touched the mirror and nightstand. Nothing. I moved toward the dresser. Something pressed against the sole of my foot. Stepping back, I knelt and lifted a heavy gold ring from the rug. The world shifted.

Petitioners flood my memory—hundreds of faces flashing past in ones and twos, far more than I could ever remember. They are ghosts, shadows—fleeting shapes acting as placeholders to represent everyone who's ever stood in their place. The faces are unimportant, as were the people they belonged to. The room around me changes too, and the throne upon which I sit. Those are *important. The ritual. The status. The respect. I roll the thick gold ring around my finger, the symbol of my office, my place in the hierarchy.*

James's face overlays the shadow, clearer than most. I relish this moment, looking down on the traitor, savoring the sensation of holding his life in my hands. A life I will soon put an end to.

I recoiled, shocked by the hatred I'd felt for the man I loved. The ring fell to the carpet, bounced once, then lay still. Grasping the edge of the bed, I sat down and rubbed my temples. That hadn't been a single, intense memory imbued from a traumatic event like the one I'd seen from Ronald. Hanzo's ring held centuries of overlaid memories imbued over time, each building on the rest, strengthening the connection—like the multiple images I'd experienced when I touched the statue at the conclave entrance.

I inhaled and coughed. I couldn't get enough air. Leaving the ring where it had landed, I bolted from the room, fighting the urge to spit on Hanzo's corpse as I rushed past.

"What's the matter?" Zuri followed me at a trot to the first intersection down the hall, where I braced my back to the wall and took several deep breaths. The recirculated air blowing through the conclave vents was an icy blast against the desert of my skin.

"Did you find something?" she pressed.

"Hanzo wore a gold ring." My parched throat turned the words into a raspy croak. I pointed to the ring finger on my right hand.

"His ring of office," Zuri confirmed. "All the councilors have one."

"It made him feel important," I continued.

"He *was* important."

"Yeah, but the ring made it real for him. He never took it off."

A small crease puckered her brow. "So?"

"So why wasn't it on his hand when he died?"

She stiffened. "Someone stole his ring?"

I shook my head. "It was in the bedroom."

The interest drained from her expression. "He must have taken it off to sleep."

I bit my lip. There was no way for me to explain my certainty without explaining that I'd actually *lived* Hanzo's memories. I'd felt his attachment to that ring. His near obsession. He hadn't taken it off. Not in all the hundreds of years he'd worn it.

"Maybe you're right," I said instead. My stomach growled, conflicting with the repulsion I felt at the smell of cooked meat clinging to my clothes. Using magic, especially the fae magic that drew its power from my own body and soul, was draining. Clamping my hands over the inappropriate grumble coming from my gut, I gave Zuri an apologetic smile. "Do I have time for a meal before my trial begins?"

Chapter 7

THE MOOD IN THE audience chamber made me hesitate when Zuri prompted me across the patch of light that spilled through the double doors that night. I'd bathed, scrubbing the scent of smoke from my skin and hair as well as I could, and changed my clothes, but the weight of Hanzo's death clung to me. Clung to all of us. The council members sat in rigid silence as I entered. Each washed, dressed, and presumably fed just as I was, but the easy authority they'd displayed the previous night had vanished. Fingers gripped armrests, eyes darted, jaws clenched. Even Esteban, whose laid-back persona so matched his title, sat at attention.

The meal of fruit and bread I'd hastily scarfed sat like a bowling ball in my stomach as I crossed the no-man's-land to the arched boundary of the council chamber. Zuri pulled the doors shut, cutting off the exit. She strode past me without a word or glance, taking her place in the center of the room. She hadn't said much since our visit to Hanzo's room. The hopeful light that had sparked in her eyes when I'd said I might be able to find out what happened had been snuffed by my failure to produce a murder suspect, or even any concrete leads. I'd tried to explain that investigations took time. Though, truth be told, I was disappointed too. I'd hoped to catch a glimpse of the killer in Hanzo's memory of the event, but apparently dying hadn't been a powerful enough shock to elicit an emotion from the stoic old man.

I squeezed my fingers into fists. *Stupid bastard couldn't make things easy for me.*

Zuri spread her hands. "Honored council. I present Alyssandra Blackwood, as requested."

She returned to my side in the shadow under the arch and nudged me forward.

I licked dry lips and swallowed, but before I could get a word out, Fatima gave a delicate cough that drew everyone's attention.

"Let us be perfectly clear," she said. "Hanzo's death in no way changes the strength or responsibility of this council. You, Alyssandra

Blackwood, have been charged with endangering the secret of our race's existence. Should you be found guilty, the sentence is death. You will now be given the opportunity to defend yourself. Make your case."

She settled back expectantly, lacing her fingers together. The other council members had similarly settled into their seats, as though cued by a rising curtain that a play was about to start.

I cleared my throat. The council members' stares skewered me in place. Resisting the urge to shift my feet or wring my hands, I took a deep breath and straightened my shoulders. This was the first step. If I stumbled here, James would lose the advantage in his trial as well.

Lifting my chin, I said in as clear a voice as I could, "When James and I confronted the PTF board of directors, we told them there were more paranatural beings in the world than they were aware of. That statement included not only vampires but any and all magical races the PTF has not yet classified, which includes a good number of fae species. Vampires were never mentioned directly. Furthermore, since the PTF was already aware that they had not cataloged the entire paranatural spectrum, it didn't give them any information they didn't already have. We merely highlighted their ignorance."

A soft chuckle emanated from Esteban.

Cecil shot him a scathing look, then turned his glare on me. "And James's display?"

"You'll have to take that up with him," I shot back, "but as I said yesterday, no one who saw him escape the meeting room in broad daylight is going to think 'vampire'."

"Indeed," Chae-Won said. "The fact that he is immune to daylight when our lore is so solidly steeped in our intolerance to the sun might actually *help* obscure our existence. Most likely, the PTF fools think James is some type of fae they haven't encountered before."

"We're not here to speculate," Cecil said. "What we know for certain is that Ms. Blackwood is collecting paranaturals for her alliance. Clearly, she wishes to add the vampires to that roster. She's trying to back us into a corner by drawing the PTF's attention to us, even if she never uttered the word *vampire*." He glared at me. "Or do you deny seeking to consolidate all paranaturals under one umbrella?"

"You're conflating two separate issues. While I don't deny that I would like to see a united paranatural community, this trial is about whether or not I've taken any specifically identifiable action that exposed your species. The fact that the PTF is still ignorant of the existence of vampires should be proof enough that I haven't."

"You raised their suspicions," Cecil said.

"People have always speculated about the existence of vampires," I countered. "There were legends of your kind long before the fae came out of hiding and magic became a fact of life in the Mortal Realm. If you want someone to blame, punish the storytellers and whatever reckless fool gave them the idea of you all those years ago."

"Oh, believe me, they were punished," Fatima said.

My brain hiccupped on that information, but I shook the thought loose and continued. "The point is rumors about your race are nothing new. I didn't provide any information that anyone with access to the internet and a half-decent imagination didn't already have."

Cecil pointed at me. "As a spokesperson for the paranatural community, your words carry far more weight than the half-baked theories of the human masses. In fact, you yourself are a registered employee of the PTF. Ergo, the PTF knows about us."

"Not at an organizational level."

"Not *yet*, you mean. After all, you came here intending to convince us to join your coalition," said Cecil.

"A coalition of *paranaturals*, not the PTF," I said. "And you're jumping topics again."

"Indeed," said Fatima. "One headache at a time. Unless anyone has some genuinely new information to bring to bear on this conversation, I propose we vote."

"Seconded," said Chae-Won.

I opened and closed my mouth, feeling as though I should provide some kind of closing argument. But what more could I say?

Fatima nodded. "All those who find Alyssandra Blackwood guilty of exposing vampire secrets?"

Cecil's hand shot into the air.

"All those who find her innocent?" Fatima raised her own hand, followed by Chae-Won and Esteban. "Alyssandra Blackwood is hereby cleared of the charge of exposing the existence of vampires."

A great weight lifted off my chest. Despite James's assurance that I was too valuable an asset to kill, part of me had worried they'd vote in favor of execution just to avoid all the uncertainty and change that seemed to follow in my wake—daywalking be damned.

"Shall we move on to the matter of alliance membership in exchange for protection from sunlight?" asked Fatima.

No rest for the weary, I thought. *This is what we're really here to talk about. The possibility of daywalking.* I frowned. *Or is it?*

You have something they want. James had been right about my potential usefulness keeping me safe from a death sentence, but maybe daywalking wasn't my only trump card. I'd come to this negotiation hoping to convince the vampires to join the alliance, but maybe I wasn't the only one who wanted that outcome.

Gambling on my hunch, I said, "You speak as though you'd be doing me a favor by joining the alliance. As if I'd somehow owe you for the honor of introducing you to the world." I set my hands on my hips. "Let me assure you that is not the case. As I said before, I'm willing to act as an intermediary, but the ultimate decision about whether or not vampires join the alliance will come down to your desire to be included and the vote of the existing members."

"Members you hold sway over," pointed out Chae-Won.

"They'll listen to my recommendation," I agreed. Going all in, I added, "Right now, I'm not sure if the alliance needs you enough to be worth the trouble it's becoming increasingly clear that you'll bring."

"You're rescinding your offer?" Fatima asked.

"I'm making it clear that I don't owe this council anything. If you decide to join the alliance, it will be for your benefit, not mine."

Cecil drummed his fingers against his armrest. "And what *benefit* can your alliance offer that would be worth risking our lives for?"

"Your lives are already at risk," I retorted. "The fae know you exist, and they hate you. They'd kill you all if they could."

Cecil shifted uncomfortably in his seat. Fatima and Chae-Won exchanged a look.

"They've been trying to do that for centuries," Esteban said. "We're still here."

"In hiding," I shot back. "Joining the alliance would mean protection. The werewolves and practitioners would have your back. You could walk the world without hiding who and what you are."

"Walk the night, you mean," Esteban said. "We'd always be at a disadvantage among those who can walk in daylight."

"That's why you need daywalking allies to guard your back, just like you use human servants to take care of your daytime needs normally."

"Except those servants are bound to us," said Fatima. "You're suggesting we trust our lives to strangers."

I pursed my lips and exhaled. "This world is becoming a very small place. The fae and werewolves already know you exist. How long do you think it will be before the humans and practitioners do, too? You may not be exposed yet, but how long can you remain hidden? And how long will you survive if you stand alone? Wouldn't you rather make a good impression yourselves than let the *fae* describe you to their new allies?"

"You actually believe the fae and humans will negotiate a lasting truce?" Cecil spoke as though mocking a child who still believed in Santa Claus.

I straightened my back and lifted my chin. "I believe everyone is going to make the deal that is in their best interest, and I believe that deal will be struck at a negotiating table that includes only the most powerful world players. At this point, the PTF, the Church, the Paranatural Alliance, and the fae will be sitting at that table. Where will you be?"

"And when would these negotiations take place?" Esteban shot back. "High noon? How can we sit as equals at a meeting we cannot attend? Or do you propose we announce our weakness by insisting the negotiations happen at night?"

"Day or night," Cecil said, "I still think revealing ourselves to the public is a terrible idea."

"What she said about the fae is true," Chae-Won said in a quiet voice. "If the fae and humans negotiate a new treaty, it's possible the fae will use that alliance to try to wipe us out."

"Again," Fatima added.

There was a moment of silence. Fatima, Esteban, and Chae-Won all seemed to be reflecting on something unseen. Then Cecil said, "Let them come."

"You are young," Esteban said. "You didn't see the carnage of the purge."

"We only survived because we could hide," said Fatima. "If the humans and paranaturals join the fae in hunting us, there will be no darkness deep enough to keep us safe."

"Which is why it may be time for us to step into the light." The corner of Esteban's mouth quirked up. "Literally. There's too much at stake for us to disregard Ms. Blackwood's invitation, but I agree that we cannot join her alliance while at such a disadvantage." He focused his attention back on me. "We require the means to meet on equal footing."

I stiffened. "I already told you, I'm not here to buy your participation in the alliance."

"That doesn't mean we can't negotiate for your services separately." Esteban smiled. "Even if you don't care about vampires joining the alliance, which I very much doubt is true, I'm sure we hold something of value to you."

James's face flashed through my mind. His trial was still undecided.

Of course they would use him as leverage against me.

I met Esteban's hungry stare and wondered, *Do I really want to give people like this more power?* But Esteban was right that I wasn't exactly unbiased in this decision. Humans had numbers and technology. Fae had powerful magic. The scattered and subjugated paranatural races had a lot of catching up to do to be seen as a legitimate power, and having the vampires on board would be a significant step in that direction . . . despite the friction it would cause with the fae. The alliance needed the vampires. Still, the fact remained that I didn't know how to make day-walking amulets even if I wanted to. If the vampires figured that out, James's life would become worthless to them. I exhaled, feeling hope abandon me on the released breath.

"Perhaps Ms. Blackwood needs to be reminded what is at stake in these proceedings," Esteban said.

Cecil smiled.

Fatima tapped one red fingernail against the arm of her throne. "If this council were to declare our intentions to join the alliance, thereby exposing ourselves to the world, the issue of James's breach of secrecy would become moot. No trial would be necessary."

Chae-Won nodded. "But only if such a declaration were made *before* the verdict of his trial. And we cannot make that decision until the issue of whether or not we will attain daywalking is resolved."

And there it was, the carrot and the stick rolled into a neat little package. Promise them daywalking, and James would be cleared. Refuse, and he was convicted.

I'd known this was coming. Even so, ribbons of anger and anxiety squeezed my chest. I let my emotions roll through me and away—a handy trick I'd learned from using my imbuing powers. I inhaled to steady my nerves and considered my options. *They may be selfish and manipulative, but they'll do what's best for the survival of the species,* I reminded myself. *Cecil is a lost cause, but the other three . . . they seem to see the merits of joining the alliance. If I'm holding two things they want, maybe I don't have to bargain with a bluff.*

I knew that if push came to shove, if there was no other way to save James, I'd promise these devils anything they asked for. Even something I couldn't deliver. But if they did end up joining the alliance, the other paranaturals and I would have to trust them, and they'd have to trust us. Hard to do that if the foundation of our agreement was a lie . . . or duress.

Once again taking a gamble that I'd guessed their motivations correctly, I put my hands on my hips and hung my head as though disappointed. "Straight to intimidation. How predictable. You claim James is on trial, but really he's just a hostage. You say you want to join the alliance"—Cecil opened his mouth, but I lifted a hand to forestall him—"*most* of you, but how can anyone trust a group that only pretends to play fair when it suits them? We've already hashed out the incidents in question here tonight and established that the PTF is still ignorant of your existence. By any logical assessment, if I'm innocent of sharing your secret, so is James."

"Except, as you yourself pointed out," Cecil said, "his trial is his own. It sounds to me as if you want us to exonerate him without even hearing the case."

"I'm only asking that James receives a *fair* trial, and that the evidence in these closely related matters is consistently applied. If you can't at least manage that much, there's no place for you in the alliance."

Esteban steepled his fingers and raised an eyebrow. "What happened to being a simple intermediary and the final decision resting with the existing alliance members?"

"Members that, as we've already established, hold my opinion in high regard. You're welcome to approach the alliance without my introduction." I crossed my arms. "Good luck with that."

Chae-Wan hissed, showing elongated fangs.

"Do not threaten us, child," said Fatima in a deathly even tone. Her eyes were liquid bronze. "I promise you will not enjoy the results."

"Not a threat," I said. "And not a promise. Esteban is right; I want vampires to join the alliance. I think encompassing all the Earth paranaturals under one umbrella will balance out the superior numbers of the humans and the incredible powers of the fae, which will help bring stability to the Mortal Realm. But only if everyone in the alliance can work toward a common goal. If any subset is too focused on their own selfish desires to do what's right for the group, the alliance would fall apart."

"And what of Hanzo's death?" Cecil asked. "James is on the line for that, too. Or do you also propose we allow a murderer to walk free in an attempt to curry your favor?"

"James didn't kill Hanzo," I said.

Esteban waved his hand. "The onus of proving that falls to Victoria, not you."

Once again, the urge to take the easy path rose up. I could promise the vampires what they so clearly wanted in exchange for James's safety and put an end to this exhausting charade. Except that wouldn't be the end. Such an empty promise would only make the situation worse later on.

"You've made your position clear." Fatima looked around at her companions. "I say we move on and let the chips fall where they will."

"Seconded," said Esteban.

Chae-Wan looked past me, to the shadows of the exit arch. "Steward, bring in the next plaintiff."

I hesitated, unsure what this sudden dismissal meant. They hadn't agreed to treat James fairly, but I was *sure* they wanted into the alliance. Fatima's words echoed in my head. *Do not threaten us, child. I promise you will not enjoy the results.* Had I just sealed James's fate? Would they execute him to prove their dominance? To punish me?

I opened my mouth, desperate for something to add, but nothing came.

Zuri caught my elbow and steered me toward the door, which was just starting to open. As we stepped into the light, she leaned close and whispered, "This is far from over. Don't let down your guard." She gave me a push through the doorway.

As I stepped into the hall, I crossed paths with James. Our eyes met. His knuckles brushed the back of my hand. Lightning shot through me as our connection burst to life.

Are you well? What did the council say? What did you tell them about my daywalking? Did you agree to anything? Thoughts bombarded my mind in rapid fire, too fast for me to respond to any, and with them came a wash of emotion. Frustration. Impatience. Helplessness. James wasn't exactly regretting his choice to leave the council all those years ago, but he definitely found his current lack of agency hard to bear.

I tried to convey all that had happened in the council chamber, as well as the gist of what I'd found in Hanzo's room, in the brief moment our hands touched. Then he was past me, marching into the council chamber, head held high, to face his accusers.

Zuri turned to join him, and the doors closed in my face.

"I'll escort you to your room."

I turned and found the Asian man Zuri had assigned to guard James staring at me. What had she called him? Yichén? I hadn't even noticed he was there. I nodded and motioned for him to proceed.

Most likely Hanzo's killer was in the council chamber, but that didn't put me beyond their reach. Not with so many thralls around and Zuri's warning ringing in my ears. I jumped at every scuff and creak as we wound through the echoing stone halls. The scent of smoke lingered in the recirculated air, though that might have been my imagination. The sooner the killer was identified, the better.

Unless it turns out to be James. I shoved that thought aside as soon as it formed. *He said he was innocent. I believe him. Not that my belief counts for much in the current situation. If only I'd been able to glean more from Hanzo's room.* I chewed at the inside corner of my lip. *The fact that he wasn't wearing his ring has to mean something . . . but what?*

I bumped into my guide's back. He'd stopped in front of a door. My door.

He turned and took a step away from me, ignoring the fact that I'd walked right into him. "Do you require anything else?"

His professionalism was commendable, but knowing he was a thrall made me wonder how much of that calm detachment was real and how much was a result of his condition. Helen's half-glazed expression drifted into my thoughts, followed by her swollen, blood-streaked face. Hanzo hadn't been the day's only victim. Perhaps the key to this investigation lay with Helen and figuring out how the security system was compromised.

I glanced at the door and pictured pacing my room in anxious anticipation of James's verdict. Maybe the council would clear him, maybe they wouldn't. Either way the accusation that he'd killed Hanzo would still need to be resolved. Better to spend the intervening time trying to remove that second sword of Damocles hanging over his head than wringing my hands and second-guessing my decisions.

"Actually," I said, "I'd like to see how Helen is doing. Could you take me to her?"

His gaze grew even more distant, and I wondered if he was asking Zuri for permission. After a long, awkward moment of silence, he said, "Very well." Then he turned and continued down the hall.

I exhaled in relief. While my insides were still tied in knots, having something useful to do put a little bounce in my step.

Yichén led me through the winding passages, past the vast entry hall with the lift Zuri had stopped and the massive sculpture of the vampires' progenitor, into a section of the compound with narrower walkways and fewer lights. I shivered, suddenly wondering if it was a good idea to follow this stranger into the darkness. I wiped my palms on my pants, swallowed my fear, and told myself I was being paranoid. Zuri had assigned this man to protect me. . . . *But no one knows who killed Hanzo, and Yichén certainly had access to the security room. Who's to say he's taking me where I asked and not some out-of-the-way corner of the compound where no one can hear me scream?*

He stopped abruptly, turning to face me.

I dropped into a loose fighting stance, arms raised to defend myself. Blood pounded in my ears.

My guide raised one eyebrow. The shadow of a smile ghosted across his lips. He motioned to the door on his left. "The food locker."

I straightened, smoothed my clothes to cover my embarrassment, and opened the door.

The room beyond stretched into the distance, though a glass wall split the area thirty feet from the entrance, its clear surface broken only by thin seams and silver hinges that marked a door at its center. The space on the near side of the glass wall was as dim as the hallway that led there. It held a desk, a cot, and a collection of comfortable-looking seats. A woman in a white jacket played solitaire at the desk. Her graying brown hair was pinned on top of her head with a large butterfly clip. She looked up as I entered. Scars puckered one side of her face. Her left eye socket was a mass of puffy pink flesh. When she spoke, only the right side of her mouth moved. "Who are you picking up for?"

"Um . . ." I swung my focus from the woman's face to the area beyond the glass wall. That section of the room was well lit. Twenty or so beds lined the corridor-like room, spaced evenly along the walls. More than half the beds held people. A few sat upright. Most were prone. IV stands stood near the head of each bed, some holding bags connected to the beds' occupants. The sharp smell of antiseptic made my eyes water. I rubbed my nose to keep the itch from turning into a sneezing fit.

Of course a vampire's "food locker" would look like a hospital ward.

"She's here to see Helen," said Yichén as he followed me in and settled into one of the chairs.

"Ah. You must be Alex. Zuri said you'd be stopping by."

I glanced at the woman, finally tearing my gaze from the quarantine room behind the glass. "Are you another one of her thralls?"

"Does that surprise you?"

"Not really," I said, though her easy manner had caught me off guard, and I once again wondered if not all thralls were as mentally suppressed as Merak's had been. My gaze lingered for what felt like too long on the ruined side of her face. I looked away.

She stood and came around the desk. "I was in a car crash." She didn't sound angry or offended, but I regretted looking just the same. "I would have died, had Zuri not found me when she did."

I turned back. She was short, standing only as high as my collarbone. The loose end of her left sleeve was pinned up where her arm ended just below the elbow. I swallowed. *That must have been some accident.* "She saved you?"

"By turning me into a thrall, yes."

"And now you guard her larder. Was it worth it?"

She turned to look through the glass wall. "I used to be a doctor, in my other life. I know nothing short of magic could have saved me." Her gaze grew distant. The right side of her mouth lifted in a smile. "This isn't quite the life I'd envisioned for myself . . . but at least it's life. Sometimes we have to compromise to save what matters most." She pressed her palm to the glass, just to the side of the door. The seams split. She pushed the door open. "Helen is recovering in the bed at the end."

I stepped through.

"Knock when you want out," she said.

I spun in time to see the glass wall seal behind me. The woman gave me a sly smile, then returned to her game of solitaire.

The antiseptic odor was stronger here, as were the smells of used bedpans and sweaty bodies. A dozen eyes swung in my direction, studying me, but no one left their bed. A few of the people seemed to be sleeping, or unconscious. Especially those with tubes in their arms. Now that I was closer, I noticed each of the beds also had a set of handcuffs attached to its frame. Nearly half of the people I passed on my slow walk down the center aisle were secured in place. They couldn't reach me if they tried. The remaining inhabitants sat or lay calmly, seemingly unperturbed by their clinical prison.

I tried and failed to swallow, swinging my gaze from side to side in an effort to keep everyone in view—a task that grew more difficult the farther into the room I walked. The hairs on the back of my neck twitched and tickled. My shoulder blades itched. No one spoke. Each creak of bedsprings or soft cough only served to accentuate the silence.

Along with the differences in their relative freedom, the room's occupants spanned a wide range of ethnicities and seeming social backgrounds. One bed held a plump woman in a sparkly black evening gown whose neck sported a diamond choker, while another contained a half-starved young man wearing a mishmash of patched garments and worn-out sneakers.

I guess, with so many vampires in one place, they wanted some variety.

My gaze snagged on Ronald lying in one of the beds. He seemed to be sleeping, though he still wore his soot-streaked clothes. Had he been brought here to recover like Helen? Or had Hanzo's death demoted him to food for the others? I considered waking him to see if he'd remembered anything more, but I'd dredged his memories pretty thoroughly in the ballroom. I shook my head. *Let the poor man sleep.*

There were a few unoccupied beds near the end of the room. I breathed a little easier once I wasn't surrounded, despite the lingering stares I could feel on my back. Helen lay with her eyes closed in the last bed on the right. The blood had been cleaned from her swollen face and a fresh bandage applied, but red stains streaked the hair near her temple and specks of blood darkened the collar of the shirt that had yet to be changed.

I drew even with the bed and patted the blanket covering her leg.

Her eyes snapped open, then fluttered to a half-closed position. "Alex. To what do I owe the visit?"

"Zuri didn't tell you I was coming?" I glanced over my shoulder, looking for the ex-doctor at the desk, but the difference in lighting turned the glass to a near mirror at this distance. "I thought maybe you thralls all had conference calling."

She chuckled softly. "Direct message only."

I sat at the foot of her bed. "How are you feeling?"

"Alive." She gave me a weak smile. "Thanks for patching me up."

I shook my head. "I just slapped some gauze over the blood."

She pointed to the bandage wrapping her head. "That's all Dyani did, and she's a doctor."

I returned her smile then glanced again at the room's other residents. Most seemed to have lost interest in me, though a man in a dark-brown suit watched my discussion with Helen as though we were a TV program. Shuddering, I turned away. "Don't you have your own room?"

"I do, but it's easier for Dyani to take care of me here. She says I have a concussion."

"I don't doubt it," I said, recalling the gaping wound on her forehead. "Do you remember what happened?"

Her head twisted side to side on the pillow. "I was alone in the security room, then my face slammed into the counter and everything went black. I woke up here."

"How could someone get into the security room without you noticing?"

"They couldn't."

"But they did."

"Yeah."

We both fell silent.

After a moment, I asked, "Who has access to that room?"

"Just Zuri and her thralls."

I frowned. "This is going to sound weird, but were you touching anything when you were attacked?"

Her visible eyebrow rose. "Why would that matter?"

"Just . . . trust me."

She gave a small shrug and said, "The keyboard, maybe. The chair I was in. Oh, and I was fidgeting with my necklace. I do that a lot when I'm bored."

Bored? There's something else I didn't realize thralls could be. "Do you still have your necklace on you?"

She pulled a thin gold chain out of the neck of her shirt. A stylized angel with a small blue stone for a head dangled from the middle.

I perked up like a dog greeting its owner. "May I hold it?"

She unclasped the chain and handed it over with a confused frown. "Why are you so excited about my necklace?"

"Because any piece of evidence could lead to a breakthrough in the case."

Her frown deepened. "I thought you were a sculptor. You sound more like a detective."

"Sometimes I'm both." I winked, then wrapped my hands around the angel and closed my eyes. *Please, show me something useful.*

I exhaled and cleared my mind of active thoughts, letting my subconscious through on a tide of magic. Doubts and fears over my earlier meeting with the council bounced around my brain, along with a swell of pride that I'd held my own in the face of their threats.

A long moment passed. I rubbed my thumb over the angel as I imagined Helen had. Nothing. I opened my eyes and found Helen staring at me under the harsh lights of the hospital-slash-dormitory-slash-refrigerator. Reluctantly, I handed back the necklace.

"Well?" she asked, securing the clasp. "Any breakthroughs?"

I shook my head.

"Sorry I couldn't be of more help."

"Not your fault," I said with false cheer.

"Dyani told me Victoria had been given the duty of finding the killer. Are you assisting her?"

I snorted. "I prefer to conduct my own investigation."

"Isn't that less efficient? Going over the same evidence? Conducting the same interviews? And how do you plan to get the council members to answer your questions if you've got no authority to interrogate them?"

I opened my mouth, closed it, and scowled. I'd hoped my imbuing magic would show me a useful memory. Without that, I was stuck trying to solve this crime the old-fashioned way. After the speech I'd made about fair trials, the councilors didn't have much incentive to help me find evidence that would clear James. Would they even agree to be interviewed if they had nothing to gain from it? And did I dare be alone with any of them? Certainly Cecil might think killing me was worth a third of his fortune if it meant staying out of the alliance. He had eternity to earn more money. I only had one life.

Helen was right; teaming up with Victoria would be more efficient and, despite my reservations about her, safer.

"Are you all right?"

I blinked and refocused on Helen.

"You've gone quite pale."

"Yeah," I said with a grimace. "Sometimes we have to compromise to protect what's most important to us."

Chapter 8

YICHÉN STOPPED in front of a door—yet another perfect replica of every other door in this place.

Honestly, can't they post room numbers or something? It's like they're trying to get people turned around. I considered that for a moment. *They probably are.*

He motioned to the door and said, "I shall have to leave you here. The second trial is ending, and I must return to my other duties."

My heart seized and rocketed into my throat. James's trial was over. I probed my connection to James, hoping for some indication of how his defense against the first charge had fared, but all I felt was the warm thrum that confirmed he was nearby. At least there was no panic or dread seeping through. That had to be a good sign. Right?

"Do you know what the council decided?" I turned pleading eyes on Yichén. "Zuri was in the room, right? Can you ask her?"

"It is not my place to share such information. Remain with Victoria or call the security office for a guide back to your room. Do not wander on your own." He gave a slight bow, then turned to leave.

Every fiber in my being wanted to follow him, to have him lead me to James. I wanted James to tell me with his own lips that he'd convinced the council to let us go. But breaking the vampire code of secrecy wasn't the only charge he needed to beat. Even if the council didn't kill him for his performance in front of the PTF, they still might if I couldn't prove he wasn't Hanzo's killer. I curled my hands into fists. *Guilty until proven innocent.* As much as I yearned for the comfort of James's arms, there were more important things to take care of.

Giving myself a mental shake, I raised my hand and knocked on Victoria's door. Whatever the outcome of the first verdict, I wouldn't let the council pin Hanzo's death on James . . . even if that meant swallowing my pride and teaming up with the slutty bitch who'd all but served James and me to the vampire council on a silver platter.

Victoria, decked out in her green dress from the ballroom, gave me one cursory look when she opened the door then immediately began to close it.

I jammed my foot between the door and the frame. "We need to talk."

She pursed her lips, rolled her eyes, and walked over to a velvet settee near the fireplace at the back of her room. I stepped inside and closed the door behind me.

"Are you here to scold me?" she asked, arranging the folds of her dress artfully around her as she settled. Curving her lips into a seductive smile, she leaned forward so far that I worried her bosom might spill out the top of her dress. "Or is this a social visit?"

I perched on a wide ottoman at the edge of the carpeted area and gave the fire crackling in her hearth an uneasy glance. My gut tightened. *How can she stand being so close to open flames after what happened to Hanzo?* Pushing the unsettling image of the vampire's charred remains to the back of my mind, I narrowed my eyes at Victoria. "Have you made any progress in solving Hanzo's murder?"

She sighed, leaning back. "Straight to business, then. How predictable you are."

"This isn't a joke, Victoria. What have you learned so far?"

She studied me for long enough that I shifted on the ottoman before saying, "Nothing."

Heat bubbled up my neck and down my limbs as I struggled to hold my frustration in check. "You've had hours. What have you been doing?"

"Well," she drawled, "I had a snack, chose tomorrow's dress, and read the first few chapters of a scandalous romance novel someone left on the bookshelf in here."

I surged to my feet, shaking with anger. "How can you be so useless? What was the council even thinking, assigning the investigation to you?"

"Isn't it obvious?" She looked at me with a pitying expression that made my skin prickle. "They assigned me this task because they want me to fail. They have no intention of raising me to a seat on the council. And by removing Zuri from the case, they've ensured she can't redeem herself. She'll most likely be executed once your trials are over, and I'll be sent back to Colorado with a reprimand rather than a reward." She shook her head and muttered, "James warned me not to overreach."

I stiffened, all other thoughts banished momentarily from my head. "He knew you were going to turn us in for a shot at the council?"

She smiled, seemed to consider her response, then let the curve of her lips relax into a more natural shape. "I'm sure he suspected, but no. He warned me to rein in my ambitions long before I discovered his naughty little secret; told me I should be content with Colorado." She flipped an errant strand of hair over her shoulder. "It seems he was right."

I returned to my seat and dug my fingers into my thighs to steady them. "How can you talk about him so casually after what you did?" I glared daggers, willing my voice not to shake. "He could *die* because of you! Don't you even care? I know you—" I snapped my teeth together so hard it was a miracle I didn't bite my tongue. I didn't want to tell her I'd seen them together in James's memories—in their younger years, when she was freshly turned—that I knew how much she'd loved him. The familiar pang of jealousy that tore at my heart when I pictured James with Victoria was nothing compared to the anger I now felt.

And still he doesn't hate her, whispered a voice at the back of my mind.

"Of course I *care*." She dragged out the single syllable like a soloist holding their final note. "But what else could I do? The council would have found out about James soon enough, regardless, and then I would have been on the chopping block right beside you." She flapped a hand in my direction as though shooing a gnat. "James understands. Why can't you?"

"Then prove it," I said. "Prove you care by helping me clear James as a suspect in Hanzo's murder."

Victoria's bell-like laugh tinkled through the room. "You think I don't want to?" She shook her head as if amused by the nonsensical gibbering of a child. "The council doesn't want this case *solved* . . . they want a scapegoat, and James is the clear target. Blaming him has the added benefit of giving them more leverage over you, so even if he manages to slip their current noose, he'll still have a knife to his throat."

"But he's innocent!"

"Are you so sure? The James I knew wouldn't have hesitated to strike first if he thought someone was a threat to him, and Hanzo certainly was that."

A flutter of doubt stung like wasps punching holes in my confidence. *Does Victoria know this version of James better than I do?* I gritted my teeth and ground out, "He didn't do this."

She shrugged. "Perhaps not, but it hardly matters. Most likely one of the other council members murdered Hanzo. Aside from James, they're really the only ones who could have pulled it off. So certainly *that* person wouldn't want the truth coming to light. The other councilors don't care about Hanzo's death beyond the inconvenience of having to fill yet another chair on the council. Most of them are probably relieved to have the old goat out of the way. They'll carve up his territory and spin a lie that paints them as heroes, or survivors, or whatever works most in their favor. They're politicians, after all. Then it's back to business as usual."

"And you're okay with that?" I demanded. "You're just going to sit back and accept their manipulations, even though it means you won't get what you came here for?"

"You really are a child. I took a gamble. It didn't pay off. Better to cut my losses and retreat than dig my own grave." She sighed. "I'll just have to find another way to distinguish myself and try again."

"Meanwhile, James gets executed," I whispered, sagging as all the heat and tension of my fury drained away, leaving only despair.

"Don't be so dramatic." She waved my comment away. "If James isn't the killer, as you so adamantly insist, someone lured him to Hanzo's room at that precise moment. And if that's the case, then the murderer most likely doesn't want to kill James. They want to control him. Or, more to the point, they want to control *you* through him."

As if that's any better, I thought. But then, Victoria didn't know I couldn't make the amulets that would buy James's freedom. She probably thought I could save James whenever I wanted, that my desire to prove his innocence was childish stubbornness. *If only things were that simple.*

I pictured the bright activity spurred by the memories in Ronald's core as he denied meeting James. "If Hanzo's servant didn't speak to James before the murder, whoever lured James to the room must be Hanzo's killer. But since the security system was off, there's no way to tell if someone used an illusion."

Victoria nodded. "True enough. With no security footage, and everyone having a reason to lie, there's no way to find out what really happened."

I chewed my lower lip, worrying it between my teeth as I considered the way Ronald's core had lit up when he answered my questions. "What if we could tell when someone lied?"

"Polygraphs won't work on a vampire," she said. "We can control our heart rate."

I hesitated, weighing my reluctance to give Victoria any additional information about my powers against my need for her help getting interviews with the council members. *Sometimes we have to compromise. . . .*

Shaking my head I said, "But not your memories."

She frowned. "What exactly are you suggesting?"

"There may be a way that we can both get what we want, but I'll need your help to test my theory."

She raised an eyebrow.

"I'll ask you twenty questions," I said. "You answer some with the truth and some with believable lies. I'll try to tell which is which."

She smirked. "You think you can read my poker face?"

I smiled back. "Something like that."

Repositioning herself on her seat, Victoria folded her hands in her lap and faced me with a cool, even stare. "Ready when you are."

Exhaling, I sank into myself, finding my magic. The rosy energy at the center of my being jumped at my call, an excited puppy ready for its walk. Focusing my attention on Victoria, I found the tangled mass of pink, red, and black that made up her core, but I didn't approach it. I needed to know if this would work from a distance. *Let's set a baseline to see if this is even feasible.* Out loud I said, "What color are your eyes?"

Victoria arched her delicately sculpted eyebrows. "That's hardly a test of skill."

"Just answer the question."

She huffed out a breath. Sparks of light flashed like fireflies tangled visible light as the memory sparks seemed to spread then fade.

"True," I said.

She rolled her emerald eyes.

"How old are you?"

Again the fireflies flickered, but this time the lights vanished before she spoke. "Three hundred fifty-two."

I considered the lack of activity in her core and said, "That's a lie."

Her gaze widened slightly, then settled back to normal. "With fifty-fifty odds, you're bound to guess a few correctly."

"What's your favorite food?"

"Chocolate." Again the lights died before she answered, leaving her core dim.

"Not true," I said. "Have you ever been homeless?"

Dozens of lights flashed, then faded. "No."

"Another lie."

A small pucker formed between her eyebrows.

This might actually work, I thought. "Did you kill Hanzo?"

"Hardly." The few scattered lights that had sprung to life pulsed.

"Well, that's good," I said. "Did you betray James?"

She narrowed her eyes. "No."

I studied the pattern of lights and frowned. "That's true."

"I know," she said with a satisfied smile, but the anger in her glare remained.

Considering, I rephrased the question. "Did you tell the vampire council that James could walk in daylight?"

"You know I did," she answered without hesitation. The light show in her soul confirmed her answer.

I tapped one finger against my armrest in agitation. *So I can only tell what a person believes. I can't identify objective truth this way, if there even is such a thing.* I scowled. *That complicates matters.*

"What's that face for?" Victoria asked. "Did you think I would lie?"

Setting the issue of subjectivity aside, I asked, "Have you ever been in love?"

Hundreds, maybe thousands of fireflies lit the threads of Victoria's soul, then winked out. "No."

"Liar."

I continued asking questions and judging Victoria's answers until we reached twenty. Then she insisted we keep going. By the time we reached fifty, I knew that Victoria had been born in Spain, she'd been a mother, she'd once worked in a gas station convenience store, she hated the smell of asparagus, she'd never chewed bubble gum, she spoke seven languages, and she'd lived in Russia at some point. Some of the exchanges had been too vague to get any information from, but those too had been useful. I now had a better idea how to phrase my questions.

"How are you doing this?" Victoria demanded, once she'd confirmed I hadn't missed a single lie.

"Magic." I rubbed my temples, swaying slightly. I hadn't noticed how lightheaded I was getting. "Can I get a glass of water?"

Pursing her lips, Victoria walked to the table and poured liquid from a crystal pitcher into a tumbler. She returned and held the glass out to me. "Can you read minds?"

I accepted the glass, downing it in one go. Wiping my lips, I said, "More like I can see memories."

Victoria blanched, porcelain skin turning a pale, sickly yellow. She backed up to her settee and lowered herself slowly, never taking her calculating gaze off me. When she spoke, her voice held none of its usual playfulness. "Then why not just look for memories of someone setting fire to Hanzo's room?"

"It would take a while to track down such a specific moment, especially over the crazy-long lifespan of a vampire, and I can't see the actual contents of the memories without the person becoming aware of my presence. From what I've experienced, people's cores have built-in defense systems that kick in when they feel me mucking about—like antigens fighting off an infection."

She frowned. "I didn't feel anything amiss."

"Because I kept my distance," I said. "Just an observer looking over the landscape. I couldn't make out any details."

"Show me the difference." She straightened. "Go deeper."

"You want me to poke around in your memories?"

"I want to know what it feels like, so I'll have warning should it happen in the future."

I opened my mouth to tell her I didn't have energy to waste on her paranoia, that I'd already used more magic than I should have with this test, but I changed my mind. Victoria and I would never trust each other, but I did need her to work with me. If I were in her shoes—impractical though they were—and she had some crazy telepathic power, I'd want some reassurance that it couldn't be turned against me.

Besides, I told myself, *it's a good idea to figure out exactly how deep I can get before I'm noticed.*

"Fine," I said. "Try to bury anything you don't want me to see."

She adjusted her position on the settee, straightened her shoulders, and fixed her emerald gaze on me. "Ready."

"Tell me when you can sense my presence."

I called my magic. The power was slower to answer this time—a lethargic slosh rather than an eager boil. My stomach growled. Ignoring my physical discomfort, I unfocused my gaze and let my senses fall toward Victoria, slowing as I approached the boundary of her being. Tiptoeing like a thief stealing the pillow from beneath a sleeping victim, I slipped between the groping tendrils of Victoria's soul, sinking closer to her core. The threads continued to drift, seemingly oblivious to my presence.

I brushed my fingers lightly along a thin strand near the edge of the main knot.

Rain streams over my cheeks, down my chin and neck, washing the thick, coppery flavor of blood from my lips. I glance once at the man near my feet, sharply dressed in an expensive suit. The fly of his slacks is open. I smile. At least he died happy.

I let the memory go, fleeing the rain-drenched alley of Victoria's past faster than she'd fled the scene of her crime. Hairlike wisps of light and color wavered in my direction, seeking the source of the disturbance, but I backed off before they touched me. Victoria shivered, vibrations running through her core, but she didn't speak.

She definitely felt something, but I guess not enough to be sure it was me.

Finding a medium-sized strand of mixed pink and black with veins of molten copper running through it, I grabbed hold.

James's flawless skin glistens in the moonlight. The Milky Way streaks the sky behind him, blending with the long, dark hair that cascades over his shoulders as if he wears the heavens as a crown. His intense gaze finds me and fixes me in place. Two tiny novas. Who knew blue could burn so hot? Sweet and citrus burst over me as our movements crush the violets, poppies, and daffodils that drape the hillside in a rainbow of muted color. He leans in. His hands grip my shoulders as I arch against his thrust. . . .

Panicked, I ran from the memory that could have been mine if not for the savage silver swirled through James's icy blue eyes and the unfamiliar hillside we'd never made love on.

Victoria swayed on the settee, one hand pressed to her heaving bosom. Her breaths came hot and fast. Pink stained her cheeks. "That was. . . . Was that you?"

I couldn't answer, not with the strands of Victoria's core thrashing around me. Some tendrils wrapped me while others pushed me away, as if they couldn't decide whether they wanted me there or not. Shaking free of the winding cords, I withdrew from Victoria's core and settled once more within my own body. A wave of dizziness rocked me. My stomach clenched, growling louder than before. Gripping my seat, I looked longingly at the fruits and cheeses on the tray across the room.

Taking the hint, Victoria brought the tray over, along with the water pitcher.

I frowned, torn between thanking her for the food and calling her a whore for what I'd seen in her memories. I settled for, "I told you to bury what you didn't want me to see."

Her lips curved up. "I did."

Picturing the many tendrils looped around Victoria's core, I wondered how many held memories of James. Had she planned that? Would I have found myself face-to-face with my lover no matter which strand I'd chosen? Heat flooded my cheeks, followed by another wave of dizziness.

I shoved a chunk of sharp white cheddar into my mouth to keep from saying anything I might regret.

"There was . . . something . . . before the memory of James. Just a flicker. Was that you?"

I nodded. "I saw you standing over a dead man in a rainy alley."

She considered. "That felt more like a stray thought than an actual memory. Now that I know what it feels like to have you inside me, I'd notice, but it didn't raise any red flags on its own."

"So I might be able to get a peek or two at the councilors' memories without alerting them." I sighed. "That doesn't solve the problem of knowing *which* memories to target, but between that and the lie-detector thing, at least we've got a chance."

"That's more than we had an hour ago."

"So what do you say?" I extended my hand. "Will you help me find a killer?"

She stared at my palm for a long moment, then said, "No."

My chest seized.

She clasped my hand before I could withdraw it and gave it a firm downward tug. "But *you* can assist *me*." She smiled. "As long as we're clear on who gets the credit."

I snorted and shook her hand. "Whatever. I just want to clear James so we can get back to our lives."

Her silver-bell laugh chimed through the room. "Oh, kitten. You don't really think they'll let you go, do you?"

"They've already cleared me of my charges. They'll clear James too," I said with more conviction than I felt.

"Death was never on the table for you. Not really. Not after what you did for James." She shook her head. "*He,* on the other hand, has as much chance of surviving this conclave as, well . . . a vampire in sunlight."

I lifted my chin. "Then it's a good thing *I'm* here. Shall we start with Cecil?"

She shook her head. "We'll interview Chae-Won first."

I gritted my teeth, sure she was overruling my suggestion out of spite. We didn't have time for these stupid power games. The sooner we found Hanzo's real killer, the sooner James's head would come off the chopping block. "Cecil was at the room almost instantly after the fire started, and he clearly hated Hanzo."

Victoria snorted. "Everyone hated Hanzo. And while Cecil may have loathed Hanzo on a personal level, they were both conservative in their votes. I doubt Cecil would have taken Hanzo out so long as their goals were aligned. Whether in the name of tradition or profit, both were firm believers that vampires should remain in the shadows."

"Whereas the other three want to join the alliance," I said, grudgingly conceding that she'd made a valid point.

"You said you'd been cleared. That wouldn't have happened if Hanzo were alive, even if it meant losing the opportunity to learn how James's daywalking works. So maybe James killed him to protect you."

"It wasn't James."

She waved my knee-jerk response away. "Or maybe someone decided preserving your unique talents was worth upsetting the status quo. Either way, I think politics is a stronger motive than personal dislike, and Chae-Won stands the most to gain from vampires joining the alliance. As a social media influencer with a huge following, she's well positioned to be the council's spokesperson. They'll want us to appear as non-threatening as possible."

I considered the petite girl's round face and child-like features. Yeah, it would be hard to look at Chae-Won and think "monster." Then again, my fae grandfather wore the body of a teenager, and he'd destroyed an entire planet. I shrugged. We'd have to interrogate them all at some point, unless we were lucky enough to strike gold with the first swing. "Fine. Chae-Won it is."

Chapter 9

CHAE-WON ANSWERED her door in the same outfit she'd been wearing during my trial, if such a farce could even be called that—loose blue slacks that billowed around her slippered feet, a white tank top with a plunging neckline that showed off a multitude of necklaces of various styles and lengths, all overlaid with a shiny silver jacket that looked a few sizes too large hanging off her slim shoulders and rolled at the cuffs. Her two-tone hair, which had been pulled into pigtails earlier, flowed loose around her face and shoulders. She looked Victoria up and down with a bored expression. "I was wondering if you'd—" She cut off as her gaze drifted over Victoria's shoulder and found me.

"Alex is *assisting* me in *my* investigation." Victoria emphasized the words *assisting* and *my* like a dog marking its territory.

Fine by me. I lowered my eyes and tried to look subservient. The less scrutiny I was under, the easier my job would be.

Chae-Won stepped back, widening the gap enough for us to pass. "Come on in."

"Where's your servant?" Victoria asked as she settled herself on the couch near the cold fireplace.

"Fetching my supper." Chae-Won sat in a deep chair, tucking her legs under her. "Have you eaten? I could instruct him to bring a second."

"Brave of you to open the door alone, considering what happened to Hanzo," Victoria said.

Chae-Won's smile was cold. "Why? Do you think you can kill me?"

Victoria matched the councilor's smile. "I'm sure Hanzo was equally sure of his invulnerability before he died."

Chae-Won's glittery pink lips turned down. "Ask your questions, Seeker. It's been a long night, and I have work yet to do before I sleep."

I watched the exchange from a wingback chair off to one side of the carpeted area. Hopefully staying at the periphery would keep Chae-Won's attention focused on Victoria. Taking a deep breath, I sank inside myself, calling up my magic. It came sluggishly. My reserves were still low from all the testing we'd done, even after eating enough to satisfy three grown men.

"Very well." Victoria folded her hands in her lap. "Please tell me what you did after the council adjourned from our initial meeting last night."

Chae-Won rolled her gaze to the ceiling. Sparks of memory flashed and pulsed along the threads of her core in a glittery light show that only I could see. "After the . . . unfortunate uproar at Alex's room, Cecil invited me to dinner in his chambers. Then I returned to my own room. A short while later, Hanzo came to visit me. We talked for about forty minutes. He left. I showered and changed clothes, ready to turn in for the day. Then I smelled the smoke and went to investigate. That's when I found Hanzo's room ablaze with several people standing outside it."

The lights in Chae-Won's core pulsed warmly.

So far, so good.

"What did Hanzo want to talk to you about?" Victoria asked.

Chae-Won waffled her head like a bobble-head doll. "This and that. Business deals mostly."

"Can you be more specific?"

"I don't see how the details are relevant."

"Then it's good you weren't put in charge of this investigation." The two women's brittle smiles mirrored one another.

Chae-Won folded first. Her gaze slipped to the side as she let out a small sigh.

I had to hand it to Victoria, despite her seeming softness, she had a vein of steel in her.

"He offered me a tract of land in Hong Kong that supports a number of successful businesses."

Again the lights flashed. She'd told the truth, but that didn't mean she'd told us everything. As I'd discovered during my tests with Victoria, there were plenty of ways to lie without lying.

Victoria, clearly thinking along similar lines, asked, "In exchange for what?"

Chae-Won's gaze settled on me. "My vote." This time, the smile she wore was that of a hunting predator . . . and I was a tasty slab of meat. "He wanted James dead and Alex caged, and he needed my vote to make that happen."

The fireworks in Chae-Won's core drove that truth home like a punch to my gut. Hanzo's hostility came as no surprise, but it was unsettling to have someone talk so casually about murder and slavery.

Especially when they were talking about me.

"Did you agree?" My voice cracked on the question. I hadn't intended to speak. Victoria and I had agreed I should simply observe while she led the conversation, but my mouth had opened of its own accord while my brain was wrestling with images of being trapped inside my own body, helpless, with James dead at my feet.

Never again. The thought circled like an echo that gained in strength rather than losing volume. *I'll die before I let them enslave me like that.* The dead Master of Denver's cackling face floated in my memory. *Never again.*

". . . of the situation." I snapped my attention back to the present, focusing on Chae-Won's answer to my unintended question. "Only a fool shows all their cards in the first round."

The warm pulse at Chae-Won's core told me what she'd said had been true, but I'd missed too much, distracted by my own dark thoughts, to make sense of it.

"What about Councilor Envy?" Victoria asked, taking back the reins of the conversation. "Did he have a similar proposition for you during the meal you shared?"

But Chae-Won hadn't taken her attention off me. She leaned onto the armrest of her seat, folding her arms over the fabric. "Now that Hanzo is gone, I suppose you think you're safe, that the main threat to your happily ever after is past. But you're wrong. The coin is still in the air."

My stomach flip-flopped like the spinning coin she spoke of. The fact that I could see she was telling the truth didn't help. She believed there was still a good chance the council would be able to cage me.

"Is that what you discussed with Cecil?" Irritation laced Victoria's words. She clearly didn't like being ignored.

Chae-Won smiled again, still looking at me. "Oh, we discussed all manner of things. The weather here in Canada. Trends in the stock market. The latest fashions of the spring lines."

The dull threads of her core marked her words as lies, not that I needed my powers to guess she and Cecil didn't share much in the way of small-talk interests.

"Or perhaps you were plotting the death of a certain surly council member," Victoria shot the remark like a cannonball over Chae-Won's bow. "It's no secret Envy wanted him dead, and I'd imagine the wealth that bought Cecil his seat on the council could go a long way toward securing allies." Victoria narrowed her eyes. "Did you have any part in Hanzo's death?"

I inched closer to Chae-Won's core—to the very edge of what we'd determined as the minimum safe distance—hoping to catch a glimpse of the contents of some of the memories Victoria's accusation had stirred up.

"I don't doubt that Cecil wanted Hanzo dead, or better yet, humiliated. But he didn't speak to me about it."

Images flashed in the sparks of Chae-Won's memories—tiny still frames and micro-films depicting moments of her life. I spotted a few altercations between Cecil and Hanzo. *No surprise there.* No clear-cut image of Chae-Won snapping Hanzo's neck or setting him on fire though. *I guess that would have been too easy.* What surprised me were the images of Fatima. We hadn't even been talking about her, but somehow the thought of plotting Hanzo's murder had brought up memories of a sobbing, mascara-streaked Fatima amid empty bottles of alcohol and silk sheets.

Darkness flickered at the edges of my vision, dimming the lights of truth in Chae-Won's core.

"What about Fatima?" I could feel Victoria's glare as I went off script again, but I bulled ahead. "Did she want Hanzo dead?"

Chae-Won's composure slipped for a second. More memories drifted to the surface like fireflies rising from a grassy field. Apparently, Chae-Won had a *lot* of memories involving Fatima. Too many for me to focus on any of them clearly without getting closer.

I resisted the urge.

"I'm not sure what her opinion of Hanzo was these days."

Lie.

"Do you know why she wasn't in her room during the fire?" I asked.

Again Victoria's narrowed gaze bore into me, but she was a shadowy distraction at the edge of my awareness as I focused on Chae-Won.

More images flickered past, winking in and out of existence in a fraction of a second, including one of her waiting outside a closed door in the robe she'd been wearing when she arrived at the fire. The one that stuck with me though—burned like an afterimage onto the retina of my magical vision—was James pressing himself deep and hard against Fatima's naked skin.

The room swam in my magically overlaid double vision. I pressed a hand to my forehead, trying to steady myself. My stomach cramped with an angry growl.

The door to the room opened, drawing everyone's attention. From the tight expression pinching Chae-Won's eyes, I wasn't the only one happy to have something else to focus on for a moment.

The bodybuilder who'd earlier had Chae-Won hanging off his arm walked into the room. He wore a pair of loose black pants that shimmered like an oil slick when he moved. That was it. No shirt. No shoes. Just raw muscle on full display.

Trailing him, drawn by the servant's hand around her wrist, was a pudgy woman who resembled nothing so much as a sparkly toad. She wore a green sweater that seemed to have glitter woven into the fabric and a black skirt that brushed the tops of her polished boots, but large blue eyes, a wide mouth, and the folds of flesh that layered her neck like a pouch waiting to expand gave the impression of an amphibian stuffed into human clothing.

Chae-Won's servant pulled up short when he saw the company in his master's room. Bowing low, he said, "Apologies for taking so long, my lady."

She waved the comment away and glanced at Victoria. "Are you through with your questions?"

Victoria glanced at the meal-on-legs who'd just waddled through the door. "For now."

"But—"

"Let's go," Victoria cut me off.

I glanced from Victoria, to Chae-Won, to the person about to be drained and her escort. Chae-Won hadn't answered my last question, but it seemed the interview was over. Clenching my jaw, I released my magic and stood. The room swayed. My stomach growled again. Louder. My knees threatened to buckle. I gripped the chair for support.

"I realize you have a history with James." Chae-Won's voice drifted across the space between us as though it were an echo shouted from the distant end of a canyon. I focused my wavering vision on her, but she was facing Victoria. "But it seems clear that he is the perpetrator here. The council accepts that. The sooner you do, the better for all of us."

I opened my mouth, but a sudden shiver that nearly shook me off my feet stopped me cold. My breath was coming in short bursts. The room swam in and out of focus. The next cramp to rack my abdomen didn't release, instead spreading to seize my ribs and lungs. My limbs turned to water as all the tension in my body dove toward my twisted center.

I have to get out of here before I end up on the floor.

I stared at the door. Victoria was already halfway to it. The servant had moved the blood donor to the side of the room. I hadn't noticed any of them move.

Victoria reached the door before I took my first step. The room stretched before me, tipping wildly as I focused on putting one foot in front of the other.

Don't fall down. Don't fall down.

My shirt snagged near my elbow. I tried to pull free, but the tug of cloth turned into fingers wrapped around my upper arm. I turned my head. The world swam.

Chae-Won leaned close at my side. She barely reached my jaw. She lifted onto the balls of her feet to cover the last few inches to my ear. I shivered as she came near my neck, twisting to shelter the vulnerable skin.

"The vote could still go either way."

My mind groped at the words, thoughts drifting as chaotically as my physical senses. Bile burned my throat. I blinked and looked again at the door. Victoria stood in the hallway beyond. She seemed impossibly far away. *I have to get out before I collapse.* That thought pushed all others from my mind. I tried to take another step, but the anchor at my elbow was still there.

Right, Chae-Won is talking to me. I tried to focus on the perky woman with her bright-pink eyeshadow and perfect bow lips, but a thick fog obscured my thoughts. My limbs felt hollow. I couldn't focus past the ache squeezing my ribs and empty stomach as if I were a washcloth that someone was wringing out.

"Change me now," Chae-Won whispered, "as you changed James, and I can protect you both from the council."

I stared at her mutely, parsing her words. My stomach cramped so tight I felt I would snap in half. I gasped, hunching. I looked again at the door. *I have to get out. Now. I can't fall here.*

"I can't." The words escaped my gritted teeth. I shoved Chae-Won off and stumbled at a half-run for the exit.

Pulling the door to Chae-Won's room closed behind me, I dropped to my knees and wrapped an arm around my heaving abdomen, gasping.

"That was dramatic." Victoria crouched so that she was at my eye level. "What's wrong with you?"

"I used . . . too much . . . magic." I panted between cramps.

She waved a hand at the closed door. "That was barely half an hour. And she was only our first stop. What good are you if you've already hit your limit?"

"I need to eat," I said. "And rest. I'll recover."

"And collapse twenty minutes into the next interview," she muttered.

"I can do this," I insisted. I sat back on my heels, taking a deeper breath. "I just have to adjust my tactics. That was my first try."

"Did you even learn anything?"

I glanced over my shoulder at the closed door. Even if the wood was thick enough to dampen our voices, sitting in the middle of a hallway didn't seem like a smart place to have this conversation. I turned back to Victoria, slowly so the movement didn't make me nauseous. "Get me to my room. We'll talk there."

"SHE WAS LYING . . . when she said she didn't know . . . what Fatima thought of Hanzo," I said between mouthfuls of succulent chicken.

Victoria's lip curled; her gaze fixed on my mouth as I tore another bite of meat off the leg. Grease slicked my lips, chin, and fingers, but I couldn't slow down. Once the meat from one segment was gone, I ripped off another, and another, tearing the bird apart.

"Though perhaps less obvious than Cecil's, Fatima's dislike for Hanzo is no less known. He tricked her out of a lucrative business deal a few centuries back, and she's never forgiven him."

"Atms ike a ritty odd mov fr uddeny keeing m'ow."

"Chew or speak. Pick one. I can't understand what you're saying with all that flesh rolling around in your mouth."

I forced the partially chewed meat down my throat with a grimace. "That seems like a pretty old motive for suddenly killing him now."

"Quite. And while I don't doubt she can hold a grudge, she's not the type of woman to let her personal feelings get in the way of practical decisions."

"Like you," I said, thinking of the way she'd betrayed James. I dropped the last cleaned bone onto a pile at the edge of the silver tray on which the roast chicken and veggies—which had disappeared equally as fast—had been served and leaned back with a contented exhale, the ache in my gut finally easing to mere discomfort rather than outright pain.

Little wrinkles framed Victoria's scrunched nose. "And people think *us* savage."

I rolled my eyes. "Hunger's a side effect of my magic."

"As it is of ours," she said.

That brought me up short. James had once compared the tearing agony of traveling through the Rift between realms to the constant hunger that drove vampires to feed on human beings. Suddenly, the chicken carcass on the tray looked like the site of a massacre, wet bones glinting amid torn ligaments and discarded cartilage. Would I be able to control myself if the gnawing hunger I felt whenever I overtaxed my magic called for human blood to satisfy it?

Clearing my throat, I wiped my mouth and draped my napkin over the carnage of my hastily devoured meal. "We should interview Fatima next. Even if the motive we know about is old, she's definitely a strong suspect."

"I thought Cecil was your top choice for Hanzo's killer."

I shrugged. "That was before I got a look inside Chae-Won's head. Now my money's on Fatima."

"It wasn't her," Victoria said in a "just drop it" sort of way.

I sat up a little straighter, prepping for an argument. "Care to share why you're so convinced? Because from where I'm sitting she had means, motive, and opportunity." I ticked off each strike against her on my fingers. The memory-image of Fatima and James together when I'd asked Chae-Won where she thought her co-councilor was remained front-and-center in my thoughts, and the voice of jealousy whispered in my ear that maybe it wasn't just Hanzo's murder I wanted to punish Fatima for. "At the very least, we need to find out where she was when the fire started, because we know she wasn't in her room."

Victoria bristled. "I'm in charge of this investigation, not you, and I say Fatima is not the killer."

"Why? What evidence do you have? How am I supposed to help if you don't share what you know?"

She lifted her gaze, as if searching for inspiration on the ceiling. Finally she said, "She was with me."

"I—Wait. What?"

"Fatima was with me. That's why she wasn't in her room when Cecil's servant went looking for help. She was on the opposite side of the complex when the fire started, so she can't be the killer."

I frowned, staring at my knuckles as I reworked my mental map of the events of that day. If Fatima had an alibi—assuming Victoria was telling the truth—she'd just dropped to the bottom of the suspect list. *I wish I'd been watching Victoria's core when she said that.*

Shifting my focus while I was still recovering gave me a headache, but I pushed through and asked, "When did she leave?"

"After the fire started. Her servant called her back when Envy's girl showed up looking for her." Lights sparked in Victoria's core. I drifted closer.

Red silk sheets slither to the floor as Fatima trades them for her clothes. I call for her to come back to bed, but she shakes her head. She looks anxious. Something is wrong.

"Stop it."

I blinked.

Victoria was glaring at me.

I drummed my fingers. "Fine. If we set Fatima aside for now, that leaves Cecil and Esteban."

"And the steward."

I frowned. "You think Zuri is a suspect?"

"She's strong enough here in the enclave to take Hanzo out, and I don't see how anyone else could have gotten into the security room unnoticed by the watcher inside."

My limbs went cold as I considered walking the halls alone with Zuri, but the idea of her as the killer just didn't sit right. She'd seemed as eager to find the truth as I was. "What would be her motive? Isn't she in a lot of trouble now that someone died on her watch?"

"True. She may well be executed for incompetence." Victoria gave a little shrug. "But perhaps she hoped killing a council member would be noteworthy enough to gain her the open seat."

I shook my head. "I don't think it's Zuri."

"Oh, please. Don't tell me you've fallen for her whole 'I'm a nice vampire' act?" She said, putting finger quotes around the word nice. She rolled her eyes. "There's no such thing as a *nice* vampire."

"James is nice."

"To *you*. But can you honestly tell me you don't believe he'd twist the head off anyone intent on doing you harm?" She lifted an eyebrow. "Or maybe light them on fire?"

I bunched my fists hard enough to leave crescent-shaped welts on my palms and said forcefully, "James didn't do this."

"Whatever you say, kitten."

"And stop calling me *kitten*," I snapped.

"Whatever," she said with a flick of her wrist. "We'll put Zuri at the bottom of the list for now. Means aside, she hasn't got a very strong motive."

"What do you know about Esteban?" I said, eager to change the subject.

"Not much. His territory covers most of Western Europe, but his title fits him well. By all accounts, he's lazy, allowing lieutenants to run his domain while he lounges in one of his many villas. He hardly seems the sort to get his hands dirty."

"How did someone like that even make it onto the council?"

"I believe he was elevated for the role he played in founding the Spanish Inquisition, a means by which he was able to accuse and murder hundreds, if not thousands, with little effort on his part and the full support and blessing of the monarchy."

My chicken threatened to come back up. "That's repulsive."

"It was efficient. Meals delivered to his dungeons on a regular basis, and a service to dispose of the bodies. All paid for by the Spanish crown."

"Do you think he's a good candidate for Hanzo's killer? He seemed all for joining the alliance, which would put him in opposition to Hanzo."

She waffled her head back and forth. "Esteban generally votes along the path of least resistance and rolls with the punches when things don't turn out his way. I can't imagine him caring about any cause enough to risk a direct confrontation with one of the other councilors."

"Then we're back to Cecil as our prime suspect. Let's go pay him a visit."

"Will you even be able to conduct another interview without collapsing?" She slid her scrutinizing gaze over me, as if assessing a broken toy to determine if it was worth fixing and deciding it was probably bound for the scrap heap.

"I've been thinking about that," I said. "I've got a trick that should give me an energy boost." Thanks to an intensive few days of training with a demon-possessed practitioner, I'd discovered that I could filter Rift energy through a net of my fae magic to draw more power. I'd only ever used that power to fuel my practitioner spells, but, in theory, I should be able to use my practitioner magic to recharge my fae magic once the energy was properly converted.

"Then why didn't you use it before?"

I looked away. "It's . . . complicated." I didn't really feel like explaining the limitations of my mixed-heritage magic—which I was barely coming to understand myself—to Victoria. I really *really* didn't want to think about what would happen if I was wrong, but it was impossible not to imagine all the burnout victims, both fae and practitioner, who'd pushed themselves too far during the war. Then there were the demons. If I messed up my filters. . . . I shook my head. "I'll be fine."

Victoria made a "hmm" sound, shrugged, and said, "Just remember to stick to your own job this time. I'm the one asking the questions."

I kept my mouth shut. If I saw something that prompted a new line of questioning, I'd definitely follow it, but there was no reason to force a conflict with Victoria ahead of time by pointing that out.

Chapter 10

CECIL DIDN'T answer his door. Instead, the young woman who looked just like the stereotypical secretary you'd expect to see at the front desk of a corporate office greeted us in a tight, pinstripe skirt, white collared blouse, and black pumps. Her orangey-red hair was swept up into a tidy bun, and thin, half-rim glasses perched on the bridge of her nose. "Can I help you?"

"I'm here to speak with your master," Victoria said.

"He's indisposed at the moment."

"It's fine." Cecil's voice carried from deeper in the room. "I figured she'd be around eventually."

The woman frowned. "But—"

"Let her in."

Cecil's servant stepped back with a soft sigh, opening the door wider to allow us entrance.

Cecil sat in a plush armchair on the hearthrug. Like Chae-Won, he'd left his fireplace cold, so the only light came from a pair of floor lamps on either side of the lavish room that illuminated his profile in soft yellow light. Kneeling between his legs was a man with matted white hair down to his shoulders that hid his face. A thin T-shirt with more holes than a slice of Swiss cheese draped bony shoulders. Spindly arms like skin-coated wire hung limp at his sides. The old man's pants were stained, the hems frayed. His pinky toe was visible through a tear in the side of one treadless sneaker.

"I was just finishing my supper." Blood stained Cecil's lips. A drip escaped the corner of his mouth as he spoke, sliding into the short hairs of his dark beard. "I'd offer to share, but there doesn't seem to be any left." He opened his hand, which had been bunched in his blood donor's shirt.

The old man folded at the knees, toppling backward like a felled tree. He hit the floor like one, too. A solid *thud* with a slight bounce. Then nothing. He hadn't even tried to ease his landing.

I took a step toward the unmoving man, thinking to check his pulse, but Victoria's arm stopped me like the wooden guard at a railroad crossing, catching me across the chest.

Cecil glanced in our direction for the first time. His gaze widened slightly when he saw me. "I hadn't realized you were here, too." He glanced at the discarded remains of his meal in a way that reminded me uncomfortably of the chicken bones I'd heaped on the serving tray in my room. "I do hope he wasn't a friend of yours."

My entire body clenched, from the tips of my curled toes to my aching teeth, to keep from doing or saying anything I'd regret, but in my head I was thinking, *God I hope he's the killer. I want to watch this son of a bitch burn.*

"If you don't leave them enough to recover, we'll run out of meals before the conclave ends." Victoria spoke in an offhand manner, as though the dead man on the floor were no more interesting to her than a glass of spilled water.

Do we really want people like this in the paranatural alliance? Sure, the werewolves kill people sometimes, but at least they feel bad about it. Vampires . . . I shook my head.

James's face broke into my thoughts, followed by a twist of guilt. They weren't all heartless. Some still remembered what it was like to be human, even after centuries. Even Victoria made an effort to prevent the vampires in her nest from killing their meals. I had a feeling that was due more to murdered locals being bad for business than an abundance of moral fiber, but the fact remained, they could adapt. They didn't *need* to kill. The ones who did . . . well, they probably liked it.

"We brought this one with us," Cecil said. He wiped his thumb along his lower lip and sucked off the gathered blood. "Not part of the shared stock."

He snapped his fingers, the sharp sound making me twitch, and pointed to the corpse.

The woman I couldn't stop thinking of as a secretary hurried over. She crouched down and, wrapping one hand around the dead man's upper arm and bunching her other at the waist of his pants, hefted his frail frame onto her shoulders in a fireman's carry. The corpse bounced as she popped up to her feet and carried her master's victim out of the room without a word.

I watched her leave with the man's limp body draped across her shoulders like a shawl. I tried to work some moisture into my dry mouth to say . . . something. But what was there to say? The deed was done. Nothing I said now would save that man, whoever he was.

If they do join the alliance, rule number one is going to be no more draining people to the point of death.

Victoria strode directly across the space the man's body had filled and settled on the couch. I circled wide of the area and sat on the far side of her, as far from Cecil as I could get without hindering my powers. Taking a deep breath, I called up my refueled magic reserves and sank my awareness past the skin of the vile man.

Victoria glanced at me and, seemingly satisfied, said, "Let's get down to business then. Did you recommend I be put in charge of this investigation because you believed I would fail?"

If I'd been more settled in my physical body, I would have glared at her. I didn't have energy to waste on her trivial points of pride.

"Not at all." Cecil spread his hands wide. "I thought you'd appreciate the opportunity to prove yourself."

There was barely any flicker of light in the tangle of his core, and even those snuffed before the end. He definitely thought Victoria would fail. But was he counting on it?

Okay, maybe not such a useless question after all.

"Tell me," Cecil said, "what do you think of this . . . alliance notion?" His furrowed gaze swung to me for a moment, then back to Victoria. "Do you believe we should expose ourselves to humans?"

"That's not the topic at hand," Victoria said, sidestepping the question.

I risked a glance at her. James thought she'd bitten off more than she could chew by asking to join the council, but maybe she wouldn't be so bad. Then again, she'd all but given up before I convinced her we could make this work, so maybe she lacked the necessary grit after all.

"It could be," Cecil said, meeting her gaze. "The council works best with an odd number. Find evidence that James killed Hanzo, and you could be in Lust's seat before the final alliance vote."

I cleared my suddenly constricted throat and croaked, "Don't you mean 'find evidence of *who* killed Hanzo'?"

Cecil's gaze never wavered from Victoria. I might as well have been a gnat trying to get the attention of an elephant.

"Would such an appointment be before or after James's sentencing?"

My heart, stomach, and other internal organs shot upward, as if I'd suddenly stepped off a cliff. I cast a worried glance at Victoria. Was she seriously considering throwing James under the bus again? *Of course she is,* I chided myself. *She's already done it once. Just because she agreed to investigate doesn't mean she won't jump to an easier path the second one presents itself. Backstabbing bitch.*

Cecil grimaced. "Looking for a way to save your ex-lover?" His gaze flickered in my direction. "Or maybe win him back?" He drummed his fingers. "Once you make your pronouncement, I'd imagine another trial will ensue. There might be enough time between the two events to declare a new councilor."

I could practically see the carrot dangling in front of Victoria's nose, laced with Cecil's unspoken promise. *Fall in line, and not only will I get you on the council, I can help you save your lover—who would of course be eternally grateful and in your debt.* It was everything Victoria wanted on a silver platter. Hopefully she realized the meal he offered was poisoned.

"We'll see where the evidence lies," Victoria's tone gave nothing away. "When did you last see Hanzo alive?"

Cecil steepled his fingers and tapped them against his lips. "I saw him leaving Chae-Won's room sometime around mid-morning."

This time the lights were brighter and took longer to fade. He wasn't lying.

"Why were you near Chae-Won's room?"

"Hers is only a short distance from here. I was returning to my own room and just happened to see him."

"Where were you returning from?"

"As the only council member who never served with James, I felt it prudent to get to know him better."

"And where is his room?"

Cecil smiled. "Planning a booty call?"

I gritted my teeth.

"Establishing how long it would take him to reach Hanzo's room," said Victoria.

"He's being housed in the south." He gave Victoria a strange look, something between humor and scorn. "Easy access to the Well."

Victoria paled, but her voice remained silky smooth as she said, "Did you encounter anyone else in the halls?"

"Nope."

The firefly memories flickered strangely, as if even Cecil wasn't sure if he was telling the truth.

I inched closer, but the relevant memories were already fading. My stomach growled.

Not yet, I growled back. Holding my focus was starting to feel like supporting a stack of books in each hand while holding them straight at shoulder height. My magic was fading faster than it had with Chae-Won or Victoria, probably because I hadn't let it properly recover.

"Esteban was in James's room when I arrived," Cecil added. "I changed my mind about speaking to James and instead invited Esteban back to my room."

"Booty call?" Victoria asked in an offhand tease.

He snorted. "Not my type. I wanted to sound out his feelings on these two"—he gestured to me—"and lay the groundwork for an alliance."

A flicker of light drew my attention to an image of Esteban's face. His lips moved in silent speech. The memory winked out before I could get closer. My physical body sagged. My magical vision and the solid world bled together like over-saturated watercolors, making me dizzy.

I licked my lips. *I'm not going to last the interview at this rate.*

"So you and Esteban went back to your room, where you passed Hanzo leaving Chae-Won," Victoria recounted. "If Hanzo wanted to speak with you, why not tell you then? Why walk back to his room only to send his servant to summon you shortly after?"

Cecil shrugged, though the bitter twist of his mouth was anything but dismissive. "Pride is . . . was . . . prideful. He liked to make others dance to his tune. Not the sort of man to change his plans for the sake of convenience or deliver a message himself."

Taking a deep breath, I opened myself to the Rift. The bluish mist that always overlaid my vision when I looked at magic grew thicker and darker, rolling in like storm clouds on every side. Faces flashed within those clouds—twisted, stretched, or incomplete. I gasped.

Cecil glanced in my direction.

I forced myself to remain still under his scrutiny, though I couldn't meet his gaze. The room had suddenly become much more crowded.

I'd expected to see a few demons—the incorporeal creatures who lived within the Rift. I always did when I accessed the source of my practitioner magic, but there were dozens of faces in this fog. The only other time I'd seen so many demons in one place was gathered around my father—a necromancer who'd promised them bridges into human hosts.

I quickly formed the filter—a mesh woven with my fae magic—that would protect me from possession as I drew in the necessary energy to keep this whole lie-detector thing going. A few demonic faces turned in my direction as I began siphoning energy, but their attention didn't linger long.

I frowned. Practitioners were like magnets for demons, both fuel and life raft. They were drawn to us as surely as a drowning man to land. *So why are they ignoring me? What are they looking at?* I twisted but couldn't see anything but the dark haze of the Rift and the solid marble of the compound wall.

"Is this conversation boring you?" Victoria's terse voice brought my attention back to the task at hand.

"Sorry," I mumbled. "Please, continue."

Victoria shifted in her seat, shot me one last disapproving look, then folded her hands primly on her lap. "Describe the events that transpired after you received the invitation from Hanzo's servant."

Frowning, Cecil leaned back in his seat, crossed his legs, and rested his arms on the sides of his chair. He took a deep breath that puffed out his chest.

I scooted to the edge of my seat, pushing my awareness closer to Cecil's core and doing my best to ignore the weirdly distracted demons surrounding me. Fireflies of thought flared. I stretched toward each spark ignited by Cecil's activating memories, careful not to actually touch any of them.

"I accepted the invitation, but I had a few matters to wrap up before heading to Hanzo's room." The flickering images I caught, and the darkness when he spoke, told a different story. Cecil had been eager for the invitation, heading to Hanzo's room as soon as the servant was out of sight.

He probably doesn't want us to know he jumped like a dog at Hanzo's call. Still, he clearly remembered Hanzo's servant inviting him.

"I smelled smoke as I approached, so I sped up. I practically collided with James as he ran out of Hanzo's room. The main area was ablaze. The carpet. The walls. Everything. I tried to reach Hanzo, but the flames were too high." Cecil shook his head, caking on remorse like stage make-up. "If only I hadn't delayed."

This time the flickering images supported Cecil's words. James's panicked face loomed large in his memories, skin pink and tight from the fire.

"Hanzo's blackened corpse was face down in the middle of the room, barely visible through the flames, arms outstretched as if he'd been crawling for the exit. I demanded an explanation from James. He claimed to have just arrived himself. Said he'd been going for help." Cecil snorted. "As if I'd believe such a flimsy lie."

Light flared around me.

My lips crack, splitting apart in the dry heat. Embers bore holes through my twelve-hundred-dollar suit. Tears stream from my eyes as I try to find a way through the flames to the blackened body on the floor, obscured by thick gray smoke. At least I don't need to breathe.

James, shielding his face with an arm, circles to the far side, but he isn't having any better luck than I am . . . assuming he's even trying to save Hanzo.

I look back at the peeling flesh of Hanzo's outstretched hands. I'd take some damage, but maybe I can grab his wrist and drag him out. Maybe there's enough of him left to survive if we douse the flames quickly.

A scream like that of a dying animal bursts into the room, making me spin. Hanzo's man, face twisted with grief, staggers through the doorway. He's walking straight for Hanzo, as if he doesn't even see the flames licking at his sleeve.

Shit! I scrambled out of the memory, wobbling in my seat as I slammed back into my physical body. I'd been so intent on catching the scene that I'd gotten too close. Had he realized what I'd been doing?

Cecil turned his narrowed gaze in my direction.

Holding my breath, I forced myself to meet him glare for glare as I eased off the flow of my mixed magics. The wisps of fog evaporated from my vision, taking the disturbingly distracted demons with it.

"Why not remove Hanzo's body from the fire?" Victoria asked. "Surely the flames hadn't done so much damage as to be irreparable in such a short time?"

Cecil's attention lingered on me a moment longer, suspicion seeping from him like a miasma. He turned back to Victoria with a scowl. "Which is why I think James must have been there longer than he's admitting."

I released my breath, freed from our staring contest.

"The flames were widespread by the time I went in, and thickest around Hanzo's body. What was left was . . . well. There's no coming back from that level of damage. Honestly, I'd have doubted anything but daylight could destroy a vampire that thoroughly."

I shuddered, recalling the brief moment I'd experienced through Cecil's memory along with my earlier search of Hanzo's room. *The killer definitely used an accelerant.*

"I tried to rouse Hanzo while Tash, my servant, went to Fatima's room for help. She came back with Fatima's thrall but no Fatima, whose absence, in my opinion, is nearly as suspicious as James's presence."

I cast a sidelong glance at Victoria, but her expression remained neutral.

"Hanzo's servant was the next to arrive," Cecil continued, "wailing like a banshee and half-mad with grief. Tash had to hold him back from the fire. He must have come running the moment he felt his master die."

Bile singed the back of my throat. Ronald had been half-mad all right, but it wasn't grief that broke him. The bindings vampires put on their thralls were like a drug, twisting deep into their core, corrupting their emotions . . . and the withdrawal was a killer.

"Around that time, Zuri showed up with two of her thralls." He curled his lip. "Sorry excuse for a steward if you ask me. Being that slow to notice a disturbance in her complex? Totally incompetent." He shook his head, looking as if he wanted to spit. "They set about dousing the fire. By then it was clear nothing could be done for Hanzo. I dragged James into the hall to confront him. Then Fatima showed up and got between us. She seems to have a soft spot for that traitor. Smart money would be on James and Fatima pulling the job together—one to take out security while the other dealt with Hanzo. Goodness knows they each had reason enough to want him dead."

The image I'd seen in Chae-Won's mind of James wrapped around Fatima's naked body sent a surge of jealousy through me, but I quickly pushed that aside. *If their past relationship makes her sympathetic to James now, I'll take it and be glad. Of course, depending on how that scene ended, her feelings might swing in the opposite direction. "Hell hath no fury," after all* . . . I chewed my lower lip. I needed to talk to James . . . about a lot of things.

"Did you play any part at all in arranging Hanzo's death?"

Caught off guard by Victoria's final question, I threw my awareness toward Cecil's core with the dregs of my purely fae magic.

"Why would I want Hanzo dead? With him gone, it'll be more difficult to convince the others not to join this one's foolish alliance." He waved a hand in my direction, then sighed and continued in a softer voice, as though speaking to himself. "If only they'd let us kill her. Without the temptation of daywalking, discussions about the alliance could have been pushed off indefinitely."

"Sorry my continuing to breathe is such an inconvenience for you," I said dryly.

He glanced at me as if he'd forgotten I was there, then smiled. "I'll manage."

Swallowing the anxiety that statement stirred inside me, I said, "I think we're done here."

Cecil turned a look of disgust on Victoria. "And here I thought you were the one investigating. Perhaps we should have offered the seat to Ms. Blackwood?"

"A good leader uses all her tools," Victoria said, smoothing her skirt as she rose. Looking down her nose at me, she said, "Come."

The command chafed, but I swallowed my pride and stood. My knees only wobbled a little.

"Do consider my offer, Victoria. There isn't much time for you to decide."

Victoria held his gaze for an uncomfortably long moment, then sauntered to the exit. Cecil's hatred burned a hole between my shoulder blades as I hurried to follow.

"AT LEAST YOU managed to keep your feet this time," Victoria said, giving me a scrutinizing glance as she led the way back to her room, which was closer than mine, to regroup. "Do we have our killer?"

I opened my mouth as we turned at one of the seemingly endless intersections but snapped it closed without speaking. Esteban leaned against the wall ahead, arms crossed loosely over his chest. Folds of creamy fabric draped his shoulders, but the shirt was left open, revealing hard muscles down to a trail of curly hair at his navel. Homespun pants in a shade of blue that made me imagine him walking in the Mediterranean surf rustled around his legs as he straightened to greet us. Waves of soft brown hair framed his golden-green eyes and olive skin. He flashed a blinding smile. "I heard you were conducting interviews. Thought I'd save you a trip."

"Are you here to confess to Hanzo's murder?" Victoria asked.

"No such luck, I'm afraid. I was sound asleep in my bed when it happened."

Cursing under my breath, I called up my magic. I stumbled as my knees threatened to give out.

Victoria grabbed my arm to steady me and hissed in my ear, "Can you do this?"

I nodded.

"Oh dear, Ms. Blackwood seems unwell." Esteban took a step toward me, hands extended as if he intended to offer his support.

"I'll be fine." I forced the words through gritted teeth. "It's just been a long night."

"Of course. Though you must be relieved, since we've decided not to execute you." He offered me another smile that I had trouble reading.

Is he mocking me? Or is this his idea of being charming?

"Shall we go in?" Victoria unlocked her door.

Esteban pushed it open and bowed as if he were a butler granting entrance to a manor. "Ladies first."

I claimed the plush chair farthest from the now-extinguished fire.

Victoria and Esteban faced off from opposite ends of the sofa, seeming to compete over who could look the most carelessly relaxed.

"Odd for you to be so proactive, Sloth. Your reputation would contradict you lifting a finger. Have you some personal stake in the matter?"

I squinted, seeking his center. Exhaustion dragged at me, but it was nothing I hadn't experienced pulling all-nighters at college. *Push through,* I told myself. *Focus.*

Light danced beneath the surface of Esteban's skin, a kaleidoscopic oil slick of twisting colors. I pulled back, dizzy.

Esteban spread his hands, splaying long fingers. "I wish only to see justice done for poor Hanzo."

Bracing my hands on the seat beside my thighs, I took a deep breath and tried again.

There *were* threads in the light, but finer than hairs and clear as dew. They were too few and far between to be called a core.

I must be too tired. Hating the necessity, I opened myself to the Rift again, channeling a slender stream of energy through the palm of my left hand and into my fae filter. Hazy clouds rolled into the room. There were even more demons present than there had been in Cecil's quarters, but once again they seemed focused on something beyond my perception.

I narrowed my focus to Esteban. He remained a being of light, held together by the finest of threads.

What the hell is going on?

"By all means," said Victoria, "tell us what you know."

I swayed, fighting the urge to throw up as the dizzying lights rippled and danced through the space where Esteban's core should have been. There were no firefly sparks to zoom in on, no sneak peeks into his memories. The entire man-shaped space that was Esteban blazed like a never-ending electrical storm.

"I dined with Hanzo that morning, after the initial meetings following your arrival. We discussed the pros and cons of change and the role of tradition in our society. We parted ways after that. I went to catch up with James; I've always enjoyed his company."

The shifting lights continued their dance with no noticeable pattern. I had no idea if he was telling the truth. *Somehow he's hiding his core from me. I need to break through this weird light barrier.* Shooting to my feet, I said "I need a drink. Would anyone else like one?"

Victoria shook her head with a scowl.

"No, thank you," said Esteban.

Ignoring the pitcher of water on the table, I set a path for the bar against the far wall. When I was two steps from the vampire councilor, I stumbled. Going down to one knee, I reached out to steady myself on the nearest object—Esteban's leg.

Please work.

The rainbow lights came into sharper focus. The nearly invisible threads surrounded me as I dove deeper, not caring if he noticed my presence. I winced, my magical vision blinded by the shifting lights. Even this close, there was no central core. It was as if Esteban had no memories, no personality, no soul.

Gasping, I yanked my hand away, but cool fingers gripped mine before I could make a full retreat.

"Allow me." Esteban, now standing, pulled me to my feet.

I tried to step back, but he tugged my trapped hand. His thumb made a lazy circle over my knuckles. My skin tingled. My right arm itched.

"What's your drink of choice?"

"Um . . ." My mind scrambled.

"How about a Manhattan? Nice and soothing. Great for a nightcap." He led me back to my seat as he spoke. After depositing me onto the plush cushion, he went to the liquor cabinet himself and mixed the drink with bartender precision.

"Here you are." His fingers wrapped mine as I took the glass, as if he feared I might drop it without his support. A shiver of energy ran through me.

I jerked, sloshing the amber liquid.

"You're more skittish than I imagined," he said. Gracing me with another of his blazing but confusing smiles, he returned to his own seat.

Had he tried to use magic on me? Or was I just freaking out about the super creepy state of his soul? What the hell was up with that anyway? How could a person not have a core? Everything had a core. Even rocks had cores! Why was his so unique?

I wish Bael was here.

I clenched my jaw, disgusted by that thought, but there was no denying I was out of my depth. Bael knew more about locating and understanding the essence of a thing than anyone alive. *If only he wasn't such a manipulative asshole.*

I released my magic, happy to let the strangely distracted demons fade. *No point burning energy if I can't trust the results. We'll just have to do this one the old-fashioned way.*

Taking a sip of my Manhattan—damn, that was good!—I asked, "Did you talk to Cecil?"

Victoria frowned but held her tongue.

Thank heaven for small favors.

"I did, actually. I bumped into him after my chat with James. We walked together back to his room."

"Did you see Hanzo?"

"Briefly. He was exiting Chae-Won's room."

"Then what?" I prompted.

He shrugged. "Envy and I spoke. A short while later, I bid him goodnight and went to bed."

"That's it?" Victoria asked. "You just 'went to bed'?"

He spread his hands. "Sorry to disappoint."

"Can anyone corroborate that you were in your room?" I asked.

"Despite my charm and good looks, I'm afraid I do spend some nights alone. Especially when all the choice prospects are . . . unavailable." He cast me a look that made my skin crawl.

"What about your human servant?" I asked.

Victoria shook her head. "Thrall testimony is useless. It's too easy to manipulate because loyalty to their master is absolute."

Esteban nodded. "Just so. The next time I left my room was when the steward woke me and insisted I follow her to the ballroom, so she can at least corroborate my whereabouts *after* the incident and that I was neither injured nor charred."

"An easy sprint for one of us," said Victoria. "You could have been back and changed by the time James and Cecil found Hanzo's corpse."

He smiled. "You'll just have to take my word; I was nowhere near Hanzo's room when he died."

Victoria glanced at me, as if seeking direction, but I had no insight to offer. I gave a small shake of my head.

"If you have no more questions," said Esteban, "I shall see myself out." He stood, bowed to Victoria, then turned and bowed to me. A golden storm swirled in his green eyes. He held my gaze for longer than was comfortable, searching my face as though I were a riddle whose answer had eluded him.

I looked away.

Straightening, he strode to the door and let himself out.

"Well?" asked Victoria after a moment of silence.

I hesitated to answer. Esteban had unsettled me on many levels. My skin still tingled where he'd touched me, and the mystery of his core made my head hurt. Top that off with the energy I'd burned that day and I felt like I was suffering the symptoms of a three-day flu condensed into an hour.

"I only agreed to this goose chase because you assured me you could identify the killer." Victoria crossed her arms, boosting her breasts. "So far you haven't given me anything I didn't already know or at least suspect."

I worried my lower lip between my teeth. "Right now, my best guess is that Esteban and Fatima worked together to kill Hanzo. Cecil's logic about her and James was sound, except we know James isn't the killer."

"Says you."

"Says him."

She sniffed. "Even better. Not like he has any skin in the game."

"Regardless, it would take two people to pull off this assassination. One to take out security, and one to do the actual killing."

"I already told you; Fatima was with me."

"Till when? Fatima was agitated when she left. Maybe that's because her thrall told her about the fire, or maybe it's because she had some-where else to be. After leaving your room, she could have knocked Helen out and erased the security footage before joining the group at the fire. At vampire speeds, that kind of detour would take what, two minutes? Three?"

"How would she have gotten into the security room?" Victoria asked.

"How would anyone?" I countered. "According to Helen, it shouldn't have been possible for anyone to sneak in and attack her, but clearly someone did. Since we don't know *how* it happened, we can't rule anyone out on that alone."

"So your theory is that Fatima used me as an alibi, then snuck off to disable the security system. Meanwhile, Esteban killed Hanzo and lit his room on fire, then ran back to bed before anyone saw him."

"Cecil did say it looked like the fire had been burning for a while. Hanzo's body was already turning to ash by the time he arrived. And James said Hanzo was dead before he got there." I shrugged. "Fatima shows up a minute later, having erased all the relevant footage. The timeline fits."

"Sure, the timeline is fine, but you could put nearly anyone in those roles. Maybe Chae-Won disabled the security and Cecil killed Hanzo. Maybe I disabled the security and James killed Hanzo. You've painted a picture with the possibilities, but *where's your evidence?* What did you see in

Esteban's interview that shot him to the top of your suspect list? And what was up with that clumsy attempt to grope him?"

I stiffened. Had my feigned trip been that obvious? Had Esteban realized what I was doing? If so, he hadn't minded. He seemed almost as eager to forge a physical connection as I was. I rubbed the phantom itch of magic tickling my skin. Had he been performing his own experiment while I'd been running mine? If so, to what end?

I studied the geometric patterns on the colorful rug that designated the seating area. I had no actual evidence that Esteban was the killer, but that strange light that blocked his core. . . . "He's hiding something."

"What?"

"I don't know," I snapped. "That's kind of the definition of hiding."

"Then what makes you think he's the killer?"

"Instinct."

"I don't give a damn about your hunch. I need evidence, enough to convince the council. If you can't provide that, what good are you?"

"We'll find it. I just need a little more time."

"James's sentencing is tomorrow night. I've got one shot to get on the council here. I can't afford to waste it on your optimism and empty promises."

I stiffened, hearing the shift in her tone. "What are you saying?"

"Time's up. We've failed to clear James's name."

"But we're close."

"You hope." She shook her head. "Hope is a luxury, Alex. What I have to be is practical. I'm taking Cecil's deal."

I opened my mouth. "Bu—but—"

Victoria steamrollered over my stuttered attempt at speech. "James is the only suspect the council will accept without irrefutable proof."

"Because they *want* him to be guilty. But he isn't."

"That doesn't matter. As it stands, James will be found guilty with or without my testimony. By confirming their choice, I might be able to claim a seat on the council. Then, just maybe, I can do James some good from there."

"But you'd still need evidence. They're not going to give you a seat on the council just for making a blind accusation, even if it is against the person they want to frame. They'll say you failed the investigation and accuse James on their own."

"You've given me enough details to paint a pretty picture. A picture that will hold up so long as no one tries too hard to poke holes in it."

And of course, no one will poke holes in a theory designed to give them exactly what they want. Cold sweat slicked my palms. My stomach threatened to send back my Manhattan.

"You can't." The words were a hoarse whisper in a voice I barely recognized as my own.

"Oh, kitten," Victoria crooned, "of course I can." She wrapped her hand around my arm just above the elbow and pulled me to my feet. "Working with you was a longshot. For a moment, I thought you might make the difference, might somehow make the situation less impossible. After all, I've seen you do the impossible before." She tugged me toward the door as she spoke. "But not this, pet. This time the house wins." She opened the door and propelled me through it.

I stumbled into the hall. Spinning to face her, I said, "We can still—"

"Better luck next time." She closed the door in my face.

I stared at the solid wood inches from my nose in stunned silence for I don't know how long. Licking my chapped lips and blinking dry eyes, I glanced up and down the empty corridor. The sun must be up by now. The vampires would be tucking in for the day. When they woke, they'd deliver James's sentence.

No. I clenched my fists. *This isn't over. It can't be.*

Shaking slightly from the combination of emotion and exhaustion, I closed my eyes.

James. I needed James. Maybe he wouldn't have any more idea about how to proceed than I did, but talking to him, just being near him, would make me feel better. Especially if this was the last—No! I couldn't let myself think that way. We'd find a way out of this, even if I had to bring this whole damned conclave down on all our heads.

There's an idea. I smiled as I pictured unleashing the full force of my unfiltered magic in one massive burst that would rip a hole to the surface above and flood the underground labyrinth with daylight. We might not get far, but if it was the difference between James's certain death and a head start, I'd do what I had to. The giddy fervor of that vision muted as reality set in. The consequences of such an impulsive action would reach far beyond this conclave. Not only would I have to kiss any hope of an alliance goodbye, James and I would spend the rest of our lives jumping at shadows with every vampire on the planet hunting us down. No more cozy home in the mountains. No more studio. No more family dinners with the misfits I called friends.

Let's hope it doesn't come to that.

Opening my eyes, I turned until the pull of James's presence narrowed like a thread pulling tight. Whatever was to come, James and I would face it together. My footsteps echoed through the eerily vacant corridors as I followed the compass in my heart.

Chapter 11

THE HAIRS ON THE back of my neck prickled as I approached another intersection and paused to orient myself, homing in on the pull in my heart that linked me directly to James. His presence was growing stronger. Strong enough that I knew he was awake, though I couldn't tell what he was thinking or feeling. I turned left and continued, swinging my attention side to side and occasionally glancing over my shoulder. The threat of running into anyone, particularly Cecil, while I was without an escort, hung heavily in my mind, but I wasn't keen on waiting around for whoever was in the security room to notice I was on my own and send a guide. I also wasn't sure a guide would take me where I wanted to go.

My feet scraped marble with each step, threatening to catch on the smooth floor and send me sprawling due to nothing more than the weight of my own body succumbing to the inexorable pull of gravity. My stomach had given up grumbling. It was now a cold, iron knot, welded into a permanent cramp that leached warmth from the rest of my body.

I reached another intersection. I turned right. Left at the next. I was halfway down the hall before I was jostled from my somnambulist shuffle by Zuri's disapproving voice.

"I told you to stay on guard. What in the Creator's name possessed you to wander these halls alone?"

I met her gaze, though my eyelids wanted nothing more than to close. Frowning, I asked, "Where's Yichén?" I'd expected to find the quiet Asian man standing guard outside James's door, not the steward herself.

"He's patrolling the surface. With one of my thralls out of rotation, and the council blocking me from investigating Hanzo's death," she added through clenched teeth, "I'm making myself as useful as I'm able."

Studying the steward from her charcoal eyes and beak-like nose, past the practical winter wear of her knit sweater and heavy jeans, to the fur-lined boots on her feet, I rolled the facts I'd been able to uncover around in my groggy brain. I liked her. That didn't mean she wasn't a killer, but I still couldn't come up with any motive for her to murder

Hanzo. His death made her look incompetent and put both her position and life in jeopardy. *Still . . . no stone unturned.*

I hadn't intended to use my magic again so soon—I hadn't counted on coming across Zuri outside James's room—but I couldn't pass up the opportunity to gain even a little more information. Not with time running out to prove James's innocence.

Opening myself once more to the Rift, I reluctantly called on my magic. My knees nearly buckled. I pressed one palm to the wall. Fatigue blew through me like a frigid wind from the snow-crusted world above. A deep ache settled into my bones, and a bluish haze drifted across my vision.

I focused on Zuri. Relief lifted my spirits as I spotted the tangled knot of her core. *I wasn't just overtaxed,* I thought with satisfaction. *Esteban must have done something to block me.* Relief at having my personal doubts silenced was quickly overshadowed by fear. *Why would he do that unless he knew what I was trying to do? But how could he? I only just discovered this trick today.*

I sighed and rubbed my tired eyes. *Save it for later. Right now I need to ask my questions before I fall on my face.*

I didn't have to fake the heavy hopelessness in my voice as I said, "If it makes you feel any better, Victoria has no idea who killed Hanzo."

She frowned. "It does not."

Lights sparkled in her core. She was genuinely disappointed by my news.

"I know I already asked this, but have you thought of any way someone could have gotten into your security room to shut down the cameras?"

"You're still investigating?"

I nodded.

She exhaled and shook her head. "As I told you before, only my thralls and I have access to that room without breaking down the wall, and there was no structural damage. Neither were the computer systems damaged, only overridden. This was an act of subtlety, not brute force."

Fireflies lit her soul. She believed every word she was saying. And yet . . . *someone* got into that room.

"If you had to guess who could conceive and execute such a plot, who would it be?"

"Any of the council members are capable of both great deviousness and great strength. While I can't imagine how they might have pulled it off, I wouldn't put it past any of them."

While her words were diplomatically useless, the first image that flashed through her core showed her true suspicions. Cecil was the most technologically savvy of the councilors. If any of them had figured out how to hack the security system, it was probably him. If he'd been in the security room when Esteban lit the fire, his vampire speed would still give him time to reach the scene in time to accuse James.

But who invited James in order to frame him? Did Esteban swing by James's room disguised as Hanzo's servant after lighting the fire? Or could there be a third conspirator involved?

My mouth went dry as a terrible thought froze my already sluggish blood: *What if all of the remaining councilors staged this plot together in order to clear Hanzo off the board and put James squarely at their mercy?*

If that's the case, Victoria was right to give up. This was never a battle we could win.

"If that's all, I'll summon Animkii to escort you back to your room."

"What?" I looked up and found Zuri's gaze fixed on me, a small pucker on her forehead and her mouth turned down at the corners. "No," I stammered. "I came to speak with James."

Her frown grew deeper. "He's a prisoner. Not a guest."

"He was also one of the first people on the scene. I need to know what he saw."

"He gave his testimony in the ballroom."

"Please," I said. "If I can't find some new evidence, there's a chance . . ." I took a choked breath, forcing words past a suddenly constricted throat as I voiced the thought I'd been doing my best to deny. "There's a chance this could be our last day together. If you're here to ensure he doesn't escape, what difference does it make that I'm locked in there with him?"

She pursed her lips, waited one heart-wrenching moment, then tapped a keycard to the lock behind her. The light flashed green. "One hour. Then I'm calling Animkii."

Even as I said my thanks, my heart shriveled at the time constraint. I'd hoped she would let me spend the day there. Now that I'd voiced my fear out loud, the reality that James could be put to death in less than a day was starting to sink in, as if I'd spoken prophecy rather than a mere possibility. Tightening my muscles to keep the tremors brought on by anxiety at bay, I passed Zuri and let myself into James's room.

His arms were around me as soon as I crossed the threshold. His lips found mine. Soft. Hungry. My abdomen clenched, but not from the mundane hunger that had plagued me all night.

"I knew you'd find a way to come." James's breath was hot on my face. He pushed the door closed behind me.

"I would have visited sooner, but I was busy trying to clear your name." My own voice rasped, heavy with need, relief, and worry. I drew back and asked, "How did your trial go? Were you able to convince them your show in front of the PTF wasn't a breach of secrecy, or—"

"Later." He pinned me against the closed door and covered my mouth with his. Energy flowed into me through that connection, reawakening numb nerves and easing cramped muscles as James shared himself to bolster my strength. The strain of the past few days was a storm in our bond as all our stress and fears mingled, but those tumultuous clouds were only a backdrop to the more forceful emotions washing over us. Our needs met and merged, blending into a single desire to be connected, as if we each held one half of a magnet yearning to be whole.

We stumbled away from the door, shucking clothes as we moved. I tripped, jeans around my knees, and James swept me up, leaving the troublesome denim behind. I wrapped my bare legs around his waist, hooking my ankles at the small of his back. Kisses traced my collarbone and traveled the valley between my breasts.

Heat pressed against my back, and I noticed for the first time that James's room was lit by the dancing warmth of the fireplace. I shuddered, but even the memory of flesh turned to ash couldn't douse my desire as he dropped to his knees on the rug. Warmed equally by the fire within and the one crackling in the hearth, I let go of all the concerns that had driven me through the night, and for one brief, glorious moment just let myself get lost in the joy of his embrace.

REALITY WAS SLOW to return. Shadows cast by the low flames in James's fireplace danced across the ceiling in playful pantomime. The rise and fall of James's chest lifted my head. Sweat slicked my cheek where it pressed against his skin and cooled on my back save where his arm cradled me. My hair, let loose from its ponytail by James's gentle hand, spilled over his shoulder. I trailed my fingers over his sternum. Once upon a time, the orange-yellow gem that protected him from daylight would have rested there. I recalled lying like this, content in his arms, before I had any idea what that amulet was, what it meant. Now its absence, something we'd both dreamed of, mocked me. We'd gotten our wish, but at what cost?

If only I hadn't insisted James undergo PTF testing. He never would have been in the fight at the PTF building, he wouldn't have been caught on film without his shirt, and the council wouldn't have known he no longer needed his amulet. There would have been no reason for them to take any notice of us. If James weren't the only vampire in history to achieve daywalking, the council wouldn't have cared about his little outburst in front of the PTF board of directors; they never would have dragged us here; Hanzo wouldn't have died; and I wouldn't be failing so miserably at clearing James of a charge that seemed orchestrated to ruin, if not end, our lives.

Once I remembered the truth of our situation, the worries and fears were all too happy to come flooding back. The mellow warmth that had soothed my muscles dissipated. The contented butterflies of my euphoria turned to suffocating ash. The nova at the core of my being fell into itself and hollowed me out. The dream was over. The nightmare of our reality had reasserted itself. I'd never been so unhappy for "later" to arrive.

Bracing for bad news I asked, "What did the council say?"

James sighed. "They're biding their time."

I frowned. "What does that mean?"

"It means the vote was split. Two to convict, two to exonerate. Fatima and Cecil seem set, but the swing votes, Esteban and Chae-Won, most likely want to keep a trick up their sleeve in case Victoria manages a miracle."

The vote could still go either way. Chae-Won's words as I ran from her room swam in my memory. *She was threatening . . . or maybe offering . . . to change her vote to break the tie.*

"So even if I find Hanzo's killer, you're still over a barrel," I grumbled in frustration. *If only I'd never changed James. Then none of this would have happened. Or if I understood my powers better, maybe I could have found the real killer or figured out how to make the amulets I need to buy this corrupt council.*

If, if, if . . . My mind ran in circles as I looked for a way out of this mess, or at least someone to blame, but every thread I followed led me back to my own choices and failures.

"Whatever happens, this isn't your fault." James's voice was low and soothing. His words reverberated through his chest. He stroked my forehead, tucking my tousled hair behind my ear and tipping my face up to meet his gaze. "You aren't the only one who made choices. And I wouldn't change one moment of the time I've spent with you for the promise of a safe eternity." He slid his thumb along my lower lip.

Joy at his words filled me, but also the dread that I might lose him. I burrowed closer, squeezing him tight. "I love you, James Abernathy."

"And I love you, Alyssandra Blackwood."

I smiled and planted a long kiss on his lips. James was the only one who could call me by my full name and make me love it. His hands slid down my back, catching at my hips. Something like a purr vibrated my throat.

Shaking my head, I pushed off his chest and sat up. "I haven't given up on you yet." I pointed a stern finger at his nose, making him go slightly cross-eyed. "Now help me figure out how to save your life."

He chuckled and said, "Yes, ma'am," while one hand traced lazy circles on my side and the other slipped lower to cup my butt.

I slapped his arm. "I'm not kidding. I don't intend to let this be our last night together."

He sat up with a sigh. "Very well. What did you and Victoria discover in your investigation?"

I told him everything we'd learned, including my newfound talent as a lie detector and Esteban's suspicious immunity to it. I also shared my opinion of Victoria and told him about the deal Cecil had offered. "She's probably going to name you the killer, even without any actual evidence."

He nodded. I could tell by the calm in our link that he was unsurprised, but a trickle of disappointment showed he wasn't entirely unaffected by her betrayal. "How do you think Esteban created the shield around his core?" he asked, changing topics.

"I have no idea," I admitted. "This is all new to me. I barely know how I'm doing what I'm doing as it is. What bothers me is that it even occurred to him to guard against me."

He nodded. "That is concerning . . . especially if it wasn't you he was guarding against."

That thought brought me up short. "What else would make a person shield their core like that? As far as I can tell, most people, even fae and practitioners, can't see that deeply into another person. It's part of my imbuing magic."

"But you said yourself, you barely understand what you're doing." He rubbed one hand distractedly over his jaw. "Vampire masters develop new powers over time. Who's to say one of the council members doesn't have a similar talent? Maybe he was protecting himself from another vampire and his defense just happened to block you, too."

I replayed my encounter with Esteban in my head, the way he'd seemed almost glad when I tripped into him, the way he'd held onto my hand when I tried to pull away. In a whisper that was barely more than a breath, I said, "Or maybe he knows reading people is possible because *he* can do it."

I'd been so focused on finding his core, it hadn't even occurred to me that I might need to protect my own. Nausea rocked me. Had he had unfettered access to my memories and deepest secrets while I was distracted?

Shifting my focus, I sank into myself, finding that tangle of delicate rose and burgundy strands that made up my core. *Nothing looks disturbed, but would I notice if it was? It's not like I've mapped this stuff out.*

"What's the matter, Alex?" James's too-tight grip on my arms brought me back to my physical body. He'd reacted to the upset he felt through our bond.

"What if he could see into me the way I can see into others? What if he knows I can't recreate your amulet or change any of them the way I changed you? He'll call my bluff. We'll lose the little leverage we've got to force them to free you."

He was shaking his head halfway through my tirade, but he waited for me to run out of breath before saying, "You said you could only glean surface memories as the person was thinking about them. Were you thinking about any of that when you were scanning Esteban?"

"No. But who's to say his power works exactly the same way as mine?"

"Who's to say he has it at all?" he countered. "We're grasping at straws here, Alex. Don't work yourself into a panic over hypotheticals."

"You're right. Sorry." I rubbed my hands over my face. "It's just been a really long day . . . night . . . whatever." I looked at the ceiling, wishing I could see the sun. Even the short time I'd spent underground had completely thrown off my natural rhythms.

"You need to rest."

"What I need is to find something that will force these self-important assholes to let us go back to our lives and leave us in peace."

"Alex."

The weight in his voice made me wary. His blue gaze, when I met it, was as deep as the sea, cast in shadow by the dying fire at his back.

"You may need to accept that the council will not be swayed, no matter what evidence you might uncover."

I shook my head. "No. Victoria can give up. Fine. But I will not allow *you* to give up. *I* will not give up."

He nodded, but the emotions feeding through our bond spoke mostly of worry, not for himself, but for me. He worried about how I would react if he was found guilty tonight.

I'll tear this conclave down and burn every vampire the council sends after us.

James's wide eyes locked on mine. A ripple of shock ran through our connection.

Maybe James wasn't the only one who'd changed since we first met. I hadn't been transformed by magic in the sense that James had been, but I'd seen, experienced, and sacrificed too much to give up on my future now . . . and my future was with James. If the vampire council wanted to stand in the way of that, well, I wasn't going to roll over without a fight.

A sly grin turned up the corners of James's mouth. "I love you."

"Yeah, well, war with the vampires isn't exactly plan A. I'm still hoping to clear your name by exposing the real killer. Or killers, I guess, since it seems like at least a two-person job." I poked him in the chest. "So help me think."

James reclined, bracing himself on his elbows. "Fatima had motive and opportunity. Despite what Victoria said, she could have made it to the security room before joining us at the fire. Cecil, as much as I hate to admit it, would have been better off with Hanzo alive, since he shared his view of the alliance. As much as those men loathed each other, it would have been a poor business decision for Cecil to kill Hanzo, and I can't see him doing that. Chae-Won didn't stand to gain much from Hanzo's death, but she didn't have much to lose either. I doubt she would have planned such a coup, but she might have been talked into it, given some incentive."

"So either Esteban and Fatima or Fatima and Chae-Won. Either way, it seems Fatima was probably involved." I ran a hand through my hair, wincing when my fingers caught on tangles. *If only I hadn't let Victoria convince me not to question Fatima.* Another thought struck me: *Did she steer me astray on purpose because they were lovers?* I glanced at James, letting my gaze travel over his exposed body. The image of Fatima and him was still fresh in my mind.

Sensing my unease, James frowned. "What's the matter?"

I cleared my throat and shook my head. "It's not important."

He straightened. "You're upset."

Stupid link.

He set a hand on my knee. "You're mad at me."

"Not mad," I said. "Just"—I plucked at a loose thread in the rug—"were you and Fatima . . . involved?"

His expression smoothed. Mr. Poker Face. "You saw something

when you were digging around in someone's memories."

"Chae-Won's."

He nodded. "Fatima and I had an arrangement for a while, as she's had with every council member at one time or another." He stroked my knee with his thumb. "It was a long time ago."

"How did it end?"

He shrugged. "Amicably, as far as such things go. We both got what we wanted out of the relationship. Then we moved on."

"So she's not holding some grudge against you that might make her want to frame you for murder?"

He smiled wanly. "Not that I'm aware of, but that doesn't mean she wouldn't if it suited her needs."

Studying the closed door that led to the hallway, I lowered my voice and asked, "What do you think about Zuri? She had access to the security room, and she'd know how to wipe the camera footage."

"I think it would have been career, and possibly literal, suicide for her to take out a guest under her protection. Killing Hanzo isn't something she'd do of her own volition, but a strong enough promise or threat from one of the other councilors might have been enough. Everyone has a breaking point."

Blowing out a noisy exhale, I stood up and started collecting my various articles of discarded clothing. "So we've got two possible ringleaders and two more maybe accomplices." My voice muffled momentarily as I pulled on my shirt. "Somehow we have to narrow it down before your trial tonight. We at least need to create enough doubt to extend the investigation."

James stood as well, though he didn't bother with his clothes. "Don't fool yourself into thinking justice is the motivating factor for most of them. These beings do not share your moral compass. It will take a lot more than mere truth to convince them to vote in my favor. You'll need to offer them something they want."

I growled as my foot snagged in the leg of my jeans. "What they want is to walk in daylight, and you know as well as I do that that's not going to happen." I forced my leg into the frustrating fabric. "Maybe if I had more time, or Bael agreed to teach me more, I could recreate your amulet. But as it is?" I dropped onto the couch. "I'm just not good enough."

The couch sank, rolling me into James as he sat down beside me. He wrapped his arm around my shoulders. "You've more to offer than just your magic, Alex."

I rolled my eyes. "Thanks, but I don't think the promise of friendship is going to sway this lot."

"Fatima and Esteban want to join your alliance. You can use that as leverage."

"Too bad those are my two main suspects."

He kissed the top of my head. "I love your sense of justice, but in this case you need to be practical. The evidence you've come up with so far can fit anyone, so pin it where it will be the most convenient."

"You want me to frame someone else, the way someone framed you?"

"Since you need Esteban and Fatima, it will have to be Cecil and Zuri."

"Those are the people least likely to be guilty."

"Which is why they're the perfect scapegoats," James said. "If either Esteban or Fatima were involved, they'll be all too happy to point the finger elsewhere, and Cecil is the strongest opposition to the alliance. With him knocked off his stride, even if temporarily, they'll be in a better bargaining position for the inevitable backroom negotiations that will ensue. We just have to make him a more tempting target than me, and that's easily done by holding your support of their application to the alliance as collateral against my life, as you've been doing from the start."

"Not that I like Cecil much, but won't the council kill him and Zuri if they're found guilty?"

"Zuri, certainly. Cecil will be able to buy his way out with a lesser punishment. A fine. Maybe giving up some territory. They won't want to destabilize the council any more than it already is."

My organs squirmed at the blasé way he brushed Zuri aside. "Can't we accuse Cecil without bringing Zuri into it?"

He shook his head. "You said yourself it had to be a two-person job. Zuri had easy access to the security room. Hell, she could have ordered her thrall to erase the footage and bash her own head in without ever setting foot in the actual room. Plus, she's expendable in the eyes of the council. They'll believe that Cecil pressured her into helping him."

"But they'll kill her."

"You can't save everyone, Alex."

I thought about the way Zuri had protected me when the councilors got out of hand, how she'd agreed to the detour to investigate the crime scene, how she'd allowed me to visit Helen instead of waiting in my room, how she'd given me this hour with James. I sprang to my feet. "No. Just . . . no. I won't be the reason an innocent person dies."

"What if she's not innocent?" he asked. "You don't know for certain that she *wasn't* involved."

"But—"

A knock at the door cut me off.

Shit, had our voices risen enough to be heard in the hall? Did Zuri know what James had suggested? The wood was thick enough to block most sound, but even I didn't have ears as sensitive as a vampire's.

The door opened. Zuri stood in the doorway. The large man who'd flown me here loomed over her shoulder.

"Time to go," she said. If she'd overheard our conspiracy, she showed no sign.

James stood, unabashed by the evidence of our lovemaking. He wrapped me in a tight embrace, burrowing his face into my hair and breathing deep. "Do whatever you feel is right, and know that I will always love you, Alex."

"I'm going to get you out of this," I promised. "We're going to go home to Colorado, and sell art, and eat dinner with our friends." Pressure built behind my eyes. I sniffed.

He cupped my cheek and pressed one more kiss against my lips, then stepped back.

I pulled on my boots, not bothering to tie them, and left the room.

"Animkii will take you back to your room," Zuri said.

I looked the steward over. She'd been maybe fifty when she was turned into a vampire. Who knew how long she'd been alive since then. She had an easy smile, and laugh lines marked the corners of her bronze eyes. She'd been nothing but kind and helpful since I'd arrived. If I had to choose between her life and James's. . . .

"Thank you for everything," I said. Turning my back on the simplest solution to my problem, I followed Animkii down the hall.

I haven't seen Fatima's memories yet. I'll eat, get some rest, and find her before the council reconvenes. She had to be involved somehow. Maybe she'll hold the key to unraveling this mess. But even as I held out hope that I would find the truth about Hanzo's murder, James's warning echoed in my mind. *It will take a lot more than mere truth to convince them to vote in my favor.* And I still had the issue of the split vote on the secrecy charge to contend with.

Truth first, I told myself. *I can figure the rest out from there.*

Animkii's broad frame filled the hallway ahead, blocking my view. Not that I bothered to look where I was going. I trailed him on autopilot, like a shadow, always two steps behind. The large thrall had swapped his charred indigo suit for a pair of pressed black slacks and a loose teal shirt with a black necktie. His polished, black combat boots made the tucked ends of his pants balloon slightly where they met.

Five turns brought us to what I presumed was my door by the way Animkii opened it without knocking and stepped back.

"Meg delivered a meal to your room when we changed shifts. It may be a bit cold, but please make do. We don't have anyone to spare on hospitality at the moment."

"That's fine."

I slipped past him and closed the door. My room was dark. My fireplace cold. I groped my way toward the floor lamp on the side of the room and flipped its switch. Pale-yellow light bloomed, but it couldn't quite banish the shadows in the corners or the cold emptiness that greeted me. A tray of cold pork, cheese, bread, and fruits sat on my table beside a pitcher of water and a bottle of red wine. Forgoing the water, I poured myself a glass of burgundy. A sharp hint of cranberry drifted off the flowing liquid. I rolled it around the glass, staring into the dark swirl, then downed it in one go. Warmth filled my stomach. The sharp edges of my prolonged stress dulled a bit.

I ate my meal on autopilot, barely registering the flavors. Bite. Chew. Swallow. Repeat. Seeing James had bolstered my reserves, both from the simple joy I felt in his company and because he'd actually shared some energy through our bond. Now that I was alone, my energy was fading as fast as the lingering warmth from his touch and the phantom pressure of his lips. My eyelids drooped. I let them close as I continued to shuttle items from the tray to my mouth by feel. It didn't matter what I picked up. It was all just fuel, and that's what I needed.

The day had to be half over by the time I crawled into bed. I would have liked a few minutes in a hot bath, but sleep was more important. I had to be up and alert before Fatima had her breakfast tonight. That would be my last chance to uncover something, *any*thing, to clear James of Hanzo's murder. Then it was up to me to make it enticing enough to stick.

I rolled over and over, trying to get comfortable, but my body wasn't the problem. It was my mind that wouldn't settle down. Esteban and Fatima. One of them had to be involved. Maybe both. I had one more chance with Fatima, but what if it was Esteban who held the key to Hanzo's death? How could I find the truth if he could block my magic? Again I pictured that strange glow I'd found inside him . . . a person-shaped void made entirely of light.

Something tickled my memory—a lecture my fae tutor had drilled into my head during the grueling hours she'd spent preparing me for life among the fae.

"Glamours aren't illusions. They're an extension of the caster, a twisting of reality that fuses all the major schools of magic. It doesn't simply fool the senses, it becomes real. That's why glamours fool recording devices where illusions cannot."

"So an illusion can never trick a camera, no matter how strong the caster?"

Hortense pursed her lips in that distinctly Hortense way of hers. "There is a level of illusion magic that can, though few have ever seen it." She pulled one of the heavy, leather-bound tomes from her collection, flipped through the pages, and set it open in front of me, tapping a picture. "The construct. It follows the same basic formula as a golem, except that instead of infusing a core into a material doll, the body is created from light, an illusion. Only three fae in history have accomplished it, and the practice was discontinued shortly after."

"Why? I'd think having tactile illusions would be super useful."

"Useful, yes. But . . . wrong. As with a golem, the only way to create a construct is to infuse it with an autonomous, living core." She frowned at my blank expression. "A soul, if you will. And the only way to give it that is to rip it from an already living being. Golems and constructs were formed either by extracting a sacrificial soul—which both killed the victim and created an uncontrollable being—or, if the caster wished to retain dominance over their creation, tearing off pieces of their own soul and stuffing those shards into dolls made from either clay or light, depending on the discipline. Both practices were banned by their respective groups, once it became clear that any fae whose soul was damaged in such a way quickly developed symptoms of madness."

From what I'd seen with my magic, Esteban certainly fit the description "doll of light." Was that why I'd been unable to find his core? To read his memories? Would a construct even have such things? But if that was true, who made him? And why? Had a fae illusionist infiltrated the vampire council? Or had a vampire found the secret to creating constructs? Fae or vampire, how had they avoided the madness that caused the fae lords to ban that magic in the first place?

Tearing off pieces of their own soul and stuffing those shards into dolls . . . That's pretty much how vampires reproduce. Maybe they're all a bit mad. But Esteban's been on the council for decades. Centuries. Why put a puppet on a throne for that long?

I rolled over, commiserating with my exhausted brain as it ran in circles. *Am I just grasping at straws?* I wrapped my arms around my pillow and burrowed my face into the lumpy surface. The prismatic glare of Esteban's core rose in my mind as sleep rolled over me. *Dolls of light . . .*

My mind drifted away on that thought.

"It's your move."

I look up and find Uncle Sol sitting across from me. Ocean waves crash on the shore behind him. A salty breeze wafts into my face, twisting my hair.

He takes a swig from his beer then gestures with his bottle, drawing my attention to the cherry-wood chessboard I gave him last Christmas. I'm already down three pawns and a rook. My king is in danger from his knight. Moving my bishop, I take out the threat.

"Beware the obvious path." Sol's voice rumbles, deep as the sea. I glance at his face. He smiles, but his eyes are sad. "It's almost always a trap."

When I look down, my pieces aren't made of metal anymore. They're flesh and blood, and each bears the face of a friend.

Sol lifts his queen, who now wears Victoria's tight red dress and beams at me with emerald eyes. Emma, the bishop I'd just used to take out Sol's knight, screams as Victoria slices off her head.

My stomach heaves. I clap a hand to my mouth.

Bael claps from atop his throne, safe on the far side of the board. Pawns in PTF uniforms and clergy robes jeer from the front rows.

I lick my lips. Victoria now has a clear path to James.

"Check."

I study the board. Sweat slicks my skin. The faces of my friends stare up at me, begging me to save them, but every move I see will result in a death.

"You can't save everyone, Alex. Decide."

I can barely hear Sol over the pounding in my ears. "There's no safe path!" I grip the side of the board and flip it into the air. Yellow leaves drift around me, torn loose to dance on the wind. Moonlight turns the rocks in the clearing silver. The air is cold. I'm less than a mile from home, but none of the gaps in the dark trees around me look familiar. I've stood in this clearing a hundred times. I spin and spin. Panic chokes me. I don't know the way home.

Something pops.

The ribbon of rockfall, stable since long before I came into being, begins to slide once more. I turn toward the trees, but I'm still not sure which way to run. I hesitate.

I'm knocked to my knees. I twist, only to get flattened to my back. The rocks tumble over me, blotting out the stars. I squirm and struggle, but my legs are trapped. My chest won't rise. The rocks stop. Silence rings in my ears.

I gasped, but no air reached my lungs. A ring of fire squeezed my throat. A weight on my abdomen pinned me down, pressing me into the suffocating embrace of my mattress. For a moment, an image of the avalanche gobbling up the starry sky hung over me in the darkness, but this wasn't a dream. I'd woken up . . . and my nightmare had come with me.

Throwing myself open to the power of the Rift, demons and all, I filled myself with energy. The blue-gray clouds that rolled in actually lightened the perfect darkness of the room, outlining the body of the person whose hands were wrapped around my throat. When I felt as if my skin would split from the energy I'd recklessly let in, I forced the magic from my body as a compressed wave. My attacker's weight lifted. The grip on my neck strained, then broke. Their shadowy form went flying away from me. A heavy *thud* and grunt sounded on the far side of the room, but I barely registered the noises past the rushing in my ears as I rolled off the side of the bed, gasping.

My knees hit the floor. My lungs inflated, starved for air, causing a coughing fit that doubled me over. My throat felt bruised, each cough scraping its way through the too-tight airway, flaying the already damaged tissue, and bringing on another bout of coughing.

Tears streamed from my eyes. Not that it mattered. I couldn't see anyway. Having released all my stored energy in that one desperate blast, the room had returned to darkness, impenetrable even to my fae eyes. My muscles shook. I hadn't rested enough to recover from my earlier exhaustion, my magic reserves were empty, and the adrenaline coursing through my system did little more than jangle my nerves.

Get up! The voice of Sarah Nazari—alpha of the newly formed PTF werewolf pack—shouted at me from my memory, cutting through the groggy haze in my mind. I pictured her standing over me, having just knocked my ass to the mat for the umpteenth time in one of our sparring sessions. *If you stay on the ground, you're dead.*

I scrambled to my feet, groping to find my bearings. My fingers smacked painfully into the nightstand. I tried to take slow breaths through my nose to get my spasming lungs under control, but snot clogged my sinuses. My heart pounded. Drying sweat from my nightmare turned my skin to ice. My damp T-shirt clung like a straitjacket.

The bed springs creaked under a sudden weight.

I backed up, bumping into a wall. Vampires could see even in pitch dark. Not that they'd need to see to find me with the racket of my relentless coughing.

Keeping one hand on the wall and the other raised for defense, I moved toward the main room. There was a lamp just to the side of the bedroom door, and if I could make it into the hall, the security team would send help.

No one helped Hanzo, whispered a cynical voice at the back of my mind.

A gust of air was all the warning I had to get my arm up. Flesh-backed fabric connected with my forearm. I'd gotten the angle wrong. My block collapsed. Instead of taking a hit, fingers tangled in my hair, yanking. A knee connected with my gut, prompting another coughing fit as my abused diaphragm cramped.

Humans rely too much on what they can see. Sarah's disapproval rolled through me.

Closing my useless eyes, I wrapped my fingers around the wrist near my temple—thick, hairy, probably male. So long as my attacker was touching me, I knew where he was. I could fight back. Curling the fingers of my free hand, I thrust my palm into the space where I imagined my attacker's face to be. My aim was off. My hand slammed into a jaw rather than the nose I'd hoped for, but it was enough to make him stagger.

The hand in my hair pulled. He'd lost balance when his head snapped back. He was open.

Dropping my weight and twisting the hand tangled in my hair to lock the joint, I stepped inside his guard and turned so my back was against his chest, as if we were spooning lovers. I tucked my shoulder in the pit of his trapped arm and, gripping his sleeve, I popped him off his feet with a bend and a twist.

A yelp sounded close to my ear. Definitely male.

There was a sickening *crack* when he landed. I didn't hesitate. Twisting his still-trapped hand, I wrenched his arm behind his back, pinning it between his shoulder blades.

Fingers gripped my shoulder.

I jerked away, calling my magic once again as I registered this second attacker. Blue fog coiled around the shape beside me. They raised their hands.

"Easy." A soft voice I didn't recognize spoke from the misty form. Light flared.

I winced and blinked, trying to clear my vision.

The nearby figure straightened. A larger person filled the bedroom doorway, silhouetted by the lamplight streaming in from the main room.

A third attacker? I blinked again. *No. Animkii. No one else has shoulders that broad.*

He stepped fully into the room. As my eyes adjusted, I could make out the details of his expression—furrowed brow, lips a thin, tight line. His gaze was fixed on the man I held pinned to the floor.

I looked down. My stomach heaved. Ronald's reddish-brown hair and slack-featured face were wedged against the foot of my bed at entirely the wrong angle. Releasing my grip, I backed away from the dead man. His unfocused gray-green eyes seemed to follow me. Blood glinted on the bedpost where his head had connected.

I raised my gaze to Animkii. "This isn't . . . I didn't mean . . ." Panic and another coughing fit choked off my inarticulate defense. I pressed my palms to my chest, fighting back a wave of dizziness.

"It was self-defense." The words came from the nearby stranger. About my height with shoulder-length black hair pinned back on one side with three barrettes, dark eyes, and sallow skin. They wore a loose sweater of navy blue and black slacks over equally dark sneakers. I recognized them from the ballroom. By process of elimination, she . . . he? . . . they had to be Esteban's thrall.

That thought sent a shiver down my spine as I once again recalled the eerie light I'd found at Esteban's center and the certainty that he'd tried to do something to me in that brief moment of contact we'd shared. Had Esteban sent his servant as backup in case Ronald failed to kill me? If Animkii hadn't come in when he did. . . .

Coiling my magic tighter, I took another step away and prodded the thrall's core as I asked, "Why are you here?"

The tangled knot at their center, such a dark crimson as to be almost black, shimmered as the threads twined and twisted, creating a ripple of gold like sunlight on water. Tiny novas flashed along the surface.

"I was passing by and noticed your door was ajar. I heard a commotion within and came to investigate." They gestured to Ronald's still form. "Though it seems you needed no assistance."

Some of the lights winked out before they spoke, but the rest shone brightly till the end. *A half-truth then?*

Anger and fear spun my emotions into a burning knot, out of proportion to what was happening. The adrenaline from the attack should have been fading, crashing my worn-out system. Instead, the overwhelming need to act seemed to be getting stronger.

James, I thought. Disjointed sensations filtered through our link. *James is fighting.*

Strong hands gripped my shoulders. For a moment, I thought the feeling was coming from James, then Animkii's face came into focus, inches from my own.

"Are you injured?"

"James." I gripped Animkii's forearms, steadying myself. My exhaustion, coupled with my abrupt awakening and the prickling certainty that

James was in pain, were making it hard to focus. "He's fighting someone. We need to get to him."

Animkii shook his head. "If the conclave is compromised, my priority is to get you out. Zuri's orders."

I pushed him away. "I'm not leaving without James." I stumbled toward the door, pressing one hand to my aching head.

"I've alerted my master," said Esteban's servant. "He will assist James if necessary. You should go with the steward's thrall until order is restored."

I shot a glare over my shoulder. *As if Esteban's presence is any kind of comfort. He's probably the one attacking.*

"Zuri will look after James," added Animkii. "If there is fighting, you would only get in the way."

"What's even going on here?" I demanded, spinning to face him. "How did Ronald get in my room? Who's attacking James?" The pounding in my head was getting worse. I felt like I was going to throw up.

"Now is not the time for discussion." He reached for my wrist, but I twisted out of his grip.

"You're right about that." I jogged through my sitting area. The door to the hallway was open. The strand of magic connecting me to James thrummed with tension. *I'm coming.* I sent the thought along our link as I stepped into the hall.

Something slammed into the back of my skull. The hallway tipped, sliding sideways. I stretched out my hand, reaching for the invisible thread that pointed the way to James. The lights flickered and went out.

Chapter 12

MY EYELIDS ROSE slowly, like curtains on a play. Light bombarded me, blinding me. I shuttered my eyes. I was sitting up, head lolling. A strange rhythmic rocking swayed me side to side. I tried to raise my hand, to wipe my eyes, but something restrained me. All at once, the mechanical hum that had registered only as white noise in my addled brain roared to the foreground. I was pressed hard into the padding at my back. I inhaled sharply. Ropes constrained my chest, limiting my lungs. Panic surged. My eyes snapped fully open.

The interior of the private jet that had carried me to Canada was awash with white warmth as it taxied, all the previously shuttered window blinds thrown open to welcome the blazing afternoon sun. The bone-jarring rattle of the ride eased off as the ground fell away. Snow glittered on the lumps and bumps of the nearby mountains, sparkling like a diamond blanket draped over the landscape, as we rose out of the valley.

My tongue felt swollen, my mouth dry. I worked up enough moisture to swallow. My head was pounding with the incessant throb of a jackhammer against my skull.

What's going on? The last thing I remember . . . An image of Ronald's blankly staring eyes drifted up from my memory, followed by the painful panic that had filtered through my bond with James. He'd been fighting someone . . . and he'd been losing. Struggling to pull my thoughts together, I called out along the magical tether that pinned James to my heart and anchored him in my soul. He was there, alive, but too quiet, and every second that the plane gained altitude, the thread between us grew thinner.

"Take me back." My voice was a dry rasp that prompted a coughing fit. My throat was swollen. Even breathing hurt.

"Awake already?"

I tipped as far sideways in my seat as I could to get a view up the center aisle. Animkii occupied the pilot's chair, just as he had on our flight here. The second seat in the cockpit was empty.

I swallowed, winced, and forced myself to say, "We have to go back." The words sliced like razors through my throat.

Animkii shook his head. "Just relax. Take a nap if you can. You look like hell."

Another memory floated to the surface—Animkii silhouetted in my bedroom door and, before that, Esteban's thrall crouched beside me in the darkness. Animkii must have been on security detail, but why was the other thrall there? I racked my brain. They said they'd seen my door ajar, but what were the odds they just happened to be passing by my room during the attack? In fact . . . the room had been pitch-black until Animkii turned on the light in the living room. If Ronald had left the door ajar, some light should have filtered in from the hallway.

Sharp pain, like an ice pick stabbing into my temple, tried to steal my concentration, but I clung to the hazy thought. I hadn't been able to see Esteban's thrall until I called my magic, and then just barely, but both Ronald and Esteban's thrall had managed to find me in the dark. I didn't have terrific eyesight for a fae, and certainly nowhere near that of a vampire, but it was much better than a human's. It made sense that Ronald would sneak his way through the dark so as not to wake me, but if Esteban's thrall came to help, why not turn on a light? Why not call out? I recalled their hand on my shoulder, calm and sure. *How had they reached me so easily . . . unless they had magic, too?*

My thoughts ground to a halt as my mind seized on that flicker of inspiration, then veered off down a new path. *Everyone is convinced only another vampire could be strong enough to take Hanzo down. No one even looked at the servants. But what if Esteban's servant isn't just a normal human thrall?*

Is that even possible? I rolled the idea around in my head, inspecting it from all angles. *Thralls are tethered to their masters, steeped in their energy, so any magical aura a vampire might pick up off a servant could reasonably be dismissed as originating with their master.* I frowned. *But even a trained sorcerer with surprise on their side would have their hands full against a vampire as old as Hanzo.*

My mind circled back to Hortense's lecture on constructs. What if the light I'd seen in Esteban's core hadn't been a shield? What if that's all there'd been to find because he *was* light? But constructs were fae magic; a practitioner couldn't do that, no matter how talented. I turned that fact over in my mind. *What if Esteban's servant is a fae?*

I felt as if the world had shattered like a dropped mirror, but the more I considered the possibility, the more sense it made. The fae had been trying to eradicate vampires for centuries, but vampires were wily, and even one could make more. But the fae could be wily, too, and they were capable of playing a *very* long game.

If Esteban had been a real vampire, already a member of the ruling council, a fae could have killed him and created a construct to run things from the shadows . . . assuming they'd found a solution to the whole "creator going mad" thing. It was the perfect arrangement for a spy. They could eavesdrop on the council, even influence its decisions, without risk of exposure. No one paid any attention to servants. Even the occasional reaction to iron would be easy to miss unless you were looking for it, and I hadn't seen a whole lot of metal in the conclave; it was mostly stone and wood. Short of posing a direct question to which they could not lie, their identity might never be challenged. Even then, the construct could step in to deflect the conversation.

I chewed my lower lip as some of the jagged edges of this puzzle slid into place. *If the puppet master killed a councilor before, murdering Hanzo would have been no problem. No one bothered to check the whereabouts of the servants because no one suspected them. While the fae was taking care of Hanzo, Esteban could have disabled the security cameras. If he's made of light and magic rather than any truly physical form, perhaps he just slipped under the door like a sunbeam.*

I turned the hypothesis over in my head. *Esteban voted to spare my life, but that could have been a misdirection to keep suspicion off him while the fae planned to take me out behind the scenes. The last thing any fae would want was for vampires to gain the ability to walk in daylight as their equals, so the fae must have been standing by to finish the job if Ronald failed. If Animkii hadn't arrived when he did . . . I shuddered. A good spy wouldn't have wanted to compromise their cover, not when they were so perfectly situated in a key position, so they played the part of the helpful bystander when they were discovered in my room.*

Certainty seeped through my bones. Esteban was a construct. His servant was a fae. They'd killed Hanzo and, with me out of the way, there was no one to stop them killing James.

Gritting my teeth, I focused on the straining tether connecting me to James and shouted, "Turn this plane around!" The words burned like acid in my battered throat.

"Or what?" Animkii called over his shoulder with a chuckle. "Are you planning to take the controls?"

Animkii wasn't wrong to assume I had no idea how to fly a plane, but he was a fool if he thought that was going to stop me. James was hurt. I didn't know how badly. Even if he'd won his fight, his life was still in danger. Esteban and his servant-slash-master were using James as a scapegoat, and no one on the council cared. Even Victoria had given up on proving him innocent, but now I had the evidence we needed.

Proving someone was fae was easy enough. One solid dose of iron, and voila! Not only would the council have Hanzo's real killer, but my exposing a fae who'd infiltrated their ranks had to be worth enough to buy off the remaining breach of secrecy charge. I could save James, if I could just get back, but every second in the air carried me farther away.

I strained against my bonds, rattling the seat. "You have to take me back; I know who killed Hanzo!"

There was a moment's hesitation, then he laughed, as someone might at a child who swore they hadn't broken the shattered vase at their feet in a last-ditch effort to avoid the inevitable.

Cold fury poured through me. Explaining my construct hypothesis could see us halfway across Canada by the time I convinced him, and I was *not* letting him carry me that far from James. If he wouldn't land the plane willingly, I'd have to take the choice away from him.

Steadying my breath, I focused on my left palm and pulled energy into my body, siphoning it through the rosy glow of my lower-than-average fae reserves to make sure no demonic hitchhikers tried to take up residence in my body. I didn't see any demons in the fog that rolled across my vision, but that didn't mean they weren't there. Funneling the clean energy into my right hand, I pointed one finger at a window on the far side of the cabin as best I could with my wrist tied to the armrest. I could burn my ropes and fight Animkii for control of the cockpit, but who knew how long that might take, or if I could land the plane in one piece. Much as I hated what I was about to do, having an experienced pilot at the controls was the better option.

Focus the energy. Picture what you want it to do. Release. Taking as deep a breath as my bindings would allow, I shot a bullet of compressed magic at the window.

Plastic shattered. A tornado tore through the cabin, stealing my breath and causing my hair to slash wildly at my unprotected face. The vortex whipped safety pamphlets, paper cups, and anything else not tied down through the cabin's interior. Emergency breathing apparatus dropped from the ceiling. An alarm sounded in the cockpit.

"What the hell?!" Animkii's voice was two octaves too high. His hands darted over the console, flipping switches and pressing buttons. The plane dropped a few feet, leaving my stomach behind, then leveled off. The mountains that had looked distant a moment ago loomed in front of us. He twisted to glare at me. "Are you insane?"

"Turn this plane around," I ordered, "or my next blast hits the engine."

He stared at me for a moment that seemed to stretch forever. The wind grew less intense as the cabin pressure equalized. Just as he opened his mouth, the plane lurched to the side. Another alarm blared in the cockpit. Cursing, Animkii turned his back on me. "Dammit! Your little stunt damaged the aileron on the left wing. I can't keep us level!"

Panic followed realization as his words sank in. *I was just trying to force him to turn the plane around . . . I didn't mean to actually crash it!*

I couldn't see what Animkii was doing with the controls, but the plane banked hard to the left and dropped with the stomach-clenching force of an express elevator, slamming me against my restraints. My ears popped. The angry hiss of air tearing past at high speeds thrummed in my ears like the deafening rush of a waterfall. A hillside loomed uncomfortably close out my window, trees and rocks breaking the blanket of snow in jagged lines of color.

"Brace yourself!" Animkii's warning was pointless, since I couldn't move in my seat, but I clenched my jaw to keep from biting my tongue and gripped the armrests my hands were tied to.

The initial impact threw me forward. The nylon cords around my chest cut deep. My chin snapped to my sternum. My eyes slammed shut. There was a moment of weightlessness as the plane bounced, then my spine was compressed into my tailbone and my head jerked forward again. A screech of tearing metal replaced the rush of wind. The cabin tipped. A piece of debris smashed into my shoulder and spun away. I ground my teeth together and prayed.

We stopped moving with the force of a head-on collision and a groan of metal. I dangled sideways in my seat as though it had been mounted to a wall. The nearest windows, now above me, showed nothing but blue sky. The window I'd broken across the way had been replaced by a gaping hole with a chunk of dark granite jutting through it. Snow drifted like glitter through the silent cabin, prickling against my skin.

I took a shuddering breath. I was still alive. My tether to James was strained, but present. I could find my way back . . . assuming nothing was broken and I didn't pass out. I lifted my head and winced. The muscles in my neck were ribbons of fire shooting daggers into my brain. My chest hurt. My shoulder hurt. Something warm slid over my ankle. I looked down to see a trail of blood dripping from the toes of one foot. Something had split open my shin. My fae blood let me recover from all manner of wounds in a fraction of the time it would take if I were entirely human, but it wasn't instantaneous, and they still hurt like hell.

Licking my lips, I called into the strangely heavy silence ringing in my ears, "You still alive up there?"

Animkii didn't answer. I squinted toward the cockpit. The pilot's seat was empty.

Great. What I really wanted was to close my eyes and let my battered body rest. Instead, I called to my practitioner magic and sliced through the cord at one wrist then the other. When both my hands were free, I braced as well as I could and used my magic like a scalpel to sever the ropes that had kept me from flying out of my seat during the crash. The bindings fell away, but I only dropped two inches. Then the lap belt cinched at my waist caught. Apparently, Animkii had taken the time to fasten my seat belt, despite my being tied to the seat.

I tightened my grip on the armrest above me, pulled the release latch, and dropped out of my seat. My elbow complained as my full weight tugged it straight. I hung for a moment, lining up my landing. Then I let go.

My knees buckled as my bare feet connected with the ice-cold stone that had torn through the side of the rotated plane. I slapped my palms to the surface to steady myself, only then realizing how shaky I was. The cold wasn't helping. I was still wearing the cotton shorts and T-shirt I'd gone to bed in—hardly ideal clothing for an arctic mountainside, even if the sunlight steaming though the windows took some of the bite out of the air.

I crept cautiously toward the cockpit, wary of any shift in the metal and the possibility that Animkii's silence might be calculated. Strips of leather, chunks of foam padding, and twisted steel brackets littered the cabin, torn loose when the rock sliced through the wall.

If I'd been sitting on the other side of the plane . . . I pushed that thought away.

Broken glass and the heady smell of alcohol filled the narrow corridor leading to the cockpit. Several cabinets in the galley had been flung open, their contents strewn about the cabin. A shattered bottle was a likely culprit of the gash on my leg. Gingerly picking my way across the minefield of glass shards and spilled snacks, I stuck my head into the cockpit.

Animkii was still in the pilot's seat, but he was slumped so far to the side as to be invisible from the aisle. Only his seat belt kept him from lying in the litter on the wall-slash-floor.

Drifted snow covered the lower half of the windshield, plowed and piled as the plane furrowed its path. No wonder Animkii hadn't seen the rock that caught us, and the landing gear would have been worse than useless in this powder. Two hundred feet in front of the plane's nose, the ground dropped into a deep bowl ringed by snow-capped peaks. Trees poked from the white ground around an icy lake that snaked down the valley to my left. The view was beautiful, and terrifying. It was the kind of scene you wanted to see in a nature documentary, safe and warm on your couch, not somewhere you wanted to be stranded.

We can't have gotten far, I reminded myself. *All I have to do is follow my tether to James. I'll be back at the conclave in no time.* The shiver that raced down my spine and raised goosebumps on my entirely-too-exposed skin called me a liar. *Two hours on this mountain, let alone when the sun sets, and I'll die of exposure. I need to take stock. There must be some emergency gear onboard. But first,* I pressed my fingers to the side of Animkii's limp neck and found his pulse. *Still alive.*

ANIMKII'S HEAD wobbled, then lifted.

I popped another handful of mini-pretzels into my mouth, cinched the silver space blanket I'd found alongside a red backpack of medical supplies in one of the still-latched cabinets in the galley, and waited.

His eyelids fluttered. The muscles in his arm tensed, as if he were trying to raise the limb, but the nylon cords I'd repurposed from my own awakening bound him tight.

"Not pleasant, is it?" I asked. My voice was still hoarse, but speaking didn't feel like I was coughing up razor blades anymore. *Go, go fae healing.*

Animkii's gaze drifted side to side, then focused on me—as much as a thrall's gaze ever focused. "We survived." He sounded mildly surprised.

"Congratulations on a successful landing," I said flatly.

He scowled. "You could have killed us."

"Do you know what the number-one rule is if someone's trying to abduct you?"

He frowned.

"Don't get in a vehicle. Once a kidnapper gets you somewhere they control, you're lost."

"Far better to die on a mountain," he said dryly. "Tell me, did you have a plan for after, or were you just lashing out on instinct."

"Get back to the conclave. That's my plan. If you'd turned the plane around like I'd asked, we wouldn't be here."

"Go back now, and whoever tried to kill you gets a second chance. The conclave isn't secure."

I pictured the blazing light of Esteban's core and thought, *It's worse than you think.* I wasn't looking forward to more vampire hospitality, but someone had to expose Esteban and his "servant" for what they truly were . . . and what they'd done. Only then would James and I have a chance at an agreement with the council that didn't involve death threats and coercion.

"Do you know what's going on there?" I asked. "Can you speak to Zuri?"

He closed his eyes, then opened them with a shake of his head. "Not at this distance, but I know she's alive. The mere fact that I still have my sanity is proof of that."

"So is James. That implies whatever danger had them fighting before has passed." *For the moment.*

"But did they win, or lose? Alive doesn't mean victorious." He narrowed his gaze at me. "Just what is the connection you have with James, anyway? You're not his thrall, yet you seem bound to him in a similar way."

"That's none of your business, and hardly the most important topic to discuss right now. We need to get off this mountain."

"Says the woman who put us here." He tipped his head toward the cockpit. "Untie me. I'll call for help with the plane's radio."

"I tried that already. It must have been damaged in the landing."

"You mean the crash . . . which you caused."

"Okay, I get it. You're mad that I crashed your plane. Get over it." I shivered and pulled the blanket tighter. The silvery fabric crinkled. "What I wouldn't give for a proper coat," I mumbled under my breath.

"You weren't supposed to get off this plane until we were far enough south that you wouldn't *need* a coat."

"Or shoes?" I shot back. He didn't respond, so I shifted the conversation back to the more pressing topic of planning my next move. "Do you have any idea how far we flew?"

"Not very," he said. "I'd barely taken off when you threw your little tantrum."

I rolled my eyes.

"Untie me," he said.

I snorted. "As if I'd trust you."

"So, what? You're going to leave me trussed up like a pig to freeze to death?"

"Don't play the victim here. *You* kidnapped *me*."

"To protect you! Zuri ordered me to get you out and keep you safe. Will you really condemn me for that?"

I took a sip from one of the plastic water bottles I'd rescued from the floor, watching him. I'd run through every scenario I could think of while I was hauling his heavy ass out of the cockpit and tying him up. How to get off the mountain. How not to freeze. How to reach the conclave before nightfall and James's sentencing. Unfortunately, no matter what other variables I changed, I was faced with one impossible choice: Trust Animkii or leave him to die.

"If you were going to leave me, you would have done it already," he said, as though reading my thoughts. "You would have stripped my clothes and been halfway down this mountain by the time I came to. You're not a killer."

We glared at each other for a tense moment. I dropped my gaze first. I *had* killed before—hell, I'd killed Ronald earlier that very day— but I'd known as soon as the thought crossed my mind that I couldn't leave Animkii to freeze to death. Killing in self-defense, in the heat of the moment, was a far cry from tying up an unconscious man and leaving him to die. I had enough ghosts haunting my dreams. I didn't want another.

"Besides," Animkii continued, "you need me. You won't survive out here alone."

I met his clouded gaze. "I'm heartier than I look."

"Fae blood may cure bumps and bruises, but can it keep you from freezing in an arctic night?" He used the steep line of his chin to gesture toward my bare toes peeking out from the bottom of the blanket. "Consider me your personal space heater."

"I wouldn't need a heater if I took your boots."

"Then you'd be back to killing me. I know this area, and I can carry you out on my back. Can you say the same?"

I took a breath to respond, then I hesitated. Animkii was acting so much like a regular person, it was easy to forget he was a thrall, that his choices weren't his own. "You're a thrall," I said at last. "Zuri ordered you to get me away from the conclave. You *can't* help me go back."

"You don't think much of thralls, do you?"

I looked away.

"We're not all the same, you know," he said. "High-level servants like personal attendants and those who run a conclave often have more . . . freedom . . . than your average cannon-fodder thrall. Sometimes we need to pass for human. Sometimes we need to make decisions in emergency situations while unable to communicate with our masters. This makes us more useful, though there's a trade-off. More self-awareness means deeper tethers. You saw it with Ronald. High-level thralls rarely survive the death of their masters. We're bound too closely to our vampires, and we know too many of their secrets, to be allowed to live beyond their passing."

"You're telling me you can disobey Zuri?" I asked, incredulous. But I had to wonder. I'd managed to attack the master who'd once enthralled me, so even a vampire seeking total control couldn't erase a person's nature entirely, and there was no doubt Zuri's thralls weren't the empty-eyed husks that had walked the halls of Merak's nest.

"Not disobey, no, but I can *interpret*." He smiled. "Zuri ordered me to get you out." He glanced side to side and shrugged. "You're out. Beyond that, she told me to keep you safe, so my next move is clear: Get you off this mountain before you freeze to death."

I gave him a flat stare. Could it really be that simple? Had he fulfilled the first requirement simply by removing me from the conclave, and now his prime directive was to keep me safe? I worried my lower lip between my teeth. Untying him would be a gamble, but. . . . *Unless I'm willing to let him die, do I have a choice?*

I stood up with a sigh, shaking pretzel crumbs off my blanket and brushing dust and dried blood from my scratched knees. "A truce then. Your word that you'll help me get back to the conclave, and I won't strip you bare and leave you to freeze. Deal?"

He smiled. "I'd shake your hand, but I'm a little tied up at the moment."

I crossed my arms.

"Deal," he said. "Now cut me loose. We're burning daylight, and it's going to take us at least a few hours to reach civilization, assuming we don't fall down a ravine or get caught in an avalanche, which I wouldn't bet against considering how this day is going."

"Cheery," I said, picking at the knot near his shoulder. The ropes fell away. I tensed, ready to call my magic if it looked like he was going to fight.

He shrugged his shoulders a few times, rolled his neck, and rubbed his wrists. Then he reached up and gingerly touched the gauze pad I'd taped over his temple when I'd cleaned his wound. He gave me a calculating look. "Thanks."

I relaxed a little, but I didn't let down my guard. Staying constantly alert was going to be exhausting, but there was no help for that. I wouldn't be taken by surprise again.

Animkii wasted no time in popping the escape hatch over the wing on what was now the ceiling and climbing out. He reached down in invitation.

Snugging my flimsy protection against the cold tightly around my shoulders, I gripped his wrist and let him pull me up. The air stung my sinuses and lungs, freezing the tips of my ears and my quickly numbing toes. I shivered and adjusted my breaths, keeping them shallow. *If I want to get off this mountain with all my digits intact, I'll need to use my magic to stay warm.* I'd never tried such a subtle effect before, but in theory it should work a bit like throwing a fireball, and I'd done that plenty of times. The trick would be control. I didn't want to roast myself. And I'd have to use it sparingly. Lack of energy could be as dangerous as lack of heat.

I turned a slow circle. Swells of snow ringed the front of the plane like ripples on a pond frozen in time at the moment a rock was dropped. The plane's one intact wing stretched toward the azure sky like the groping fingers of a drowning man. The other wing was crumpled and twisted, barely attached. Metal debris littered the snow along the trough we'd gouged into the mountain, revealing brown grass and hard dirt beneath the snow. I stopped my pivot when the pull of James's presence was strongest. A white ridge loomed before me, taller even than the shelf on which our plane was perched.

"So much for a straight line," I grumbled.

"Considering how far south we flew, our fastest way out of the mountains is probably to the southwest. There's a town at the southern edge of Nááts'įhch'oh Park."

"That's in the opposite direction from the conclave."

"Exactly. It was along our flight path, so we're closer to it than to the conclave. If we reach the town, we can get a vehicle then circle back."

I shook my head. "We might get out of the mountains faster, but we'll waste too much time backtracking if we have to drive around the southern end of the range." I didn't voice the real reason I had for taking the most direct route back to the conclave: that I couldn't bear the thought of moving any farther from James. Not just for the ache it would cause in my own heart, but because he'd feel the strengthening or weakening of our bond from the conclave, just as I could feel him here on the mountain. I couldn't tell him with words, but he would know from my movements that I was coming back, that I hadn't abandoned him. "We'll go east along the valley at the base of this cliff, then turn north once the terrain levels out. There must be settlements on that side."

"Farther. Smaller."

"But they do exist," I said triumphantly. "Even a single homestead will do. Anyone who lives in the wilderness should have a reliable means of travel."

"And if we freeze to death in the extra hour it takes to reach civilization in that direction?"

"I should be able to keep us warm with my magic, at least for a while."

"How long is a while?"

I shrugged. "Until I lose my concentration or pass out from exhaustion." I pointed to the east, along the frozen valley. "I'm going this way. If you're backing out of our deal, I suppose we can waste time fighting over your boots, but we're both going to need that energy later. What do you say?"

He shook his head, looking disgusted. "Stupid, stubborn . . ." He flapped his arms. "Fine. East it is. There's a tiny settlement to the southeast of the conclave that we might be able to find. I can't guarantee they'll have anything more useful than a fire to get warm by, but that's going to be our best bet."

I smiled, pleased by my minor triumph and desperately hoping I'd made the right call. If we got caught in the mountains after sunset, even my magic might not be enough to keep us from freezing.

Animkii rested his hands on his hips and peered over the side of the plane, past the crumpled wing. "That's a steep descent."

I joined him in inspecting the hillside. It would be hard to keep your feet, and if Animkii slipped with me on his back, we'd both go for a tumble that likely wouldn't end until we reached the bottom. I snapped my fingers and turned to Animkii. The mental image of an uncontrolled tumble had brought to mind something I'd seen in the cabin. "I have an idea that might help . . . and shave some time off our trip besides."

He cast me a skeptical look. "Oh?"

I lowered myself back into the cabin and grabbed the heavy cube of folded orange plastic I'd found in the locker beside the red backpack and space blanket. The words "In case of water landing" accompanied a series of cartoonish pictures depicting how to inflate the plane's emergency raft. I lifted the parcel for Animkii to see. "How do you feel about sledding?"

I PEEKED OVER the lip of the inflated orange plastic of the raft. Reflective silver tape mimicked the glitter of ice beside my fingers. I'd tied my silver blanket around my neck, like a superhero's cape, to free my hands and tucked the bottom around my folded legs. The red backpack, stuffed with first aid gear and as many snacks and bottles of water as we could fit, rested against my side.

"Maybe this wasn't such a great idea."

"Too late," Animkii huffed, breath streaming from his nostrils as he positioned the raft at the top of the smoothest chute leading into the valley below. Assuming we missed the handful of trees scattered over the hillside that were large enough to pose a threat, we'd have a clear stretch of frozen lake at the bottom to bleed off the momentum of our descent. And so long as we didn't rip any holes on the way down, we'd float if the ice turned out not to be solid.

"Hang on."

I tightened my grip on the rubbery plastic, wishing it had handholds like a proper sled.

Animkii bulldozed a half-dozen steps through the calf-deep snow, propelling the raft in front of him. He dove into the back as gravity took over.

Cold wind rushed into my face, billowing my blanket like the childish cape it resembled despite its lower edge being pinned under my butt. Tears streamed from my eyes, leaving frozen tracks across my cheeks as I squinted forward. Stunted trees and the bare branches of dormant brush folded under our stampede, bumping beneath my ankles, only to spring up, bent but not broken, in the wake of our passage. Larger mounds shifted our course or popped us into the air only to drop us with a jolt that left my stomach in my throat and threatened to flatten my nose on the raft's outer tube.

Despite the cold freezing my limbs in place and the ache of bruises that hadn't yet healed being slammed repeatedly against the uneven terrain, the rush of speed and the bracing shock of the air made me grin. I threw my head back and let out a *whoop* of glee.

"You really are crazy!" Animkii hollered over the howl of the wind.

I glanced over my shoulder. The bulky man was sprawled in the bottom of the raft, arms and legs splayed to create as many points of contact as possible.

I gave him my best Cheshire Cat grin.

"Look out!" He pointed forward, eyes wide.

I twisted in time to see the thick trunk of a tree directly in our path. It had been hidden from view by a shallow rise until we were nearly on top of it. Its snapped-off upper half lay partially buried a little to one side. This wasn't some stunted growth that would bow at our approach.

This was a brick wall with deep roots.

"Lean," I shouted, throwing myself against the side of the raft and digging my hand into the snow in an attempt to pivot the vessel.

I felt Animkii do the same, bouncing me with his weight. His hand plunged in beside mine. Micro-daggers of ice grated my chapped skin. I gritted my teeth and pushed deeper. The raft veered to the left, but not enough. The right edge caught the side of the trunk, sending us into a spin. My hand left the ground as I fell back hard enough to feel the ground beneath the raft's cushion of air. Animkii landed beside me, bouncing me up.

The sun and sky continued to spin. An unseen drop stole the raft from beneath me, only to find me again on the next rise. Animkii's knee found my ribs, and I was pretty sure my elbow found his unmentionables at one point. Nausea clawed at the back of my throat. I scrunched my eyes closed and held my breath. The snap and flap of my blanket ends cracked in my ears. Fresh powder sifted over me, prickling my skin.

Eventually, the rush of the wind eased off. The bumps rippling under my back became distinct swells whose passing I could mark and measure. I opened my eyes. The sun had settled to a single point in the sky above. The scrape of ice on plastic slowed, then stopped. The ride was over.

Animkii sat up first, draping himself over the edge of the raft with a moan like a seasick sailor. "I am never doing that again."

I pushed myself upright. The raft might have stopped, but my head was still spinning. I twisted to look in the direction from which we'd come. We'd traveled about one-third of the way across the frozen lake. It seemed solid enough, but the creaking of the ice and the gurgle of moving water that I hadn't been able to hear from the ridge above made me eager to get to surer ground. The crash site was barely visible, marked only by the thrust of the plane's wing.

"At least we made good time." I turned my attention back to the long stretch of valley that would hopefully, eventually, take me back to James. "Now for the hard part."

Chapter 13

I SWAYED TO THE rhythm of Animkii's steps as he trudged a trail through the ankle-deep snow. My blanket, once more tied and tucked around me, now encompassed the pack on my back as well. An occasional grunt from Animkii was his only concession to the weight. Over an hour, maybe closer to two, had passed in silence since our wild ride down the hillside. Since then he'd needed every breath to make progress through the treacherously snow-masked terrain. We'd briefly discussed having him drag me in the raft, but that decision was made moot when a faint whistling noise drew our attention to a slow leak in the raft's outer wall. It seemed we hadn't come out of our encounter with the tree trunk entirely unscathed. The increasing density of trees as we moved down the valley would have put an end to that plan pretty quickly, regardless.

The air wasn't quite so bitter in the valley as it had been on the ridge, helped by the fact that there was less wind. That didn't make it warm by any means. Clouds had rolled in from the west, bringing new snow that drifted in lazy flakes among the trees. My nose was a constantly running faucet crusted with ice. My lips chapped and split. Even the surface of my eyes stung, either from the dry cold or from the reflected glare off the snow.

If not for my extreme discomfort, worry for James, and the press of time as the sun slid below the upper basin, I might have enjoyed the hike. Quiet and solitude had always been my happy place. The stillness of the forest around me, so similar to the area near my home, was a comfort that soothed my tumultuous soul. The shadow of an eagle swept across the snow. An echo of tumbling rocks brought my attention to a herd of sheep with curved horns, their white fur making them all but invisible against the hillside. They stood still as sculptures carved in ice, watching us pass from their rocky vantage.

My legs swung to either side of Animkii's waist. He'd donated his socks to the cause of saving my toes, but even the thick cotton provided little warmth. When the painful ache of the cold was replaced by the more worrisome absence of any feeling at all, I'd experimented with magical heating. Singed clothes and a dunk in a snow drift had pretty quickly shown that fire was *not* the way to go. Instead, I found that using magic to monitor and control the flow of blood through my veins—like a police officer directing traffic during a crowded event—did the trick. When a section of my body grew colder, I found the blood there to be sluggish. I'd push more blood into the affected area, speeding the flow, and feeling would come back. Unfortunately, I couldn't offer the same treatment to Animkii. Even if he was okay with the idea of me taking control of his bodily functions, a ridiculous amount of focus was required just to keep my own system running. I probably couldn't handle two. I might not even have managed walking with so much of my concentration aimed inward.

"Now that your trial is over, I'd have thought you'd be happy to get away from the council." Animkii's voice splintered my focus, jarring me out of my cardiovascular juggling. He hoisted me higher with a bump and tightened his grip around my thighs, fingers laced under my butt.

"I'll be happy when I'm free," I said. "That's not the same as getting away, and I'm not foolish enough to believe the council will leave me alone just because they decided not to execute me. There's also the unsettled matter of the alliance to consider. Oh, yeah, and saving James before they execute him for a murder he didn't commit."

"Fair enough. But you'd be in a stronger negotiating position on neutral ground or, better yet, your own home turf. Make them come to you."

"Except I'll have lost the chance to save James by then."

"You've already lost that," he said, "if you ever had it. Between the show he put on in front of the PTF and taking the fall for Hanzo's murder, he's at their mercy, and that's not something the council is known for."

I considered his phrasing—*taking the fall for Hanzo's murder.* "You don't think James killed Hanzo?"

"You do?"

"Of course not," I snapped. "I'm just surprised to hear you taking his side."

"Whether or not I believe he's innocent is beside the point. Maybe if Zuri were still in charge of the investigation, justice would matter, but she's lost control of the conclave. Her authority started slipping the second Hanzo was killed. She can't protect you there. Either of you. Not from a council member. James's fate is already sealed. Returning is pointless at best; more likely, it's suicide."

My confidence wobbled under the weight of his words and my own doubts. Maybe going back wouldn't accomplish anything. Maybe James would already be dead by the time I arrived. Maybe I was wrong about Esteban's servant being a fae, or the council already knew, and they were playing a game of their own. Maybe they'd figure out that my ability to provide daywalking en masse was an improbable dream and decide to kill me after all. Maybe another assassin would slip into my room while I slept and finish the job Ronald had botched.

My mood grew darker with each scenario, but in the end, those fears and doubts were burned away by one blazing truth. I cleared my throat as my conviction turned to stone, shutting out the whispers of doubt blowing through my mind. "Whatever happens, I won't abandon James."

"That's noble and all, but would your lover want you putting yourself in danger for his sake?"

No, I thought, *he wouldn't. But he'll understand.* James had stood by my side against a tide of undead soldiers, trusted me to tinker with his soul, and risked being torn apart in the unfiltered chaos of the Rift to save me from exile in a dead realm. I'd trusted him with the true name I'd earned in my fae trials and had infiltrated a vampire stronghold to save him from eternity in a light-lined box. He was my anchor, and I was his.

"Risking ourselves is part of loving each other," I said.

"So what do you intend to do when you reach the conclave? Someone there still wants you dead."

"That happens more often than you might think. I'm getting kind of used to it." He chuckled, and I joined in. Not that there was anything funny about the number of people who'd tried to kill me in the past few months, but it felt good to laugh at the insane mess my life had become. Better than the alternative.

"I'm going to negotiate," I said. "The council may not be known for its mercy, but the members are self-serving opportunists, every last one of them. I have something they want."

"And they have something you want . . . want enough to die for, apparently. That's why you should negotiate from a place of strength. Return and they'll have the upper hand."

"They'll always have the upper hand," I said with resignation. "But I'm used to being the underdog. Don't count me out just yet." Even as I spoke, my mind was a whirl of activity. *I have more to offer than just the promise of potential daywalking, inclusion in the paranatural alliance, or evidence of a spy in their midst. There's also the stick end of the equation. I'm kin to a fae lord with an army at his back. I'm friends with some of the most powerful werewolves and practitioners in the world. I have allies in the Church and on the PTF board of directors.* I'd been letting the vampires set the tone of this engagement with their farce of a trial from the moment they'd caught me off-balance with their summons. No more playing defense. If reason wasn't enough to sway them, I'd see how they responded to threats.

The biggest variables in the equation, though, were Esteban and his servant. . . . I was eighty percent sure I'd interpreted the situation correctly—that Esteban was a construct, and his servant was a fae pulling his strings—but there were still some gaps in my theory. How long had it been since the real Esteban was replaced? Was the spy acting at the direction of a single fae lord, as part of some multi-realm scheme, or were they a rogue element? And what was their endgame?

I glanced at Animkii's head bobbing under my chin. Snow was collecting in frozen clumps along the silky black strands of his hair, turning them white. I frowned. As a thrall to a conclave steward, Animkii must have met the council members before. Maybe I could get more information before facing the fae impostor again. "How long have you been a thrall?"

"Why do you want to know?"

"I'm curious how many vampires you've met."

He shrugged, bobbing me against his back. "A few dozen have been brought to the conclave. Other than those, not many. Vampires tend to keep to their own groups."

"Have you met Esteban before?"

"I have."

"How long ago was that?"

Another shrug. "A decade, perhaps."

"Did he have the same servant?"

Animkii's foot caught on a thick branch hidden by the snow. I clutched tighter as he stumbled then regained his balance. Once he'd straightened and resettled my weight on his hips, he said, "Why do you care who Esteban's servant was?"

I hesitated. If I was right about Esteban's nature and Hanzo's killer, the truth would not only clear James but help redeem Zuri as well. How could she have prevented a security breach from a being made of light and magic? A being that by all rights shouldn't exist? But I didn't want to share my suspicions until I had a chance to verify them . . . and decide how best to use the information to my advantage. "Just curious," I said with a nonchalant shrug.

"Well, I don't recall. High-ranking vampires have many thralls, often used interchangeably. It isn't worth remembering them all."

I scowled. I'd hoped another thrall, especially one with a master as lenient as Zuri seemed to be, might pay more attention to their peers. *Let's try a different angle.* "What keeps the conclave safe from discovery?" I asked. "Surely, having all your leaders in one place would be a tempting target for the fae."

"Secrecy, mostly. Very few people know the location of even one, let alone all, of the conclaves. Beyond that, magic. Vampire powers may not be as varied as those of the fae, but they're quite good at illusion and misdirection spells."

A grouse called into the silence that followed his statement. Snow cascaded from a nearby tree as the fat brown-and-white bird took wing.

"Have you ever heard of someone casting an illusion that could fool a camera?"

Animkii's laugh seemed strained, as if the very idea of such a spell made him nervous. "You have quite the imagination."

I tracked the path of the grouse overhead until the angle grew too steep and the tickle of fluffy white flakes against my lashes made me blink. The snow was picking up. Matte-gray clouds hung low over the mountains. A storm was coming.

"Have you, though?" I pressed. "A rumor? A legend?"

"The oldest vampires boast many unique and powerful abilities, but I've never heard of that one."

So the vampires might not know constructs are even possible.

Animkii came to an abrupt stop. "Smoke."

I sniffed and, sure enough, the blessed scent of burning wood filled my nostrils. I swiveled my head, searching for the source. A thin stream of gray smoke, nearly invisible against the cloud cover, rose above the tree-lined ridge to our right. I pointed. "There."

Animkii turned toward the beacon of civilization and started to climb, boots sinking deep in the drifts.

I wiggled my toes to make sure I still could. Numbness had put a worrisome distance in the sensation. My fingers, too, had lost some feeling. Calling my magic once more, I urged my sluggish blood to move a little faster. *Just a bit longer.* Fantasies of warming my hands by a crackling fire filled my head. *A steaming drink. Maybe some soup.* My mouth watered at the thought. *Maybe they'll even have some boots to spare.*

I glanced west. Between the shadow of the mountain and the growing storm, it was hard to tell how far the sun had dropped, but the sky to the east had faded to bruised indigo.

The vampires will be up soon, if they aren't already. How long will they take to sentence James? And how long till they carry that sentence out? The need for haste lodged like a boulder in my throat.

The crest of the ridge revealed our salvation. Animkii hadn't exaggerated the smallness of the settlement—a bare handful of single-story houses with smoke rising from their chimneys.

"Take off your blanket," Animkii said, crouching behind a rocky outcropping.

"Why?"

"You can stand on your blanket or stand in the snow."

"You're putting me down? We're nearly to the town. Why are you stopping?"

"You don't think it'll raise a few eyebrows if a half-naked American woman walks out of these mountains?"

"Who cares if they're surprised so long as they help?"

"And waste our time with a lot of awkward questions. Not to mention alerting the local authorities, who'll no doubt have questions of their own. In case you've forgotten, vampires are a secretive lot. No one knows the conclave is near here, and it needs to stay that way. You wait here. I'll pop down to the settlement, get what we need, and come back."

"And a lone wanderer out in a storm at dusk won't raise suspicion?"

"At least I look like I belong here."

I wanted to argue more, but the few streaks of burnt-orange sunset highlighting the underbelly of the storm were fading, and the snow was getting heavier. Every second we wasted would make this trip harder.

"Fine. Lean over." I tugged loose the knot at my neck and spread the silver blanket over the snow in front of him. He straightened and turned so I could step onto the square of fabric. I settled at one edge and wrapped the remaining blanket around me like a cocoon. "Hurry."

He trotted down the ridge without a backward glance, moving faster now that he didn't have my weight to slow him down. My chest tightened as his shape grew small, flitting in and out of sight as trees and gusts of snow filled the distance between us. Not that I'd miss Animkii himself. My head still ached from the blow he'd landed, and I was freezing my butt off on the side of a mountain thanks to him. Okay, that part was a little bit my fault. But watching my only companion, flawed though he was, walk away was hard. There'd been a time, not so long ago, when I'd gone for days, even weeks, without speaking to another human being, when I'd worn solitude like armor and believed that made me strong. Now I knew it only made me more vulnerable.

Without my friends, I never would have come to grips with my convoluted family history and learned to accept magic as a part of myself. I never would have been able to face my father and stand strong against the temptation of joining him. I never would have had the courage to call out the PTF directors and take the first steps in building a world where people like me—freaks and outcasts—had a place to belong. But my friends weren't here. They were scattered, some as far as other realms. All of them out of reach. Loneliness more bitter than the cold seeped into my bones.

"I'll find my way back." The wind snatched my whispered promise, carrying it to the sky. Emma, Kai, Chase, Maggie, David, Sarah. Each of their faces smiled, chided, or teased from my memory. I had people waiting, a place where I belonged. Those memories, and the sense of connection they carried, spread through me on a wave of warmth stronger than my magic trick. "And I'll bring James with me."

James had never quite felt like he belonged among my friends. He hadn't said so in words, but he wore a barrier of aloofness when he interacted with them. And who could blame him? The fae viewed vampires as abominations. Most tried to kill them on sight. At least Kai and Chase seemed to accept that James wasn't an enemy, though I wasn't sure they'd ever see him as an equal. My human friends had trouble seeing past the whole "vampires drink blood" issue, even though he'd never fed from any of them personally. And now, with his daywalking, he'd been set apart even from other vampires. I'd once thought James was a charismatic gallery owner who seemed to be friends with everyone, when really he was even more isolated than I was. But if I could make a place for myself, I could make a place for James, right by my side. I'd poured the foundation for a community that didn't treat practitioners and werewolves like monsters. I could bring the vampires into that fold. There had to be space in this world for all of us.

I shivered and shifted my attention to trying to stay warm until Animkii returned. The snow, the wind, the cold—all my discomforts—faded into the background as I focused on keeping the sluggish blood flowing through my numb body.

The growl of an engine jarred me out of my concentration. I blinked, unsure how much time had passed.

A dark shape rushed toward me from the direction of the settlement, swerving between trees. The houses were gone. The storm had picked up as night settled over the land, driving the snow horizontally in a blinding curtain that clipped the horizon, turning my hiding spot on the ridge into an island and making the very air seem claustrophobic.

Animkii came into focus a bare dozen feet from my location, sending up a gout of fresh powder as the snowmobile he was riding skidded to a halt.

"Put these on." He threw a wadded bundle at my feet.

I lifted a puffy lavender coat long enough to reach my knees. A pair of beige boots tumbled out. I nearly danced for joy. The fur-lined boots pinched both my toes and heels. I wouldn't be able to walk any distance in them without getting blisters, but at least they were warm. I slipped my arms into the jacket sleeves. The material stretched uncomfortably across my upper back, limiting the range of my shoulders, and left a good two inches of my wrists exposed, but it broke the wind and kept the pelting snow off my skin.

"How did you explain needing a woman's boots and coat?" I asked, fumbling buttons with numb fingers. "I doubt any of those buildings was a department store."

"Who says I explained anything?"

I shot him a dark look. "You stole them?"

"You needed them."

"And this?" I gestured to the snowmobile. "Did you steal that, too?"

"Do you want to get out of here, or not?"

"We could have bought it or borrowed it."

"A settlement this size? They only have one, maybe two of these between them. They wouldn't have parted with it to help a stranger."

"You don't know that."

"Are you coming, or not?"

I bunched my fists, fighting the urge to slug him across the jaw with enough magic to shatter bone. But James was waiting, and the storm was growing worse.

Grumbling, I shoved my blanket into my pack and climbed onto the seat, snugging up to Animkii's back in almost the same position I'd been in for the trek out of the pass, except that I wrapped my arms around his waist instead of his neck.

"Hang on." He let out the throttle, and the snowmobile rocketed forward.

I tightened my grip as the machine tried to throw me off the back and ducked my head to keep the snow and wind from blinding me as we plunged down the slope.

"How can you see where we're going?" I shouted as he swerved around a tree close enough to cause a cascade of pine needles and snow.

"What makes you think I can?" he called back.

I tightened my grip, pressing my cheek to Animkii's back. Where my ill-fitting coat ended, my knees and thighs burned from the cold as ice shards flayed my raw skin. I clenched my teeth, afraid I might bite through my tongue as we careened down the ridge toward the mouth of the valley.

How long would it take to reach flat enough terrain to turn north? And how much longer till we reached the conclave? We'd only been in the air a few minutes, but planes could cover incredible distances in that amount of time. The storm had quickened the onset of dark, but behind the oppressive ceiling of clouds, the stars were surely shining. I clung to the man who'd put me in this predicament and willed the snowmobile to go faster.

I'm coming. I reached out to James along our bond, taking comfort in the thin strand of connection as I plunged through an ocean of swirling white and darkness. The thread of our connection pointed like an arrow to the northwest. As Animkii and I bumped along the blurred ground, the tether stretched, cutting like fishing line tied around my heart. We were moving farther away.

"We need to turn north," I shouted into Animkii's ear.

He shook his head.

I glanced to my left, the direction of James's signal. The snow was a wall of swirling white that stole distance and geography. There might be a ridge or cliff blocking our path, or we might have reached the shallow hills at the mouth of the valley and have a clear shot all the way to James. "Turn north," I said again.

"Not yet," he called back.

The snowmobile jerked right, narrowly missing a pine tree that sprang out of the blizzard. Needles slashed my leg. I choked back my first impulse, which was to tell him to slow down. Barreling full throttle through a dark forest in the middle of a storm was suicide, yet I felt the need to go faster, to reach my destination *now*. Or as close to now as I could manage. The sun was down. The vampires were up. James was alive, for the moment, but how long would he remain that way if the council thought I'd run away? If they decided James no longer had tactical value. . . .

I dug my fingers into Animkii's shirt as the snowmobile careened first right, then left, dodging trees that seemed to be growing denser by the minute as we left the ice-capped peaks behind. The swells of land became less severe. *Surely, we've cleared the valley by now.* But far from turning north, I got the impression Animkii was angling us slightly to the south.

I stretched to bring my mouth as close as I could to Animkii's ear. "We need to turn north. You're going the wrong way."

This time he simply ignored me.

I jolted in my seat as the snowmobile flew off the top of a hill and slammed back to earth, bouncing on its shocks, but the sour taste at the back of my throat wasn't from this kamikaze rollercoaster ride. The ground was flat—as flat as it was going to get—but judging by the compass in my heart that led unfailingly to James, we were turning more and more to the south . . . away from the conclave.

He never had any intention of taking me back. The thought stabbed like a knife through my soul. Not the betrayal—I'd half-expected that—but the fact that I now had yet another obstacle keeping me from where I needed to be, that this delay might be the reason I didn't reach James in time. Closing my eyes, I considered my options.

I could form my magic into a blade and slide it between Animkii's ribs. Quick, clean. I could pierce his heart with a single thrust, assuming I could account for the bumpiness of the ride. My moral center cringed from the idea of cold-blooded murder . . . but a darker part of me, a part that had been growing louder lately, liked this plan. I'd given Animkii a second chance by not leaving him hog-tied on that mountain. He didn't deserve a third.

The snowmobile jerked to the side again, nearly dislodging me. I'd let my grip loosen as I contemplated killing the man wrapped in my arms. Pine needles showered my hair and back as Animkii and I clipped a branch brought low by the weight of the snow.

If I kill the driver while we're going this fast, we'll crash. My practical side struggled with the choice between a quick kill without a fight versus my need for an intact vehicle to reach my final destination, not to mention the potential injuries of a head-on collision with a tree.

He's big and he's fast, but I've been training with werewolves, and I have magic on my side. I should be able to win a straight fight. I just need him to stop the snowmobile.

Locking my left arm against Animkii's ribs, I called to my magic. A little bit of practitioner energy to fuel the spell, a little bit of fae to hone it. Magic coated my index finger, tapering to a needle point. Bracing against his shoulder, I tapped my invisible weapon against the side of his throat and gave him a small nick, just enough to get his attention. I couldn't risk holding it there lest a sudden bump derail my plan.

"Stop now, or I drive this blade through your throat." I had to shout to be heard over the storm and engine, which made me sound more like a kid throwing a tantrum than a serious threat, but needs must.

"Where'd you get a blade?" he called back without slowing.

"I made it. Stop the snowmobile."

"Not gonna happen."

"I *will* kill you."

"You didn't on the mountain."

"Consider this strike three." I gave him another nick, enough to lace the wind with the scent of blood. "Stop, now."

"Kill me and we crash." He swerved around a tree as if to prove his point.

I rocked with the motion, trying to keep my hand a steady distance from his throat, but I'd already lost. I had hoped surprise would keep Animkii from processing his options, but he'd called my bluff, just as he had at the crash site. An empty threat was no threat at all, and I wasn't willing to risk the consequences of killing him. The only other course of action I could think of was to take away the one thing he'd seemed determined to keep close through this whole ordeal. . . . Me. Zuri's order had been to get me out of the conclave and keep me safe. He'd been able to play along with our deal because he'd still, technically, been following that order . . . up until the moment when I demanded he turn north. If I was right, he wouldn't be able to drive away without me.

Better a few bruises than to keep going in the wrong direction. Willing my muscles to relax, I used magic to bolster my body and kicked off the back of the snowmobile.

Chapter 14

I ROLLED AS I HIT the ground, tucking my limbs close as I tumbled over and over through the fresh powder. The growl of the snowmobile grew fainter. I sat up, head spinning. Light shone in my face, blinding me. Animkii had turned around, though he and the idling machine he straddled were all but invisible behind the glare of the headlamp.

Thank god. I'd hoped Zuri's standing order wouldn't let him abandon me, but I hadn't been sure.

"Seriously, are you *trying* to die?" he shouted.

I stood up. Snow slipped from my coat into the tops of my boots, freezing my ankles. "I'm going north, whatever it takes."

"It'll take you all night to get there on foot, if you can even find the place."

I filled my palms with crackling energy. "Which is why I'm taking that snowmobile."

"You'll kill me to get it?"

"I'd rather not, but I won't let you stop me from getting back to James."

Animkii gave a soft whistle. "That must be some binding he put on you."

"It's called love."

"Like Ronald loved Hanzo?"

I curled my lip at the thought. "I'm not enthralled."

"James never shared his blood with you?"

"Get off the snowmobile."

"He has, hasn't he?"

"I said, get off."

Animkii turned off the machine, plunging the snowy forest into darkness for a second before my eyes adjusted to the ambient glow provided by the millions of tiny mirrors filling the air.

"Step away," I said.

"You don't need to serve him." He crunched toward me.

"I don't serve him; I love him."

"If you say so."

"I do," I snapped.

"But can you really be sure?" His voice drifted like the snow. "He's had your blood. You've had his. That's a binding, like it or not."

"Maybe, but not anything like what you're imagining. My magic changed our connection. He can no more control me with it than I can control him." Of course, I'd given James my fae true name, which *did* allow him to control me, but there was no reason to share that little nugget of information . . . ever . . . with anyone.

Animkii cocked his head. His tone turned thoughtful. "So that's why."

"Why what?" I asked.

"But nothing has changed," he said, not answering my question. "Whether for love or by compulsion, you cannot save James any more than I can save Zuri." His voice hitched on Zuri's name, making me wonder if he felt more for the woman than simple servitude. "There's nothing left for you at the conclave . . . for either of us. James will be executed for Hanzo's murder, and Zuri for her failure to prevent it. After that, well, you saw what happened to Ronald." His voice caught and he looked away. "The least I can do is fulfill my master's final wish before I lose my mind, and that's to carry you to safety."

I chewed my chapped lower lip, weighing my options. I could sympathize with Animkii's position. The vampire he was bound to was going to die, and natural or not, the grief of losing her would destroy him. Despite my argument that love was not a binding, I felt the same way about James. "What if told you I could save both James *and* Zuri?"

He laughed. "I'd say you're either a fool or a liar."

I glared at him.

He shook his head. "You'd have to provide irrefutable proof that Hanzo's murder was executed in such a way as to be wholly unavoidable and in no way a result of incompetence or negligence. Suicide perhaps?"

Or a magic that no vampire would ever expect to find in their most sacred sites. I took a deep breath, weighed my options, and said, "Hanzo was killed by a fae."

I expected Animkii to laugh again. Instead, he remained quiet so long that I began to wonder if he'd heard me over the howl of the wind.

"What makes you think that?" His words echoed through the storm, bounced about by the lashing snow until they seemed to come from all around me.

No turning back now. If I failed to convince Animkii, I'd fight him for the snowmobile, but if I couldn't convince someone who *wanted* me to be right . . . what were the odds the council would listen?

"My magic lets me see inside people, see what they're made of, what makes them *them*. If I go deep enough, I can see their memories, tell if their lying, stuff like that."

"That's what you did to Ronald in the ballroom?"

I nodded. "I did it during Victoria's interrogations of the council members, too. And there's something really wrong with Esteban's core."

"Oh?"

"He doesn't have one." Another long silence stretched before I continued. "I think Esteban is actually a creature called a construct, a being created with light and magic by a high-level illusionist."

"But Councilor Sloth has form, thought, permanence. He's far too complex to be an illusion."

"Hence the 'high-level' part of my theory. It would have taken an incredible amount of magic to pull off something like that."

"In this theory of yours, who made him? And why?"

"The one person guaranteed to stay close to him. His servant."

"That's why you asked about them earlier." Animkii's silhouette nodded and crossed his arms. "Can you prove any of this?"

"Fae are allergic to iron. They can't lie. There are any number of ways to prove what they are."

"Assuming you're right," he said. "What if you're not?"

"If I can just get another look at them, I'll know for sure. Even if I'm wrong about them being fae, which I doubt, I'm sure they're involved in Hanzo's death. I should be able to find something that will convince the council."

"For someone who only recently discovered they have magic, you're very confident in your abilities."

I wanted to laugh. I was anything but confident, however, admitting that wouldn't help me convince him to hand over the keys. "I can prove the council has been duped, all of them, not just Zuri. They can't blame her for being deceived if they were as well. I just need to get back before anyone dies." I held out my hand, asking for the keys. "Will you get out of my way?"

"If your theory is correct, wouldn't you be better served siding with the fae? You are, after all, part fae yourself. For all you know, this fae could be a spy from your grandfather's court, and likely very powerful. Is it wise to cross them?"

"Wise went out the window when they framed James for murder."

"For the sake of your lover, you'd side with the vampires over the fae?"

"Why are people so obsessed with sides?" I let my arm drop. "I don't do sides. I deal with the situation in front of me. That's it. Maybe that's a limitation of being human, but I can't scheme like an immortal. I'm not acting *for* the vampires or *against* the fae. I'm just trying to make the best of a bad situation."

Animkii remained statue still for a long exhale. "You're a stubborn fool."

I held my breath to stop the pressure in my chest from coming out as a sob. I'd failed to convince him. I was going to have to take the keys by force . . . and think of a better argument before I reached the conclave. I tightened my grip on my magic, readying for the fight.

"I'll take you back."

My magic scattered as my concentration broke. "Wait—What?"

"I'll take you back," he repeated, turning his back on me and walking toward the snowmobile. "Hop on."

A laugh burst from my lips. "As if. You fooled me last time because I was desperate to get off the mountain without becoming a murderer, but you're still under orders to get me *away* from the conclave. That's why you couldn't turn north."

"I *didn't* turn north, because I believed going back was suicide and Zuri wanted me to protect you. But circumstances have changed. If there's even the slightest hope that you can save my master . . ." He shook his head. "I still think you're insane, but I'll take you back."

"You're a thrall," I spat the word like an insult. "Granted you're more normal-seeming than other thralls I've met,"—*or been*, I thought darkly—"but you're still a thrall. You can't disobey orders. Admit it; you're still trying to get me away from the conclave."

"I told you before, not all thralls are created equal. It's true that I tried to keep you away from the conclave. And yes, I did that because my master desired that I keep you safe. The conclave is not safe. But it's also true that I have the ability to interpret the meaning behind my master's orders and do what I think best serves the spirit, if not the exact letter, of those orders. In this case, Zuri ordered you away because she thought the situation at the conclave to be hopeless. But you've given me a reason to hope. I believe Zuri would wish to live if she became aware that was an option. I certainly do. Therefore, I'll take you back."

I narrowed my focus, gathering my magic once more to examine Animkii's core. I couldn't trust his words, but he couldn't lie inside his soul. The red ribbons of his core were tangled with black, as all thralls were. One trailing thread faded out, stretching to the north. That had to be his binding to Zuri. A thinner strand, more crimson than black, with a metallic sheen, twisted around the connection like a vine growing around a tree trunk. *A second connection to Zuri?* I recalled the hitch in his voice when he declared she was doomed. *Perhaps a deeper one?* If his feelings were strong enough. . . . *Maybe his relationship to Zuri isn't so different from my relationship to James after all.*

"No tricks this time. You swear you'll take me straight to the conclave?" I pointed one numb finger at him. "I'll know if you go the wrong way."

"Keep the knife to my throat if you like. We can do all this again if I veer off course."

"Swear it," I demanded.

He exhaled a puff of frozen breath. "I'll take you straight to the conclave. No tricks." Lights flashed in his core, burning bright through his promise.

I considered taking the keys and leaving Animkii in the snow regardless of his vow, but he had a stake in this too. Not only Zuri's life, but also his own and those of his fellow thralls were on the line. And misguided though his actions had been, it did seem true that he'd been trying to protect me.

Cautiously following his tracks to the snowmobile, I climbed aboard and wrapped my hands around his waist. "Don't make me regret this."

Nodding, he opened up the throttle. The snowmobile launched into the storm.

"HOME AGAIN, home again," Animkii sing-songed as he cut the engine.

I released my death grip around his waist, bending my fingers to make sure I still could. The snowfall had eased from whiteout conditions to fluffy flakes that danced playfully on the wind, which was a blessing for my raw skin. Sections of green-tinted darkness peeked through cracks in the cloud cover, freeing what little heat had been trapped below that ceiling to escape into the ether.

Animkii parked the snowmobile in the same field where the plane had landed that first night, though it took me a moment to recognize the clearing, since the runway was now covered in snow. The pull of James's presence was stronger, and I turned my stiff steps in his direction, projecting as loud as I could, *I'm coming.*

I stumbled on numb legs that felt like clumsy stilts and tripped over a rock hidden under the snow.

Animkii grabbed my arm to steady me. "Pity to fall so close to your goal."

I smiled. Despite all our mishaps, it felt good to have an ally at my side—something I'd been notably short of lately. We'd cleared the air, we were on the same page, and we were going to save our vampires. Together, we trudged toward the trees behind which the little cabin that hid the conclave waited.

"Thank you, Animkii." A shadow stepped out from behind a towering pine. Light glinted off metal as they lifted their hand. "Your services are no longer required."

I called up my magic, but I was too slow.

A crack like thunder split the snow-muted forest. Warm spray splattered my cheek, burning against my frozen skin. I turned in horror. Animkii stayed upright for a moment, then sagged to the ground as though his skeleton had turned to water. One of his eyes and the side of his face were missing. I blinked, filling my lungs only when the burn in them became too much to bear. A familiar sense of isolation settled over me like an unwanted embrace.

Pulling more energy from the Rift, I wrapped magic around myself like armor, though the feeble protection was little better than the silver blanket I'd worn earlier. I'd been casting almost nonstop for most of the day to keep from freezing. My body was worn out, and my reserves were laughable. If I tried any high-level practitioner magic at this point, I'd risk a burnout—a backlash of uncontrolled energy let loose in a body too weak to safely contain it. That was how Emma had lost her sight, Garrett had lost the use of his legs, and a great many sorcerers had lost their lives during the Faerie Wars.

Esteban's servant lowered their gun as they moved closer, clearing the trees to join me in the glittering glow of the field. They wore the same dark attire as they had in my room. It was hard to believe less than a day had passed since Ronald tried to kill me. Their hair was pulled back in a high ponytail that made the angle of their cheeks more prominent under the deep pits of their dark eyes. Their skin seemed to glow with the same eerie light as the snow. They hadn't bothered with a coat despite the cold, so they must not have planned on being outside long. *How did they know I was coming back?*

A shiver that had nothing to do with the cold racked me as my mind raced to process the implications of finding the person I suspected was a fae spy and assassin waiting for me outside the conclave. *Do they know I suspect them? Why else would they be out here? But why kill Animkii now and not in my room earlier? Are they tying up loose ends? At least this proves my suspicions were right.*

I settled into a fighting stance and raised my hands. Not that fists, or even magic, would be of much use against a gun at this distance, but I wouldn't give them the satisfaction of seeing me cower.

Frowning, they glanced down as though they'd forgotten the gun was in their hand. They shook their head and waved the weapon as if it were no more than a toy that sprayed water and not the reason the snow around Animkii's crumpled form was the wrong color. "Relax. If I wanted you dead, you'd be dead. In fact, I've been working quite hard to keep you alive. Not that you're making it easy."

Keeping my guard up, I glanced at Animkii. Snow had started to collect on his cooling skin. He'd probably be buried in an hour, just another lump hidden under the white blanket that masked the land. He'd said almost the same thing when I accused him of kidnapping me. *Is that why the fae allowed, maybe even helped, Animkii to take me? Because he was keeping me safe by removing me from the conclave?*

"Why are you out here?" I asked.

"Are you speaking to me, or the corpse?"

I shifted my glare to Animkii's killer.

"I thought it prudent that we speak . . . in private."

I balled my fists. "Is that why you shot him? For privacy?"

"Partly."

"And the other part?"

"He'd become a liability." They holstered their gun and took a few steps closer, resting their now empty hand against their chest. "First, let me introduce myself. You may call me Ash."

You may call me. Not, my name is. A very fae introduction, considering how finicky they are about names.

"You've surprised me, Alex," Ash said. "Several times, in fact. That's not an easy thing to do."

Because you're ancient, I thought. *Fae and vampires, even the shorter-lived werewolves . . . they all say the same thing. Eternity is boring, because there are no surprises left.*

"I never imagined that you'd crash a plane to make your point, or that the bond you share with James was so . . . equitable."

I frowned. "How did you . . .?"

"The same way I know that you suspect me of being a fae." They smiled. "A truly inspired deduction on your part. My hat's off to you. Though it does seem you had a bit of a cheat." They shook their head. "I never imagined there was someone who could actually *see* souls. Tell me, what do they look like?"

A cold deeper than the snow numbing my toes filled me. I hadn't come up with the theory that Esteban's servant was a fae until after Animkii took me out of the conclave. Ash knew about the plane crash. They knew I'd be here, now. The only person other than myself who'd known all those things was Animkii.

Your services are no longer required. . . . "Animkii was working for you."

Ash shrugged. "Only so far as a puppet works for the hand that controls it. He was largely unaware of me pulling his strings."

"The weird tendril on his tether to Zuri," I whispered, picturing the ivy-like vine I'd seen wrapped around the thread of Animkii's enthrallment. I'd taken it for a manifestation of his emotional connection to Zuri . . . but what if it was something else? Something more insidious?

I hadn't bothered checking Ash for truth since fae couldn't lie, and I'd need what was left of my magic if it came to a fight, but now I had a reason to delve into Ash's core. Dredging the remains of my magic reserves, I shifted my focus. Ash's core was a massive tangle of dark crimson, larger and more complex than most I'd seen, but it matched the color of that thinner tendril perfectly . . . right down to the ripple of gold that seemed like a trick of the light. "That was yours. You piggy-backed on their bond, infecting it like a parasite so you could keep tabs on me. That's how you found out your cover was blown and where to ambush us so I couldn't expose you."

"Very good." They clapped their hands.

"Why haven't you killed me?"

They arched an eyebrow. "Do you want me to?"

"Of course not. But there must be some reason you're keeping me alive despite the threat I pose to your secret. Fae are never kind without a reason."

"Too true." A shadow of grief stole across Ash's expression. "I want to make a deal."

Of course. That, too, was a very fae trait.

"You'll be pleased to know, the council has not yet pronounced James's fate."

I sagged in relief, exhaling a cloud of frozen breath.

"If the council had met as planned, he would have been sentenced already, maybe even executed, but everyone's in an uproar about your escape."

The word "escape" rang like a gong in my head. "They think I left by choice?"

"I don't think anyone really cares *how* you left. Only that you're gone. The councilors have been making calls nonstop, stationing agents at airports and landing strips, staking out your house in Colorado." Ash chuckled, a melodic sound that made me want to lean into it. "Ironically, despite all your racing against the clock to get back here, you *were* the clock. Now that you've returned, the council will stop fretting, and the sentencing can get back on track."

"Which leaves us where?" I asked. "We both know James is innocent."

"And we both know that doesn't matter in the slightest as far as the verdict of this trial is concerned."

"I assume this is where your deal comes in?"

Ash smiled. "Just what are you willing to sacrifice to save your lover?"

"What are you proposing?"

"I have what you need to save James."

Lights danced in Ash's core, but not just the firefly memories that said this offer was real. That metallic, golden sheen I'd witnessed earlier caught my eye, distracting me. *What's causing that?*

Adjusting my focus, I tried to find the source of those flashes of color. It was as if Ash's core had been dipped in a thin, metallic coating that infused the crimson ribbons with golden highlights. *I've never seen a core like this before.* My mind stuttered as I realized that was a lie. I *had* seen something like this before. Once. After I changed James.

In order to grant him daywalking, I'd had to integrate the separate elements of James's core, fusing his vampire and mortal traits on a level that made them indistinguishable from one another. The end result was that the silver coils that had previously bound and strangled his mortal threads were now a silvery sheen infused evenly throughout his entire core . . . just like the gold in Ash's.

"You're not a fae," I mumbled in numb disbelief of the words leaving my lips. "You're a vampire."

"Oh dear," Ash said. "I suppose this means you really can see into my soul."

Chapter 15

"BUT . . . THE CONSTRUCT," I stammered. "Vampires may be illusionists, but that level of magic is . . ." My mind reeled. Splitting their soul was child's play for a master vampire—that's how they reproduced, after all—but compared to the fae, even old vampires rarely had enough magic for more than petty parlor tricks. To pull off a fully functioning construct . . . that would require both immense power and a masterful knowledge of illusion magic.

I braced my feet in the snow, as if solid footing could somehow make my position less precarious, as all my previous theories blew apart. Ash wasn't a fae spy looking to undermine the vampire council.

"You're trying to figure out where you went wrong." Ash smiled. "Don't be too hard on yourself. Your assessment wasn't entirely inaccurate."

I frowned.

"I'll let you in on a little secret." Ash slipped behind me, too fast to track.

I fought the urge to spin to face them. They were toying with me. I wouldn't give them the satisfaction of seeing me flinch.

"Consider it a reward for entertaining me." Their breath warmed my cheek, dropping to a barely audible whisper. "I'm not just any vampire." Fingers curled around my shoulders. Lips brushed my ear. "I'm the first."

My brain stalled, groping to make sense of the words. *The first vampire. A hybrid. Part fae, part demon-possessed practitioner.*

"You can't be." I hadn't meant to whisper, but there wasn't enough air in my lungs to put any force behind my denial. "That would make you . . ."

"Ancient? Dangerous? Powerful beyond your feeble comprehension, and so far out of your league as to make any action you might take against me laughable?"

My knees went weak as the surety in their voice settled over me.

"I am all of those things." They stepped away, moving so quickly that the loss of support I hadn't realized I was relying on almost dropped me on my ass.

I stumbled, turning to face them. "Then why the charade?" I demanded. "If you're as strong as you say, why create a construct and pretend to be a human servant? Why not just take the council seat yourself?" I thought of the androgynous sculpture in the conclave entry hall. The likeness wasn't far off from the person before me. "Hell, you could disband the council and be an emperor. They'd worship you."

Ash turned their face up to the drifting snow. I followed their gaze. Stars peeked from patches of aurora-streaked darkness as the storm broke up. "Worship is all well and good for a while, but . . . well, let's just say it gets old." They dropped their gaze. "Plus there's the pesky matter of the price on my head. Even with the best of intentions, this lot wouldn't be able to stay quiet. All the loyalty in the world won't stop rumors from spreading, and it's not hard to imagine what the fae will do if they catch wind I've resurfaced."

The fae had tried, and failed, to put the first vampire and all their progeny in the ground when the species first started spreading. If the fae found Ash, they'd hunt them to the ends of the Earth, and they'd slaughter anyone in their way. No wonder Ash was all for accepting the protection of the paranatural alliance. "So you're hiding from your descendants as well as your enemies, but you like to keep tabs, maybe nudge a vote now and then?"

"Parents must give their children room to make their own choices. That doesn't mean we don't care about the outcomes. Hence my more-direct-than-usual participation in this conclave."

"You call them your children, but you killed Hanzo."

"I'm both mother and father to an entire species. I can't play favorites. Tradition breeds stability, and that's served the council well, but Hanzo's inability to adapt puts all my children at risk. We can't remain isolated in this shrinking world, but a motion to join the paranatural alliance would never have passed with him in the picture. He held too much sway over the others."

"That's why you murdered him?"

"I did try to change his mind first. But he was determined to end you, snuffing the barest possibility of daywalking to ensure vampires had no choice but to remain hidden. I couldn't allow that."

I swallowed the lump in my throat. Ash had killed Hanzo to save me—or at least to save my influence and abilities—but I couldn't muster a single drop of gratitude. "Then you framed James because he was convenient and expendable."

"Not at all," Ash said, as though surprised I would think so little of them.

"Then why?"

"You," they said simply. "James is powerful, brilliant, a child any parent would be proud to call their own, but you were proving . . . difficult." He pursed his lips and gave me a quizzical look. "I can't control you."

I laughed. "You thought you could?"

"I should have been able to."

"You can start a club with Bael, Shedraziel, and all the other puffed-up assholes who've tried to put me under their thumb."

Ash shook their head. "What do you know about thrall bonds?"

That wiped the laughter from my lips. Memories of being trapped in my own body, unable to resist the commands of that sadistic bastard Merak, pressed on me like an avalanche, squeezing the breath from my lungs. I knew far more about being a vampire's thrall than I'd ever wanted to, though I now knew not all thrall experiences were the same.

"The process of creating a thrall is not dissimilar to that of creating a vampire." Ash spoke as though lecturing a child. "Only the ratios differ. A small amount of blood and a healthy host are all that's required; even a few drops is enough to snare most humans, at least for a while. Long-term servants have stronger, more complicated bonds. The more blood a vampire gives, the stronger the bond, and the longer it lasts. That means every vampire and every thrall carries a piece of the original vampire's soul—*my* soul—and the bond that forms between them relies on that connection, like to like, with the higher concentration holding the reins."

I rolled that idea around in my head. "Wait, are you saying you can control any vampire and any thrall?"

They smiled again. "Animkii was more than a window to spy on you."

I shivered, though I'd long since grown numb to the cold. "That's how you disabled the security cameras," I whispered. "You never needed to get into the room. You just used Helen."

Ash gave a self-satisfied little bow, though they didn't lower their gaze.

"Then you sent Ronald to attack me so Animkii could play the hero, thinking I'd follow him to 'safety' outside the compound."

"Wrong on all counts this time." Ash shook their head. "I had no idea Ronald was going to attack you. It wasn't until James went berserk trying to reach you and I intercepted a communication from Zuri to Animkii that I learned of the threat. I ordered Animkii to your room with all haste, but feared his mortal limitations might prove too slow. So, without any suitable pawns to call on, I raced to your side myself."

"My hero," I drawled. "If you didn't use Zuri's thralls to override the security, how did Ronald get into my room? How did he even get out of the food locker?"

"That was Cecil's doing. And while it would have been convenient if you'd gone along with Animkii's chivalrous attempt to whisk you to safety, after witnessing the fervor with which James tried to reach you, I assumed you would show equal relentlessness in trying to reach him. Hence the need to knock you unconscious. Though, as I've already admitted, I never expected you to crash the plane."

"So the council, this conclave, it's all an act. You can control them all." I frowned, spotting a flaw in my logic. "But you said you couldn't change Hanzo's mind. That's why you killed him."

"Once the original soul takes root in a vampire, it grows, changes, becomes a new, powerful entity in its own right." Ash set their hands on their hips. "The fae believe killing me would eradicate all my race, but I'm not so sure. My progeny have grown beyond what they were. I think they might survive." They chuckled. "Though I'm not willing to put that theory to the test."

They shook their head. "The point is, even I have difficulty influencing a fully realized vampire. Especially those as powerful as the ones on the council. Attempting such a feat would risk my exposure even if I were successful; but thralls . . . they're predisposed to serve. The path is already there, like slipping through a back door. I act as a switchboard operator, connecting, crossing, or dropping calls as I see fit. Except with you." Ash sighed. "By all accounts, James shared enough of himself to turn you into a full vampire, and the fact that your bond is still active would seem to support that scenario. There's definitely a binding between you, yet when I reach for it . . ." Ash extended one hand, fingers stretched as if to grab me even though they were standing too far away. "There's nothing. No resonance to connect with."

I shuddered, disturbed by the idea that James had accidentally implanted a backdoor into my soul, and pleased beyond measure that it seemed to be locked. "So you can't control me through my link to James the way you did with Animkii."

"Hence needing to find another point of pressure to ensure your cooperation."

"You framed him for murder."

"Plan B, as it were. I assumed you would offer the council daywalking to save your master."

"He's not my master," I said.

Ash smiled. "So it would seem. I was intrigued to discover you'd managed to alter the terms of your binding." They gave me a calculating look. "Fortunately, this offers new possibilities. For example, since you're not truly enthralled to James, there's no risk of losing you if he dies."

I glared. "You said you wanted to make a deal. I won't agree to anything that results in James's death."

"I believe you'll find my terms quite reasonable," Ash said with a toothy smile. "You and your beau both get to live, and the vampires lend their considerable influence to your fledgling alliance." They spread their hands. "You see? Our goals are not so very different."

"And the cost?"

"Normally, a human can be bound to only one master, otherwise vampires would be usurping each other's servants all the time to learn their rivals' secrets. Once a person is enthralled, the existing link prevents another from being formed so long as it's active."

I thought of the black snake of Hanzo's influence in Ronald's core, active even after he died. Leash, telephone, cyanide capsule, guard dog . . . enthrallment was much more complicated than I'd first thought.

"I'd assumed this was the case with your link to James," Ash continued, "but since your bond doesn't follow the usual rules, I'm hopeful it will not interfere with the formation of a second, more traditional, thrall binding."

"You want to enthrall me." The words fell like weights from my shivering lips. I bunched my fists. *Never again.*

"I won't have you following me like a lap dog, if that's your concern. You can go back to Colorado and live your life however you see fit . . . until such time as I deem it necessary to call upon you."

"At which point I'll have no choice but to obey." Bile rose in my throat as images of Merak and his minions flashed through my memory. My limbs began to shake. I jerked my head side to side. "I don't have to play your game." My breath was coming is short, sharp stabs. "You want to join the alliance. You want daywalking. You need me more than I need you."

"That may be, but don't imagine that gives you any kind of advantage. I could take you now, consent or no. I could have overpowered you the moment you stepped into these woods."

I thought of the speed with which Ash had gotten behind me and knew their words to be true. "Then why haven't you?"

"You've surprised me twice when I relied on force and deception. I thought a more direct approach might yield better results. And if I'm right about your ability to absorb a second bond . . . well, why waste a subject as exquisite as James if it's not necessary. You've made it plenty clear what James means to you, and the lengths to which you'll go to keep him safe. Join me willingly, and we both get what we want. Otherwise, your lover won't leave this conclave alive."

My freedom or James's life. Dark specs danced in my vision as pressure grew in my chest. *Isn't there anything left to bargain with?* I groped desperately for any leverage, any hope that might save me from this terrible choice . . . or at least delay it. I latched onto the only thread I could find, thin though it was. *Ash is hiding.* "Bindings take time. Even killing takes time." My voice cracked, but I pressed on. "I have a connection to James that you can't touch. I can tell him what you really are even as I'm dying. You may be fast, but nothing travels faster than a rumor." I shot the words like bullets from a wildly waving gun, praying they'd hit, that Ash would accept silence in place of servitude. "An alliance isn't out of the question, but try to enthrall me, and everyone on the council learns what you really are."

Ash nodded, not seeming at all concerned by my threat. "You *could* do that, but do you really want that much blood on your hands?" Ash's sharklike gaze bore into me. "If a single person here, aside from you, learns my identity, they all die. The vampires, the attendants, the food. All of them. Including your precious James. It'll be a pain in the ass to wipe the slate and rebuild the council from scratch . . . but it's nothing I haven't done before." Their dark gaze remained steady, unblinking, as they spoke, and I believed every word. This person could, and would, do exactly what they described, without malice, and without regret.

I couldn't look away from that stare—so full of years, yet somehow empty of life. I swallowed, trying to work moisture into my parched mouth. "If it's a secret worth killing your own people for, why tell me at all? You could have let me keep thinking you were just some random old vampire."

Ash tipped their head to one side, considering. "Because you and I are alike."

I stepped back, putting more distance between us. "I'm nothing like you."

"Oh? Were you not born of bloodlines that should never have mixed? Do you not know what it is to walk the world alone? Rejected? Abandoned? We are abominations, you and I, relegated to the barren between. We can play at life, for a time, but the act grows thin upon close inspection. You fight for a united world—in truth, you've accomplished more than I would have thought possible. Do you know why? It's because you can't find a place where you fit. And you never will. You may be able to broker peace between the races, but that won't soothe the ache in your soul. The humans will never truly accept you, not so long as there is a drop of magic in your blood. The fae will never accept you, not only for your human heritage, but for the taint of Rift you carry. Your practitioner father, a necromancer, burdened you with that contamination, just as my necromancer father did me when he raped my mother and brought me into being. And you've compounded that by bonding with a vampire. Don't forget, the blood that ties you to James, that saved your life, came from me. To each side, all sides, you will always be 'other.' So tell me, Alex, where do we belong if not together?"

Ash's words rang through the night, carried on a cloud of frozen breath.

"I can't say you're wrong." My voice shook slightly. I inhaled, straining against the tightness in my chest. "Many humans seem to think I'm an agent of the fae. They constantly question my motivations and loyalties. And plenty of fae have called me an abomination. If not for my imbuing, I doubt Bael would ever have claimed me as a relative. I can't say I've ever felt exactly welcome at his court. But the bureaucrats and lords don't make up the whole world. You're right that I work toward peace in order to create a place where I belong, but it's not just for me." My thoughts turned to Emma, who had a magic no one understood; Maggie, who loved magic despite not having any of her own; Kai, who gave up a stable future for the sake of curiosity and friendship; Targe, who settled in an inhospitable realm in order to provide a safe place for travelers; and the werewolves, who were still trying to hold onto some semblance of normal life after "normal" was stripped away.

"You say I'm alone," I continued. "I used to believe that was true. But not anymore. Abominations with powerful bloodlines aren't the only people who feel like outcasts. The future I'm trying to create is for all of us." I closed my fists, not tight, but as though I was holding onto something, some invisible lifeline. "I know exactly where I belong now, and it isn't with you."

They nodded. "A pretty speech. I had hoped you'd see the logic of joining me, welcome it even, but perhaps you're too young yet to understand. I too tried to pretend in my youth. I joined a community. Played a role. I even fooled myself into thinking it was real . . . for a while. Someday you'll come to see the truth. When the friends you think you have show their true natures, when the family you've built becomes the pyre on which you burn, you'll find that not all outcasts are created equal. You'll be glad of me then, because there are no others like us."

I shook my head. "I'll never be like you, cold and calculating, willing to murder my own kin for the sake of keeping a secret."

"It's all right if you can't see the appeal of my company yet. That's not the only reason I told you who I am." They stuffed their hands in their pockets and sauntered a few steps away, then turned back. "You need to understand how hopelessly outmatched you are. You've put on a good show, but it's time to accept your fate."

"Fate is just an excuse for avoiding choices."

Ash smiled, their eyes full of pity. "Then tell me, Alex, what choices do you imagine you have left?"

I licked my chapped, cracked lips and tasted blood. *I could run, but I wouldn't make it two steps before Ash caught me. I'd be right back where I started. I could tell the vampires who Ash really is. Then they'd be dead, James would be dead, and I'd still be caught. I could attack, but that'd be like a kitten challenging a lion . . . or a steamroller.* I opened my mouth. No words came out. Ash was right. There was no choice. *There's no way out of this clearing other than under Ash's control.*

"Please," I whispered, broken. "I'll do what you want without being bound. You don't have to enthrall me."

"I wish I could believe that." Ash gave me another pitying smile. "Now that you understand your position, shall we discuss the details of our arrangement?"

I couldn't muster the energy to respond. My mind had gone blank. Nothing short of death would keep me out of Ash's hands. I glanced at Animkii's ruined face. I hadn't always liked him, but he and Zuri were the closest thing I'd found to allies in this place. I never imagined he would end up like this. *Are we all just flies dancing on Ash's web?*

"We don't have time for a full bonding at the moment, so we'll start small," Ash said. "Just enough to keep you in line lest that rebellious streak of yours rears its head." They patted me on the shoulder. "No more sabotaging airplanes and the like."

Ash brought their hand to their mouth, then reached out and smeared their thumb against my chapped lips with enough force to part them. Coppery warmth filled my mouth.

I pushed away, spitting as I stumbled backward, knowing it was already too late. I wiped my mouth with the back of my hand and glared at the ancient creature who'd claimed my sovereignty.

"Come," Ash said, seemingly unconcerned by my impotent rage as they walked toward the cabin and its conclave entrance. "Let's get inside before you freeze to death."

I would have preferred another blizzard to the cold certainty in Ash's command, but my stolen boots crunched bloodstained snow before I even realized I was moving. Had that been a compulsion? Ash pulling my strings like a marionette? Or had my body simply accepted the inevitable sooner than my mind? Either way, there was no point resisting. Ash had won.

Chapter 16

THE ELEVATOR lurched to a halt. I half-expected to find a mob of angry vampires bearing down on me when the doors opened, but the entrance hall was still and silent save for the gentle tinkle of the waterfall.

"You can just come and go as you please?" I asked. "What happened to the lockdown?"

"After your disappearance, the council relieved Zuri of stewardship. Two such catastrophic failures could not be overlooked. They're interrogating her as we speak, trying to decide if she was actively undermining them or simply incompetent as a steward."

Resentment twisted my gut and curled my fingers. Ash had killed Hanzo and kidnapped me, yet it was Zuri and James who were being punished. "Meanwhile, you get off free and clear."

Ash spread their hands. "Such is the inequity of life." They stepped out of the elevator and headed down the hallway on the left.

I followed grudgingly, casting a glance at the towering statue of the vampire progenitor. The cheeks were a little too narrow, the eyes too soft. Otherwise, the likeness was uncanny. "If Zuri's been fired, who's in charge of security?"

"The councilors' aides. I'm on patrol duty. Fatima's and Cecil's people are watching the monitors together, because no one could trust anyone else's thrall to do the job. They will have seen us come in, but Esteban is already explaining the situation to the council. Chae-Won's man is guarding the food, which now includes Zuri's three remaining thralls."

"Three?" I stopped short, matching faces to names in my head. "Shouldn't there be four?"

Ash didn't slow. "Sadly, Meg was killed during your escape."

By process of elimination, Meg had to be the petite brunette who'd carried Victoria's bags. "Killed by whom?"

"Animkii."

Cold sweat slicked my skin. I hurried to catch up. "You made Animkii kill his fellow thrall? Isn't that like murdering his sister?"

"Very much so. But I blocked the memory, so he was none the wiser. Zuri, however, was beside herself. She'd been trying to contain James at the time, but when Meg died she just about brought the whole conclave down in her grief. The councilors had no choice but to bind her." The hint of a smile curved Ash's lips. "That added confusion gave Animkii plenty of time to get you strapped in and take off."

"Did she know it was Animkii?"

"No. I blocked Zuri's connection to Animkii as soon as I decided to have him abduct you. She probably thought he was dead, too."

Crimson snow and warm spray flashed though my memory. "Which he is . . . now."

"As I said, he'd become a liability. I couldn't have people wondering how he'd acted against his master's orders. Such a thing is supposed to be impossible." Ash winked at me over their shoulder.

I struggled with the urge to pound that smug smile off their face. Animkii had followed what he thought were Zuri's orders without ever realizing Ash could rewrite those orders at will, and the reward for his obedience had been a bullet in the brain.

"After you." Ash opened a door and motioned for me to enter.

I hesitated on the threshold. They'd brought me back to my own room. Stepping inside, I glanced toward the bedroom. There was no sign of Ronald's corpse, and the blood where his head struck the post had been cleaned up, but I could still see him there in my memory. I hugged myself and proceeded to the sitting area. "What happens now?"

Ash closed the door. "Have a seat."

I did as instructed, selecting one of the plush chairs by the cold fireplace and wishing there was a flame in the hearth. The biting cold of the surface world no longer stung my raw skin, but with the numbness of prolonged exposure fading, my shivers grew worse, and a hollow ache settled into my bones.

Bypassing the sitting area, Ash entered the bathroom and turned the taps on the tub before joining me.

"Lean back." The noisy rush of water from the other room masked their voice.

"Why?"

Ash dropped to their knees in front of me.

I stiffened. "What are you doing?"

"Completing the bond." They arched an eyebrow. "Did you think we were done?"

"You said we didn't have time for a full bonding."

"We don't, but even a weak bond requires an exchange in both directions." They frowned. "Are you saying James never drank from you?"

Memories of James, starved, weak, and out of his mind, plunging his fangs into my neck made me feel suddenly lightheaded.

"Don't worry," Ash said. "A few sips should do. But we can't have people seeing bite marks on your neck." They gripped my legs, fingers warm against the backs of my calves, and tugged my butt to the front of the chair, forcing me to recline. The motion hoisted my jacket and shirt up to my hips.

Before I could protest, or even regain my balance, Ash's teeth plunged into the soft flesh of my inner thigh. Faces from my nightmares loomed in my memory, overlaying Ash's dark hair as Merak and his fear-loving followers took turns tearing my flesh and making me scream. Cold sweat broke out across my clammy skin. I tried to stay in the moment, to remind myself that those scars had long since healed, but the lamplight seemed to dim as the blue flames of Merak's throne room invaded my mind and femoral blood left my body, sapping what warmth I'd managed to retain during my long trek back to the conclave. Shivers turned to cramps. Strength bled out of my muscles. By the time Ash lifted their head, I could barely keep my eyes open.

Ash exhaled, sitting back, and trailed one hand over their blood-stained lips. Their skin had turned nearly transparent, highlighting the dark veins pumping my stolen blood through their body. "Exquisite." They offered me a fang-filled smile as a flush of color returned to their skin. When Ash stood, they looked once more like the unremarkable human they were pretending to be.

To my horror, I found I could feel Ash's pleasure, their triumph, just as I could sense James's emotions when we were close. Ash had completed the circle. We were bound. Panicking, I slammed every mental ward I'd learned from James into place.

"Go take a bath," Ash said. They moved to the fireplace. "Get clean and warm, but don't take too long. We have a busy night ahead of us."

Once again, my body moved before I registered any intention to do so. This time I knew the driving force was Ash's command. As physically and emotionally drained as I was, it should have taken a forklift to get me out of that chair, but my bedraggled muscles responded to the resonant order coursing through my core as the familiar desire to please that I remembered from my time with Merak rose inside me. It wasn't the strongest compulsion I'd ever felt, but I didn't even try to fight it. If I had the strength or stomach to look, I was sure I would see a gold-tinted crimson tendril binding me to Ash. Instead I let my body autopilot to the bathroom, stripped off my clothes, and sank into the scalding heat of the tub.

As the hot water brought me back to life, my mind, stunned to blankness by the overwhelming events of the past few hours and the seeming hopelessness of my future, finally rebooted. I dragged a soft sponge over my windburned skin and tentatively turned my attention inward. My magic was a dim flicker, drained nearly to nonexistence. It would take days of rest to replenish it naturally. Opening a single point of vulnerability on my left palm, I started the process of filtering Rift energy, slowly adding the converted energy to my natural magic reserve.

Touching the Rift wasn't the safest thing to do when my guard was so low. I might not be able to defend myself from even a weak demon in my current state, but I couldn't risk missing an opportunity to turn the tables on Ash because of something as pathetic as a depleted battery.

Shifting my focus to look for threats, a blue-gray haze drifted through the room, almost indistinguishable from the steam produced by the bath except for the distorted faces peeking out from the curling eddies. The shadowed faces I'd grown used to seeing when I touched the Rift seemed to fill the small room, a crowd watching a concert . . . or a train wreck. None spoke or approached. They all seemed to be waiting for something, but it wasn't me they were watching. All eyes were turned toward the sitting area where I'd left Ash. Nice as it was not to be the center of demonic attention for a change, the tableau left me shaken. The only person I'd ever seen demons flock to in such a manner had been my father, a necromancer. Were the denizens of the Rift hoping Ash might fill a similar role?

Once I'd stabilized the trickle of energy feeding my reserves, I nervously turned my magically augmented awareness to the cluster of strands that made me the person I was. Most of the threads were a deep purplish-red. A heavy cable of darker purple laced with silver twisted between the brighter strands—my link to James. I strummed that ribbon. James's presence was there . . . but dulled. Was he shielded, unconscious, or had my new connection to Ash somehow damaged this preexisting bond? Perhaps my defenses were locked so tight that I wouldn't hear him even if he were screaming.

Every fiber of my being wanted to call out to James, to throw open my barriers and let his presence fill me, but I dared not lower my guard. I could feel Ash in the other room—a nearer, stronger connection. One mistake and they might slip inside, gaining access to my thoughts and memories. Was that why they'd offered the bath? Hoping I'd relax? Once past my defenses, how deep would the link they'd established allow them to get? And what if my connection to James gave Ash a backdoor into him, as it did into the councilors' thralls? Dread and despair washed through me, dousing the pleasant warmth of my bath and the momentary comfort I'd gained from James's nearness.

I gave myself a mental shake and scrubbed with a vengeance at the grime under my fingernails. If I gave in to despair, that would be the end of me. *Stay calm, Alex,* I chided myself. *If you keep your head, you'll find some way out of this mess . . . You have to.*

Taking a deep breath, I turned my focus on the other foreign strand in my core. This one didn't twist and twine with the others. The gold-tinged crimson thread remained apart save for one point of connection anchored like a barbed harpoon right at the heart of me. I knew at a glance that I couldn't just tear it out, not without causing massive damage. And damage to a core . . . well, that might kill me. Still, I tucked the possibility away. Depending on what Ash demanded of me, I couldn't say with certainty there wouldn't come a time when death was preferable to obedience.

I didn't touch my tether to Ash. I didn't want their attention on me any more than it already was. Releasing my magical sight, I scrubbed shampoo into my hair, happy to have something physical to attack, and plunged beneath the surface to rinse the suds. The world beneath the water was a warm cocoon of muffled echoes that pushed reality to a safe distance. *If only I could stay like this forever.*

I remained submerged until my chest burned with a heat that had nothing to do with the temperature of the water, then I broke the surface with a gasp. Just like that, all my problems snapped back into place. Ash was standing beside the tub, a fluffy green towel in one hand, underwear, jeans, and a white hoodie decorated with pink cherry blossoms that I recognized from my own hastily packed bag in the other.

"Time to work." They held out the towel.

Giving my hair one last rinse, I stood. Steam rolled off my lobster skin. Ash's gaze didn't waver or stray. I might as well have been an insect for all that my naked body seemed to affect them.

I snatched the towel and stepped onto a plush rug set on the tile floor. "What *work* are we doing, exactly?"

"Daywalking, of course."

I froze in the process of wiping down my legs. Of course Ash wanted daywalking, that was no surprise, but I'd hoped to have some time before the demand came up . . . time to think of some clever work-around or stall tactic. With our newly forged bond, there was no way I could hide the truth of how I'd changed James, or the fact that I likely couldn't reproduce his success.

"Shouldn't we focus on placating the council first?" I asked.

Ash thrust the stack of clothes against my still damp chest. "Come along."

Again that need to please swelled inside me. I wrapped the towel around my hair, pulled on my clothes, and padded on bare feet back to the sitting area. A fire now crackled in the hearth.

Ash settled in the chair I'd claimed earlier and folded their fingers together over one crossed knee. "Explain the process you used on James."

This time, when the compulsion filled me, I pushed back, pinching my tongue between my teeth to keep from blurting the first thing that popped into my mind. It was a small rebellion, yet even that success was a pleasant surprise. Ash's confidence and the sheer magnitude of their nature had shaken me, but this hesitation proved their power was not absolute. Perhaps their offer to spare James's life was not as magnanimous as they'd made it seem. If they weren't as confident in their ability to control me, even with a blood bond, as they'd led me to believe, that might explain their offer to keep James alive. Ash needed him as insurance against my continued good behavior if our bond proved insufficient.

That thought gave me hope. When I'd been enthralled to Merak, I'd been helpless to resist his commands when his attention was fully on me, but that was before I'd bonded with James, before I'd faced a siren, and before I'd earned the true name buried deep within my heart that offered some protection against compulsion. Even without that arsenal, I'd managed to fabricate a ball of sunlight when Merak's focus wandered, seriously injuring the vampire and allowing me to escape. The fact that I could resist a direct command from Ash, even for a moment, meant their hold over me was not complete. If I could distract them, perhaps I could find some opening to take advantage of, as I had with Merak.

I sat at the end of the couch nearest the fire, directly across from Ash, careful to keep my thoughts locked behind the wall protecting my mind. Whether from blood loss, prolonged exposure to the elements, or the heat from my bath, I felt feverish. That, coupled with desperation, gave rise to a wild, reckless idea.

I'd nearly killed James the first time I tried to change him.

I couldn't overcome Ash physically even before they'd bound me to them, and I couldn't outmaneuver them politically . . . not with the threat of a massacre hanging over me if I spilled their secret, even accidentally. Ash had boxed me into a corner. But if they wanted daywalking, they'd have to give me the keys to their soul. If I was fast enough, and deep enough, I might be able to tear apart their core before they could strike back. Then I could root out the broken threads they'd anchored in my own core, as I had with Ronald. Ash's binding was not nearly so well-established as Hanzo's had been. With Ash out of the picture, I could expose them as Hanzo's murderer to the rest of the council without fear of reprisal. I'd be on even footing again.

"I'm waiting." Ash spread their hands and drummed their fingers against an armrest.

Licking my cracked lips, I said, "Showing would be easier."

Ash frowned. "Explain the process first."

"I can't." I spread my hands and shrugged. "I only found out I had magic a few months ago, and even with a tutor, I know next to nothing about how it works. Almost everything I've done has been trial and error or instinct. I don't know the theory behind what I'm doing, so I can't explain it." I opened a crack in my mental defenses, pushing sincerity along our bond and highlighting my own ineptitude, while shoving my murderous intent deeper to the back.

Ash's lips pursed then turned down again. "But you understand it well enough to repeat the process?"

"Like muscle memory," I said. "You'll see once I start."

Watching me warily, Ash waved a hand in invitation.

I stood, took two steps, then dropped to my knees in front of Ash, flipping our positions from earlier.

"Understand that if you attempt to deceive or harm me during this exchange, you will lose any good will you currently have with me. I *will* make you suffer."

I swallowed the sudden lump in my throat. Did they suspect . . . ? No. If they did, they would never invite me in. I set my shaking hands over the vampire's pale fingers on the armrests, strengthening our connection. I had to be quick.

Will Esteban simply cease to exist when Ash dies? I wondered. *If the construct survives its master's death, that might be a problem.*

I pushed the thought away, trying to clear my mind so I could focus on the task at hand. I was only going to get one chance at this. But as I called up my magic, another thought struck me, rattling my resolve. The fae believed killing the first vampire would destroy all those who came after. If they were right, and I managed to kill Ash . . . James would die, too.

"What's the matter?" Ash's brow furrowed. "You're upset."

I tightened my grip on my emotions, trying to prevent any more leakage through our bond, and once again blessed James for the experience in mental control I'd gained over the past few months.

Killing Ash might kill James. Was it worth the risk? I could almost hear James in my head, telling me to go for it. He'd gladly exchange his life for my freedom. He'd proven that before. That didn't mean I was okay with those terms.

Ash said vampires had evolved, that they might survive their creator's death . . . but even Ash hadn't been sure. There was no way to know which theory was correct, and if the fae were right, it wasn't just James who'd be affected. Victoria, Zuri, the council, all of them. Every vampire in the world, potentially wiped out at once. Genocide. If that happened, I'd be a hero among the fae . . . just like my grandfather. Hell, he might give me an iron throne right beside his for a feat like that. An abomination on a throne. Wouldn't that be a sight?

Then there were the thralls. Ronald lost his mind when Hanzo died, and Fatima said most thralls didn't survive the death of their masters, but Animkii had implied that was only true of high-level servants with deep, long-term bonds. Still, there was no way to know how many humans the vampires would take with them if they died.

No. I was as unwilling to kill Ash as they were to kill me. The stakes were too high. I'd have to find another way out from under the vampire's thumb. Luckily, I was seconds away from first-hand access to all their secrets. There had to be something buried in Ash's memories that could give me the upper hand . . . or at least hope.

"It hurts," I blurted, fully aware that I'd been silent too long.

"What?"

"This process. It hurts."

"I'm accustomed to pain."

"You threatened to make me suffer if I hurt you, but I'm telling you right now, this *will* hurt. I have to burrow deep into your core. It's going to be uncomfortable, and it's going to stir up all kinds of old memories and buried trauma."

"Why?"

"A change like this needs to happen at the very center of your being. Anything less won't stick. That's why James's transformation didn't take the first time. He fought me when it became uncomfortable. It's very important that you don't fight me. You have to let me in." I let the truth of my words flow between us.

Ash stared at me for a long, calculating moment. "Very well."

Exhaling, I called up my magic and dove toward the tangle of Ash's core, trailing my fingers along the threads of their soul. I'd never seen a core so dense before, so cluttered with the weight of years. Faces and places flitted by like swarms of butterflies, flaring up to draw my attention and pull me off course.

I dance in the candlelight of a gilt ballroom, heavy folds of crimson fabric brushing my legs as my dress swishes. My partner is a head taller than I am, with broad shoulders made more rigid by the gold braids sewn there. His polished shoes clack in time to the music as the orchestra leads us through another waltz. All around us couples match our steps, dozens of perfect copies. More perfect than he knows.

The grandfather clock at the edge of the room chimes the midnight hour. I smile. My dance partner smiles back. His blue eyes twinkle. As the final toll of the clock mingles with the last strains of the waltz, I sink my teeth into the duke's flesh. Hot, sweet life flows between my lips and down my chin, darkening the red of my bodice.

My children strike all around me, one for each noble in the room. The fae crave power, so I will show them power. I'll rule the entire region before daybreak and earn my place as a lord among them. I continue to dance with the near-corpse in my arms, spinning out the steps of the waltz to a symphony of screams.

I pulled away from the pulsing memory. Even from within Ash's perspective, and despite the lovely dress they'd worn on that night of carnage, I hadn't gotten any clear sense of gender from them—or rather, I got the sense that they'd played both roles so often that such labels held no meaning for them.

Drifting toward a deeper memory, I let it envelope me.

Ice cuts my bare feet. Snow stings my arms. The tatters of my stained brown tunic do nothing to block the wind as I trudge down the road. Moonlight turns the white fields to mirrors, reflecting my isolation. I continue to put one frozen foot in front of the other.

"By all that's holy," shouts a man. He swings down from the mule he's riding and slings a thick, fur-lined coat around my shoulders. "What in God's name are you doing out here, child? We're days from town."

Six days . . . or six nights. Who's to say which was longer. Six nights of lonely wandering since the last bed, the last meal, the last spoken word. Six nights since I fled the matron's basement and the rows of sleeping children with nectar singing in their veins, afraid that the hunger would get the better of me.

The kind stranger drops to one knee so he's closer to my height and pulls his coat tight around me. The sable hem brushes the snow. "Come on with me now. My farm's just over the next rise." He gestures to the left. "Along with my wife and bobbins. You'll be safe there." He moves to stand, but I place one tiny, dirt-crusted hand over his arm. He hesitates.

"Thank you." My atrophied voice rasps through the winter night. I lean forward and wrap my thin arms around his neck in a grateful embrace.

He secures the coat as it tries to slide free and pats me on the back. "There, there. We'll get you sorted out."

I press my lips to the kind man's neck, breathing in the heat of his skin. Closing my eyes, I break the surface. The man jerks, but his size is not the advantage it should be. He cannot pry me off. His second knee hits the ground. His weight settles against me. His arms drop to his sides. I step back, and he falls. I resisted for as long as I could, but the hunger won. The hunger always wins. Still it burns inside me, insatiable. Taking the mule's reins, I turn toward the rise beyond which I will find the kind man's farm.

I climbed free of the memory, shaken. Guilt and joy, pain, anger, satisfaction . . . Ash's emotions bubbled around and through me, muddying my own. Giving myself a mental shake, I considered the memory. Vampires stopped aging the moment they were transformed, but Ash had been a child. Then again, Ash wasn't a vampire in the usual sense. Fae grew from children to adults over the course of a century, and Ash was as much fae as anything else. How long had their childhood lasted? Could that hint of mortality be a weakness?

I forced myself deeper. Threads of reddish-gold lashed my incorporeal self, sensing a threat. Even with Ash's invitation and our forced bond, I didn't belong here. Ash's core knew that on an instinctive level. I just had to hope their rational mind would keep their defenses down long enough for me to find something useful in all these densely packed memories.

More faces flitted past. I caught Hanzo's profile and held fast, falling into the memory.

". . . outweighed by the benefits she could offer," Esteban says.

"The threat is too great," Hanzo replies, waving a hand and settling back against the couch cushions. I see him both from the front, a deep scowl on his face, and from behind, where his neatly trimmed, gray-streaked hair crests the back of the couch.

The memory twisted as though trying to buck me free, but I dug in, wondering how Ash could stand seeing through two sets of eyes at once like that.

The me of memory glances at the door, though I can still see Hanzo's face through Esteban's eyes and the shadow that is myself standing behind him.

Hanzo's servant will be back soon. If I can't convince him . . . I finger the toxin in my pocket, potent enough to overcome even the ridiculously overactive metabolism of a vampire.

"But daywalking! Surely any risk is worth that?" Esteban recites, voicing my words as I bide my time in the background, willing the stubborn old fool to take the offer.

"Secrecy is paramount. The Blackwood girl would drag us all into the light, consequences be damned. Mark my words, if we trust her, she will be our downfall. She must be eliminated."

Esteban shakes his head, reflecting my gesture. I had hoped it wouldn't come to this, but the fact that I'd prepared the toxin belied my optimism. I'd known Hanzo wouldn't fold. It wasn't in his nature.

Sighing, I pull the syringe from my pocket and remove the cap. Sensing the threat, Hanzo twists, bracing against the back of the couch. He's fast. I'm faster. None of my offspring can match me. They are but faded copies. Still, Hanzo is old. He's strong. He will be difficult to replace. But Hanzo is a dinosaur. There is no space in this world for those who cannot adapt. Not with the survival of the species at stake and my goal so close at hand.

The needle delivers its dose of sedative before Hanzo can rise. His eyes widen. His mouth goes slack. Black lines spread from the injection point, tracing Hanzo's veins. He lifts an arm, but it only flops in feeble protest. He slides sideways off the couch, smacking his head on the coffee table on his way to the carpet. A breathy whimper escapes his lungs.

The part of me that was separate, that was Alex, rejoiced at discovering this hidden gem. *Ash used a chemical to incapacitate Hanzo. That's why he couldn't escape the fire even though he hadn't suffered any wounds. A drug that affects vampires. If I could get my hands on that . . .* My mind reeled at the possibilities. *I could take Ash out of the equation without killing them and risking the others.*

"Tuck him under the bed," says my memory self. "We can't have his servant finding him early."

Esteban stands, lifts Hanzo, and carries him away.

My waking mind watched Esteban shove the unwieldy body beneath the bed through Ash's split perspective, tucking his limbs out of sight and straightening the covers. *This must be why I found his ring on the bedroom floor.* But Hanzo's corpse had been in the sitting area. Had he recovered enough to crawl out from under the bed and halfway through the apartment before the fire bested him?

I move to the open space between the couch and the door. Setting one hand on the floor, I pour energy into my palm and slowly lift my arm. Light fills the room. Weak light, an impotent cousin to the death that burns the world above. I concentrate on Hanzo's face, picturing every detail, every craggy fold and strand of gray. The tilt of his teeth. The weight of his eyelids. The curve of his lips. The drape of his clothes. When I can no longer tell the difference between the man under the bed and the one standing before me, I reach into myself and call up a thread of life.

Agony tears through me like a tidal wave. There is no avoiding it. No stopping it. All I can do is hang on and weather the storm. I open my eyes. I'm on my knees. I don't remember falling.

Getting up, I tie the final piece of magic into place within my creation. Hanzo blinks. My perspective splits again. I see long black hair framing a pale, fine-boned face. I'm looking at myself through Hanzo's eyes. Frowning, I reach out and straighten my black tie, nearly invisible against my matching shirt. I'm not particularly fond of black, but fewer people pay attention to shadows.

Esteban emerges from the bedroom, and I watch myself straighten my tie from across the room.

The door opens. Hanzo's servant comes in.

Esteban gives Hanzo a nod, then walks out the still-open door as the servant scrambles out of the way. I follow my Esteban-self, perception fracturing further as I simultaneously walk through the halls and stand in Hanzo's room. The me that is a Hanzo-construct stops Ronald from closing the door. "I wish to speak with Chae-Won." Hanzo's perspective enters the hall as well, and I catch a glimpse of my own retreating back. I have a sudden sense of vertigo, as if I'm looking into an infinite mirror, then I turn away from myself and walk in the opposite direction.

I tumbled out of that memory feeling as though my skull had been split open by an axe. *Is this how Ash feels all the time, with their awareness split between multiple people? Were they on the mountainside with me, watching through Animkii's eyes, speaking through his mouth, while also wandering the halls here as Ash and speaking on the council as Esteban?*

Forcing my thoughts into order despite a lingering dizziness that reminded me of my college hangover days, I grabbed onto the fact that the memory I'd just witnessed hadn't ended in a fire. That scene had to be earlier in the day, which meant it was Ash's construct and not Hanzo who'd made the rounds to talk to the other councilors. But why bother if they were going to kill Hanzo in such a public way? Why not dispose of the body quietly and maintain the clone, thereby holding two of the council chairs?

Then I remembered the splitting headache, the lingering effects of which were still making it hard to think. Two perspectives was hard. Three was torture. Maybe Ash could handle it, but *I* wouldn't be able to maintain that for very long without wanting to blow my brains out. Then again, I wasn't an ancient being living with a demonic taint that constantly devoured and regenerated my body. Vampires were used to discomfort; it was a fundamental part of their existence.

I replayed the scene I'd just witnessed, drifting for a moment in the space between memories, careful not to brush against any of the weblike threads. Ash must have needed to speak convincingly through Hanzo's mouth, if only for a little while. Once they'd accomplished their goal, the construct made sure to be seen returning to Hanzo's room, alive and well, only to start the fire a few hours later. *Ash must have lit the fire to destroy evidence of the drug in Hanzo's system.* I pictured the black lines tracing Hanzo's veins. To the best of my knowledge, vampires couldn't even get properly drunk, let alone poisoned. Their constantly renewing bodies burned through everything. *I have to find out what Ash used and recreate it. That will give me the advantage I need.*

Chapter 17

I TURNED MY attention back to the web of core strands encircling me. They rippled and pulsed, not happy, but not yet attacking. I could feel Ash's presence, a dam holding back the tide. Their patience was wearing thin. They wouldn't tolerate this invasion much longer if they didn't start seeing results.

Bricking away my true intentions as tightly as I could, I projected a sense of confident reassurance and dove deeper. I was making progress. There was treasure here, if only I could find it. The woven threads of Ash's core grew tighter, denser, closing around me as I burrowed into their central memories. Pressure built, choking me, slowing me down.

"Don't fight me." Even though I'd shouted the words in my head and along my connection to Ash, only a weak copy left my physical lips to echo in the real world.

"Then hurry up." Ash's reply came from everywhere and nowhere.

An angry thread lashed out, too fast to dodge, and I fell into a city of narrow streets and stone buildings.

I wear the body of a child, though several centuries have passed since I could rightly be called that. I run with other children who thrive in the night. They are not like me. They do not burn in the light of day, but they choose the darkness. Purse strings and throats alike are cut more easily in the dark. We rule the alleys and rooftops of the outer city, but tonight I venture beyond the boundary of our domain, to the very wall of the keep.

Soiled burlap pants and a tucked-up shirt that could have covered a grown man snap against my wiry limbs as I creep along a cold stone ledge just under the lip of the bridge. The rhythmic march of boots pounds above as a patrol of guards heads into the city, creating my opening. My bare feet slip and slide on the dewy moss clogging the cracks where my toes and fingers fight for purchase. The others are shadows along the shore—lookouts, they say, against the guards' early return. The truth is they are afraid. Afraid of the gibbets and the guards' batons should we be caught.

Halfway across the bridge, I whistle to the second in the line of man-sized cages swinging overhead. Their rusty hinges grind out an eerie song of longing and loss. A thin, dirt-crusted face presses against the bars. Wide eyes reflect the flames of the bridge torches as the prisoner spots me clinging to the wall below.

"That you, Scuff?"

"Who else would bother saving your pitiful arse?" I shoot back, responding to the name Briar had given me the first time we met.

"Thanks all the same, mate, but these bars is thick. Ain't no squeezing through."

"Leave that to me." Tensing my muscles, I spring away from the bridge, wrapping my fingers around the base of the cage. Iron squeals and chains rattle as the cage swings wildly. Someone stirs in the next cage over—a man looks up from the knees tucked against his chest. His eyes shine with hunger above a thick, black beard.

"You can't pick a lock with one hand," Briar hisses.

Ignoring him, I climb high enough to wrap my fingers around the heavy iron lock. Twisting a thread of magic into Briar's mind, I make him see lock picks in my fingers that aren't really there. One good yank and the latch snaps open. I grin. "Who says I can't?"

Briar stares in open-mouthed wonder.

It's dangerous to show my strength, even under the cover of an illusion, but there's no time for subtlety if we want to get off this bridge before the guards return. Briar brought me into this group, gave me a home. I won't let the crows have him.

The man in the next cage rattles his bars. "Me, too." His voice is strained and dry. Blood seeps from gashes on his arms and face. The crows have been at him already. He jerks the bars again, making the cage groan. "Take me, too."

I turn my back on the man, opening Briar's cage. I'm here for my friend. Nothing else.

Briar barely makes the leap to the bridge, catching his shin against the edge. He rolls into the road with a soft curse.

"Me, too," the man says, louder now.

I spring lightly onto the bridge and stoop to help Briar up.

"Guards!" shouts the man in the cage. "Escape! Escape!" He's standing now, rattling his bars like a man possessed.

Guards swarm out of a door set in the keep wall.

"Run!" I push Briar toward the far end of the bridge. If we reach the city, we can disappear, but Briar is limping and human slow.

I hesitate. Briar and the others believe I'm like them. They accept me. Would they still if they knew the truth?

Enough bird calls to fill a menagerie erupt from the end of the bridge. The patrol is back. Our exit is blocked. Shadows scamper over the distant shore, invisible to all eyes save mine. At least the cowards sounded a warning before they ran away.

"Sorry, Scuff." Briar shakes his head. "You shouldn't have come."

Lifting my friend over one shoulder, I sprint toward the approaching guards.

Briar screams as we cover the distance at a speed that must seem impossible to him. A volley of arrows peppers the bridge. One pierces my leg, and I stumble. Briar slips from my grip, rolling. I snap off the shaft of the lucky shot and spring to my feet. A guard has Briar, one knee wedged in his ribs while his arms are pulled behind him. Another guard swings his baton into Briar's unprotected face. There's a wet thud and a sickening crack.

    I howl in rage, releasing my hold on the gnawing hunger that is always with me. I've been careful in the city. Never too many. Never close together. Just enough to keep the hunger in check, to keep my friends safe. But not tonight. Tonight, no one lives.

    I leap onto Briar's attacker and sink my fangs into his neck, tearing flesh and veins alike as I gulp down the liquid fire that fuels me—the only thing that soothes the constant aching hunger. There's no time to gorge on the glorious flavor. Kicking off my first victim, I pivot mid-air and land on the back of the guard pinning Briar. Another bite. Another blessed gulp of euphoria sliding down my throat.

    The other guards raise their clubs, but they are puppets moving in slow motion. I ricochet from body to body, on to the last before the first hits the ground. I straighten. The stones of the bridge glisten red in the torchlight.

    Briar struggles to stand. His cheek is split and swelling. His flowing blood calls me like a song, but I can resist. I've had my fill. I take a step toward him, but he jerks away, eyes wide and frightened. He hadn't looked at the guards like that, even when they tried to kill him.

    "What are you?" Briar's voice is too high, his words slurred by a fractured jaw. His rapid heartbeat rings like a hammered anvil in my sensitive ears.

    "I'm your friend," I say.

    "You're a freak! A monster!" Tears leak from Briar's unblinking eyes. He backs away until he bumps the low stone wall. He glances over the side, as if considering the long drop into the icy river below.

    "Calm down."

    "Leave." He winces, choking on the words.

    "I only—"

    "Get away from me!" He grabs a nearby torch from its cradle and brandishes it before him.

    His expression, more than the fire, stops me in my tracks. His look of absolute hatred breaks my heart, made all the more potent by the love and acceptance I'd grown accustomed to seeing there.

    "I said be gone, demon!" Briar thrusts the torch at me, igniting the thin fabric of my clothes.

    I could snuff the fire in an instant. I could kill Briar as easily as breathing. Instead, I run from the rejection on Briar's face as my skin blisters and peels.

    Ash's grief and rage pressed against me as I climbed out of the memory, and I recalled their earlier words: *When the friends you think you have show their true natures, when the family you've built becomes the pyre on which you burn, you'll find that not all outcasts are created equal.* Pity swelled within me for the person Ash had once been, the life they'd longed for and lost. I tried to squash the emotion. I didn't want to sympathize with the person who'd trapped me, who dangled James's life like a treat offered to a well-behaved dog.

I twisted away from the thrashing tendrils, searching the endless stream of memories flashing past. So many memories. So many years. The weight of it all threatened to crush me as I scanned for a glimmer of recognition among images more plentiful than stars in the sky.

Focus on the drug, I thought, trying to home in on my target like a divining rod. *It would have taken time and tests to make, and probably magic. I'll bet some vampires died while Ash was perfecting it.*

I slid by more memories until I spotted a fang-filled scream. A vampire with long blond hair tied up in dozens of braids writhed in pain. I grabbed hold of the flickering image.

Screams fill the noonday air. Animal wails without thought or hope. Battle cries of rage and desperation. Sounds of fear. Sounds of hate. The air is thick with them.

Creatures of myth and legend stride through the city. The earth shakes with each step from a massive stone golem as it topples buildings. Dust and smoke shrink the world. The cursed light outside flickers as a winged shadow crosses the sun. A gout of green flame engulfs the neighborhood across from my hiding place. Some of my children are flushed from the collapsing buildings alongside humans caught unawares by the war that now consumes their tiny world.

Not that we were much better. I knew the fae were hunting us. They always were. But to expose themselves like this? I never thought they would go so far.

Sunlight turns the pale skin of my offspring to ash as they scream. Bones burst into charred powder against the cobblestones. Ash drifts on a wind that smells of burned flesh, blood, and the electric zing of magic.

The sharp features of a sidhe reflect the bonfire as she scans the carnage. She prods her mount, a six-legged beast with massive antlers, and raises one hand. Her voice carries to every corner of the city, amplified by magic. "Leave no stone unturned. We'll eradicate this plague before they can spread."

I retreat from the window, deeper into the shadows of my sanctuary. But even the shadows are not safe. Fae flit through the darkness like a thought. One springs out of thin air beside me, his sword halfway to my throat before he fully forms. But I am faster than this distant cousin. Even my children are faster. I duck beneath the blade and thrust my fingers between the fae's ribs, splitting them apart. He falls at my feet. But there are more where he came from, and there is nowhere to run in the toxic daylight.

"We cannot beat them." The words fall hollowly from my lips, drifting like dead leaves on the wind.

"Then you must escape." Bright eyes of molten silver stare up at me. The girl they belong to has been with me nearly a century. She was one of my first, once I decided to build this family. "You must survive."

I cup her cheek with my free hand. "To what end?"

She grips my fingers with hers. "To prove we were not a mistake."

I shake my head. "I would need to stop the sun from shining. Even I am not strong enough for that."

"Then use us." Another of my companions steps forward. He gestures to the handful of refugees who share my sanctuary. "Take what you need to cast your spell."

My heart twists. It might be possible, but . . . "The drain would kill you, and it still may not be enough."

"Our lives belong to you," says the girl. "Use them while they still have value."

An explosion rocks the earth. Dust sifts from the ceiling. Half the city is already gone. The fae will not stop until every structure is razed, every life snuffed. I turn to my children. "Very well."

Using charcoal, I sketch one of the runic circles my mother taught me as a child, large enough to hold the half-dozen of my children who are about to die. "Step inside."

Touching the control rune, I reach my other hand toward the ceiling and the blazing death above it. I begin the siphon. Energy courses through me. My children scream and writhe on the ground. I draw more. The sky grows dark as an illusory moon crosses the face of the sun. The spell flickers. My children stop their convulsions. They have nothing left to give. The magic that animated them has gone to feed the spell . . . but it's not enough. I can feel my illusion unraveling around the edges. It will blow apart in moments. Desperately recalling my mother's stories of our family's power, I lift the dead fae's sword and slice my arm, offering my blood to the circle. I feel a ripping in my soul. The spell snaps into place. The flickering light outside the window comes solely from the fires that blaze throughout the city. I cast one look at the corpses in the circle, turn, and run. I do not know how long the spell will hold.

The last of my children break from cover under the shield of my eclipse, charging to meet the fae head on. I itch to join them, to cry out the injustice of my life in a futile and violent end, but I must survive. The fae will pay for what they've done here. What they did to my mother. What they did to me. They were meant to be my people. Their blood outweighs the human or demon in my veins, yet this genocide is their response to my very existence. They will be made to see their error . . . but not this day. If I am to have any hope of retribution, I have no choice but to play the coward.

I turn mutely from this arrogant injustice as the blood of my children flows through the streets. Next time I will keep them safe. I will keep them secret, hidden in the cracks of society until we are strong enough to face the fae and win. My feet pound the earth until the sounds of battle grow distant and the city I'd claimed is a bare smudge of rising smoke under the shade of the eclipse.

Drowning in despair, rejection, and rage, I shot out of that memory so fast that I stumbled right into another.

I gaze up at my mother's face as she smooths back my hair and says, "Our family home lies at the heart of a forest where two streams meet above a waterfall. The trees are as tall as mountains, and their prism leaves sing lullabies when the wind stirs them."

"When can we go there?" I ask, as I do every time Mother describes her home in that heartbroken tone.

"Once my family realizes they were wrong." Mother smiles as she repeats her stale response.

I frown. I am the reason Mother can't go home. "Why do they hate me?" My question, like her promise, is an echo of an old conversation repeated so many times the words have lost their meaning.

"Because they do not understand you. But fae understand power. You will be powerful, my child. Then you will be accepted." She pats my cheek. "Then we can go home."

I know her promise is true. Mother cannot lie. Someday, I will find the place where two streams meet at the heart of a prism forest. I will walk in the land of my mother, and I will be home.

The memory froze and flickered, as if a second film were being projected onto a shared screen. The smiling woman—slender, pale, with pastel-pink eyes and a cascade of white-blond hair—morphed into the face of a nightmare. Her glassy gaze stared in silent accusation. Tear trails streaked her blood-spattered cheeks. The area below her slack mouth was an open, glistening wound that mocked her missing smile.

A ball of grief and rage slammed against me so hard that I tumbled back into my physical body and fell to the floor. The air burst from my lungs in a startled gasp cut short by an iron vise around my throat.

Ash no longer looked human. Molten gold flecked with swirling crimson glared from sunken sockets. Tapered ears poked through the curtain of purplish-black hair framing their angular features. Translucent skin clung to the sharp lines of their face and stretched over an elongated jaw filled with fangs that were far too close for my liking. Even as those details sank in, my world shrank to a tunnel and began to dim.

Chapter 18

I CLAWED AT THE fingers cutting off my air supply. My heels scraped the carpet.

Stop! I pushed through the fog closing in on my mind. *You're killing me.*

My tether to James stirred, flaring in response to my plea, but he wasn't the vampire I needed to reach. Another wave of panic, fear, anger, and grief slammed into me, amplifying my own emotions. What I needed was calm. Enough calm to reach Ash, to sooth their frenzy.

Forcing my limbs to be still and ignoring the burning vacuum in my lungs took everything I had, but I grabbed the cord connecting me to Ash and desperately sent out a ripple of calm wrapped in magic.

My thundering pulse slowed as my oxygen-starved blood turned sluggish.

Ash's grip loosened. The pressure pinning me down vanished.

I sucked in all the air my lungs could hold and blew it out in a noisy *whoosh* that turned into a cough. Rolling to my side, I curled in a ball and continued to gasp and cough until the spasms in my diaphragm subsided.

Wiping tears from my eyes, I looked for Ash.

They stood with their back to me, seeming lost in their study of the crackling fire.

I pushed to a sitting position, still trying to catch my breath, not only from the second abuse of my battered throat, but from the overwhelming mass of emotions I'd experienced in Ash's core. Worst was the disturbing sense of familiarity as their memories mixed with my own. Traveling from place to place without any sense of home or family. Ash's earlier words hammered like a drumbeat in my ears. *Do you not know what it is to walk the world alone? Rejected? Abandoned? We are abominations, you and I, relegated to the barren between.* Ash had been rejected by their blood, betrayed by their friends, and forced to watch as the family they'd created was cut down around them. I knew those first two well enough. I could only imagine what I might become if the third came to pass.

Staring at Ash's back, I wrestled with my pity for the stone-cold killer who'd shot Animkii in the face and lit a helpless Hanzo on fire, who even now was dangling James's life like a prize to be won.

"You needn't pity me." Ash's whisper cracked the silence.

I climbed to my feet, straightening my hoodie. "I don't." My voice rasped. Being strangled twice in as many days couldn't be good for my vocal cords.

They inspected one hand in the light of the fire, studying the lines of light and shadow across their palm. "I feel no different."

"You kicked me out before I could finish."

"You overstepped."

"I *told* you it would be unpleasant."

Ash was silent for a long moment—a black hole of despair pulling the warmth from my body. When they spoke again, their voice was empty of all emotion, though I could feel it simmering beneath the surface. "How much more do you need?"

More time? More magic? More memories? I wasn't sure what Ash was referring to, but it didn't matter. Even if enabling them to walk in daylight had been my primary focus on this little stroll through their core, I would have failed, and that had nothing to do with quantity. No amount of magic or personal insight would be enough. Not in this case. I couldn't change the other vampires because I didn't know them as intimately as I knew James. I couldn't change Ash because there was nothing to change. They had no memory of walking in sunshine to tap into, no life before their change to act as a bridge. They were never changed in the first place. They were simply born, and their core was as complete and harmonious as it was ever likely to be.

"You can't do it, can you?" Their depthless eyes stared into me.

Shit! I needed Ash to believe there was still a chance . . . for James's sake as well as my own. Thinking of the drug Ash had used on Hanzo, of how close I'd come to finding a weapon that could even the odds against this ancient creature, I said, "We were almost there. If we try again—"

"You're lying." They strode forward and gripped my wrist.

Panicking, I bolstered my mental defenses, but I was too late. The moment Ash made physical contact, they'd felt my doubt as plainly as I'd felt their despair.

"Open your mouth."

I frowned. "Why?"

"That." They pointed at me. "That hesitation. I felt it earlier, too.

You shouldn't be able to do that." Their dark gaze grew more intense, as though they were trying to see through me. "I had hoped to keep the effects minimal, but . . ." They shook their head. "You'll need more."

Rolling up one black sleeve, they dragged a clawlike nail over their own wrist, parting the flesh. Blood gushed from the wound, but even as they raised it to my lips the gash began to seal.

"Drink." Ash's insidious voice slithered through my soul.

I shuddered at the compulsion. Every instinct screamed for me to fight, to push away the abhorrent liquid that would anchor this foul creature even deeper within me. But Ash could physically overpower me without breaking a sweat. I was alone and outmatched. Struggling would only convince Ash to open another vein, pouring his poison into me until I lost the will to resist. Better to comply and save my rebellion for when I had either the tools or allies to stand some chance of success.

Hating myself, I choked back my revulsion and opened my mouth.

The blood was thick and salty. It coated my tongue.

Ash cupped my chin with their free hand, stroking their thumb down my neck with each convulsive swallow.

I grew lightheaded as Ash's blood entered my system. The warm glow of my magic rose up to meet it. Pain flared like an electric shock through my whole body as my veins were set alight. A scream bubbled up in my throat. Then the pain receded. My magic settled back into its reservoir.

Ash pulled their arm away, the bone-deep cut now a fading scrape across the inside of their wrist. A sticky copper coating lingered in my mouth, but the desire to rinse it away was a distant, hazy thought.

Better.

Ash's satisfaction filled me, and it took a moment for me to register that their lips hadn't moved. A tiny voice shouted from the edge of my awareness that this was a bad thing, but mostly I was just happy that Ash was happy, and that I had played some small part in achieving this pleasure.

"If you lie to me again, James will not only die, he will beg for death. Do you understand?"

I nodded.

"Then let's try this again. Can you change me to walk in daylight?"

"No." Disappointment swept through me, though whether mine or theirs I couldn't tell. That one word had stolen hope from both of us.

Ash paced the room. "But you changed James to walk in daylight?"

"I did."

"What's the difference?"

"He was human."

Ash frowned. "Explain."

"I don't know that I can."

"Try," they said darkly.

I laced my fingers and stared at my palms. "James's core was part vampire, part human. I used the human half to . . . protect the vampire half." I shook my head. "Your core is already integrated."

Ash made another circuit of the room. "But the others . . ." Hope crept into their voice. "The one's made from humans. You can change them?"

I hesitated. If I admitted my uselessness, James was as good as dead. But if I lied, there'd be no hiding it. Closing my eyes I said, "Probably not."

There was a long moment of silence. I opened my eyes to find Ash studying me.

"That's why you didn't use daywalking in your earlier negotiations," they said. "It's an empty promise."

I nodded.

"And yet . . ." Again they paced. "And yet you clearly succeeded with James."

"What I said earlier was true. I have to change a person at the very center of their core, and I can't do that unless they trust me completely. Do you think any of the councilors are capable of that?"

They smiled, a tightening of their mouth with no warmth or humor. "What about the pendants you promised Victoria?"

Again I hesitated. "I've been trying," I said, "but I haven't managed to recreate the one James destroyed."

Ash nodded. "So you *might* be able to change a vampire's core if they could overcome their own mistrust. And you *might* be able to create daywalking amulets given more time and knowledge. But as things stand now, you're pretty much useless."

I swayed under the judgment. The part of me bonded to Ash reeled with self-loathing. The part of me that was still free buckled under the weight of failure. I'd held the bluff as long as I could, but this was the end of the road.

Ash walked to the fireplace and flipped a switch. The flames sputtered out. "The council is growing restless. We'll continue this discussion once we're safely away from the conclave."

I frowned. "You're not going to kill me?"

This time their smile carried a hint of mirth. "Your power, incomplete though it may be, is the first hope I've had of daywalking in centuries. I'll not throw it away so easily. Whatever the obstacle, we'll find a way around it." They crossed their arms. "But it does seem premature to make any promises to the council. Cecil in particular won't waste the opportunity to derail our plans if he discovers your shortcoming." They tapped one foot against the carpet. "Once James's trial is behind us, Esteban will suggest that the issue of joining the paranormal alliance be postponed to a later date. That will give you and me time to work out the kinks in your transformation process. When the results are repeatable, it will be an easy sell to convince the council to join the paranatural alliance in exchange for daywalking. Then vampires will finally sit as equals among the other races."

I could sense the hunger behind their words, the long-burning desire to take vengeance upon the fae coupled with a child's need for acceptance. I'd come to this conclave hoping to convince the vampires to join the paranatural alliance, but discovering Ash's identity changed everything. If Ash gained a seat at the table, their personal vendetta against the fae might irrevocably shatter the already volatile balance of power in the Mortal Realm. Yet I was in no position to stop them. They had power, purpose, and perhaps the most dangerous attribute of all . . . patience. What I had was a harpoon in my chest that guaranteed obedience.

I licked my lips, afraid to voice my next question. "What about James?"

Ash watched me until my skin began to itch. I shifted my weight.

"I think it best we keep James around for the time being," they said at last.

My knees threatened to buckle as relief rocked me.

"You will inform Victoria that Zuri is the murderer. She lit the fire in Hanzo's room after incapacitating him with her unique environmental advantage then commanded her thrall to erase the camera footage and injure herself to divert suspicion. She invited James to Hanzo's room under the illusion of Hanzo's servant—unverifiable with the cameras off—thereby framing him for the murder."

I pictured Zuri enacting the plan as Ash described. It was plausible, as it had been when James suggested the same tactic earlier, but the lie made me want to vomit. Zuri had been as kind a vampire as I'd ever met, good to her thralls and fierce in her sense of justice. She didn't deserve the fate Ash had dealt her. Every fiber of my being recoiled at the thought of being party to this charade. "They'll kill her."

"Nothing less than an execution will satisfy the council at this point. A sacrifice must be made, and there are only two options. James or Zuri. Choose."

I shook my head. "How can I? How could anyone with a heart?"

A small frown creased Ash's mouth. "If it eases your sense of moral outrage, Zuri will likely die regardless. She's proven herself inept as a conclave steward, having allowed the murder of one distinguished guest and the abduction of another. The council cannot overlook such gross negligence."

"But she wasn't negligent," I retorted as the indignant whisper that was my suppressed inner voice gained in strength. "Her only shortcoming is that she has you as a relative."

Ash narrowed their eyes. "Which would be a terrific argument, if you were capable of telling anyone that."

I curled my lip, unsure if my disgust was more for Ash or myself. Perhaps it didn't matter. There was plenty to go around. I might be able to shake off Ash's control to some extent, but that didn't change my options. I could point fingers all I wanted, but I'd choose James over Zuri every time.

"What's her motive?" The words rang hollowly in my ears, heavy with defeat. I'd known since Ash led me across the bloodstained snow that I wouldn't escape this conclave intact. My freedom, James's life, my moral integrity, the future of the alliance . . . I couldn't save them all. I could only hope to mitigate the damage and pray I could still bear to look at my reflection when all was said and done.

"The usual," said Ash. "Tired of her lot in life, she sought to sow enough confusion to whisk you away, killing one of her own thralls to make it look like another's doing."

"Will the council believe that?"

"The question isn't, 'What will they believe?' The question is, 'What can you sell?' They don't need to believe the story, so long as they benefit from it. All we require are their votes."

"Okay," I said, hating myself. "Let's get this shit show over with."

Chapter 19

ASH LED THE WAY down one hall, up another, and came to a stop in front of a door. I trailed two steps behind, pulled in their wake like a balloon on a string. Ash knocked twice. A long moment passed, then Victoria stood in the doorway, resplendent as always with her lustrous black hair and emerald eyes. Tonight she wore a shimmering blue, form-fitting dress that parted to show her shapely calves and the intricate lacing of her knee-high, equally shiny, matching blue sandals. She glanced at Ash, barely registering their presence, before her gaze settled on me.

Her eyes widened in surprise. "You're back."

I looked at Ash. Victoria had no idea of the power standing before her. Ash was her creator, a god among vampires, yet she paid them no more mind than a piece of furniture. Of course, I'd been the same. I'd barely given Ash, given any of my fellow humans, a second thought when trying to identify Hanzo's killer. Ash wore anonymity like a shroud, hiding in plain sight—unthreatening, unassuming, and unnoticed.

"You are summoned by the council," Ash said, motioning for Victoria to join us in the hall.

Victoria gave my damp, unbrushed hair and bare feet a scrutinizing look. "You look like a drowned rat."

"It's been a long day," I replied.

"Yes, I imagine there's quite a story there. I hadn't expected to see you again."

"You thought I'd abandon James?"

"I didn't think you'd have a choice." The corner of Victoria's plump, red lips quirked up. "So, which was it?"

"Huh?"

"Which councilor arranged your abduction?"

"We must proceed to the council chamber now," Ash interjected.

Victoria waved her hand in their direction as though shooing a fly. "We're coming." Addressing me, she said, "Are you sure you wouldn't like to borrow something a little more . . . appropriate? Something in black, maybe?"

Get her moving. The command shivered along the thread tethering me to Ash, soothing yet horrific. I rejoiced and recoiled simultaneously at the contact.

"I doubt my clothes will have any bearing on the outcome of this trial, Victoria. Let's get going."

"You're that eager to see your lover burn?" A hint of acid crept into her honey-sweet tone.

"He's innocent."

"Hmph." Victoria stepped into the hall and pulled the door closed behind her. "So you've said. But *I'm* the named Truth Seeker, and I say he isn't." She narrowed her eyes. "Or have you learned something useful on your little outing?"

I turned with Ash and started to walk. Balling my fists I said, "If you want to claim your seat on the council, name Zuri the killer."

Only the muffled sound of my footsteps filled the hall as Victoria mulled over my words. Ash, like all vampires, moved with soundless grace. How had I not noticed that before? How did Victoria miss it even now? *Because we weren't looking for it,* I chided myself. *One thing humans, vampires, fae, and probably every species in the universe seems to have in common: We can miss even the most obvious things simply because we aren't expecting them.*

"Do you have evidence," Victoria asked, "or is this simply a last, desperate attempt to save your paramour?"

"The evidence was in front of us the whole time." Ash's words fell from my lips as if I were no more than a ventriloquist's puppet. "No one else could have accessed the security room."

"Neither could Zuri," Victoria countered. "Not when she was busy putting out the fire in Hanzo's room."

"Why can't thralls be used as witnesses?" I asked.

"Because loyalty to their master supersedes all else." She stopped. "Oh, I see. That *is* clever." She turned her hungry smile on me. "The thrall in the security room was never really attacked."

I nodded, stopping with her. "She erased the security footage, then slammed her own head against the desk to make it look as if she'd been attacked."

"And there's no way to verify the truth, since her testimony can't be trusted."

"No way to refute it either," I said, continuing down the hall and wishing, as my bare feet padded against the cold marble, that I'd taken the time to put on socks and shoes. "In the end, it will come down to what each councilor wants, and whether you can sell the story."

She pursed her lips and followed. "Some on the council may still prefer the other version, the one in which James plays the villain and comes to a tragic end. Cecil for certain. Probably Chae-Won. I'm not sure about the other two." She gave Ash's back an assessing look. "I'll need better than fifty-fifty odds if you expect me to put my future on the line."

Ash cleared their throat. "My lord Esteban is willing to testify that he saw Hanzo's servant, or someone who looked like him, inviting James to Hanzo's room as he walked from Cecil's room back to his own that day. Since this would have been at nearly the same time as Cecil himself received his invitation, this lends credibility to the fact that James was being set up by someone who both possessed high-level illusion magic and knew the security cameras would be disabled."

Victoria cast me an approving glance. "Been making side deals, Alex?" She smiled. "Nice to see you're learning the game."

"And you can add kidnapping to the list of charges," I said to seal the deal. "Animkii wasn't killed during my so-called escape. He's the one who abducted me, which he could only have done on Zuri's orders."

"Then the steward is to be applauded for her acting skills. Her anguish seemed quite real." Victoria's gaze grew distant and her cheeks paled. "For a moment I feared she would bring this whole structure down on our heads."

"Perhaps that's why she had Animkii kill Meg," I said. "To make her pain believable."

Every argument I made, every half-truth I revealed, burned like acid on my tongue, but Ash kept a stranglehold on my reins, speaking with my voice . . . and I let them. *I'm no better than the council, twisting facts to suit my ends, justice be damned.* I'd sold my soul to a devil. All I could do was ride the wave and beg for forgiveness from the ghosts left in my wake.

"Where is Animkii now?" Victoria asked. "I assume he didn't return with you."

I hesitated, unsure what Ash intended to do about the body under the snow. Then their words filled my mouth. "Our plane crashed in the mountains. He died on impact."

"Yet you survived, intact, and you made your way back here all by your lonesome in less than a day?" She raised an eyebrow.

I met her gaze. "You know what James means to me. Will you proclaim Zuri the killer, or not?"

She let out a long, languid exhale and looked toward the ceiling. "Very well. I shall inform the council that I have discovered the murderer in their midst. With Sloth's testimony to confirm James was lured to the crime scene, a reasonable explanation of the security breach, and your insights about Animkii, I should be able to convince them that Zuri was behind it all."

I exhaled. "If the council wants to maintain the image of being a reasonable governing body, they'll have to clear James of the murder charge."

"Don't get too excited," Victoria said. "They've still got him for breach of secrecy, and with Cecil's deal off the table, I doubt they'll delay the second vote until I've been appointed to my new rank."

I stared at Ash's back. We only needed one vote to break the stalemate. Now that Ash had what they wanted, Esteban would switch sides. To Victoria I said, "One step at a time."

Ash stopped in front of a door that looked nothing at all like the others we'd passed. This door was made of steel. A spoked wheel framed by a series of four thick rods, two vertical and two horizontal, sat at its center. When Ash twisted the wheel, the rods retracted with a *clang*. The door swung smoothly.

I peeked into the revealed room and winced, shielding my eyes. My first impression was that the walls were made of diamonds. A few blinks cleared my vision. The walls were, in fact, mirrors—hundreds if not thousands of tiny mirrors lined the curved walls of the cylindrical room, reflecting and amplifying the light that leaked in from the hall. The floor, too, was reflective, though it seemed to be a highly polished metal. In the middle of the room, anchored by a pair of manacles on a thin silver chain to one of three heavy steel rings set into the floor, knelt James.

Ash bowed like a butler announcing me to a ball. "Welcome to the Well."

I flew over the threshold, dropped to my knees on the unyielding floor, and wrapped my arms around James. He tried to return the embrace, but the chains restricted his hands, so he had to settle for burying his face against my neck and shoulder.

"I feared—" his voice cracked.

"I'm all right," I whispered. "And you will be, too."

He cleared his throat and straightened. "What happened?" The previous moment's vulnerability vanished from both his expression and his voice.

I gripped James's bound hands and stared into his eyes, strengthening the cord stretched between our souls. I could feel him, as I always could, yet when I touched his mind, his heart, it was as though I were pressing against a flexible wall that kept me at a distance.

"It's the chain," James whispered. "This room is designed expressly for the purpose of containing and killing vampires. The chains are enchanted to dampen magical abilities—strength, speed, regeneration . . . telepathy. All shielded."

I looked up. The mirrored wall rose at least forty feet, ending in another reinforced door set in the ceiling. "Is that . . . ?" I couldn't bring myself to voice the question.

"This is how executions are carried out. The top hatch is left open at dawn. There is nowhere to hide in here, and the chains ensure there is no escape."

"But if the chains void magic, shouldn't that include—"

"Dampen," James corrected. "Not void. Sunlight still burns, though I understand it takes a while to truly kill in these circumstances."

I recalled the mirror-lined box in which Merak had imprisoned James, filled with just enough light to keep a vampire on the cusp of death indefinitely as their cells were burned away and regrown. Then I imagined Zuri—kind, practical, innocent Zuri—chained to this floor as the sun rose. How long would it take her to die as the flesh peeled off her bones?

I gagged at the mental image, and a freezing hollowness settled over me. Could I really condemn a person to that?

"What's the matter?" James didn't need telepathy to realize I was upset.

I looked into his worried eyes and steeled my nerve. *Sometimes we have to compromise to save what matters most.* I might never know a night's peace after this, but to save James, I would do it.

He frowned.

I looked away. Had he seen my guilt, or had he noticed the hazy sheen of enthrallment in my eyes?

"Say thank you, James," Victoria called from the hallway, clearly unwilling to set foot in the mirrored room. "I'm about to save your life."

His frown deepened. "How?"

"By naming Zuri as Hanzo's killer."

He looked from Victoria, to Ash, to me. "You agreed to this?"

Even with our bond dampened, I could feel James's disbelief. The last time we'd spoken, I'd argued for Zuri's innocence.

"We found new evidence," I said.

"What evidence?"

"It doesn't matter."

"Whoever set me up was meticulous, calculating. If you found evidence, I have to believe they wanted you to."

"Just take the win and let it go," I said.

"What happened to not being responsible for an innocent person's death?"

"You said it yourself; I can't save everyone."

"That's never stopped you from trying." He narrowed his eyes. "What changed?"

Even through the muffling effect of the enchanted chain, I could feel him prodding at my mind, trying to find the truth. I tightened my defenses. I couldn't risk him seeing the real reason behind this deal, or the identity of the unassuming servant standing beside Victoria in the hall.

"Can we get him out of here?" I called over my shoulder.

Ash stepped into the Well. They dangled a ring of old-fashioned keys as they approached. "Nice and calm now, yes? No reason to struggle since you're about to be cleared."

James nodded, though he kept his focus on me. Shame kept me from meeting his gaze. For all my schemes and speeches, I'd had to compromise my morals in the end.

Ash opened the ring holding the chain to the floor. James's hands were still bound, but he could get off his knees. I helped him up.

"Something's wrong," he whispered. "You don't believe Zuri is the killer."

"The evidence fits," I said, willing him to drop the matter.

"That wasn't enough before."

"It's enough now."

"Which means there's something else at play. Something you're not telling me." Again I felt James pressing at the edges of my awareness, seeking a way past that flexible wall. "You've made some kind of deal."

"Let it go." I turned away, but he caught my arm and pulled me back to face him.

"A deal you don't like," he said. "Because of me."

I glared at him, suddenly angry at his imperious attitude. Of course I didn't *want* to sentence an innocent woman to death, but what choice did I have? "This is the way it has to be."

He narrowed his eyes. "There's more to this, isn't there?" He cupped my cheeks between his bound hands, causing the silver chains dangling from his wrists to rattle. "Tell me what's really going on, Alex." He pressed his forehead to mine. The whisper of a word, a name, shivered through my soul. Even with our bond dampened by the magical chains, James could reach me. He possessed a skeleton key to my soul, the deepest secret of my heart—my true name, gained in the fae ritual that pitted a person against their darkest self.

I thrilled at the contact, the gentle caress of his presence. His request for the truth burned through me. I opened my mouth, eager to comply. Then I felt Ash's presence, poisoning the connection, straining to understand this new dynamic. I snapped my teeth together as reason returned. James wasn't pressing his command, but he could, and I would be helpless to resist. I would spill Ash's secret, and James would die. They would all die.

"Please." My voice shook. "If you love me, don't push this."

I stepped away from James, breaking the contact. Not only was there a danger that James might learn Ash's secret despite the muffling effect of the chain, there was also a chance Ash would notice the existence of my fae name through my connection to James. That name was likely all that stood between the sliver of self-determination I retained and total subservience. I couldn't risk its discovery.

"The council is waiting." Ash gave James's chain a tug, pulling him into motion.

James kept his steady gaze on me as he left the execution chamber, a deep frown arching his lips and a furrow on his brow.

"Smile," Victoria said. "You're about to be a free man."

He turned his assessing stare on her. "What deal did you two make?"

"I earn my seat on the council; she gets to keep her daywalking boy toy." She traced one crimson nail over his cheek and down to his chest. "Though I can't say she'll keep you all to herself."

James knocked her hand away.

Victoria pouted out her lower lip. "You're no fun these days, James. Elise's court may have been a nightmare at the end, but at least you had a sense of humor back then. Where has all your playfulness gone? Your sense of adventure?" She narrowed her eyes. "All dried up with Elise's blood?"

James lunged, but Ash yanked on the silver chain, bringing him to heel.

Victoria's silver-bell laughter echoed off the marble walls as she did a little half-twirl out of his reach and led the procession up the hall, a flirty bounce in her step.

I brought up the rear, dragging my feet in trepidation of the moment when we'd reach the council chamber and I'd come face-to-face with the woman I'd condemned.

OUR GROUP CAME to a stop outside the large doors behind which the council was waiting to receive my lies. I shifted my weight and stared at the floor between my bare toes.

James leaned close, brushing my shoulder, and whispered, "You're afraid."

"I'm nervous," I whispered back.

"I've seen you nervous, and I've seen you scared. This is the latter. You don't scare easily, so what's going on?"

I barely resisted the urge to look at Ash as they pushed the chamber doors open and ushered us across the narrow bridge of light that led into the council room.

The four remaining council members waited on their thrones. All looked grave and weary as they watched our entrance. Zuri knelt, nearly prone, just off-center in the lit area. Her face was hidden by her thick, black curls. Her wrists were bound by manacles connected by a thin, silver chain identical to James's. Three fingers on her left hand were swollen, purple, and at entirely the wrong angles. She lifted her head as we approached. A long gash split one side of her face, bisecting an empty eye socket and twisting her upper lip into a toothy grimace. Rusty stains streaked the front of her cream-colored blouse. Her remaining brown eye caught my gaze.

Both hands flew to cover my mouth as bile rose to the back of my throat. I turned away. James hesitated beside me, but Ash dragged him onward. Even Victoria let slip a quiet oath as her gaze settled on Zuri's ruined features.

A drug that knocks them out. A chain that strips their speed, strength, and ability to heal. Vampires aren't nearly as invincible as they pretend to be. At the moment, I didn't find that fact nearly as comforting as I might have otherwise.

"Finally," Fatima said, at the same time that Cecil proclaimed, "You certainly took your sweet time cleaning up."

"Not that she's managed it," Chae-Won added with a look of disgust as she took in my stringy hair, bare feet, and plain clothes. She turned to Esteban. "I thought you said your servant was getting her ready."

"As I understand it," Esteban replied, "this is a vast improvement upon the bedraggled state of her arrival. But if you'd like to postpone yet longer while she changes into proper attire, by all means—"

"That won't be necessary," said Fatima. "Her lack of social grace is not the issue here."

"Indeed," said Esteban. "Let's settle the matter of Hanzo's killer once and for all so that we might put an end to this most unsightly gathering."

Cecil gestured to Victoria, meeting her gaze with a meaningful look. "Step forward, Truth Seeker, and share your findings."

Victoria preened at the title, holding her already impeccable posture a little straighter as she strutted onto center stage. She stood to one side of the middle of the room, opposite Zuri, and carefully arranged her feet to avoid touching any of the specks of dried blood that dotted the floor.

"Lords and ladies of the council, as you know, I was assigned the task of identifying the culprit behind Councilor Hanzo's death. I'm pleased to report that I have succeeded."

Cecil glanced at James with a smile.

"Not only will I provide the name of the killer," Victoria continued, playing to the crowd, "but facts and witness testimony to back up the allegation, so there can be no doubt as to the thoroughness of my investigation and my worthiness of the promised prize." Her gaze fell hungrily on the empty council seat beside Cecil.

Thoroughness, I thought bitterly on the verge of laughter or tears, I couldn't tell which. *As if she actually did anything.*

James slipped his hand around my wrist, making me twitch. Our numbed connection pulsed weakly, but I could feel his concern. Not that I needed magic to guess what he was feeling. He leaned close and whispered in my ear, "Victoria wouldn't risk this road without a councilor on her side. Who did you make a deal with?"

I compressed my lips.

"Since it's my life we're saving, shouldn't I have some say in this decision?"

"There is no decision," I said hollowly.

He tried to catch my gaze, but I kept my eyes on the scene playing out in the center of the room. I couldn't bear his scrutiny.

"The person who turned this conclave on its head," Victoria said with a sweeping gesture, "was the very person in charge of running it smoothly." She turned and pointed. "The steward, Zuri Yahaya."

The councilors stirred in their seats. Cecil half rose from his. All wore frowns. Fatima leaned over and whispered something to Chae-Won. Even Esteban looked agitated, though I knew his shock was an act.

"What is your evidence?" Cecil demanded.

As Victoria launched into her story about Zuri overpowering Hanzo, Helen's self-inflicted wounds, and Animkii's attempt to kidnap me, James leaned even closer and repeated in a gravelly voice heavy with frustration, "Who did you make the deal with?"

I could feel him scrabbling at the edges of my mind, trying to find a handhold, but the magic-dampening chain held him at bay. I silently thanked the device for providing that buffer, unsure if I could fend off James's persistent scrutiny on my own. I couldn't afford to have him discover the truth. Burying Ash's identity as deep within my barricaded mind as I could, I shook my head and tried to pull my hand from James's grip.

Even without his full strength he managed to hold me in place. "What did you have to promise in return?"

"It doesn't matter." My words made hardly any sound at all, disappearing into the backdrop of Victoria's speech.

"It matters to me. What exactly is my life worth?"

"Everything," I hissed, turning to glare at him.

James stilled, studying my face. "A binding," he whispered. "You've promised to serve."

My lip quivered. Had that been a lucky guess, or could he see the spell clouding my eyes? Sense the second anchor in my soul? "You may be willing to roll over and let them kill you, but I'm not."

He pressed his mouth to mine, stealing my arguments and my anger. His lips were warm and soft against my chapped skin. He tasted like blackberries and cloves. "For that, and for so many other reasons, I love you, Alyssandra Blackwood." He spoke the words against my lips, sharing my breath. "But I know you. You have a strong sense of justice. If you've agreed to something that burdens your conscience, the weight will consume you."

Tears leaked from the corners of my eyes. "And what would losing you do to me?"

He shook his head. "I will not be the chain that binds you."

"It's already done." I closed my eyes. "This is the only path forward."

I felt him smile. "One of the many things you've taught me during our time together is that a person always has options, even in impossible situations. I could easily bear the guilt of Zuri dying for my freedom, but I cannot accept the price that decision would extract from you."

James's resolution washed over me as he backed away.

I clutched his sleeve. "What are you going to do?" The dampening effects of the magical chain that protected my mind were now a hindrance as I struggled to see James's intentions.

"What I have to." Turning to face the councilors, he announced in a booming voice that cut Victoria short, "I'm terribly sorry to interrupt this lovely fantasy, but I can't allow this charade to continue." He shook me loose and strode to the center of the room, stopping directly between Zuri, who was shaking her head in denial of the charges being laid against her, and Victoria, who'd been in the middle of telling the council how Zuri ordered one of her thralls to kill another in order to divert suspicion.

I took two steps forward, but Ash gripped my arm just above the elbow, yanking me to a halt. "What's he planning to do?"

I shook my head, at a loss for words, though a giddy pleasure filled me at the look of concern on Ash's face. As hopeless as my situation seemed, Ash wasn't omniscient or omnipotent . . . which meant they could be defeated.

"Mr. Abernathy," Esteban said in a threatening tone, "you will return to your place until called upon to speak."

"You want to know who killed Hanzo." James raised his hands as high and wide as the chains would allow. "Here I am."

My breath caught. My heart stuttered. I took a step forward, but the barbed harpoon Ash had anchored in my core pulled me back.

"We have to stop him," I hissed at Ash.

"And how exactly do you propose we do that?" they replied. "James has gone off script. He's on his own."

I found the cord tethering my core to Ash and wrapped my awareness around it. *The deal was my servitude for his freedom.*

Which I provided, came the terse response. *If your paramour decides to burn his free pass, that's on him.* I could feel Ash's disappointment at losing James, but they weren't distressed enough to intervene. Not when that might draw unwanted attention in their direction.

"You're confessing?" asked Cecil. He looked around at his equally stunned counterparts. "Why?"

James glanced in my direction, then returned his focus to the council. "Because I cannot watch a good woman be destroyed by the whims of this court."

The words hit me like a hammer. James didn't care about Zuri. It was me he was trying to save, my "goodness" he was protecting. I gritted my teeth. *Why does he have to be so damnably noble?*

"No." The outburst came from Victoria. "No, that's not right. Zuri is the killer."

James gave a little shake of his head. "I'm afraid not."

"It seems your investigation wasn't quite up to the task," Cecil said. "Though you did weave a convincing tale."

"What are you playing at?" Victoria demanded.

James shrugged, rattling his chains.

She bared her teeth, then turned it into a smile and faced the councilors. "He's lying."

Fatima frowned. "Why would he lie when the result would be his own death?"

Victoria laughed, though the strained sound was a far cry from her usual silver bells. "Clearly he has some game in mind to wind this council up."

"To what end?" asked Chae-Won. "What possible benefit could there be in confessing?"

Victoria's smile looked more like a grimace. "I'm not sure, but I have eyewitness testimony that James was lured to Hanzo's room the night of the fire by someone disguised as Hanzo's servant—someone who knew the security cameras would not be able to detect their illusion."

Another round of mutters erupted around the room as the councilors processed this information.

"And who might this witness be?" asked Esteban, leaning forward in his seat to draw Victoria's gaze. "What fool would pit their word against a flat-out confession?"

Victoria gaped. She stared at Esteban for a moment, then shot a glare at Ash and me. Focusing once more on James she demanded, "Then tell us, James, how did you disable the security cameras?"

"What kind of trial is this," he asked, "where a person must prove their own guilt?"

"I've heard enough," Cecil said. "Victoria, you've failed. Accept your defeat with some grace and step aside."

"But—"

"Clearly you aren't cut out for a seat on this council." Cecil's words seemed to take all the fight out of Victoria. She swayed on her feet, then backed into the shadows, for once not swishing her hips as she walked. She stood like a ghost under the arch with Ash and me.

Cecil turned his focus on James. "James Abernathy, you stand accused of the murder of Councilor Hanzo. How do you plead?"

"Guilty," James said without hesitation.

"No," I shouted. Ash grabbed my second arm as I made to step forward, pinning both elbows behind my back. Their surprise at my outburst swept through me.

The councilors looked in my direction. Cecil frowned. Chae-Won smiled. Fatima said, "Do you have something to add before sentencing, Ms. Blackwood?"

Ash's voice pounded through my mind, painful in a way that James's never was, as they sought control. *Stand down.*

I fought the compulsion even as my limbs relaxed under Ash's grip. *Let me save him,* I begged. *I won't reveal your stupid secret!*

Nothing can save James now that he's confessed, unless you're prepared to grant them all daywalking here and now?

You know I can't.

Then you're out of options, and so is James.

You need him if you want my cooperation, I projected, grasping at any available leverage.

You have other loved ones. Ash's words were cold, calculated, and brought up a disturbing montage of Emma, Maggie, Kai, and the rest of my friends waiting for me back in Colorado and elsewhere. If Ash got hold of them. . . .

A great weight settled in my chest, constricting my lungs as I sought a path forward. The doors of my future seemed to be closing around me.

"Well, Ms. Blackwood?"

Fatima's prompt jostled me out of the dark spiral sucking me into despair. This was my last chance. I had to say something. Anything. I would not abandon James to his fate, even if it was a fate of his own making.

Casting about wildly, I latched onto the only fact that offered a glimmer of hope: James had killed a council member once before, and he hadn't been punished for it. In fact, he'd been rewarded. What was it James had said? When he killed his maker, he'd done it for the benefit of all vampire kind.

"He did it for you!" The words were out of my mouth before the thought was fully formed.

"What do you mean?" Chae-Won asked.

Cecil cut her off with, "He killed Hanzo to save his own skin."

"No." I shook my head, struggling against Ash's hold both inside and out. "He was protecting the council . . . protecting all the vampires. Hanzo's archaic notions of tradition would have seen your people stagnate. You're being left behind as the other races move forward. You have to grow, to change, if you hope to survive. James knew Hanzo's stubbornness would destroy you all, just as he knew the leverage Hanzo held over each of you would make you too weak to overrule him." I lifted my chin. "He did what none of you could, because he cares about the future of his people."

It was a weak argument, a last, desperate gamble, but it was all I had. I could see the wheels turning in the councilors' eyes as they weighed my words, assessing risks, calculating rewards. It wasn't enough. *I've given them an option, but I have to make it enticing enough to take. I need some kind of incentive to back it up.*

Once again my thoughts snagged on the only thing I held that was of any real value to this council . . . myself. I couldn't clear James's name, but I might still be able to save his life. At the very least, he wouldn't go down alone.

I opened my mouth, but Ash was there, pulling my strings, blocking my path. My teeth snapped painfully together.

I can afford to lose James, Ash's voice whipped through my soul, shoring up their tethers until I felt cocooned within my own body. *You, I cannot. You will tell the council that you have nothing more to say.*

Once again I opened my mouth . . . and once again I slammed it shut, this time on *my* command.

Time seemed to slow as I sank into myself. The council chamber faded, along with the impatient stares of the gathered vampires. Letting the rest of the world disappear, I huddled around the tiny glowing ember in my deepest core. There was no sign of Ash here, no barbed anchors polluting me. I could still feel them, twisting the cords that bound us, trying to make me obey, but this one corner of my soul was safe. This was the reason I was still able to resist, the last stand of my rebellion.

My true name thrummed in my soul, filling me with strength and confidence. So long as my name remained protected, I stood a chance, but for how long? How many compromises would it take before I was no longer me? Before this name no longer fit, and I lost even the desire to fight back? But if I exposed this most secret part of myself and failed to push Ash out, they would own me . . . completely. There would be no chance to find the drug I'd witnessed in Ash's memories or the secret to forging power-dampening chains.

I curled tighter around the light, seeking its comfort, its council. Did some future advantage matter if James was out of time?

No. I refused to lose James. I refused to lose myself. This was one compromise that I would not make.

Breathing deep, I cradled the glowing seed of the name hidden deep within myself—the truth at the heart of my existence, bound by magics even older than Ash. The suffocating hold of Ash's control loosened, though their tethers cluttered my core like cobwebs. Energy flowed back into my usurped limbs.

What are you doing? Ash's words carried a hint of warning . . . and a hint of worry. I'd surprised them before.

Let's see how they like this surprise.

Concentrating all my magic, fae and practitioner alike, I poured every drop of energy I possessed into the blazing sun that was my fae name. As the inferno swelled, it burned away Ash's anchors, leaving only those parts of my core that belonged, the parts acknowledged and protected by my name. Two anchors, three, four popped like rubber bands as the blaze spread.

No! Ash's consciousness dove toward the brilliant glow of my name, my truth, reaching out to claim it.

I braced myself. This was the danger, the moment of decision. The outcome of this single, infinite moment would determine who owned my soul.

Chapter 20

ASH'S CONSCIOUSNESS slammed into me, and the two of us tumbled into the light. I spun uncontrollably for a moment, then my back slammed into what felt like solid ground. Gasping, I struggled to my feet. The world around me was a wash of white marked only by a soft haze, as if I were standing in a cloud. My nose tickled with the scent of slightly ionized air that brushed my skin with a feather-light touch.

"You think you can defeat me?" Ash's voice came from everywhere at once, but a tingle on the back of my neck made me turn. Their clothes matched those they wore in the waking world, but that was where the similarities ended. The vampire progenitor was taller and thinner in this realm of thought and magic. A silky curtain of black hair hung to their knees and drifted as though stirred by a wind I couldn't feel. The angles of their face were sharp, and the tips of their tapered ears protruded a good three inches above their veil of hair. "I'll put an end to this rebellious streak of yours, even if I have to replace every drop of blood in your veins."

A dark lash snapped out from Ash's hand, a whip of ebony that slashed like black lightning across the white world. The cord wrapped around my neck tight enough to strangle, but I wound my forearm into the crackling darkness and held fast before Ash could pull the line taut.

"You may be an intriguing mix of magics," Ash said, "but you are still mostly mortal. This"—they gestured to the light around us—"sanctuary will not save you. Every fortress you erect will fall to my will. As will you." They yanked viciously at the whip.

I stumbled, dropping to one knee as the cord of magic dug into my flesh.

Ash was stronger, faster, more experienced . . . in the real world. But we weren't in the real world. Here in the core of my soul, we were beings of thought, intent, and magic. Speed and strength had nothing to do with muscles in this place. The power of my name and the magic of this fortress of light pulsed through me, clearing the constant whisper of doubt that had taken root in my mind. In this place, I could be as strong as I could imagine. I only hoped I had the will to match the cold confidence in Ash's eyes.

Tightening my grip on the dark lash, I gave it a yank of my own. Ash jerked forward, not quite falling. I took the reprieve to unwind the cord from my neck. When Ash regained their balance, I faced them on even footing.

Ash lifted their upper lip in a snarl. The whip vanished. Ash blurred into a streak of shadow and flowed toward me, a swirling stain against the white mist of this non-place. But here, with no cumbersome flesh to weigh me down, I could move with the speed of thought . . . speed enough to match even the oldest of vampires.

I stepped back, dropping into a fighting stance. Ash's clawed hand raked the air a breath from my face. I shifted my weight, coming in for a counter, but Ash was already moving. My blow brushed the fabric of Ash's sleeve. Their hand came down on my arm, but I twisted out of their grip and pivoted to their exposed side. They ducked and spun, striking out with a blow that scraped my ribs.

Around and around we went, two evenly matched specters locked in combat in this space outside of space, fighting for the key to my soul. Exhilaration turned to dread. I could keep up. I could hold my own. That in itself was a miracle. But I wasn't making any headway. And while I wasn't yet feeling fatigue, how long could this boxing match last? I had the vague sense that time could not touch us here, but surely we could not remain in this unnatural state indefinitely. Yet with every parried thrust, every sidestep, every counter, it became clear that even here, where I was practically a god, I could do no more than keep up with Ash, and only just.

I called my magic, desperate to get the upper hand . . . but nothing came.

Surprise made me hesitate. Ash's fist connected with the side of my face. Pain exploded through my cheek as bone broke under the impact. Tears blurred my vision. I spun away, raising my arms in wild defense, but Ash followed my retreat, closing for the kill. A second strike entered my field of vision, coming from the opposite side.

I threw myself backward in a sloppy dodge that saved my face but dropped me on my ass.

I rolled through the mist, scrabbling across the invisible ground. Ash's polished shoe came down on the space where I'd landed, stirring the billowing mass of cloud on which we fought.

Ash's frustrated growl was muted by my own heavy breathing and the pounding in my ears. I might not have a physical body in this place, but the pain in my cheek proved these bodies of light and magic could still be hurt, maybe even killed. And the adrenaline, the panic, those were as potent as ever.

Continuing my roll, I sprang to my feet. Once more I reached for my magic, not to harness it this time, but simply to find it, to understand what had changed. Realization washed over me as I studied the flow of energy swirling through and around me and my relationship to it. I'd failed to find the magic contained within me, because *I* was inside *it*.

Ash and I warily circled each other once more as I struggled to understand this new relationship to my magic. *At least, if I can't use magic here, Ash shouldn't be able to either.*

The two of us had fully entered the ancient spell that bound my fae name to my soul. The glowing light we'd fallen into wasn't just a representation of my name . . . it was the spell itself that bound my name to my soul. This mist and light that surrounded us *was* my name, my truth. Even now, if I focused, I could hear it, like a whisper carried on the wind. A shiver raced down my spine. If Ash defeated me here, they too would be able to hear that name. Then I would never be free.

Ash lunged. I pivoted. Knuckles brushed my damaged cheek and tangled in my hair as I stepped inside Ash's guard and twisted, wrapping both hands around their extended arm. Ash's momentum carried them into my throw. I thought about dropping to one knee for the split second that Ash tumbled over my back, trying to add a finishing blow or a hold, but a whisper through my mind told me to keep my distance. I released my hold before Ash's impact sent up a billow of white mist. Their hand lashed out in a counter that would have toppled me if I hadn't already been moving away. As it was, their fingers only brushed my leg.

Backing up a dozen steps, I took a deep breath and tried to sort my thoughts. *This place is a part of me. It* is *me, and I'm it.* Something clicked. I was holding too tightly to the idea that I was separate, that I was in charge while the magic was a tool, when in reality we were one and the same.

Ash, back on their feet, snarled. Fury burned in coal-black eyes swirled with crimson and gold.

I took another deep breath, grounding my stance. *I am the tool.*

Ash covered half the distance between us in three long strides.

I opened myself to my magic without trying to force it along preconceived paths, letting it lead me where it wanted to go, where it knew it *needed* to go. Power surged through my veins and infused my muscles. I clapped my hands together. The sound cracked like thunder around us. My body broke apart.

Two steps away, Ash's eyes went wide as their target turned to glittering dust, then mist, then light itself.

I was an arrow. I was the mist and the light of the world. My name rang in my ears, simultaneously a welcome home and a call to battle. I relinquished all control, trusting my name, my truth, to see me through. I shot forward at the speed of thought.

Ash skidded to a stop, but they couldn't change direction. Not this close. Not fast enough.

I pierced flesh that was not flesh. Ash screamed. Their manifestation staggered, splitting apart. Tissue, bone, and sinew parted as I passed completely through the Ash of this place and out the other side. They stood for a second with a ragged hole through their center, then they too turned to dust. But they were not welcomed into the mist and the light. They were not a part of this place. Even as my body reformed, theirs blew apart. Dark particles blurred past, thrust away as though repelled by a magnet.

I rose more slowly out of the light, reluctant to leave its warm embrace. But this fight wasn't over. Ash hadn't been killed. Only evicted. A distant part of me could still feel the barbs anchored in my core, and the physical prison of their hands on me in the real world. The past few days had forced me to compromise on a great many things, trading one loss for another in an effort to save what mattered most. But some things were too important to lose, because losing them meant losing everything. This time, there would be no compromise. I wouldn't stop until I was entirely free.

I couldn't quite tell if I swelled or the light shrank, and in truth it didn't matter. I once again hovered in the tangled cords of my core with the light of my name cradled against my chest. Holding that tiny nova aloft, I let the light fill me, and where the light fell, it burned away everything that didn't belong. The dark harpoons Ash had anchored within me charred and fell to dust, while my bond to James—accepted and cherished—remained intact, though still muted by the magic-dampening restraints he wore.

I continued to rise, leaving my glowing core, until the physical world came into focus. I inhaled, filling my lungs to capacity, and let it out in a long, slow breath as I took in the scene before me. The council chamber was just as it had been. The entire dreamlike conflict for my soul had taken place in the space of a blink. Yet I knew it was no dream. My thoughts and actions were once again my own. My cheek, the one Ash had broken in that spectral fight, ached, but the bones were intact. Only the pain lingered. *My pain's probably nothing compared to what Ash must be feeling.*

Ash panted behind me. Their hands still pinned my arms, but they sagged, and their grip wasn't as tight. Even if it happened in that strange in-between place, getting torn apart and scattered can't have felt good. Not that they didn't deserve every twinge of discomfort for what they'd done . . . and tried to do.

James frowned at me. Once again I could feel him pressing from the other side of the barrier the chains erected between us. He knew something had happened, but he had no idea what. And to keep him safe, he never would. No one could ever know. Because besting Ash in the fight for my soul changed nothing here in the real world. Well . . . almost nothing.

Hooking my foot behind Ash's ankle, I sank my weight and twisted. One hand left my arm as Ash, already reeling from their defeat, struggled for balance.

One more pivot, this time in the opposite direction, and a circular sweep broke their grip on my remaining arm, freeing me completely.

Ash gasped as their back hit the ground. Esteban jumped to his feet. Chae-Won swore, but her tone sounded more appreciative than concerned.

"Order," shouted Fatima.

I bent over Ash. Here in the real world, they could kill me in a heartbeat, but not without revealing what they were. And not without losing the quickest path to everything they wanted. I held the promise of daywalking, incomplete though it might be at the moment. I was their pass into the alliance, to sitting across from the fae as equals, protected and powerful. They needed me.

Unfortunately, I also needed them, and not just for the vote they held in deciding James's fate. There would never be peace in the Mortal Realm until all the races were represented equally, and allying with the vampires meant allying with Ash. The two were inseparable. But, before we went any further down that road, I had to make one thing perfectly clear. Leaning closer I whispered, "You will never control me."

Ash stared up at me with a mixture of hatred and respect. Then they smiled. "We'll see."

Turning my back on that unsettling smile, I strode toward James and addressed the council. "Victoria brought up an interesting point earlier." I drew even with James so that we were standing side by side. He tried to catch my gaze, to warn me off this path. Even with our bond muted, I could sense his unease. I kept my attention on the council and forced a light confidence into my voice. "How did James disable the security cameras when he was busy killing Hanzo?"

The four councilors stared at me with narrowed eyes, expressions varying from curiosity to outright antagonism. Esteban lowered himself back to his seat.

"Don't keep us in suspense, Ms. Blackwood," said Fatima. "How were the cameras disabled?"

I lifted my chin. "I did it."

"What are you doing?" James hissed from the corner of his mouth.

"Saving you," I whispered. I'd already accomplished the impossible today. Maybe I could pull off one more miracle.

"She's obviously lying," said Esteban. "There's no evidence to support such a claim."

"Since when do defendants have to prove their own guilt?" I asked, echoing James's earlier argument.

"How then?" asked Fatima. "If you were James's accomplice, how did you manage to break into the security room and overpower the thrall on duty without the steward realizing anything was amiss?"

I licked my lips, playing back what I knew of the attack and the relationship between vampires and their thralls. If I was going to make this confession stick, I needed a believable story to back it up. "After the ruckus in my room on the night I arrived, I called the security office and told Helen that I didn't feel safe staying by myself. I said I'd prefer some human company and asked if I could join her in the security room during her shift."

"And she agreed?" Fatima asked. She turned to Zuri. "Were you aware of Alex entering the security room with your thrall?"

Zuri looked up, though her shoulders remained hunched. Blood oozed from the split lip that the magic chain was preventing her from healing. She glanced from Fatima to me.

"Helen didn't report my presence." Recalling Animkii's words when he convinced me he could make certain decisions on his own, I said, "It was such a small concession, she said it wasn't worth bothering Zuri about."

Fatima narrowed her eyes at Zuri. "Is this possible?"

I curled my fingers into fists, willing Zuri to play along, to understand that I was trying to save her, too.

"My thralls are semi-autonomous," she said. "I do not require that they check in with every decision they make unless there is a clear need for direction."

I exhaled. My pulse was racing. I wanted to wipe my palms, but I forced myself to remain still. One thing I'd learned from interacting with the fae was that any sign of weakness could prove deadly when dealing with people more powerful than yourself. The weaker your position, the more you needed to project strength, and my position was precarious as shit at the moment.

Chae-Won clucked her tongue. "Even for an aide, you give them too much freedom."

Zuri lifted her chin a fraction, though the gesture was easily missed from her position on the floor. "I find my team works better with a certain amount of freedom."

"Because your 'team' has handled this conclave so well," droned Cecil sarcastically.

"Regardless," Fatima said, "it *is* possible that Ms. Blackwood was in the security room that night."

"Has your thrall recalled anything that might confirm this?" Chae-Won asked Zuri.

Again Zuri glanced at me, as if weighing her options. She shook her head. "Helen's recollections from that day are a mess due to the head injury she sustained. It's possible Alex was with her, but she cannot say for certain either for or against."

Fatima swung her attention back to me. "Continue."

Sweat prickled my palms. I fought the urge to shift my weight from foot to foot as I spoke. "Once I was through the security door, it was easy enough to slam Helen's head against the desk while she watched the monitors." I suppressed a flinch as an image of Helen's blood-matted hair and bruised face induced a wave of nausea. "With her knocked out, I disabled the security cameras and erased the footage that would have shown me entering the control room and James killing Hanzo."

Every nerve ending in my body itched with the lie, but I fought to remain still. If these people knew me at all, they would have seen right through this farce. I could barely make my own computer do the most basic of things. I certainly didn't have the technical skills to hack a security system.

"So you and James worked together to kill Hanzo," Fatima said, "and you would have us believe you did this for the good of the vampire species rather than out of a simple desire to save yourselves?"

"Then why insist on your innocence?" Cecil demanded. "Why not tell us from the beginning why you'd done it?"

"This council is not known for its mercy, even in the face of logic," James said before I could think of a comeback. He glanced at me. "And Alex has a habit of playing the reckless hero. I knew she would have difficulty allowing me to shoulder this burden alone. I intended to get her to a position of relative safety before taking responsibility, so I played for time in the hope that a solution would present itself."

"Which it did," I cut in as inspiration struck. "Thanks to Ronald's unforeseen assassination attempt." I smiled. "I'm not sure which one of you tried to kill me"—I settled my stare on Cecil—"but thanks. That disruption was exactly what we needed. Because of that attack, Animkii took me out of the conclave to keep me safe. Both the security footage and Esteban's servant, who heard the commotion and came to investigate, can corroborate this."

One glance at Zuri's furrowed brow confirmed that Animkii's "orders" had actually come from Ash. Did she think he'd acted on his own? Or might she suspect something larger was at play? Fortunately, whatever her thoughts on the matter, she was clever enough to keep her mouth shut, and the councilors were too distracted to pay any attention to their other prisoner.

All eyes turned to Esteban who, after a moment's hesitation, gave a terse nod.

"Seeing a chance to escape," I continued, "I ambushed Meg, who'd joined us outside the conclave, and used her gun to kill both her and Animkii."

Zuri's soft whimper broke my heart. I hadn't actually killed her thralls, but I was still the reason they were dead. Especially Animkii. His odds would have been better if I'd left him tied up in the plane. This time I kept my gaze carefully averted. I didn't want to see the grief I'd caused.

Chae-Won arched an eyebrow. "You overcame two highly trained vampire thralls with just your bare hands?"

"I've bested a serial killer, a necromancer, and the fae general who led the army of Enchantment against the Mortal Realm in the Faerie Wars." I held her gaze, ensuring she absorbed the full weight of my words. "Do you really think I'd come up short against two mind-fucked humans?"

She glanced at Fatima, who shrugged.

"If you need more proof," I continued, "you can find Animkii's body near the landing strip outside. He died of a bullet to the head. Not a plane crash."

Victoria made a choking sound from the shadows near the exit. Animkii's body would prove beyond doubt that the version of events she'd fed the council—the version I'd encouraged her to share—was false . . . assuming Ash didn't have the other thralls move Animkii's corpse before the council could verify my claim.

"Unfortunately, flying a plane proved more difficult than I thought it would be," I continued. "I didn't make it very far before I crashed."

"So you came back here?" Cecil said. "To the very place you'd just escaped?"

I shrugged. "Not ideal, but better than freezing to death on the mountain."

The council members exchanged looks, as though gauging each other's reactions. My story was hardly watertight, but it didn't have to be. It just had to hold together long enough to get me to solid ground. As I'd seen time and again throughout this trial, what the council actually believed didn't matter nearly so much as providing a story they were willing to accept—a story that aligned with their goals.

"Let's say we believe you," said Cecil. "That makes you personally responsible for the injury of one thrall and the death of two others."

"Three, if we count Hanzo's man," said Chae-Won.

"That was self-defense," I said.

Cecil waved his hand. "Regardless, you've killed. And James has admitted to murdering a council member . . . again." He turned in his seat to address the other councilors. "Our path is clear. Both must be executed."

"Unless, as she claims, Hanzo's continued existence posed a measurable threat to the vampire population," countered Fatima.

"Which I contest," said Cecil.

"You've been particularly quiet today, Esteban." Chae-Won said, turning to him. "What are your thoughts on the matter?"

I resisted the urge to glance over my shoulder at Ash, who'd regained their feet. I could feel their stare like a nagging itch on the back of my neck. I only hoped pride wouldn't prevent them from accepting this solution. I was counting on Esteban's vote to keep me alive. Ash had lost their hold over me, but they could still have a seat on the alliance and force a parley with the fae. They wouldn't get everything they wanted, but they could still walk away with *something*.

I bunched my fists. *It's your turn to compromise.*

Esteban's fingers tapped against his armrest. The rhythmic sound echoed around the chamber. "There can be no denying that Hanzo was set in his ways."

"That is no crime," Cecil said.

Chae-Won laughed. "As if you didn't complain about that very trait every time we convened."

"His shortsightedness cost us on a few business deals . . ."

"More than a few," Fatima said under her breath.

". . . but he also brought stability to this council."

Esteban frowned. "You think this council will fall to chaos and rampant impulse without him? Those of us who remain are not so young as all that."

"I only meant—"

"If I may?" I interrupted. "Hanzo wanted to keep you all in the dark indefinitely. When presented with the possibility of joining the rest of the races that share this world, of being involved in making the decisions that will shape all our futures, he preferred to hide and let others dictate his fate. Is such a person really fit to lead you? Would you trust your interests to be served by the werewolves? By the fae? Who will speak for your people if you are too frightened or stubborn to stand up and speak for yourselves?" I stood a little straighter, lifting my chin. "Hanzo was afraid of change, and he had his hooks so deep into all of you that you fell in line behind him. James and I cleared a path so that this council could make an informed decision about what would most benefit the vampire population, whatever that decision might be. You're welcome."

Silence fell over the chamber like a blanket.

I glanced from one stony expression to the next. Only James smiled when our eyes met. Pride trickled through our sluggish bond. Whatever happened next, I'd put on a damn good show.

Esteban erupted in laughter, shattering the spell my speech had cast. Fatima scowled. Chae-Won shook her head, rubbing fingertips against her temples as though easing a headache. Cecil narrowed his eyes and laced his fingers over his crossed knee.

"But now we come to the crux of the matter," Esteban said. "Even if we accept that this council, and by extension the vampire race, has been aided by your actions, we're still faced with the dilemma of being unable to join the paranatural alliance on equal footing with the other members. Not so long as we're hindered by daylight."

"I'm still not convinced Hanzo's death was for the best," Cecil said.

"Not convinced Ms. Blackwood should live, you mean," countered Chae-Won.

"Even if Hanzo's death *was* for the best," Cecil continued with a glare at Chae-Won, "it's not up to the likes of an exile and an outsider to decide that. An attack on a council member is an attack on the council. They must be punished for their crime."

"My dear Envy, I believe you may have touched on a solution there," Esteban said.

Cecil leaned back in his thronelike seat. "What do you mean?"

Esteban looked at me and smiled. Despite the difference in shape and color, I could feel Ash's gaze through those eyes. "James never truly relinquished his seat on this council," he said. "He simply stopped performing his duties."

"Not so simply as all that," Fatima interjected.

"Granted," Esteban said, "but the result is the same. For all that he chose a life of exile, James never ceased being a member of this council. As such, he had as much right to question Hanzo's fitness to serve as any of us."

"But not his sentencing," Fatima said. "A death order cannot be issued by one council member alone."

"I agree," said Esteban. "He deserves to be punished."

"As does Blackwood," said Cecil with glee.

Esteban raised a placating hand. "But a punishment fitting his station. One that might clear up the second dilemma we face. If we are to join the alliance—"

"We should not," Cecil said.

"—we will need an advocate resistant to sunlight."

Fatima's eyes widened to saucers. "You wish for James to speak on behalf of our race?"

"How is that a punishment?" Chae-Won demanded.

Esteban made a shushing motion. "When James left, he made it clear that he valued nothing so much as his freedom. He washed his hands of politics and power and settled down to a life of pointless mediocrity, even accepting the bans this council placed upon him."

I bristled. James had sacrificed his status, his wealth, and his community to live a life he could be proud of, a life free of the guilt and carnage that had plagued most of his existence. Granted he'd managed to regain some semblance of those things since leaving the council, but he'd had to start from scratch. After two centuries of hard work, he still held only a fraction of what he'd given up.

Perhaps sensing my outrage on his behalf, James pressed his fingers against my wrist. The silver chain binding his hands brushed my fingers, sending an electric tingle through my skin.

"Therefore," Esteban continued, "losing that autonomy will indeed be a punishment for him. I propose we reinstate James to full status on the council . . . with a few caveats in place."

"Caveats?" Chae-Won asked.

He nodded. "When James parted ways with this council all those years ago, we banned him from creating any more of our kind, founding a nest, or holding territory. I believe those earlier impositions should remain in play. And as he is now a king without a kingdom, I propose that each of us take turns hosting James in our own territories. He will serve at the will of this council until such time as we deem his sentence fulfilled."

My heart seized.

"At how many years would you value Hanzo's life?" Fatima asked.

"That depends on Ms. Blackwood." Esteban's gaze settled squarely on me. "So long as James is the only vampire who can walk in daylight, he is our figurehead. He must speak for us until such time as we can speak for ourselves. Therefore James will remain with us until Ms. Blackwood provides each and every council member with the means to walk in daylight. After that, James will be allowed to return to his exile."

My mouth went dry. Esteban, no . . . Ash, had outmaneuvered me. I could see my own earlier argument reflected back at me. I wouldn't be able to leave this room with everything I wanted, but if I accepted this deal, I could still save *some*thing. James would be alive. I would be free. We just wouldn't be together. Not until I provided the councilors with the means to walk in daylight . . . which I wasn't confident I'd ever be able to deliver. I gritted my teeth. *Another fucking compromise . . .*

"While we're negotiating terms," said Fatima, "I suggest we kill two birds with this stone. The seat of Lust has been open too long, and no potentials have distinguished themselves as worthy candidates."

All the councilors looked behind me.

I didn't turn, but I could feel the seething humiliation rolling off Victoria like ocean waves knocking against my legs, threatening to topple me.

Chae-Won nodded. "So we give James the seat of Lust and announce that Wrath is now officially vacant. That buys us a few more centuries to find an acceptable councilor."

"The new title also fits this softer version of James," Fatima said.

"Probably a better look if he's to represent our people to the world."

Cecil snorted. "Rebranding. As if that will make anyone forget his bloodstained past."

"Humans have short lives and shorter memories, and the wolves and fae hardly care how many he's killed. Their hands are as red as ours."

"Very well," Esteban said. "All those in favor of reinstating James to the council as the seat of Lust, and playing intermittent host to him, until such time as Ms. Blackwood provides us all with daywalking, in exchange for dropping all current charges against him?"

Esteban, Fatima, and Chae-Won raised their hands.

"Motion passed," said Chae-Won.

"All those in favor of joining the paranatural alliance, with the understanding that James will represent us in negotiations until such time as one or all of us are able to attend the meetings ourselves?" asked Fatima.

Again three of the four council members raised their hands.

Cecil crossed his arms, looking disgusted. "This exposure will be our ruin."

"Motion passed," said Fatima.

Esteban leaned forward in his seat. "James Abernathy, formerly known as Wrath, do you agree to henceforth serve on this council as the seat of Lust and submit to the will of this council in all our judgments and edicts, without hesitation or countermeasure, until such time as your debt is paid in full?"

James shot me a sidelong glance, then he dropped to one knee and lowered his chin to his chest. "I accept."

I shook my head. The motion traveled down through my body until every inch of me was shaking.

"Ms. Blackwood," said Esteban.

My gaze snapped to his, and again I felt the uncomfortable certainty that Ash was staring at me through those eyes. Even without the now-severed connection, I could feel their hunger, their anger, and their triumph. I'd surprised them; I'd found a loophole in their plan . . . and they'd found a loophole in mine. They didn't get to keep me. I wouldn't get to keep James.

"Do you agree to provide every member of this council with the means of negating the effects of sunlight on our kind, and to do everything in your power to induct vampires into the paranatural alliance, as penance for the crimes you have confessed to here tonight?"

I'd known the demand was coming, but the words struck me like a blow. I swayed on my feet. For one wild moment, I wrestled with the urge to shout Ash's secret into the silence; let them burn it all. Then sanity reasserted itself. So long as James and I were both alive, there was hope. It might take years, but I would find a way to recreate the amulet that had protected James for centuries. I would win his freedom and bring him home . . . even if I had to negotiate with Bael to do it. One way or another, I'd see James again.

I didn't drop to my knees or lower my gaze. I stiffened my shoulders, set my jaw, and glared. "So long as James is kept healthy and treated well, I'll get you what you need."

"Agreed," said Fatima. "I'll host first."

"We should draw lots," Esteban said.

"I don't think Cecil should be included in the rotation," said Chae-Won. "He might execute James to serve his own ends."

Esteban nodded. "Let us agree now that killing James would not serve the council's interests, and anyone acting against the spirit of this agreement will be held guilty of treason without trial."

Fatima and Chae-Won both said, "Agreed."

"I'll not harm him," said Cecil. "But I insist on getting equal time with him. If he's to represent our interests, I'll not be the only one without access."

"We can work out details on the time and location of James's accommodations later," said Chae-Won. "For now, I move that we declare this conclave concluded."

"There is still the matter of the steward's negligence," said Esteban.

"She's already lost two thralls," said Fatima. "I say we strip her of her rank and call that done."

"Her ineptitude resulted in the death of a council member," Esteban argued. He looked at Zuri, but I got the distinct impression it was me he was trying to punish.

"A death we only moments ago deemed beneficial to our race," said Chae-Won. "Why punish her more severely than those who committed the act?"

"I side with Esteban on this," said Cecil. "The steward's crime was not Hanzo's murder but the negligence that made that death possible. The two are distinct and should be sentenced accordingly. I vote to execute the steward."

"Seconded," said Esteban.

"I move to exile," said Fatima.

"Exile," said Chae-Won.

Cecil sighed and crossed his arms. "The council is split."

James cleared his throat.

All eyes turned to him.

He climbed slowly to his feet, brushed off his knees, and strode to one of the empty seats. Sitting down, chains dangling between his knees, he said, "I have not yet cast my vote."

The others exchanged glances.

"I have been reinstated, have I not?" James asked.

"As a hostage and a figurehead," said Cecil.

"But a full council member, nonetheless."

"James is indeed a member of this council," Fatima said. She nodded to him. "Cast your vote."

James lifted his chin and stared impassively at Zuri, who kept her own stare focused on the floor. "Exile."

"The sentence is exile," Fatima proclaimed.

"*Now* can we end this conclave?" Chae-Won asked with an overly dramatic eye roll.

"Seconded," said Cecil.

Fatima waved a hand at me. "Ms. Blackwood, Victoria, you are dismissed. We'll call a plane to retrieve you."

Light bloomed behind me. Victoria had wasted no time in fleeing the room.

I looked at James.

He gave a nearly imperceptible shake of his head.

I hesitated a moment longer.

Ash wrapped their fingers around my upper arm.

I jumped and tried to jerk away, but their grip was vampire strong. They steered me toward the exit.

I cast one last glance over my shoulder. James's cool gaze met mine. Then I was through the door.

"Congratulations," Ash said.

I shot them a sideways look. "I thought you'd be angry."

"Oh, I am. That doesn't mean I can't appreciate a game well played. And I still got most of what I wanted. The rest . . ."—they shrugged—"time will tell."

I kept my mouth closed to prevent the snakes writhing in my insides from climbing up my throat. My skin itched under Ash's grip. I didn't want any connection to this person, not after the way they'd tried to corrupt my core, but we weren't in that timeless place anymore, and I'd lost the element of surprise. Physically, I was no match for Ash, so I let them guide me back to my room like the good dog they'd wanted me to be. I had to choose my battles, and my dignity wasn't important enough to risk unbalancing the Jenga tower I'd managed to construct.

Ash stopped in front of my door. Releasing my arm, they flashed their key card against the lock, pushed the door open, and gave a small bow. "Until the next round."

I clenched my jaw and curled my hands into fists as I watched them walk away.

At the intersection, Ash gave a little wave and called without a backward glance, "I look forward to hosting your lover."

My fingernails pressed eight perfect crescents into my palms.

Chapter 21

I GRIPPED THE couch cushions on either side of my thighs while one leg bounced nervously, rocking slightly as I waited. I'd felt the moment the magical chain was removed from James's wrists, felt the surge of emotion as our bond reasserted itself. That had been more than an hour ago. Ants crawled over my skin as the constant hum of his presence grew stronger. I could feel the moment he turned the final corner. Anticipation swelled within me.

Rising, I crossed the room and opened the door.

James swept me into his arms without hesitation, pivoting to kick the door shut behind us as his lips connected with mine. Electricity surged through my body, supercharging my nerves while simultaneously turning my muscles to melted wax. The scent of cloves and fresh soap washed over me. I let out a little moan and tangled my fingers in James's hair, pressing my knuckles against his scalp. His desire mixed with mine, drowning me. There was so much to say, so much to plan, but those thoughts evaporated as we came together, fusing into a single being held too long apart. He carried me into the bedroom, and we fell onto the mattress.

Clothes hit the floor in a flurry of limbs. Heat swelled where our flesh met. All the fear of the last few days, along with my new worries about what the future would hold, crashed over me and split apart, scattered on a wave of relief. For this moment, James was in my arms. For this moment, my life was my own. For this moment, all was right with the world.

I arched, breaking the seal of our lips with a cry of release. James took one shuddering breath as he moved against me, then went rigid with a cry of his own. My body turned to liquid. James lowered himself to my side, one arm pillowing my head while his other hand cradled my sweat-slicked hip. We clung together in comfortable silence until my breathing and pulse returned to normal. Lying like that, I could almost believe we were back at home, waiting for dawn to break over the Colorado mountainside. Oblivion tugged at my consciousness.

"The plane will be here soon."

I twitched, jerked back from the edge of sleep. With those six words, James had shattered the illusion. The safety and warmth of the moment passed. I shivered on the covers and burrowed closer to James's side. I was once more a pawn and James a captive. There would be no coffee and conversation as we watched the sun crest the eastern horizon.

I closed my eyes and curled my fingers against his bare chest. "I'm so sorry."

"For saving me?" His voice rumbled against my ear.

"For coming up short."

He stroked my hair. "I was prepared to die rather than see you bound directly to any one of them. By comparison, this temporary separation is a small price to pay for your freedom." He kissed the top of my head. "Make no mistake, my love, you *did* save me."

Another moment of silence stretched between us, then James cleared his throat. "What exactly happened in the council chamber? The chain prevented a true connection between us, but just before you knocked Esteban's servant to the ground—most impressive, by the way—there was a . . . resonance. I thought—" Frowning, he brushed his knuckles over my cheek. *I thought I heard your name. Your* secret *name. It was as if you were calling to me from across a ravine. I could sense you struggling, but I couldn't reach you.*

Shame and regret flitted through our connection.

"I made a deal with one of the council members to secure your freedom," I said quietly. "I let them bond me to them in exchange for testimony that would convict Zuri."

"Esteban," James guessed. Anger and violence boiled just beneath the surface of his calm exterior. "Their servant was the only person you had contact with after your return to the conclave."

It was dangerous to point James in Esteban's direction . . . but not so dangerous as letting him suspect Ash was anything but the servant they appeared to be. I shrugged. "Once you so chivalrously trashed my plan, they tried to use that bond to stop me from helping you."

"They underestimated you."

"They didn't know I had a true name." I shuddered, recalling how close Ash had come to claiming that final spark of light in my core. "I fought them, and I won, but now they know my name exists." I twisted to look up at him. "They also know I love you, and I trust you."

"They'll assume I know it, too," he said quietly.

"And they'll be right." I pressed my palm against his naked chest.

"I can't reproduce the amulets. Who knows how long you'll be at the mercy of the vampire council. At Esteban's mercy." Fear swept through me, threatening to drown me. I wasn't so naive as to believe the terms of my agreement with the council would stop Ash from torturing James to get what they wanted. "We have to find some way to protect my name."

He sat up, pulling me with him. "Alex, I would die before I let any harm come to you."

I snorted. "I've noticed. But you can't know everything they're capable of. Good intentions aren't enough."

His clear blue gaze bore into me. "You think I'll break."

I hated the feeling of inadequacy I felt through my connection to James, but then I recalled the ferocity with which Ash had fought to take possession of my name. If they'd succeeded. . . .

James would endure captivity and even torture for me, but his will alone might not be enough to resist the progenitor of his race. Ash couldn't control a master vampire of James's power the way they could manipulate a human thrall. That didn't mean they couldn't crack James like a walnut for the split second it would take to find the information they needed. Of course, James would fight to protect my secret, but could he win?

"I know you would never betray me on purpose," I said, "but if they have some trick, some magic . . ."

James pressed tentatively at our connection.

I shielded Ash's identity but let James feel my fear.

"If there is any doubt," he said, "any chance . . . then you must not leave your name with me."

I shot him a skeptical look. "It's not like I can take it back."

"You cannot," he agreed, "but I can erase it."

I frowned.

"Vampires rely on secrecy," he said. "We'd quickly have been discovered if we killed every witness to our existence, so, as a race, we've become quite adept at manipulating the memories of others. It's one of the first skills we hone. Though, as with all abilities, some find more success with it than others."

"You can erase *your own* memories?"

It was his turn to frown. "Not normally, no, but the process should work so long as I have someone else to guide the spell." He stood up and began pulling on his clothes. "Memory manipulation is delicate magic. We must remove all traces of the targeted information while leaving everything else intact. Take too little, and my mind will piece together the missing information and reconstruct the memories. Take too much, and I could lose whole segments of my life. Since the information we're seeking to remove pertains to you . . . I could end up forgetting you entirely."

"Then it isn't worth the risk," I said automatically. "We'll build a wall around the information in your mind."

He shook his head. "As you yourself said, we cannot know what our enemies are capable of. So long as I hold the information, there is a chance someone could find it." He smiled. "Don't worry, I'm quite adept at memory alterations. I will, however, require your help."

"I have no idea how to erase memories. I might lobotomize you!"

He sat down again, now fully clothed. "I'll provide the magic. All you have to do is guide the spell. As I lose the memories connected to your name, I will also lose focus on what I am trying to erase. I literally won't be able to remember what I'm looking for. That makes it too likely I'll overlook some crucial connection and the memory wipe won't last. I need you to be my eyes, as it were. I need you to follow the connections and make sure every last reference to your true name is eradicated."

"If I mess up . . ." I shook my head. "You said you could forget me."

He set his palm against my cheek. "I trust you."

"I'd have to dig through your core again."

"There's no corner of my soul you have not already seen."

"What if—"

"Alex," he cut me off, "if this adversary is as strong as your fear seems to suggest, erasing my memory is the only way to protect your secret, short of my death."

Pressing my lips tight, I nodded, stood, and dressed. "What do you need me to do?"

He patted the bed beside him.

I sat down.

"I'm not sure how your imbuing magic works exactly, but you seem able to observe more than most," he said. "I'm going to prepare the spell. Look within me and tell me if you can see it."

I shifted my focus, sinking beyond the surface of reality, and followed our bond into James's core. Silvery light flared around me, blinding me for a moment before shrinking to a fist-sized silver glow crackling with blue lightning that hovered near James's center.

"I think I see it," I said.

"Good. I am going to start with the night you shared your name with me. From there, you should be able to trace the connections to other memories pertaining to your name."

The zappy ball of light streaked toward one of the ribbons of James's core. I hurried to follow. Sinking into the memory behind the electric glow, I saw myself through James's eyes as my perspective shifted.

Alex sits on a blanket in the dim cellar of a fae waystation. I press a damp rag over a cut on her arm, wiping away mud and blood. She hisses and sloshes her pumpkin cider.

"Sorry," I mumble. I'm trying to be gentle, but the wound is deep. It must be cleaned.

I can feel her gaze upon me, studying me as I set the rag aside and pick up a bandage.

"Did you hear it?" she asks. "When I came out of the trial?"

I frown. "Your name?"

She nods.

"Almost. You were wide open when you stumbled out of the trial. I had to slam down the link to keep it from spilling over into my mind."

"You didn't want to know?"

"A true name is precious, and dangerous. You need to keep it hidden."

"Not from you," she whispers. "I want you to have it."

A word whispers through my mind, just at the edge of perception. No, not a word. A name. The woman before me comes into sharper focus as I see her not as a physical being but as a soul laid bare.

Lightning crackled and arced through the memory. Sear marks became holes, and the holes spread until the entire image turned to ash and drifted away. I remembered that moment in the cellar. It was the first time I told James that I loved him, the first time I'd allowed myself to be that vulnerable. It was the best decision I ever made, and it had saved my life more than once. How much of that night would James retain? Would he remember me saying "I love you?" Would he recall that feeling of absolute trust despite not knowing the details? Or would these erasures undermine the foundation of our relationship?

Follow the connections, James prompted. *Direct the spell.*

I don't like this.

Yet it is necessary.

A blackened section of ribbon marked the place where the erased memory had been. Moving closer, I found hair-thin tendrils stretching out from it. Connected memories. These strands were thinner than any

I'd noticed before, forming a transparent web between the core threads. The first fiber led to a memory of James and me sitting side by side on a porch. The second showed James standing beside Morgan as he gave the command that would later save me from falling victim to a powerful siren. Then came the moment when I made James promise never to use my name to control me.

Out and out the fibers arced, branching and thinning until I had to trace them by touch. Sometimes the memories circled back to others that had already been burned. Sometimes they split multiple times before anchoring again, and I had to backtrack to make sure I followed every path to its end.

About halfway through the process, I felt James lose focus. He didn't understand why his memories were being erased, but he trusted me. He gave me full rein over his magic, and I directed it down every path related to my true name, no matter how thin the connection. The final memory to burn away was this very moment, the knowledge that the knowledge had been taken from him.

I released my hold on James's spell. Without a target, the magic dissipated. Drifting up and out, I had one final glimpse of James's core and the dozens of scorch marks I'd created before settling back into my own body. My cheeks were wet.

James wiped my tears away. "Why so sad?"

I shook my head and tried to smile. James had no idea what he'd just lost. The magic had cleaned up after itself. For James, those memories and the knowledge they contained had never existed. "I'm just going to miss you, so much."

He wrapped his arms around me. "I'll miss you, too, but this isn't goodbye."

I strummed the bond anchored in my soul, and James responded, resonating with me. Even without my name, we were connected. We always would be. So why did I feel like I'd been cut adrift on the ocean?

Breaking his hold, I rose and left the bedroom, looking for a pliable material. My gaze settled on the tassels at the edge of a woven rug. Kneeling, I snapped several of the threads free.

"What are you doing?" James stood over me, a deep furrow between his brows.

I sniffed and smeared my tears with my palm, trying to clear my vision. "Neither of us knows how long we'll be apart, so I'm making you something."

He raised an eyebrow but settled on the couch to watch.

I had yet to successfully recreate James's original daywalking amulet—the one made by Bael—but months of failed experiments had given me a somewhat clearer grasp of my imbuing abilities in general, and this was the perfect opportunity to put that knowledge to the test.

Calling up my magic, I let the loss and loneliness of what I'd just done wash over me. I let those emotions go. Next came anger, frustration, resentment. The vampires, and Ash most of all, had threatened me and the people I loved. They'd forced me into a corner. Inadequacy reared its ugly head as all my doubts and second guesses crowded in, but those emotions, too, I released. They were not what I needed right now.

Once the powerful negative emotions swirling through my psyche had their say, they drifted to the background, allowing me to focus on the feelings I wanted to harness . . . the ones I wanted to share. Reaching for James's hand, I wrapped a single thread around his ring finger and tied it off. Then I removed the loop and added a second strand at the connection point.

I licked my lips. I'd never tried to make something like what I had in mind, but I had a good idea how it should work. Calling up my own memories of the lovemaking session James and I had just shared, I started tying knots, thickening and strengthening the loop. I added knot after knot, working my way around the ring, and with every knot I tied in another sensation. Another memory. Another emotion. I dug deeper. Every conversation. Every stolen moment. Each knot carried another aspect of my feelings for James, growing deeper and stronger as I worked. I could feel my love for James reflected back through the strands, resonating deep in my soul as I approached the beginning of the loop.

Sweat slicked my forehead, and my stomach was starting to cramp, but I wasn't done yet. I had one more trick to perform to make the ring function the way I intended it to. I needed to add a trigger. I didn't want just anybody who touched the ring to get a voyeur's display. The memories I'd imbued into this thread were immensely personal, meant to be shared by only two people—James and myself. Setting the final knot loosely in place, I slipped the ring back onto James's finger.

"Picture our time in the bedroom just now. Remember how it felt."

James closed his eyes and complied. I could feel his lust rise with the memory, calling to my own, but I couldn't let that distract me. I followed the sensations back along our tether to the memory, fresh and vibrant, in James's core. Plucking one of the gossamer threads attached to that memory, I hooked the strand through the final knot on the ring and pulled it closed, locking it in place and completing the loop.

James gasped, swaying. He gripped the couch with his free hand.

I smiled. The imbuing had taken root, and, if I was right, it was anchored to a specific memory.

James shuddered, exhaled, and opened his eyes. "That was . . ."

"Anytime you want to feel it again, just remember that moment. The sensations I imbued into the ring can only be accessed through that one specific memory." I grinned. "Now you won't have to miss me quite so much."

It was poor compensation for what he'd lost, but the hollowness I'd felt when James forgot my name didn't feel quite so sharp.

"I appreciate the gesture." He pulled me onto his lap. "But nothing compares to the real thing." He locked his lips to mine, warm and wet.

I squeezed my knees against his hips and ran my hands over his back, memorizing every curve. I fully intended to make myself a matching memory-anchor ring, but there was no harm in collecting a few more sensations first.

"SORRY FOR MAKING you wait," I said as James and I entered the vaulted chamber that would carry us to the surface, though I wasn't sorry at all. Who knew how long it would be before I saw James again. I was happy to claim every precious moment.

Zuri and her three remaining thralls huddled together, each holding a single backpack. No evidence remained of the vampire's wounds save a fabric patch over her left eye. It seemed even vampires couldn't grow back new body parts beyond a certain point, or maybe it would just take longer. I couldn't meet Helen's gaze. Did she know my confession was a lie, or did she believe I'd tricked and attacked her? Did she think I'd killed Meg and Animkii?

Victoria stood with her arms crossed, one toe tapping rhythmically against the marble floor. Her luggage was already in the elevator. She'd traded her evening gown for a more practical wool skirt and a knit sweater. Her feet were clad in black fur-lined boots. Ash stood apart but stepped forward when I approached. I couldn't help comparing the fine-featured person before me with the colossal statue of their legacy once more. How old were they really? The weight of their memories had been suffocating, and I'd barely scratched the surface. Was that what a fae soul would feel like if I ever had occasion to touch one?

"The council bids you call this number when you have need to communicate." Ash extended a white business card.

A single phone number was printed on one side. The other side was blank. I tucked the card in my pocket.

Ash looked at James. "You are not to leave the compound. Say your goodbyes here."

James squeezed my hand. "We already have."

I cradled his jaw, rough with stubble from his stay in the Well, and kissed him one last time. "I love you."

"I love you, too," he echoed.

"Gag me," Victoria muttered from across the room.

Ash caught my eye. "Safe travels. I'm sure we'll meet again soon."

Taking my bag from James, I crammed into the elevator between the vampire I'd almost condemned and the vampire I'd betrayed. Zuri hit the button. The doors closed. The last I saw of James was him standing next to the originator of his race, completely oblivious to the threat beside him. I bit my lower lip and swallowed the warning struggling to escape.

"You must be loving this," Victoria said.

I glared at her. "My boyfriend is being held hostage."

"He's back on the council," she shot. "Not only that, but now he's the spokesperson for our entire race. Am I supposed to believe you didn't plan this from the beginning? Clearly he realized his mistake in giving up his position, and the two of you set me up to fail so he could swoop in at the last second and claim the prize."

"Weren't you listening in there? He doesn't *want* to be on the council."

"Well I do," she shouted. Her chest heaved with angry breaths. Her fingers curled.

"Don't be a sore loser," said Zuri. "It's unbecoming."

Victoria laughed. "And what about you? Were you in on the joke? Did you know the whole time who killed Hanzo while you watched me make a fool of myself? Did you know James would step forward to save your pitiful life in the end?"

Yichén made as if to strike her, but Zuri placed a hand on his arm. "I fully expected to die," she said. "Though, for the sake of my thralls, I'm glad I did not." She smiled at Victoria. "I'm also glad you did not earn a seat on the council."

Victoria's lips compressed to near invisibility.

The elevator doors opened, and those of us with backpacks filed out, leaving Victoria to haul the mountain of luggage she'd brought on her own.

The night sky was alive with the lights of the aurora as our party tromped through the trees to the runway. I glanced at the place where Animkii had fallen. Someone had cleared his body, and fresh snow hid the blood.

"What about the people?" I asked Dyani, thinking of the rows of cots she'd guarded. "The . . . food."

She took three more steps before answering. "Normally it would fall to the steward to wipe the memories of the general stock and see them safely returned to the places where they were collected."

"And now?"

"The council won't waste the energy. Far simpler to end them here."

I missed a step.

"They'll kill them all?"

"And burn the remains," she said.

My insides twisted. "I wish I hadn't asked."

The plane waiting on the runway was similar to the one I'd arrived on, and my pulse spiked as I climbed aboard. A pudgy woman in a blue uniform sat at the pilot's station, while a man with the build of a stick insect sat beside her. The man waved in welcome. The woman ignored us as she ran through her preflight checks. I moved to the very back of the plane, as far from the section that had been ripped open in our crash landing as I could get and reminded myself that the only reason that plane had gone down was because I'd made it.

Zuri and her entourage clustered on the opposite side of the plane. Victoria, bringing up the rear, took a seat near the front. I glanced at the empty seat next to me and felt my chest tighten.

Once Victoria was strapped in, the stick man secured the door. The engines whined. The plane lurched forward. The wheels left the ground. As the plane climbed, the tether connecting me to James stretched, just as it had when Animkii tried to kidnap me. This time I didn't fight it. I pressed my forehead to the cool plastic window as we rose into the glowing ribbons of the aurora. It felt wrong to be going home without James, but this wasn't over. Not by a long shot. I twisted the fabric ring on my finger. *We'll meet again soon.*

The adventure continues in
Shadow's Bastion
Book 8 of The Magicsmith series.
Coming soon...

Acknowledgments

Thank you for reading my book! I hope you enjoyed it.

This story was a lot of fun to write, but it did tie my brain into knots a few times. I want to thank my family, and especially my husband, for being patient while my mind was elsewhere trying to patch plot holes and weave twists rather than paying attention to my immediate surroundings.

Thanks to all the early readers who helped me polish this book, and to Steve for helping me figure out how to crash a plane. Thanks to all my lovely ARC readers for being a part of my launch team, and to the folks at Bell Bridge for bringing the book to life.

I also want to shout out a big THANK YOU to everyone who has posted a review of any (or all) of my books. Reviews really are a wonderful (and free) way to support authors. They help others find our work and give us motivation to keep going when the seeds of doubt start to creep in. So thank you!

Until next time,

—L.R.

About the Author

L. R. Braden is a bestselling, multi-award-winning author of dark-yet-hopeful urban fantasy stories. Her published works include the *Magicsmith* series, the *Rifter* series, and several works of shorter fiction. A bit of a recluse, she enjoys collecting skills that may (or may not) prove useful in the event that she is suddenly transported to an inhospitable alternate reality. Since that hasn't happened yet, she mostly spends her days weaving fantastic tales, playing with her family, and getting lost on purpose. Her writing has won many awards, including the Eric Hoffer Book Award for Sci-fi/Fantasy, the Next Generation Indie Book Award for Paranormal Fiction, and the Imadjinn Award for Best Urban Fantasy.

Connect with her online at lrbraden.com

www.ingramcontent.com/pod-product-compliance
Lightning Source LLC
Chambersburg PA
CBHW031212260626
47169CB00007B/2027